"I think you still owe me,"
Preston whispered.

His demand teased her, but she didn't dare look at him. Become ensnared, entangled in that wicked, dangerous gaze of his.

"What do you say, Tabitha?"

He looked down at her, and suddenly it wasn't just that he held her, that he surrounded her—his arms wound around her, his hands warm against her gown, his body pressed to hers—all of it left her breathless.

"More?" More was dangerous. Ruinous.

And suddenly all too irresistible.

She had started this evening knowing nothing of men and now she had come all the way to this—to this passionate, dangerous madness. And that next step, to letting him steal her first kiss, was hardly as cavernous a leap as it might have seemed…

And if this is madness…some newfound part of her heart clamored…*then let me drown in his kiss*.

Preston pulled her closer, and it was as if time itself came grinding to a standstill—pressed as she was against his chest, her legs brushing against his hard thighs.

Then everything upended and he was kissing her.

By Elizabeth Boyle

Rhymes With Love series

ALONG CAME A DUKE
AND THE MISS RAN AWAY WITH THE RAKE
IF WISHES WERE EARLS
THE VISCOUNT WHO LIVED DOWN THE LANE

LORD LANGLEY IS BACK IN TOWN
MAD ABOUT THE DUKE
HOW I MET MY COUNTESS
MEMOIRS OF A SCANDALOUS RED DRESS
CONFESSIONS OF A LITTLE BLACK GOWN
TEMPTED BY THE NIGHT
LOVE LETTERS FROM A DUKE
HIS MISTRESS BY MORNING
THIS RAKE OF MINE
SOMETHING ABOUT EMMALINE
IT TAKES A HERO
STEALING THE BRIDE
ONE NIGHT OF PASSION
ONCE TEMPTED
NO MARRIAGE OF CONVENIENCE

ELIZABETH BOYLE

Along Came a DUKE

Rhymes With Love

A V O N
An Imprint of HarperCollins Publishers

This is a work of fiction. Names, characters, places, and incidents are products of the author's imagination or are used fictitiously and are not to be construed as real. Any resemblance to actual events, locales, organizations, or persons, living or dead, is entirely coincidental.

AVON BOOKS
An Imprint of HarperCollins*Publishers*
10 East 53rd Street
New York, New York 10022-5299

Copyright © 2012 by Elizabeth Boyle
ISBN-13: 978-0-373-60179-0
www.avonromance.com

First Avon Books paperback printing: June 2012

Avon Trademark Reg. U.S. Pat. Off. and in Other Countries, Marca Registrada, Hecho en U.S.A.

HarperCollins® is a registered trademark of HarperCollins Publishers.

Printed in the U.S.A.

To LeHang Huynh,
for her love of a good romance,
the chase that ensues and
all the scenes in between
that lead to true love.

Thank you for your
enthusiasm and your support.

Chapter 1

Kempton, Sussex
1810

The day dawned like it always did in May in the village of Kempton, with a bright sprinkle of sunshine, a hint of dew on the grass and the birds singing happy choruses in the garden.

There was no indication whatsoever that on this day, Miss Tabitha Timmons would not only find herself betrothed, but fall madly and deeply in love.

And not necessarily with the same man.

No, the only thing on Tabitha's mind as she stepped out of the vicarage that afternoon, closing the door quietly behind her on her way to the Tuesday afternoon meeting of the Society for the Temperance and Improvement of Kempton, was that she was escaping her aunt's demands and her uncle's complaints for the next blessed three hours.

"Ho, there," Miss Daphne Dale called out cheerily from the garden gate where she had been waiting for Tabitha. "I was beginning to fear she wasn't going to let you come," Daphne continued in a loud whisper as she reached down and gave Tabitha's ever-present dog, Mr. Muggins, a scratch behind his ears. The large Irish terrier gazed up at Daphne with pure admiration shining in his large, expressive brown eyes.

"Then Aunt Allegra would have to go in my stead, and heaven forbid she be assigned some task to attend to," Tabitha said, glancing over her shoulder and thankful that the curtains were all still drawn—which meant her aunt wasn't there peering after her, trying to come up with some excuse to call her back.

"Wretched notion that," Daphne declared, linking her arm into Tabitha's and towing her friend away from the vicarage that had once been Tabitha's happy home.

It should still be such a place, sitting as it did, stubby and content in the shadow of St. Edward's Church, a large and ancient relic from the Norman times, with its high stone walls, long nave and a bell tower that was only dwarfed by the heights of Foxgrove, the Earl of Roxley's nearby estate.

Instead, with her father's death two years ago of a heart ailment and the installation of her uncle as the new vicar, Tabitha's beloved childhood home was naught but a dreary, dreadful place.

At least, Tabitha mused, she was still allowed to attend the Society meetings, if only because her aunt found the mission of providing charity baskets to Kempton's many spinsters a tedious chore.

They ambled along Meadow Lane, the narrow track that led from the vicarage to High Street, while Daphne chattered on, bringing Tabitha up to date on the local gossip.

"—Lady Essex will never allow Louisa and Lavinia to have their way on this matter. The buntings for the Midsummer's Eve Ball have always been lavender. Apple green, indeed!"

Tabitha smiled and let the idle talk wash over her like a great balm, for when she was with Daphne or at the weekly Society meetings, it was easy to believe that nothing about her once idyllic life had changed.

"—I even called on the twins yesterday and tried—most politely—to explain how they will only raise Lady Essex's ire if they persist." Daphne huffed a sigh. "Oh, how Louisa and Lavinia love trouble!"

Tabitha eyed her friend. "You honestly thought you could deter them?"

"I had hoped," Daphne confessed. "And if that failed, I thought my new bonnet would distract them." She tipped her head to show the green silk bonnet with its gray ribbon off to advantage.

Tabitha was used to Daphne's preening and laughed. "You convinced your father to advance your allowance, didn't you?"

Her friend grinned unrepentantly, blue eyes alight, her gloved hand rising to touch the jaunty brim. "Yes, and worth every shilling," Daphne declared. "I was afraid Papa wouldn't relent before Miss Fielding discovered it and snatched it up for herself, and you know how ill she looks in green!"

Tabitha laughed. The rivalry between Daphne and Miss Fielding grew deeper with each passing year.

"I think it would look perfect on you," Daphne said, in an offhanded way. "You could try it on when we get to Lady Essex's." She glanced over at Tabitha, her gaze filled with kindness, her teeth holding her lower lip as she waited.

Knowing exactly what her friend intended, Tabitha shook her head. "You know I cannot consider such a thing. You recall how my aunt was when you gave me those gloves last winter."

"They weren't charity," Daphne declared, her brow now furrowed. "And neither would this be. 'Tis only that you haven't had a new hat in…"

"Two years," Tabitha replied. Or a new gown. Or shoes. Or stockings. "Truly, I don't mind."

"Well, I do!" Daphne shot back. "Your aunt and uncle should be ashamed of how they begrudge you even scraps."

What could Tabitha say? It was all true—her aunt and uncle had been more than happy to gain the elevated position of her father's living when he'd died, but the guardianship of his penniless daughter? Not in the least, being childless themselves. Aunt Allegra, who had not a motherly bone in her body, even liked to complain that her niece took up too much space in the corner of the attic they'd graciously allotted for her to sleep in.

Not that Tabitha minded her attic hideaway, for it was where her mother's trunks were tucked away. Their closeness allowed Tabitha to occasionally catch a hint of her mother's violet perfume—those moments as elusive as her memories of the willowy beauty who had died of a fever when Tabitha had been so very young.

"Every time your uncle gives a sermon on charity,

I want to stand up and call him an overbearing hypocrite," Daphne said.

"You're incorrigible," Tabitha scolded, though only halfheartedly—for if anyone had her best interests at heart, it was Daphne.

"Who is incorrigible?" Miss Harriet Hathaway asked as she joined them where Meadow Lane met High Street. In true Harriet fashion, her hem was muddy, her gown slightly rumpled, her bonnet askew and on one of her pink cheeks was a smudge of something. She'd probably realized the time and come dashing out of the Pottage stables without a second glance toward a mirror.

Lady Essex was guaranteed to be put out by her protégée's untidy appearance. Her ladyship had high hopes of taking Harriet to London and finding her a grand match, though hardly anyone in Kempton put much stock in such notions.

After all, this was "Harry" Hathaway they were talking about.

"I am," Daphne told her and then deftly changed the subject. "I bought a new bonnet."

Harriet spared it a glance. "Oh, yes, so you have. Isn't that the one you showed me last week in Mrs. Welling's window?"

Daphne nodded. "Lovely, isn't it?"

Taking another look, Harriet asked, "Yes, but I thought it had a feather trim on it."

"I removed it," Daphne said quietly, tipping her head nonchalantly at Mr. Muggins.

Tabitha cringed. She loved her dog dearly, but he had no notion that a feathered trim on a pelisse or a jaunty quill tucked in the brim of a hat was not attached to an actual bird.

When he'd ravaged three of Aunt Allegra's hats not long after she'd arrived, the lady had threatened to have the grizzled-faced beast cast out—only to find the entire village of Kempton and a good portion of the population from the surrounding villages refusing to take "that red devil of a dog" in, much to Tabitha's relief.

Eventually, the indignant lady had done as Daphne had and removed the remaining feathers from all her hats. Even the indomitable Lady Essex removed the feathers from her favorite turban before she would wear it to a Society meeting.

No feather was safe when Mr. Muggins was close at hand, much to Tabitha's chagrin. Whyever couldn't he possess such an enmity for squirrels or rats like other terriers?

As it was, Tabitha was compelled to take her roguish companion with her everywhere, for fear Uncle Bernard would find some unsuspecting passerby who would be unwitting enough to take the dog with them.

"You look tired, Tabitha," Harriet remarked. "And thinner. You are working too hard."

Tabitha glanced away. "I had to have the scrubbing done before I left, so I got up early."

Daphne slanted a look at her. "And I suppose you also polished the silver and washed the dishes and got the table laid for supper and the vegetables cut for Mrs. Oaks."

That was nearly all of it, but she'd also done the ironing as well. Still, she rose up in the face of their concern. "Don't look at me so. The work is nothing."

Harriet's jaw set. "Someone needs to remind your aunt that you are a lady and not the charring girl."

"I would prefer they didn't," Tabitha said. At least she had a roof over her head, a point her aunt and uncle liked to point out on a daily basis.

"You can always come live—" Harriet began, but Tabitha stopped her with a sharp shake of her head.

You can always come live at the Pottage.

Just as Lady Essex had offered her a place at Foxgrove, and Daphne a room at Dale House, but her uncle and aunt had refused to allow Tabitha to move out, convinced she would turn wanton and licentious without their ever-present protection.

That, and they would lose a free maid.

But there was also the simple fact that Tabitha loved the vicarage—it had always been her home, and though she now had naught but a small corner under the eaves and ate in the kitchen, at least she could still tend her mother's flowers in the gardens and gaze upon her father's sure handwriting as she made entries into the parish record.

It was the closest thing to a home she would ever have.

"If only we weren't from Kempton," Daphne said, sighing loudly. "Then you could marry and escape your aunt's demands."

"Let us think of something more merry," Harriet proposed as if she'd spied the shadow crossing Tabitha's face. "Such as how scarlet Lady Essex's cheeks will be when the Tempest twins make their ridiculous motion—yet again—to change the color of the Midsummer's Eve Ball buntings."

They all three laughed and continued contentedly

along, for which Tabitha was glad. At least some things never changed.

They were approaching the smithy, where Mr. Thury's hammer rang sharp and clear as he worked steadily at some task. The sound was familiar, but nonetheless, Daphne came to an abrupt halt.

"Oh my!" Her gasp was followed by Harriet's stumbling to a stop, the heels of her boots digging into the gravel. She let forth with an oath most obviously learned from one of her five brothers and finished it with a rather unladylike, "That's a demmed fine rig!"

Tabitha stopped and glanced back at them, then put her hand to her forehead and squinted into the sunlight until she was able to focus on the sight that held her friends captive.

For indeed, there before Mr. Thury's forge sat a fancy carriage—a phaeton, she believed it to be—but she'd leave that designation to Harriet, who was far more informed about such matters. Whatever it was, the expensive contraption now sat lopsided with one wheel removed, as it was most likely being repaired by the village smith.

The grand oddity was unlike anything usually seen in Kempton.

For while Kempton had quite the abundance of spinsters and unmarried ladies, it rather lacked a population of gentlemen—so much so that such masculine trappings were a rare sight indeed.

"Goodness, have you ever seen anything so admirable?" Daphne whispered.

Tabitha slanted a glance at her friend. "I doubt even your father would cozen such a conveyance."

"I wasn't looking at the carriage," Daphne confessed. "Rather at the gentleman in that splendid jacket." She slanted her glance toward a tall, elegantly attired man standing under the smithy's awning. His superfine coat was thrown open, revealing a snowy white cravat tied in a great display of lace, above a bright checked waistcoat, an ensemble far too over-done for Tabitha's sensibilities. The gentleman in ques-tion, holding a large pint in his hand, lolled against the wall, and worse, grinned in their direction. "Whoever could *he* be?"

"Oh, that's just Roxley," Harriet supplied. Then much to Tabitha's horror, her friend waved at the no-bleman like one might hail the grocer or a passing peddler. "Ho, there, my lord. Have you come to visit your aunt?"

Without any propriety or thought of good manners, Harriet plowed on ahead, extending her hand to Lord Roxley—the all-too-infamous and ruinous Lord Rox-ley—so very rarely seen in these parts that it was no wonder he could arrive and not be recognized.

"He's the earl?" Daphne whispered under her breath, her gaze fixed exactly as Tabitha's was on Lady Essex's nephew. Her ladyship's house, Foxgrove, was one of Roxley's many properties. The earl, who had been raised in London, only came to Kempton on brief, annual visits—usually unannounced—so his wily aunt couldn't wrangle him into some large ball or other en-tertainment meant to match him to a local lady.

"I didn't know you were coming to Kempton, Rox-ley," Harriet said with comfortable familiarity. Then again, Tabitha was always a bit awed at Harriet's easy manners with the opposite sex. She supposed it was because her friend, having grown up with five broth-

ers, saw them not as mysterious and dangerous prac-
titioners of ruin but good company.

Odd notion, really, to Tabitha's way of thinking.

"Chaunce wrote me just this week and didn't mention you were coming down from Town," Harriet continued to scold.

"Sssh, Harry! 'Tis a devilish secret that I'm here."
The handsome fellow winked at her.

The girl straightened and shook her head. "You
know you musn't call me that! You will have your
aunt in horrors! I am Miss Hathaway now." She struck
a pose that would have made even Lady Essex proud.

But Roxley appeared unimpressed. He leaned
closer, like a conspirator. "Miss Hathaway, indeed! Not
to me, Harry. Never." He reached over and tweaked
her cheek.

Harriet shooed his hand away and laughed. "You
never change, Roxley."

"I hope not. I fear I would disappoint my family utterly if I turned up one day all stodgy and straitlaced
like your brother Quinton." He laughed again, then
glanced over at Tabitha and Daphne before giving Harriet a pointed look.

Remembering her manners, Harriet said quickly,
"My lord, may I present Miss Timmons and Miss
Dale."

"You most certainly may," he said.

Tabitha gave the man some credit, for though she'd
heard his character lamented over and over again by
his great-aunt, Lady Essex, he made an elegant bow as
she and Daphne dipped into proper curtsies.

"And who is this?" he asked, reaching out a hand to
give Mr. Muggins an amiable pat on the head.

The large dog replied with a low growl.

"Noble beast," Roxley managed as he drew his fingers back warily.

"I am so sorry, my lord," Tabitha rushed to say, "I fear he is uneasy around strangers."

"'Tis the feather in your brim," Harriet told the earl.

"The what?" he said, eyeing the full-grown beast, who was now watching him like a wolf might a lost lamb.

"The feather in your hat," Harriet repeated, reaching up and plucking the white quill from his brim.

"Hey, that's my souvenir—"

But whatever its meaning, the feather was gone as Harriet quickly dispatched it, tossing it to Mr. Muggins, who caught it deftly and looked up at his mistress with an overly proud expression in his eyes at having caught his prey.

"You can thank me one day," Harriet told Roxley, as if that was enough of an explanation.

"Whatever happened to your carriage, my lord?" Tabitha ventured, changing the subject.

"Not my carriage, Miss Timmons. 'Tis Preston's." The earl waved his hand over toward the smithy. "I warned him not to take the corner by the great oak at that speed, but would he listen? As ill-mannered and stubborn as your dog." He shrugged and grinned as if their dangerous and foolhardy misfortune was a badge of honor.

Harriet laughed. "My brother George did the same thing last spring. Hell-bent he was, my father says."

"Harriet!" Daphne gasped. "Remember what Lady Essex said about language! She'd double her lessons if she were to hear you say such a thing."

"No, Harry!" Roxley lamented, glancing from Daphne back to Harriet. "You aren't letting my aunt ruin you?"

"Not ruin, my lord," Harriet told him. "Just round me out. My mother has given up. But Lady Essex is determined. She has plans to bring me to Town next month."

"To Town, you say?" Roxley asked.

"Yes, didn't she write you?"

"Never does," he told her. "Just shows up and bedevils me for weeks on end." He grinned at her. "Now I am forewarned and in your debt."

"Yes, well you can dance with me at Almack's."

"Never!" he said with a shudder. "I shall be away all next month. Yes, away. Hunting."

"It isn't the season for hunting," Harriet told him, folding her arms over her chest.

"It is somewhere," he teased back.

"If you are so resolved to avoid Lady Essex, whatever are you doing here in Kempton?" Harriet asked.

"Racing! We're trying to beat that coxcomb Kipps back to London, and I told Preston that we could use the Kempton road as a shortcut. Bet Dillamore a monkey we'd get to Town first." He raked his hand through his dark hair and looked again at the lopsided carriage. "Warned Preston about that corner by the oak," he said with a rueful shake of his head.

"Dear me," Tabitha said. "Five hundred pounds?"

Daphne's eyes went wide at the amount. "I do hope Mr. Thury knows how imperative it is that you get your wheel repaired."

"Oh, he does," Roxley told her. "Preston has even pitched in. Prestigious fellow that he is. Though might be 'cause he's got twice that wagered and he'll be in the suds with his dreary uncle if we lose." Lord Roxley craned his head toward the smithy's forge and called out, "We'll beat Kipps yet, eh, Preston?"

There was a low growled muttering from behind the forge where a bent-over figure worked.

The earl shrugged, a rather apologetic motion. "He's in ever-so-foul a mood. Ho, there! Preston! Come meet some of the local ladies. There are few gentlemen in these parts and we are considered a rarity."

On that, Roxley had the right of it.

Gentlemen left this sleepy, forgotten corner of England for school as soon as they were out of short pants, and few returned—the lure of the army, the navy, and even the clergy offered far more exciting venues than the quiet meadows and green hills of Kempton. Hadn't all of Harriet's brothers—save George, her father's heir—hied off to the four corners of the world rather than remain in the place of their birth?

And they did so because they could.

Tabitha had to wonder at this friend of Lord Roxley's—for she knew well enough from his aunt about the earl's licentious character—what of this Mr. Preston? What sort of man would bet so much on a carriage race?

It was scandalous, but at the same time, Tabitha felt a frisson of envy that these men had the freedom to wager such staggering amounts and jaunt about the countryside at will, while she was…she was…trapped.

A few moments before she would have described herself as content—overworked, tired and slightly underfed, yes—but suddenly she chafed at the inequity of it all.

Yes, trapped. Trapped by her circumstances…by a lack of opportunities. Never before had she ever felt the lure of London, but looking at this swift carriage and the freedom it lent its owners, Tabitha's heart beat with a rare note of rebellion.

And while London was only a two-day drive, whatever would she do once she got there? Her relations in Mayfair would only send her back to Kempton.

Now Tabitha saw the real danger of men. They put the most impossible notions in a lady's head. For once she was rather glad that Kempton was not overrun with them.

"Preston, this will only take a moment," Roxley was saying, still attempting to lure the man away from his labors.

"Yes, well, you needn't bother your friend, my lord," Tabitha said as politely as she could. "We should be on our way. To our Society meeting." Besides, who knew what sort of unsettling notions this Mr. Preston would inspire. "We would not want to keep you and Mr. Preston from your…your—"

Oh, bother, how did one describe a wager that was naught but foolish and a grand waste of time, money and effort?

"Oh, it is no trouble," Roxley said grandly. "Would do Preston some good to meet some respectable ladies. His aunt is forever harping on about it." Arms crossed over his chest, his boot tapping impatiently, the earl turned to his friend. "Come now, Preston! Make your bow or word will spread that I keep uncivilized company—Lady Essex will never let me hear the end of it." The earl turned and waggled his brows at Harriet.

Tabitha suspected that Lady Essex would not be

happy to discover them in the company of this "Preston" person, no matter how prestigious Lord Roxley thought him.

Prestigious, indeed. From all accounts, the man must be the worst sort of...

Then she spied him, this Mr. Preston, rising up from beside the forge, bellows in hand, and prestigious was not the word that came to mind.

Everything Tabitha suspected about him—that he was not fit company, that he was a scandalous, dangerous rogue—ignited like sparks from the hot fires, bright and sure one moment and gone the next.

Oh, Mr. Preston might well be a gambler and a rake, and quite possibly as rapscallion as they came, but much to Tabitha's greatest horror, he was utterly intoxicating to look at.

Sinfully so.

And no, the word that came to mind was definitely not prestigious, but rather something more simple and straightforward.

Ruin.

He rose up, no ugly Hephaestus, but like a very Adonis. This she knew for certain, for Lady Essex kept a statue of this legendary hero in her morning room, one her father had picked up on his Continental tour so many years ago.

At least this version had the decency to keep his breeches, boots and shirt on—though barely. The white linen shirt that might once have been fashionable was open to his waist and plastered to his body, his smooth, muscled chest gleaming from his labors.

A gentleman would never appear in public so— without his cravat, without his gloves, without all the

proper trappings. Why, this Mr. Preston was nearly...
Dare she even think it? There was no other word to
describe the man.

Undressed. Unadorned. Naked.

Not that he needed anything to gild his form—for
it was perfect.

Tabitha pressed her lips together in shock. Good
heavens, what was she thinking? Wasn't it bad enough
her limbs burned as if she'd been dipped in the very
flames of the forge? Her heart pounded with an odd
twitter, and she knew she should glance away, not gape,
not stare, and yet she couldn't...didn't want to.

He shook his head, and his tawny hair fell about his
shoulders like an unruly mane. His dark eyes flicked a
glance toward her, and for a moment, Tabitha had the
rare feeling of being pinned in place—like one of her
father's specimens—as if this man's very gaze could
capture her. But his regard didn't last very long, for he
all-too-quickly looked away, dismissing her as hardly
worthy of his attentions.

Something very feminine inside her ruffled with
annoyance. How dare he! Not that she cared one whit
as to his opinions, but whoever was he to think his regard was such a boon?

Nor was she the only one to witness his hasty re-
jection.

"Don't be such a curmudgeon, Preston," Roxley
complained, rocking on his boot heels, his hands now
folded behind his back. "It is bad form. Besides, you're
utterly safe from the advances of young ladies here in
Kempton. Not one of these misses has a hope or prayer
of ever finding a man to catch in the parson's mouse-

trap." The earl winked at the ladies. "Cursed, the entire lot of them."

Cursed. This brought the man's gaze up, a flicker of interest in his dark eyes.

Tabitha, who was rather proud of the Kempton Curse, nay tradition, suddenly felt rather embarrassed. Why, Lord Roxley made them sound like country simpletons, and nothing could be further from the truth.

"Cursed?" Preston asked, setting the bellows down, one of his dark brows tipping with amusement and his piercing gaze once again fixed on Tabitha. "Is that so?" He reached for a rag and began to wipe his hands clean.

"Very much so," Roxley teased, winking again at Harriet. "Been that way for centuries. Can't find a man to marry a one of them. Not and live to tell you about it. Why, they still recount the tale of poor John Stakes, and he's been dead nigh on two centuries. Named the demmed public house for him after his Kempton bride—"

Tabitha could take no more. "My lord! No one puts any faith in those old myths."

Daphne stepped forward and added, "Certainly not! Why, four years ago, Miss Woolnoth married Mr. Amison, and they were perfectly suited."

Harriet's eyes widened, and she looked about to reveal the truth.

That Mr. Amison had drunk shamelessly and only married Miss Woolnoth because he had sought a cheaper means to buy her father's best ram. He might have gotten the sheep, but he'd also gotten a wife who'd nagged endlessly.

Worse, the Amisons' short-lived marriage only seemed to fortify the last remnants of the Curse's legacy that a marriage to a girl from Kempton would only end in tragedy. Mr. Amison had been found floating in the mill pond after a particularly merry night at the pub and a less-than-happy homecoming.

Not to say that Mrs. Amison had anything to do with his unfortunate accident, but this was Kempton, after all.

"Indeed, my lord. We are certainly not cursed," Tabitha rushed to say. Tucking her nose in the air, she added, "We simply choose not to marry."

Of course, the general lack of marriage partners in Kempton, the dowry to tempt one or the opportunity to gain a man's attention also factored into her bravado.

There was a moment of silence from the gentlemen, then Lord Roxley let out a loud laugh, which was grating to say the least, but it was Mr. Preston's reaction that set Tabitha's teeth on edge.

The man actually let out a loud snort of derision. As if he had never heard such nonsense.

"Ladies who choose not to marry!" Lord Roxley laughed again. "Ah, if only the females of London would adopt such forward thinking, eh, Preston? You might be able to attend a ball or a soirée without causing a complete stir."

There was another snort from Mr. Preston, which only grated on Tabitha more so. And given what the earl had just revealed—that Mr. Preston was a source of scandal in Town—she knew him for the mean creature he was: the type of man who disavows marriage yet spends his time ruining young, innocent ladies of their virtue as a matter of course, robbing them of any future chance of happiness; the very lowest sort of beast.

"Mr. Preston—"

Roxley barked out a laugh. "Miss Timmons, you should know—"

"Now, now, Roxley, let the chit have her say," Preston told him. He crossed his arms over his chest. "Yes, Miss Timmons?"

Tabitha drew a steadying breath. "Sir, I will have you know, I never intend to go seeking a husband and am quite content with the notion." There, she'd managed that much; it had been a long time since she'd spoken her mind, and, fortified by her first success, she continued unabashedly, "Marriage offers no benefits to a lady, save leaving her a servant to a man's fickle whims and his selfish demands."

Her uncle would have apoplexy over such a brazen statement.

Much to her shock, this odious Preston looked more amused than put in his place, for he grinned at her, stalking forward like a lion, the king of the forest having discovered easy prey within his lazy reach. "Truly?" His gaze swept over her again, and when he finished his quick appraisal, one brow rose in an arched bow, as if poised to strike.

She dug in her heels and gulped. "Yes."

He nodded. "And you and your companions have no intention of marrying?"

"I cannot speak for Miss Dale or Miss Hathaway, but I consider myself quite happily situated if I may be so frank."

Then again, any woman foolish enough to marry a man like this Mr. Preston would most likely find herself abandoned and her heart broken.

And yet…for a moment, she wondered how a

woman could naysay him, for even her stalwart resolve to send him on his way with a thorough
dressing-down began to waver as he came even closer
to her—until he stood with his bare chest just a hand's
width away from her wide-eyed gaze.

So close she could see the rivulets of moisture running down the muscled expanse before her, nearly feel
his pulse as it raced from his heart. He smelled of
his labors, of the charcoal in the forge and of something else, something so masculine that it wrestled
with Tabitha's better nature and left her bereft of common sense.

It left her wanting to inhale deeply and reach out
and touch him, if only because suddenly she had the
sense of the ground beneath her shifting.

Then to her horror, he leaned over and whispered
in her ear, "If I might be so bold, Miss Timmons, what
exactly do you know of men's whims or, for that matter, the desire a lady feels?"

The implication of his words hit her with the same
force as if he had struck her. Tabitha stumbled back,
out of his reach, her cheeks flaming. "Ooooh! How
dare you!"

The wretched fellow laughed and turned his back
to her, returning to his labors, dismissing her in much
the same manner as he had earlier. Halfway back to
the forge, he stopped and glanced over his shoulder.
"Miss Timmons, if you had ever dared, you wouldn't
make such a foolish statement."

She sucked in a deep breath, her hand resting over
her stomach, which seemed to have filled with butter-
flies. Catching hold of what little bit of composure she
still possessed, she let fly with a hot retort.

"There is nothing wrong with a lady who knows her own mind and chooses not to be ruled by a man and his arrogance."

"You speak your mind quite freely, don't you, Miss Timmons?" Mr. Preston barely looked back as he tossed this question over his shoulder. Yet then he paused and turned. "And do all the young ladies of this town share that trait?"

On either side of her, Daphne and Harriet nodded their heads in sisterly unity.

Lord Roxley began to chuckle, but when he found himself facing three outraged misses, and perhaps knowing that this furious trio would in all likelihood be reporting this encounter to his great-aunt, he coughed and stepped aside, leaving his friend to bear the wrath of their fury all alone.

Preston picked up the bellows and then looked over at them. "Then I would say it isn't the ladies of this village who are cursed, but every man within fifty miles."

Chapter 2

Instead of returning from her Society meeting content enough with her life to endure another week in the vicarage, Tabitha stormed through the door in a mood that defied her uncle's dictums for reserve and order.

In fact, she closed the door with a decided rattle.

Her temper wasn't from the near brawl the Tempest twins had launched over the Midsummer's Eve Ball buntings—truly, lavender or green hardly seemed to matter as much as it had earlier in the day.

Before…before…

"That…that…odious, odious man," she told Mr. Muggins as her dog rushed past her, the exuberant waving of his tail neatly clearing a nearby tabletop of its knickknacks. "Whatever is wrong with speaking one's mind?"

It wasn't as if she didn't have occasion to hear the

very same lament—the burden of a spinster niece and her tart manners—from her uncle on a daily basis, but her uncle's ranting she could manage.

From that wretched Mr. Preston? Why, it was unbearable!

Utterly so, if she was being honest. Not only were his mocking glance and smug tones unsettling, but she also had the horrible suspicion that he could see right into her heart and know without a doubt that she was lying.

"Certainly there is nothing wrong in remaining unmarried," she said to Mr. Muggins.

Especially if it meant not being under the control of such a man. A handsome, overbearing brute like Mr. Preston.

Certainly he was the sort to ruin a lady without any remorse, what with those leonine flashes of power of his, that sharp, piercing gaze and his commanding stance. Why, he could probably convince some unwitting gel that he was a gentleman, perhaps even a baronet.

A baronet, indeed! Now that was funny.

What wasn't amusing was the way his whispered words had left her all ashiver with something that could only be described as "want."

Want. She glanced at her reflection in the mirror. For what? For Mr. Preston?

Tabitha shook her head. If she had any desire to see that wretched bounder ever again, it would be for one reason and one reason only.

"To give him a piece of my mind," she told Mr. Muggins. "The wigging I should have given him."

And she would have, right there and then, if she

hadn't been so tongue-tied after he'd made his out-
landish remark. "If I had brothers like Harriet," she
explained, "I would have been capable."

Mr. Muggins tipped his grizzled red head and gazed
up at her quizzically.

"Yes, I suppose you are right. I'll never know, for
I'm not likely to see the likes of him again," she conceded. And thank goodness for that small favor.

That should be a comforting thought—never having to see him again, never stand so close to him that
she could reach out and touch him, feel that bare chest,
the muscled planes, the rigid strength...

Winding her arms around herself, Tabitha shivered.
Oh, heavens, she must be imagining things. He hadn't
been *that* handsome. No man was. He'd simply left her
overcome by his...rudeness.

"Yes, that was what it was," she told Mr. Muggins.
"He was ever so ill-mannered."

But there was little time to debate this lie, as the
heavy steps of the housekeeper came down the hall.

"Oh, there you are," Mrs. Oaks declared as she
bustled into the room. The large, sharp-eyed woman
had arrived with Tabitha's aunt and uncle, and, like
her master and mistress, found Kempton without any
charm and the old vicarage a terrible trial. "I thought
I heard the front door close." The lady's brows arched
in condemnation of such uncharacteristic violence in
the vicarage. "Just as well I did hear you come in, the
vicar has been in quite a state since *I* had to go fetch
the post for him," she said, frowning darkly because
that was one of Tabitha's many tasks.

Woe be it for her aunt or uncle to have trotted themselves up to the post office.

Mrs. Oaks glanced at Tabitha's flattened hat and discarded gloves, clucking her tongue. "Reverend Timmons said I was to send you to the parlor the moment you returned. Now that I've gone and told you, best not tarry."

Against her better sense, Tabitha asked, "Whatever is this about?"

"How am I to know?" the lady huffed as she waded her way around the furniture and went to straighten up the toppled knickknacks. "I don't pry, nor do I gossip, but it can't be favorable. Never heard any good tidings come from one of those London thieves." The brows arched again.

"Thieves?"

Mrs. Oaks heaved a great sigh and then went on to elaborate, clearly exasperated that Tabitha hadn't more information to add. "Solicitors. From London."

Lawyers? Tabitha paused and then recalled that her uncle had been receiving sporadic letters from a London solicitor over the past few months—though she hadn't given it much regard, for it could hardly concern her.

Yet now it seemed it did.

"Well, what are you waiting for?" The housekeeper clucked her tongue again and shooed her toward the hall.

"Yes. Indeed," Tabitha agreed as she smoothed down her skirt and took a deep breath. "I'd best see to this." Hurrying down the hall, she stopped before the parlor door for just a moment to compose herself, shaking off any last vestiges of Mr. Preston and his debatable charms before she rapped on the panel. "Uncle, I have returned from the Society meeting."

"Come in, come in, dear girl," he replied.

Dear girl? Tabitha drew back from these cheerful tones. Oh, good heavens, this couldn't bode well in the least.

And her fears were not abated when she pushed the door open to find—to her dismay—not only her uncle but her aunt as well, sitting on the settee, the tea tray set before them and both of them wearing wide, uncharacteristic smiles on their faces.

Well, Aunt Allegra's lips were *almost* tipped into a real smile. As near as Tabitha had ever seen the lady manage.

Suddenly she felt like a canary with a broken wing left in the barn with a clowder of hungry cats.

Uncle Bernard waved Tabitha inside and toward an empty chair. "There you are, our dearest niece. We have been waiting most anxiously for your return."

"I told you, Bernard, we should have sent the carriage to fetch her home," Aunt Allegra said. "She looks completely parched." At this her aunt busied herself with filling a teacup for Tabitha and handing it over to her.

"Is there something wrong?" Tabitha asked, her hands trembling as she held the good china, which, up until this moment, she'd only been allowed to wash.

Her aunt and uncle shared a glance, then Uncle Bernard set down his teacup and began shuffling through a collection of papers scattered beside the tea tray. Having made his selection from amongst the notes, he said quite bluntly, "I fear I have bad news," at which he held up one letter and, reaching for another, continued by saying, "and some rather shocking news. Which do you prefer?"

With the afternoon she'd had, Tabitha didn't find either one preferable. But apparently "neither" wasn't a choice. "Perhaps I should fetch you more tea," she suggested, starting to rise.

"Heavens, Bernard, you've frightened the poor child," her aunt chided, once again smiling at Tabitha. Well, nearly smiling.

Her uncle nodded in concession, for the only person he deferred to was his wife. Then again, according to family rumor, he had only married the former Lady Allegra Ackland because she had come with a tidy income, so necessary to the third son of a baronet with few prospects. "It is my sad duty to inform you that your mother's brother, Winston Ludlow, has died."

Uncle Winston? Why, his name was barely spoken in this house, and certainly not by her father's relations.

Her mother's brother had been dead set against his sister's marriage to the second son of a baronet, whose slim prospects had risen no higher than the vicarage in Kempton. Having had his heart (and business dealings) set on his beautiful sister marrying well, Winston had abandoned her and England altogether for his holdings in the West Indies when Miss Clarissa Ludlow married the Reverend Archibald Timmons.

"Oh, dear! How very sad," she managed, digging in the pocket of her gown for a handkerchief which she truly didn't need. All she'd ever known of her uncle was what could be discerned in the miniature of him that had been her mother's. And now that handsome, smiling fellow, the one at whom her father had clucked his tongue in censure on more than one occasion, was gone, never to be known in person.

Tabitha looked up at Uncle Bernard and Aunt Allegra, who were both still smiling.

And while she wouldn't expect a grand show of sympathy from the pair before her, whyever did they both continue to smile over this news?

"There now," Aunt Allegra said, brushing crumbs from her lap. "That untidy business is over with. Now tell her the good news, Bernard."

Uncle Bernard cleared his throat and read in his most nasal vicar voice, "According to Mr. Pennyman, of the offices of Kimball, Dunnington, and Pennyman, your uncle has left you the entirety of his estate." He paused and glanced up at her. "It seems you are an heiress of some worth."

Aunt Allegra burst into happy tears. "Our dearest girl an heiress! What this will mean for all of us!"

"An heiress?" Tabitha whispered. Suddenly the room grew far too close and she had, for the second time this day, the sense that someone was tugging at the carpet beneath her feet.

"Well, yes. But that is hardly surprising, with your mother gone and you the only family Ludlow had left," her uncle was saying. "Death has its way of taking and at the same time giving—both to the deserved and the undeserved."

She had no doubt in which of those categories her aunt and uncle considered her, but suddenly her heart fluttered with a rare freedom.

An heiress. No longer would she be at her aunt and uncle's beck and call. As an heiress, she wouldn't have to reside on their bitterly doled-out charity.

She rose, biting her lip as she stood there considering what needed to be done next. Suddenly she was back in control of her life. "I will need a mourning gown. I haven't anything that will be proper—"

"That is not necessary—" her aunt said, sharing another quick glance with her husband, then waving Tabitha to sit back down.

"Whyever not?" Tabitha asked. Certainly this news had taken some time to reach England and then wind its way to Kempton, but… "He was my uncle, and a proper observation—"

"Your aunt is correct. The time for mourning is over. Besides, there are more pressing matters that need to be settled."

Tabitha stilled. "More pressing? How so?" Why, Harriet had inherited a modest sum from a maiden aunt not two years ago and the solicitor had merely sent along the money in a letter. Nothing to be settled or sorted out, just a neatly conveyed inheritance.

Certainly an entire estate would be a more complicated affair, but it could hardly—

"Your uncle had grave concerns about turning over his vast fortune to a young lady with no experience in the world."

"A most thoughtful concern," her aunt added.

"Precisely," Uncle Bernard agreed. "Which, I daresay, is a sentiment I can commend him for."

Tabitha sniffed at such a notion. Unable to manage her own affairs, indeed! Her uncle ought to take a look at the household accounts and parish records. It wasn't his smudged and lazy tallies that were to be found in the ledgers.

"Mr. Pennyman, of the offices of Kimball, Dunnington, and Pennyman," her uncle intoned, "as well as I and my esteemed brother and the head of our family, Sir Mauris, are of the opinion that before the will be made public, certain provisions needed to be handled. Discreetly."

"For which you should be most grateful," Aunt Allegra told her. "A young lady with a fortune is subject to all sorts of untoward attentions by the worst sort of vagrants."

Why was it that Tabitha instantly thought of Preston?

She shook off the image of that handsome rogue and focused on what her uncle was saying. "I hardly think I will be of much interest to any man."

"You needn't worry on that account!" Uncle Bernard burst out laughing. "My dear, you will be married before Midsummer's Eve."

"A summer bride," her aunt enthused.

Tabitha glanced at both of them. "However is that possible?"

Her uncle, no longer smiling, having taken off his glasses and characteristically frowning at her, said, "Your uncle's will only allows you to inherit if you are married." He studied his spectacles for a moment more before he began to clean them. "The entire inheritance is void if you are not wed before your twenty-fifth year to—"

The words echoed past her, each one banging into the other until it was naught but a cacophony. *Married. Twenty-fifth year.*

Twenty-fifth year? Tabitha froze. "But that's only—"

"Yes, a little over a month's time."

"Then the money is lost," Tabitha said, throwing up her hands. "However am I to find a husband in so short a time? There's not even enough weeks left to read the banns properly, let alone find a suitable *parti*."

"Not in the least," Aunt Allegra told her, smiling anew. "It has all been arranged."

If Tabitha thought her life had been turned upside down by her encounter with Mr. Preston, she suddenly realized she was about to be overturned yet again.

"Whatever do you mean, Aunt Allegra?" Tabitha glanced at her uncle. "Sir?"

"All is not lost, my dear," Uncle Bernard said with a renewed cheer. "Your Uncle Winston was kind enough to also bequeath you a husband."

"What the devil is all this I've been hearing all over Town?" Lord Henry Seldon asked, standing before the bottle-covered table at White's where his nephew, Christopher Seldon, the Duke of Preston, and the duke's rapscallion friend, the Earl of Roxley, were holding court.

Small court that it was, for most of the other members of the club were giving them the cut direct. Not that either man cared.

"I beat Kipps!" Preston crowed. "No one thought my nags could take that fancy set of cattle Kipps has been prowsing on about, but I've been collecting vowels all night." His hands swept drunkenly over the pile of notes before him.

Roxley reached in his jacket and plucked out a handful as well. "Rich as Midas, we are!"

"Damn near killed us doing it—" Preston began to explain.

"Pulled up short on a bunch of geese—" Roxley added.

"Goslings—" Preston corrected.

"Might as well have been a litter of pups," the earl told Lord Henry, "but you know how your nephew is about a woeful pair of brown eyes. Gets him into trouble every time."

"Roxley, I don't think geese have brown eyes," Preston posed.

As the pair began to argue the point, Lord Henry lost his patience and temper. "Whatever possessed you to do something so foolhardy? You could have been killed. Not to mention you've beggared half of the *ton*. Ruined Kipps, I suspect."

Roxley and Preston exchanged glances.

"Because we could," Preston told him, roaring with laughter. Roxley joined in, and the pair of them brayed like jackasses.

"You are both pot valiant now," Lord Henry said, shaking his head, "but tomorrow will be another story. Hen will have your head for this, Preston."

Preston's reply was another dismissive wave of his hand.

"She'll not be naysaid this time," Lord Henry continued. "She'll insist you take a bride, if only to spare us all from ruin."

"Ruin? Hardly that, Henry." Preston plucked his boots off the table and rose unsteadily to face his uncle. "Haven't you heard? I've come into a fortune tonight."

Lord Henry shook his head. "Marriage it will be, whether you like it or not."

"Not," Preston proclaimed, wavering for a moment, and then flopping back into his seat. "I won't take a wife."

"You're drunk," his uncle complained.

"Utterly foxed," Preston corrected, wagging a finger at him.

"I might get married," Roxley said to no one in particular.

"You?" Preston laughed.

The earl nodded. "I have to imagine I've passed the perfect woman time and time again. If I were merely to open my eyes, I would discover her."

"It might help if you stopped drinking and carousing," Lord Henry advised, waving at one of the attendants to come clean up the litter of empty bottles.

"If I were you, Roxley," Preston slurred, "I wouldn't open my eyes."

Roxley laughed. "I think such a sentiment makes me romantic."

Lord Henry's gaze rolled upward. "That is the last thing anyone would call you."

"Rake," Preston observed. "That might work."

This time the earl shook his head and leaned forward to whisper. "No, that's Henry. Devilish rake if ever there was one."

Preston smirked. "No, I think he's a scoundrel. Coming here and using that word when we're celebrating."

"What word?" Roxley asked as he poured himself and Preston another round. He held up an empty glass for Lord Henry, who just shook his head.

"Marriage."

Roxley shuddered. "You sound like my Aunt Essex."

Lord Henry threw up his hands. "Preston, I am trying to tell you, you are ruined. Go home, sleep this off, and then come to your senses." He turned and stormed off. Probably off to the dull, empty halls of Boodles. Good steaks, but the cellar wasn't as fine as White's.

Preston watched him leave with a wry glance. "Come to my senses, indeed! He's older than me—why doesn't he get married?"

"Exactly," Roxley agreed. "Dip his toe in first. Test the waters for us."

"However does one find a wife for such a dull, practical fellow?" Preston posed, leaning back in his chair and propping his boots back up on the table.

Roxley rubbed his chin. "Since neither of us is of a mind to set foot in Almack's, I don't think we'll ever find out."

Just then, a gray-haired Corinthian came by. Lord Mouncey. Nay, Murrant. No, that wasn't it either. Preston tried to shake the man's name out of his brandy-soaked brain.

And he might not have had to worry about it if the fellow had just ambled right past. Yet that wasn't the case, for while the man did cast a shuddering glance at the state of Preston's muddy boots, it wasn't the lack of gloss that stopped the fastidious old dandy in his tracks.

"I say there, Preston, is that today's paper under your boot?"

Preston leaned forward and eyed it. "It is, Lord Mulancy." That was it, Mulancy! There, he wasn't *that* foxed.

"Might I borrow it? Baldwin mentioned an advertisement for a fine batch of fillies coming in from the countryside this week. Want to get the particulars."

Preston tugged his boots off the table once more and handed over the paper. But before he went to hoist the muddy Hessians back up, he stilled. Whatever had Mulancy said?...*an advertisement for a fine batch of fillies...* "That's it!"

Roxley's head bobbed up, having dozed off during the lull in conversation. "What's it?" He blinked owlishly at his surroundings and looked ready to doze off again.

"Oh, wake up," Preston said, giving his boon companion a hard shake. "That's how we find Henry a wife. We advertise for one."

And this time when he waved the attendant over, he ordered not only another bottle of brandy, but pen and ink.

"Preston, this is absolutely unacceptable!" Lady Juniper, the former Lady Henrietta Seldon, declared as her nephew came into the Red Room a few days later. "You cannot continue to use London society as your personal circus."

Despite Hen's best efforts to sound severe and forbidding, Preston didn't appear the least bit affronted by his aunt's scold. Rather, he laughed as he came into the room which served as her favorite place to take tea.

Lady Juniper turned to her twin brother. "Henry, help me out."

Lord Henry got to his feet, tucked his hands behind his back and began to pace across the carpet. "Hen is right. You must rein in these impulsive bouts of scandalous behavior and start behaving with some decorum—"

"Decorum?" Preston shuddered. He glanced over at his relation, who was a walking advertisement for the notion—from the perfectly respectable cut of his coat to the carefully tied and knotted cravat. No grand waterfall of linen, no intricate *Trone d'Amour* that would make him the envy of every Corinthian, just a steady Mailcoach that lent an elegant, orderly air to Henry's expensive, yet simple, ensemble.

"Yes, decorum," his uncle repeated, eyeing his nephew's interest and striking at it like the finest of batsmen. "Decorum is the new order."

"Truly, decorum is the new order?" Preston asked. "Shall we have this room redone so we can be a bit less ostentatious?"

The Red Room could only be described as the height of extravagance—gilt and red velvet and gleaming mahogany. Thick Turkish carpets and silk coverings on furnishings. A tea urn—no simple pot but a great towering silver urn, complete with cherubs and a dragon at the top—stood grandly at the end of the long table.

He shot a glance over at his aunt, Lady Juniper—it was Juniper, wasn't it? Or was it Michaels? Taking a moment, Preston did a momentary tally. No, Michaels had been her second husband. So it was indeed Juniper.

Like her mother before her, Lady Henrietta had the unwitting fate of picking husbands who turned around and cocked up their toes.

And like her brother, she was done up in the latest stare. Though all in black, for Lord Juniper had only been gone for six months. Nor did the suggestion of redecorating her beloved parlor seem to redirect her attentions. Rather Hen looked anything but diverted. Not in the least.

"Decorum!" Henry repeated.

"Grandfather must be rolling over in his grave to hear that word uttered in this house," Preston replied.

"Well, perhaps it is about time the Seldons adopted the notion," Lord Henry countered, wagging his finger at his nephew.

Once Henry got going, there was little one could do to stop him. Not even when one was a duke.

So Preston settled back in his chair and folded his arms across his chest and did his best to appear both interested and conscious.

Not an easy feat when Henry was on one of his tears.

"Times are changing," Lord Henry rattled on. "We can no longer afford the negligent airs and misadventures that have marked—"

The duke stopped listening, for he knew exactly how this tirade was going to continue. Yes, yes. *The misadventures that have marked this family for eight generations. Eight generations of dalliances and revelry and scandals that have constantly put us at the very fringes of society and the king's good graces...*

Preston knew it by heart. He'd heard it enough times since his grandfather had died five years earlier to recite it verbatim.

But of late, it had become nearly a daily harangue. Mayhap it was time to send Lord Henry on some emergency review of the ducal holdings in Ireland.

Preston perked up at the notion, that is until he recalled that he'd already done that once before—last fall, to be exact. He glanced over at his uncle, who was still sermonizing on and on with no hint of an end in sight.

No, Preston couldn't hope that such a ruse would work twice.

Especially since Henry now knew there were no ducal holdings in Ireland.

"—honor, respectability, nobility on your part and in the eyes of the influential members of our society and we may, and I emphasize 'may,' regain what we have lost." Thankfully, Lord Henry paused to draw a breath, as did Preston.

Respectability? Honor?

Some would argue those were traits the Seldons had never possessed, though it wasn't an argument Preston was in the mood to broach with Henry. Not today.

Now Hen wasn't above a bit of scandal now and then. Look at the fuss she'd kicked up when she'd married her second husband. So he flashed a grin in her direction hoping upon hope she would save him.

But no luck there. His aunt looked as dour as Henry sounded. And as prosy. Worse, if he wasn't mistaken, the slip of paper she was plucking from her reticule had all the appearances of a list.

Which could only mean one thing.

Oh, dear God, this is an ambush, he realized all too late, struggling to get to his feet.

"Sit, Christopher," Aunt Hen ordered.

And Preston did. When she used that tone and resorted to his Christian name—not "Preston" or "Your Grace"—it was always best to do as Hen advised. He'd learned that early in life.

Lady Juniper glanced over at her brother. "You as well, Henry. Your pacing about is giving me a megrim and I daresay will give Christopher a bout of hives."

Lord Henry retook his place on the sofa and took the offered cup. "It is high time that—"

Preston cut his uncle off mid-scold. "I won't discuss this."

"You need to stop causing scandals," Lord Henry continued as if Preston was still in short coats. "This ruinous situation with poor Kipps has brought us all down."

Kipps? This was all because of his race with Kipps? "Will blow over," the duke averred, even as an odd breeze ruffled at the back of his neck, sending the hairs there standing on end.

No, it won't.

He did his level best to ignore that niggling frisson of doubt. That voice of reason that had little or no place in his life.

He was the Duke of Preston after all.

"Kipps is utterly ruined," Hen said plainly. "It is a wretched disgrace."

"His difficulties are hardly my concern," Preston told them, trying to sound as coldhearted as he could muster, but once again his conscience got the better of him.

You knew better and still...

"It is most decidedly a matter of our concern when all of society blames you—and us in turn—for his ruin," Hen shot back.

Who needed a conscience when one had Hen in their life?

She paused for a moment, which unfortunately allowed Henry to leap right in. "Good God, Preston, you haven't just ruined that poor lad; now his family hasn't a feather to fly with, and everyone blames us."

Preston shifted in his chair. He'd certainly thought something had been amiss last night when he'd gone to

White's—he'd been snubbed by more than one member, which wasn't so unusual given his reputation— yet it had been easily forgotten once Roxley had come along and they'd spent a companionable evening drinking and playing cards.

"If Kipps was so far in the River Tick," Preston told them, "then he had no business making such large wagers. He's a foolish cub." He waved them off and turned his attention to the tea tray.

"You took advantage of poor Kipps, Preston," Hen said, her brows furrowed into an angry, disapproving line. "He trusted you. You took him under your wing."

Preston glanced away. He rather liked Kipps. The young earl was an affable fellow and always up for a lark. Certainly, he'd never meant to lead Kipps astray...

"You nearly got that poor boy killed!" Hen said, her finger wagging. "Making such an indecent wager and then racing all that distance. What did you think would happen? He had to reach London before you. Instead, he crashed his carriage, nearly broke his neck, and now he's got everyone calling in vowels he can't afford."

"Then I won't call in what he owes me," Preston told them. Not that he had planned on doing so—after all, it had been nothing but a grand caper. Glancing at his aunt and uncle, he doubted they would call it such. "I'll pay off his debts."

"Out to ruin his pride as well, eh, Preston?" Henry said, letting out an exasperated breath. "Besides, have you looked at your own pockets of late? You haven't the ready blunt. One more of these romps of yours and we will all be in the same straits as poor Kipps."

"Poor Kipps! Poor Kipps!" Preston burst out. "I nearly wrecked my carriage, sent Roxley flying over a hedge, and demmed near lamed my best set of bays, but I don't see anyone wringing their hands and wailing 'Poor Preston.' I said it before, and I'll say it again, I am not responsible if that wet-behind-the-ears child is naught but a fool to have wagered so much. If he'd been reasonable and cautious…" His words trailed off even as Hen's brows arched with an indignant angle.

"Kipps wasn't foolish, he was desperate," Hen told him, rising to her feet, her temper getting the better of her. "Do you know that his sister has been ill? That the surgeon's bills have nearly run them under? That he has four more sisters who are to come out in the next three years? His father left him in dire straits. A situation you of all people could appreciate considering the tangled mire Father left behind."

That previous niggle of guilt suddenly felt more like a nudge. Given Hen's furious expression, it might well turn into a well-placed boot in his arse.

Henry waded in again. "Now Kipps has no choice but to marry and marry quickly. The first *cit's* daughter who will take him."

Preston's gaze swung toward his uncle. "Marry? Whatever for?"

"So he can pay his bills," Henry said, getting to his feet in the same fit of exasperation that Hen was exhibiting. "He needs a fat purse to fill his coffers."

"Well, he won't be 'poor Kipps' then, will he?" Preston tried to quip, but his jest fell on deaf ears. Unfortunately, like the thud of his joke, he felt his own future close around him like a pair of leg-shackles.

"It is no laughing matter," Henry said. "It's that or debtor's prison for him."

"You have ruined us with this escapade, Preston,"

Hen said, resuming her seat and staring him straight in the eye. Her usually affable blue gaze was deep and serious. "Every tongue in Town is blaming us for Kipps's fall. Have you noticed that the doorbell hasn't rung once this morning? The salver sits empty."

"Hardly empty," Preston corrected. "I just came in and it was buried with letters."

Henry's face turned red and he began to bluster. "Because you and that idiot went and placed that demmed advertisement—"

Hen stopped her brother with a wave of her hand. "Preston, there are no invitations arriving—not even from the few mushrooms who would dare to presume. The only scrap I have received this week was to inform me that my vouchers for the Season had been revoked. I am banned from Almack's! Me!" The lady reached for her handkerchief.

Preston knew it wasn't to douse tears, for Hen never cried. Still, here was his aunt, making a great show of dabbing at something in her eyes.

"You don't even like Almack's," he reminded her.

"What has that got to do with anything?" she said. "No respectable family wants to be associated with you, with us." There it was again, that dramatic pose with the handkerchief stuffed to her supposedly quivering lip.

But as he looked closer, he could see Hen was truly distressed, and something in his chest clenched into a knot.

The same sort of knot that had had him driving his carriage into an oak to avoid a flock of geese and dragging home strays he found on his meanderings.

Demmit! His aunt knew him too well.

And to that end, Henry picked up where his sister had stopped. "Hen and I have discussed this and are in agreement that the only thing that will save us all is for you to take a wife."

"Why don't *you* go out and find a wife," Preston suggested just as Henry was taking a sip of his tea.

"I think you and Roxley already took care of that," Hen said with a wry, disapproving shake of her head.

Lord Henry sputtered a bit. "Your wretched advertisement has brought out every spinster and lonely heart within a hundred miles of London."

Preston looked from one to the other. "Advertisement?"

His uncle's brow rose into an imperious arch. "The one you and Roxley penned?"

This time it was Preston's turn to sputter a bit. Oh. *That* advertisement.

The duke leaned over and nudged his uncle in the ribs. "Don't like the bit, but you are more than happy to see me saddled, eh, Henry? Besides, you're six months older than I, so it only seems right that you dip your toe in first. You should be thanking me. I've done you the favor of fattening the pot."

He knew better than to push Henry too far, for the next time they met at Gentleman Jim's, Preston was going to take a devil of a beating. As it was, Henry was rising to his feet, hands fisting.

Perhaps he wasn't going to have to wait...

"Preston, this is hardly helping!" Hen told him. "You! Sit!" she ordered her brother.

"It is a matter of keeping the family together, you reckless fool," Henry replied, even as he sat as his sister had bid. He might be able to pummel Preston in the boxing ring, but neither of them could out argue Hen. "I could marry, but then what? You'll still be gadding about causing one reckless scandal after another."

"In other words," Preston began, "I need to be as dull and sensible as all those mushrooms and *cits* you pander to in the House of Commons."

Hen pressed her lips together and narrowly avoided smiling at this insult. "Henry does have a point. You must consider the lineage. And our position in society."

"Hang Almack's and the rest of them," Preston replied. "Besides, I don't see the rush. Grandfather added you two to the family tree when he was well into his dotage."

The old duke's marriage to the young and comely widow Lady Salsbury had been yet another *on dit* in a long life of scandals, especially when she'd gone and produced a spare heir and a daughter all at once. Society had been shocked. Who would have thought the old duke capable, let alone Lady Salsbury—who'd had four husbands before her marriage to the duke and not a child to show from any of those unions?

"Dash it all, Christopher," Lord Henry said, completely forgetting himself, "you need to infuse some cash into your estates, and I am trying to help you do just that. These *cits* and mushrooms you mock have more ready brass than you do. Than any of us do. The world is changing, and mark my words, one day it will be the merchants and shop owners who run this country."

"Good heavens, what a distasteful notion," Aunt Hen declared, her nose wrinkled at the very thought. "Really, Preston, it is simply a matter of getting married to a proper lady and securing an heir. Then Henry will do the rest, and all of us will be redeemed."

There it was. Get married. The solution to everything.

Why couldn't his aunt be more like one of those chits from that little village Roxley had dragged him through? If it were true—that none of them had any desire to be wed—he might consider moving there. Permanently.

But his momentary plans for escape were for naught, for Lord Henry reached across the table and caught up his sister's list. "Hen has the perfect lady in mind. She comes with a decent bloodline and a goodly inheritance."

"How kind of you," Preston replied.

Hen ignored his sarcasm. "I cast this paragon in your direction with much trepidation, Preston. There are others there as well. Just in case."

"Truly, Hen, I am no monster," Preston told her, avoiding even a glance in the direction of Henry's outstretched hand. Wherein lay his future bride. "I hardly see why one bit of scandal should force me into the parson's trap."

"One bit of scandal?" Hen shot back. "Look behind you, Preston! You've left a wake of ruin in your path this Season and it is only the first week of May!"

"Isn't that doing it up a bit, Hen?" he dared. Even as the words fell from his lips he knew he'd fallen into a dangerous mire.

"Lord Holdwin's daughter?" She held up her hand and ticked off one finger. The rest of her fingers fell in quick succession. "Lady Violet, Miss Seales, the Earl of Durston's twin daughters—"

"They only count once, for I could never tell them apart," he tried to joke.

Hen appeared ready to douse him with her tea. Or rather the entire urn. "And shall I remind you of how this Season began? With Lord Randall's daughter?"

Preston scuttled up in his seat, rising to his own defense. "That foolish chit shouldn't have followed me out into the garden. At her own debut ball, no less."

"You ruined her!" Aunt Hen shot back. "And put a blight on our reputations because you couldn't control yourself."

"I didn't ruin the gel. I kissed her," he corrected. "I hardly call that ruin. Besides, isn't she engaged now to that Scottish fellow?"

"Yes, but he's a mere knight, and hardly the lofty and well-connected prospect that Lady Randall had her heart set on," Aunt Hen complained, refilling her brother's cup of tea and adding the two lumps of sugar he liked in it.

"Wasn't Michaels a knight?" he prodded, referring to Hen's second husband.

"A baron," she corrected.

"Same difference," Lord Henry muttered, for he hadn't been in favor of his sister's impetuous marriage to a man whose elevation had been so recent that there had hardly been time to let the ink dry on the Letters Patent.

"As it is, Lady Randall is going to have a terrible time when she tries to bring out her other daughters," Hen said, steering the conversation back to the subject at hand.

"Then Lady Randall ought to have kept a better eye on that minx," Preston told them. "And I will note I wasn't the first one into that pasture. The gel knew exactly what she was doing. Damn near had my breeches open before I could—"

"Oh good heavens!" Hen sputtered. "I don't think *that* needs to be repeated."

"Well, she did," he told them. "Mayhap I did let slip I was going out for a cigar, but I can hardly be responsible if she is hen-witted enough to follow. Or offer to show me what she learned at school." He glanced over at Hen. "Imagine my surprise to discover the girl's lessons included a variety of courtesan's tricks. Is that what they teach in Bath? I thought the order of the day was dancing and poetry. Or have we men been mistaken all these years about the curriculum of a Bath education?"

Aunt Hen, who had spent three years at Lady Emery's, rolled her gaze upwards. "I hardly think what a girl learns in finishing school is the point."

Henry, who had no desire to know what "tricks" his sister might have learned in her time in Bath, pulled the conversation back on point. "I can't go over to White's these days without being buttonholed by yet another aggrieved father or brother who claims you've slighted some female member of their family."

Preston huffed a grand, exasperated sigh and threw up his hands. "Now I'm responsible for the maidenhead of every young lady in London?"

"This," Hen said, "is getting us nowhere. Those names are what we are here to discuss." Taking the note out of her brother's grasp, she handed the slip of paper over to Preston with her usual determination and leaving him no means to object. There just was no refusing Hen when she set her mind to a subject.

Hence the three husbands.

Reluctantly, Preston accepted her proposal and took a glance at it. The first name sounded vaguely familiar in a dull sort of way, but before he had a moment to put a face to the memory, Hen continued, "These ladies are not to be kissed. Not to be ruined. Nor to lure to some secluded alcove—"

A direct reference to Lady Violet. And in his defense, that chit had caught him by the arm and hauled him behind that curtain. Last time he'd turn his back on some country miss. That one had possessed the grasp of a plowhand.

"—but to *court*. With the intent of marrying one of them." Hen settled back in her seat and smiled at Preston, then at her brother.

For they both knew that once Hen had Preston married off, she'd set her cap on seeing Henry settled as well. She'd always held that her position as the eldest of the three gave her license to rule over her brother and nephew.

It had been that way since the day she'd taken her first step and lisped her first "mine."

The duke sighed. "And if I refuse?"

Then to his surprise, it was Henry who answered. "We'll move out."

Preston glanced over at the man who was more a brother than an uncle. "Leave?"

"Yes," Hen said, with all the determination of a Seldon. She had inherited that much from her father. It was a Seldon trait that never failed to find its way into the blood.

"You'd abandon me?" Preston asked, though he knew he needn't. Once a Seldon made a declaration, it was carved in stone—no matter if it drove them into deeper waters and left them drowning.

"Yes," Hen told him, giving every bit of proof he needed to know she would. And Henry as well.

But they couldn't! It was only the three of them left. Mulish obstinacy they had in spades, but sadly the Seldons weren't a prolific lot. And the three of them had always stuck together. Henry and Hen had been his only family since…well, since always.

Preston glanced around the large room and the rest of the vast rooms in the house and shivered. They'd be cold and hollow without them. No one coming and going. No one to take his meals with.

Something he hadn't felt in years too many to count rose up inside him. Not since the day he'd come to live in this house. Alone? They couldn't do this to him. They wouldn't.

One look at the set of Hen's brows, the line of Henry's jaw, said only too clearly they would.

"You've left us no choice, Preston," Hen said, rising from her seat and setting her napkin down on the table. "Either you marry and take a respectable place in society, or we will leave and never come back."

Worst of all, they could do it. They'd both inherited a tidy fortune from their mother—Hen having added to her own coffers with three advantageous matches— so neither of them truly needed him.

And neither did society, for that matter. The *ton* would blackball him without a second thought and he'd be *persona non grata* in London.

Glancing down at the paper in his hand, he asked, "Is this the only way?"

Hen's gaze rolled skyward. "Oh, good heavens, Christopher! Whatever is wrong with marriage?"

"I'd say we ask your late husbands," he muttered.

Chapter 3

"This will never do," Lady Essex declared as she stared out the window of her carriage. The lady, who had planned to take Harriet to Town, had agreed to bring along Tabitha. Unwilling to be left behind, Daphne had managed, in true Dale fashion, to reason and arrange her way into the party.

Now their grand trip to London, which should have taken only two days, had come to a grinding halt a good half a day away from the city gates, much to Tabitha's relief and dismay. After pressing on in a terrible spring squall earlier in the day, all their hopes of reaching the city before nightfall were dashed. The mired roads had slowed their pace so much so that as evening had fallen, Lady Essex had declared they must take shelter, news that had brought a sigh of relief from a beleaguered and exhausted John Coachman.

"Tomorrow! I cannot believe we shall have to wait until tomorrow to reach London!" Daphne said as she secured her pelisse and checked her hat to make sure it didn't blow off.

Tabitha said nothing. After all, ever since her uncle had declared that she was to be married, Tabitha had found herself in the middle of a maelstrom, with her aunt and uncle refusing to listen to her protests against this match.

"Your uncle has chosen well for you," Aunt Allegra had stormed. *"A man well connected, and an heir presumptive to a great title. Think of how you will be able to help your family, your dear cousins!"*

Then they had proceeded to treat her with such overreaching care and kindness—after all, one day their very own, dearest Tabitha would be a marchioness!—that Tabitha had found herself wishing for her corner in the attic and the solitude of her former chores.

"Come now, Tabitha. You cannot tell me you aren't the least bit disappointed about not getting to London tonight," Daphne asked as they dashed across the inn's muddy yard. "Of meeting *him*. Mr. Reginald Barkworth." Daphne couldn't say the man's name without adding a soft sigh. "It is all so very romantic."

Much to Tabitha's chagrin, Daphne had taken the position that Tabitha's arranged marriage was the most efficient and practical means of finding a husband. And Mr. Reginald Barkworth? The heir to a marquisate? Well, obviously the perfect gentleman.

Harriet, however, was not so optimistic and liked to remind them both of the fate of Agnes, the most infamous bride of Kempton. Poor Agnes had gone mad on her wedding night to the unfortunately named John Stakes, a man her parents had forced her to wed.

Agnes, Daphne would argue, *knew nothing of men.*

And a little too much about how to wield a poker, Harriet would mutter back.

Yet there it was. Whatever did Tabitha know of men? Or as that wretched Preston had put it...*of men's whims or, for that matter, the desire a lady feels?*

Nothing. Absolutely nothing. Save how unsettling it had to been to meet Preston.

Preston with his open shirt and bare chest. Preston with the broad shoulders. Preston with the tangled mess of chestnut hair. Preston, whose eyes burned with a wicked light.

Even the very remembrance left her a little breathless and off-kilter. Oh, he was the path toward madness if ever there was one.

And she blamed him entirely for her reluctance to get married. Whatever would she do if Mr. Reginald Barkworth was merely half as handsome?

"Tell me you are thoroughly excited at the prospect of meeting Mr. Reginald Barkworth," Daphne pressed as they got inside and waited while Lady Essex ordered up rooms. "Or I will be most disappointed with you, Tabitha."

"Mayhap a little," she admitted. Terrified might be a better description.

"I wonder what he looks like," Daphne said, her hands clutched in front of her. "Do you think he will be handsome? Did your aunt or uncle say anything about his countenance? As long as he doesn't have a wen. It is quite impossible not to find oneself staring at one, especially if it sits there like a button in the middle of their forehead. That could be quite worrisome. If he has a wen."

While Daphne seemed to ponder this possibility silently (thankfully), Tabitha realized that a wen had been the least of her concerns, but now that she thought about it, she added that to her ever-growing list of fears.

"Whatever will you do if he does have a wen?" Daphne posed.

"Who has a wen?" Harriet asked, dashing up from behind, having returned to the carriage to fetch her reticule.

"Tabitha's betrothed," Daphne told her. "Well, actually we don't know if he has one, but we were considering the possibilities."

"Oh, that would be dreadful," Harriet agreed. "I still say you forgo all of this nonsense and move into the Pottage. Marriage is fraught with peril, or so my brothers vow."

On this dour note, Lady Essex returned and declared their surroundings "suitable." The indomitable spinster had bullied the landlord into giving her and her young charges the best room—the one with a parlor. Once they'd climbed the stairs, "away from the rabble," as Lady Essex said, she took to her bed and left her three charges on their own.

For the next few hours, Tabitha paced the room as she had every night for the past two weeks—torn between her anxieties of continuing on and the prospects of what, or rather whom, would meet her there.

Mr. Muggins, who could not be left behind in Kempton, watched his mistress from the rug before the fireplace with an air of curiosity, while Harriet snored softly from a narrow couch.

"Whatever is the matter?" Daphne finally asked, glancing up from the London newspaper she'd purloined from a downstairs table. "You aren't still worried about Mr. Reginald Barkworth, are you?" She laid her paper aside. "Surely your Uncle Winston would not desert you to some terrible roué."

"He all but abandoned my mother when she married Papa." She'd loved it when her mother would tell her how she had been destined to marry a lofty lord and then run away with Tabitha's father instead. It was such a romantic story and spoke of true love, not this willed union and business agreement her uncle had devised.

"Perhaps your Uncle Winston is making up for his shortcomings by providing you with an exceptional groom." Practical to a fault, Daphne found Tabitha's arranged marriage ever so tidy. "At the very least, Mr. Reginald Barkworth can be counted as a gentleman of good breeding." With that said, she went back to her paper.

Who was willing to marry me for my fortune, sight unseen, Tabitha resisted pointing out.

Though Harriet would have, if she were awake.

Not that Tabitha was in the mood to hear them begin debating the subject yet again, not when she was tired and famished. As if to punctuate that thought, her stomach growled. Loudly.

"Good heavens!" Daphne declared, peering over the edge of her paper. "Whatever was that racket?"

"My stomach. I'm famished." While her friend gaped at her, Tabitha tried to fathom how it was that

Daphne and Harriet and Lady Essex could subsist on tea and toast all day.

Even Mr. Muggins appeared unsympathetic—but then again, the innkeeper had sent up a bone for the terrier, most likely to keep the dog from chewing up the furniture in his best room.

"However do I get something to eat?"

Daphne was no help; enthralled as she was by some notice in the paper, she barely looked up. "How would I know? Father usually goes down and then the trays are brought up. Not that I ever partake. Never do like to eat when I'm traveling."

Tabitha wished she shared that inclination. But being hungry only intensified the nervous gnawing that had been churning in her gut for a fortnight.

"Do you want me to come with you?" Daphne asked, all the while looking longingly at her newspaper. She read the ads and legal notices like Harriet devoured serial stories and Miss Briggs's infamous Darby novels.

"No, no, you enjoy your paper," Tabitha told her.

"It does seem quiet down there," Daphne said, tipping her head toward the door. "Lady Essex will be none the wiser if you were to just pop downstairs to ask for a quick supper."

"Do you think it would be proper?"

"You could take Mr. Muggins with you," she suggested. "There isn't a man alive who would come between you and that beast. A far better chaperone than Lady Essex."

They both laughed, for their towering guardian, with all her rules and strictures about proper decorum, most likely wouldn't wake until dawn—leaving them quite unprotected.

Tabitha's stomach growled again, and Daphne shook her head. "Do you like being hungry?" With that said, she continued on, "I might remind you that Lady Essex does not believe in taking breakfast while traveling— or did you forget about this morning?"

How could Tabitha have forgotten? The lady had hustled them out the door and into the carriage without even a warm scone.

Or a bite of bacon. A slice of ham. Not even a hard-cooked egg. Oh, she'd arrive at her aunt and uncle's house tomorrow afternoon on her last legs.

And what if Mr. Barkworth was there? Awaiting her? She'd be a sullen, hungry, bedraggled wreck.

She'd probably be so delirious with hunger she'd marry him without a second thought just to get to the wedding breakfast.

That decided the matter. Tabitha nodded and went to the door. Immediately, Mr. Muggins was on his feet, following his mistress.

"Oh, Tabitha, before you leave—" Daphne began.

"Yes?"

"Will you fetch my writing desk?" Daphne pointed at the black box near her valise.

Tabitha retrieved it, and as she handed it over, she glanced at the long line of advertisements. "Found something worth inquiring about?"

"Nothing of note," Daphne replied. "But it might be worthwhile—" Already she was pulling out a sheet of paper and organizing her pen and ink.

From the doorway, Tabitha said, "If I find the company unseemly, I shall bring a tray upstairs immediately."

"If you run into any handsome gentlemen, practice your wiles," Daphne teased.

"I possess no wiles," Tabitha reminded her, but by now Daphne wasn't listening, only waving her hand in a distracted flutter and settling back into composing her inquiry.

Thus dismissed, Tabitha made her way down the dark stairs, Mr. Muggins tight on her heels, only to be dismayed to find that the common room was empty. The storm had chased everyone to the cozy warmth of their beds.

But as she rounded the corner, a bit of light illuminated the end of the hall, the one that led toward the kitchens. Someone was in there.

Oh, yes, please, she thought as the singular and enticing smell of roast beef wound around her.

Even Mr. Muggins perked up, his wet brown nose tipped in the air.

If there was roast beef, there might even be Yorkshire pudding. Tabitha sighed with something between hope and rapture. *Yorkshire pudding!*

She hastened her steps, hurrying along the corridor, visions of pudding and roast beef luring her forward, so that she swung around the corner and instead of finding the kitchen as she'd hoped, she found herself colliding with a large man. The two of them became an immediate tangle of limbs—her hands grasping at his coat lapels to keep from toppling backwards, his arms winding around her to keep her upright.

Truly it was rather like hitting a side of beef. As her fingers splayed out to steady herself, they found a wall of unmistakable male muscle that rose like the walls of Jericho beneath his wool coat.

She might be just a spinster from Kempton, but the woman inside her recognized that unmistakable power surrounding her, and something, oh, something like that odd, tempting hunger she'd felt once before reawakened.

Tabitha tried to breathe, tried to even remember how or why she'd gotten to this place. For this man hadn't just kept her from falling but he was also holding her still, intimately so, his fingers moving over her back, his warmth enveloping her on this cold night, curling inside her limbs and enticing her to edge closer. Her feet, instead of finding their footing, wavered, her toes curling inside her boots.

This feeling, this languor, good heavens, it was utterly...

Familiar, she realized, looking up and shocked to discover by whom she'd been undone yet again.

"Oh my!" she gasped. "You!"

Preston.

Scrambling backwards, she nearly tangled with Mr. Muggins, and again, the man reached out to catch her from falling, but this time she managed to save herself and avoid his clutches.

"I suppose I am," he replied, leaning back against the doorjamb and crossing his arms over his chest. "And you are not the maid with my supper."

"The maid? I think not," she sputtered, feeling even more put out and catching up Mr. Muggins by the collar, just in case he felt the urge to bite this villain.

Which apparently he did not. Mr. Muggins shook off her grasp, ambled inside what appeared to be a private dining room and settled down by the fireplace, absolutely unworried at having entered such a den of iniquity.

Preston eyed the interloper who had just taken up a place on the rug and then back at Tabitha. "No, definitely not the maid."

"Which I am heartily thankful I am not, since it seems you are in the habit of accosting them." She brushed her hands down her sleeves, as if wiping away his touch.

"Accosted? I hardly think so," he told her, looking quite amused and proud of himself. He pushed off the wall and walked past her. "Not in the least, miss. And not with you." Then he leaned forward, peering through the shadows. "Good God! You're that scrawny, saucy minx from that village—"

Scrawny, saucy minx? Well, I never—

"Miss—Miss—" He tipped his head to one side and examined her, an assessing glance that landed on her as if he were running his hands over her.

"Miss Timmons," she reminded him, repressing the shiver that threatened to leave her quaking before him.

"Ah, Miss Timmons," he replied, "if I had truly accosted you, you wouldn't have escaped." That rakish grin of his spread from his lips and lit his eyes with a wolfish gleam. "Nor would you have wanted to."

No, you wouldn't have, something inside her agreed.

Tabitha took another step back and bumped into the wall, which kept her from toppling over. Thankfully. That rakish look in his eyes had her knees wobbling again. "Oh! You are a—"

Her scolding admonishment was interrupted by another. "Miss Timmons! Did I hear you say 'Miss Timmons,' Preston?" Inside the room, a tall, athletic figure rose from a chair near the fireplace. "Why, it is you!"

"Lord Roxley," Tabitha said, not surprised to find the earl in this man's company, but ever so thankful to see him.

"Good heavens, what are you doing here?" he asked, coming forward and taking her hand. "How is it you are so far from Kempton?" The earl led her into the room, sweeping her past Preston, whose arched gaze followed her every step.

Right now she would have wished herself back in Kempton and well away from this devil's snare.

"Your aunt, Lady Essex, is bringing me up to London," she said in a rush, but not so much of one that she finished that sentence...*to get married*. For she well remembered her last encounter with Preston.

Sir, I will have you know, I never intend to go seeking a husband and am quite content with the notion.

How her life had turned upside down since she'd declared those fateful words.

She'd meant them then and would mean them still if it hadn't been for Uncle Winston's will.

"My aunt?" Roxley echoed, glancing at the doorway as if he expected Lady Essex to come barreling into the room.

As it was, the poor earl nearly leapt out of his skin when someone did—at that moment—come through the door. "Good heavens, I'm done for," he declared, closing his eyes.

"Oh demmit, Roxley, shore up your reserves," Preston told him. "'Tis only the maid."

Roxley cracked open one eye and then sighed with relief at the sight of the kitchen girl—the one Pres-

ton had been on the prowl for—arriving, large tray in
hand. Behind her came a serving lad with an equally
laden tray.

"Is there anything else you'd be needin'?" said the
girl—well, she was hardly a girl, Tabitha realized, as
she tossed an obvious glance at Preston, her hips sway-
ing like a saucy cat in heat.

"No, the meal looks excellent," Preston said, tossing coins to both of them. "Thank you."

The boy caught his deftly, grinned and departed.
The maid caught her coin just as easily but lingered
a bit longer.

Remembering what Daphne said about speaking up,
Tabitha managed to get her request in. "Please, I would
like a tray brought up to my room, if that is possible."

The girl slanted an assessing glance at her and obviously found her sadly lacking. "Sorry, miss. That's
all there is left," she said, tipping her head toward the
trays. "Until morning."

Morning? Tabitha glanced over at the bounty they'd
brought in and discovered that without so much as
an "if you don't mind," Preston had begun filling his
plate, the maid, Roxley and Tabitha all but forgotten.

The maid huffed off, most likely going to seek her
bed and certainly not a supper tray for Tabitha.

Meanwhile, Roxley had evidently forgotten any
thoughts of dining, what with the news of his med-
dlesome relation so close at hand. "Are you saying that
Lady Essex is *here*?" The note of panic was impossible
to miss. "In this inn? Under this roof?"

"Yes, my lord," Tabitha replied, trying to focus on
the earl even as the enticing smell of roast had her
reeling much as Preston's grasp had. "She's upstairs—

asleep. But I assure you, it is unlikely she'll rise before morning."

"If my luck holds until then," he muttered under his breath, raking a hand through his hair. After a few moments of silence, he shot a worried glance in her direction. "Did you say she's coming to London?"

"Yes. I believe she intends to stay with you," Tabitha told him, a bit distracted by the vision of Preston heaping his plate with roast beef…and yes…a second generous portion of Yorkshire pudding.

Even Mr. Muggins had noticed, having moved over to the table and sitting perfectly still, exhibiting a rare feat of manners—for which he was rewarded when Preston tossed him a piece of the roast.

Tabitha wrenched her gaze away, managing to get back to the discussion at hand. "Yes, that is her plan. To stay at your house. If you recall, Harriet mentioned it when last we met."

The earl paced back and forth, raking his hands through his hair. "Yes, yes, now I recall. Slipped my mind. Don't know how," he confessed, pausing for a second. "But I am in your debt, Miss Timmons. Ever so much." Roxley glanced over at the table, but apparently the decreasing amount of roast was the least of his concerns. "Preston, I need a place to bunk down, at least for—" Roxley glanced back at Tabitha. "How long does she intend to stay?"

"A fortnight, I believe."

Roxley glanced back at Preston. "Do hate to impose, my good man, but I did take you in last year after Henry got back from Ireland."

"Yes, yes," Preston told him, waving his fork in the air. "But if the old girl comes looking for you—"

"I doubt she will darken *your* door," Roxley replied, moving about the room and gathering up a coat, a hat, and other male trappings.

Preston paused, his fork and knife in midair. "What the devil are you doing?"

"Going into hiding. Must seek my room, my good man. Can't risk running into the old gel. If she finds me here, or worse, in your company, I'll never hear the end of it, nor will I be able to escape her for the next fortnight." The earl shuddered. "She'll insist I escort her about Town—shopping, soirées, the theater." He spared a glance at Tabitha, and then his eyes widened in shock. "Good lord, man, mayhap even Almack's. Best if we set out early—first light I think."

Preston set down his knife and fork. "You can't leave now. You know I deplore eating alone."

But Roxley was already to the door, having swept past Tabitha. "You aren't alone. Miss Timmons's arrival is more than just timely."

Both the men turned their gazes toward Tabitha. Roxley's full of pleading and Preston's holding nothing but skeptical regard.

"Miss Timmons, if you would take my place—" the earl began.

"Dine with him?"

"With her?"

The two sparring partners glanced at each other and then turned their aggrieved expressions on the real culprit.

"Good God, Roxley. Where is your manhood?" Preston said, rising to his feet and tossing his napkin down on the table. "Fleeing from a decent meal on the off chance your maiden aunt rises from her bed?"

Roxley's jaw worked back and forth. "Hardly so. If anything, I think I am taking a cold." He sneezed for good measure, but it was hardly convincing evidence.

Certainly not for Preston. "Roxley, this is ridiculous. She's naught but a spinster, and hardly leading a barbarian horde. Sit and eat."

The earl hardly appeared chastened or insulted. "Shall I tell Hen what you were doing today gamboling about the countryside? I do recall we had to rise before daylight to escape her notice."

Tabitha had no idea who this mysterious "Hen" might be, but the lady had the power to cow even the indomitable Preston. The man's brow furrowed darkly and he sank back into his seat. He waved off the earl. "Then scurry off and hide from Lady Essex, but leave Hen out of this. Oh, and I shan't forgive you for abandoning me."

"Of course you will," the earl said. "I am currently your only friend." Then taking Tabitha's hands and squeezing them, he continued. "And thank you, dear Miss Timmons, for keeping Preston company for me. He'll be in an ill humor tomorrow if you don't stay, while I will be forever in your debt."

Tabitha tugged her hands free before she found herself bound by some unspoken promise, even as her gaze flew about the private, intimate chamber. Just her and Preston? Alone? Dining? Vow or not…

She caught hold of Roxley, anchoring him in the room. "My lord, it wouldn't be proper! I am a respectable lady. The daughter of a vicar."

"There you have it," Preston pointed out. "You are leaving a lamb to be devoured by the Lion of Harley Street. You'll be held responsible."

This threat glanced right off Roxley. "You should know by now, I'm never held accountable, Preston."

Tabitha glanced from one man to the other. "I will not stay here alone with this...this..." Her finger wagged toward Preston, who had the temerity to appear affronted.

"Good heavens, I have no intention of ruining you, Miss Timmons."

"He's quite tame once you get to know him," Roxley assured her.

As if one could truly ever call a lion tame. Tabitha didn't trust the man in the least.

"I quite simply deplore eating alone," Preston declared as he sniffed the wine in the decanter. Apparently it met his discerning taste, for he poured himself a glass.

"That is hardly my concern," Tabitha said, even as the smell of roast curled around her nose, leaving her stomach rumbling with an unladylike churn. Or perhaps it was his adamant statement that she was completely safe in his company that had her unnerved.

Whatever was wrong with her that he wouldn't count her in what she suspected was his long list of conquests?

Tabitha shook off that thought, because she certainly didn't want to be one of his conquests. Or any man's, for that matter.

She was intended for a respectable gentleman worthy of her unblemished virtue. If this wretched Preston didn't want her, that was most excellent news.

At least it should be.

"Miss Timmons, you are quite safe with Preston. He has given his word. Besides, it looks to be an excellent supper, and I have to imagine having traveled all day with my aunt, you are famished."

She pressed her lips together, for he had her there. But to dine with Preston? Alone?

"Why, it would be ruinous," she told the earl. At least it should be. Then she made the mistake of taking another glance at what remained of the Yorkshire pudding and felt her resolve crumbling.

Just like the crust would when she stuck it with a fork...

Meanwhile, Roxley had managed to work his way to the door in a quiet effort to take his leave, when he paused and added, "And you won't mind keeping my presence here out of my aunt's ear, will you?"

Tabitha's jaw worked back and forth, but the earl had the most engaging smile, and it was impossible to say no to the man.

A fact that Lady Essex declared on a regular basis—that Roxley, rapscallion that he was, would never be ruined in the eyes of society, since no one could naysay one of his pleading smiles.

"I won't, my lord, but if she discovers that I have lied to her—"

"It isn't a lie, Miss Timmons, not unless you are asked directly," Preston remarked as he once again settled into his meal. Obviously he was also familiar with Roxley's persuasive powers and took it for granted that so asked, she would stay.

Not that he looked overly pleased at the prospect, that is until he took another bite of that roast beef and his expression changed to one of sated happiness.

Was it truly that good? She'd never know unless she...

"Miss Timmons, you know my aunt—" Roxley implored.

Oh good heavens, between her own pangs of hunger, the delicious odor of roast beef and pudding whiling at her senses, combined with Roxley's charm, it was nearly impossible to think straight.

"Not a word to Lady Essex," she promised in a distracted state.

Roxley's relief was immediate, and he made a quick bow and fled, scurrying off to his room as if he were escaping a press gang.

Which, in a sense, he was.

"Well, what are you waiting for?" Preston asked, grudgingly waving at the seat across from his.

So much for a mannerly and elegant invitation. Then again, she could hardly expect the manners of a gentleman from this rogue.

"You must be hungry," he added.

"Why do you say that?"

"Because there is no other reason for you to be wandering about an inn at this hour of the night unless you haven't had your supper yet." He paused. "That, and you don't look the type to tipple quietly on the sherry bottle when no one is looking."

"Oh!" Tabitha gasped. "I do not imbibe. My father was a—"

"Yes, yes, a vicar, so you said earlier," he said as he scanned the bowl of mashed 'nips.

Unwittingly, she took a step toward the table. Oh, good heavens, there were turnips! However had she missed those?

She glanced up and found him staring at her, a wry smile on his handsome lips—for he had caught her out.

"Actually you look like you could use a good meal," he said, before an odd look of dismay passed over his face. It was quickly extinguished and replaced by his usual stony expression. "Sit. It is still hot, and I refuse to stand on ceremony, especially if it only serves to let my supper grow cold." Then he dug into the bowl before him, piling the mashed 'nips on his plate and devouring his supper with all the gusto of a lion.

No, he certainly wasn't going to offer a kindly bow and a well-spoken invitation, or hold her chair and select the finest bits from the platters for her like a gentleman might.

Like Mr. Reginald Barkworth most certainly would.

Then again, Tabitha suspected the honorable and esteemed gentleman her Uncle Winston had chosen for her would never in his wildest moments suggest such an arrangement—dining alone with an unmarried miss in such an intimate setting. The notion that it was scandalous and quite possibly ruinous (no, truly it was entirely ruinous) would leave such a situation beyond the pale for her betrothed.

Not so for Preston. Tabitha glanced quickly over at her host. Such improper assignations were probably so commonplace for the man that this night was barely worthy of note.

Oh, if only she wasn't so hungry to the point of being beyond reason…at least that was what she told herself, for when she looked at Preston and that handsome visage of his, the twinkle of mischief in his eyes—dark like raisins in a tart—she felt an entirely different sort of hunger.

Tabitha drew a deep, steadying breath. As it was, she'd spent the last fortnight telling herself that her memory of the man—how handsome he was, how the sight of his muscled frame, so broad and powerful, had left her breathless—had been naught but foolish fancies.

Yet here he was again, as handsome as ever. Though thankfully, with a shirt on. And a waistcoat. His jacket lay negligently across the back of a chair. His voice still held that deep, sinful tone—as if it could whisper across one's skin, carrying all sorts of scandalous notions in its wake.

And there was his promise—*I have no intention of ruining you, Miss Timmons*.

Certainly that counted for something.

Worst of all, the well-filled platters on the sideboard and the one on the table told the truth; the kitchen staff *had* emptied the larder for Preston's consumption. She'd be lucky to find a crust of bread. Let alone a tin of tea.

That is if she could even rouse that surly maid.

So, it was this or nothing.

And Preston was right about one thing, nothing was worse than a cold supper. Or dining alone. She'd done that enough since her father had died.

So against her better judgment, she sat down in the lion's den.

Preston knew better than to invite some innocent miss to dine with him. Alone. In a dark, cozy inn. Hen would flay him alive if she were here.

Then again, if Hen were here, he wouldn't be in this predicament.

For the truth of it was that he truly hated dining alone. Detested it. So much so that the very thought

of Hen and Henry moving out and leaving him to pot-
ter about No. 6 all by himself with no one but the servants and his butler, Benley, to keep him company
had him doing his best to keep his name out of the
scandal sheets.

So there it was. Have to dine alone (dreadful notion)
or risk scandal by dining with Miss Timmons (dreadfully dull notion).

Preston took a glance at the lady in question. Certainly, she wasn't the marriage-mad type who had
plagued his very existence this past spring. No, given
the set of her jaw and the furrow of her brow, she certainly showed no signs of being one of those wily Bath
misses who would do her demmed best to lure him into
some scandal, if only in hopes that he would then be
induced to marry her.

No, this Miss Timmons had absolutely no charms
about her. Skinny and wearing an ugly, ill-fitting dark
gown, she frowned too much, eyeing him with a wary
disdain.

Better that, he reasoned, than the covetous glances
she tossed at the roast beef.

Nay, there was no risk of him being lulled by soft
glances and fluttering lashes from this miss.

In fact, it was probably to his advantage that Miss
Timmons thought him no more than a nefarious gambler, the worst sort of ruin. Nor would she arrive in
London and start nattering on to anyone who would
listen that she'd dined privately with some ne'er-do-
well roisterer of no consequence.

Not her. Not a respectable vicar's daughter.

He sat back in his seat as he came to a stunning realization: perhaps he had discovered the perfect dining

companion. Well, mayhap not perfect, but decidedly better than Roxley, who tended to drink all the wine and take extra helpings of the Yorkshire pudding as if it were his due.

No, if Preston were inclined to be honest, he might admit he rather liked her disdain and her lack of fawning obeisance. Right down to how she addressed him in that voice dripping with haughty scorn.

"Mr. Preston."

Preston only wished he would be able to see the expression on her face when one day—very soon if she was indeed going to London—she learned the truth. In the park or at a ball, someone would nudge her and point him out—for he saw the looks and finger wagging that the matrons and misses of London cast in his direction.

"That, my dear, is the most ruinous man in London. The Duke of Preston. Avoid him at all costs."

She'd look once, perhaps twice, and then come to the stunning realization that she'd been a hoity-toity little snob to none other than the Duke of Preston.

Not that she'd be able to tell anyone—for then she'd be ruined.

Preston perked up. Good heavens, this made Miss Timmons with her impertinent remarks and baneful glances entirely perfect.

"Believe me, I am no more happy to have your company than you are to have mine," he told her, feigning indifference and enjoying it all that much more as her brow furrowed even deeper, "but I am afraid you are stuck with me and my offer for supper."

She had sat down with a thud and now surveyed the table like one might the choice of pistols at a duel.

"Come now, whatever is the matter?" he asked, settling back in his chair. "They've set an excellent table."

"Everything looks delicious. It is just that—" She fidgeted in her seat and glanced away from the table.

"Just what? Whatever could be wrong?" He looked over the platters, thinking he might have missed something.

Then she looked him squarely in the eye. "I've never dined alone with a man. Well, other than my father. If it were to become known—"

So that was it. Her reputation. Most likely it was all she possessed.

Poor bedraggled kitten, he mused, and even as he thought it, a familiar pang twisted in his chest. The same one that had him bringing home flea-ridden mutts or that litter of kittens Hen had viewed with horror.

His Achilles' heel, and damn Roxley to hell, for he'd played on those sympathies when he'd urged Preston to feed her up a bit.

Preston took another glance at the lady. *She is rather skinny,* his conscience prodded. *No one is looking out for her.*

He dug into his dinner and fought back the urge to overfill her plate.

This chit was not his bloody responsibility.

"What? No witty remark? No scoffing jest?" she posed as he realized how long he'd been sitting there mute.

"No, none of that. It is just that I have never dined alone with a vicar's daughter, so I suppose we are even."

This didn't seem to appease her either, only furrowed that brow of hers into an even deeper crease. How unfortunate she'd never learned to smile.

"Miss Timmons, since you have no intention of ever marrying," he told her, forking a piece of roast and sliding it onto the plate in front of her, then selecting servings from the other platters until her plate was quite full—for perhaps her ill manners were nothing more than a case of being overly peckish—"then you needn't waste your time being concerned about your reputation."

She opened her mouth to protest, but he cut her off, continuing quickly by adding, "You can count on the fact that I will not be relating this evening to my compatriots or the scandal sheets. Dining with a vicar's daughter, indeed—why, they'll think I've gone round the bend." He shook his head and helped himself to another piece of roast beef.

"I don't know whether to be insulted or relieved, sir," she replied, her gaze taking in the heaping plate before her.

"I would say, since this is a very good joint of beef, you might try 'relieved' and eat. Besides, you are not a typical miss, and I doubt you have ever been confined by what is expected of you."

Her eyes widened beneath her furrowed brow. So she'd gone with insulted.

"Oh, don't go all miss-ish on me," he told her. "I meant it as a compliment." And to add a stamp of approval to her company, he poured her a glass of wine, ignoring her earlier protestation that she didn't imbibe. "Please, Miss Timmons, eat your supper. The roast is most excellent."

She picked up her fork and knife and tentatively cut

a small bite. Once she tried it, she returned with gusto, eating her supper as if she hadn't eaten so in years. The next time he glanced at her, she'd nearly cleaned her plate and was reaching for another portion of the Yorkshire pudding.

And took the largest piece, putting even Roxley to shame. Preston couldn't help himself. He grinned and tucked into his own plate.

How utterly refreshing, he realized. Spinsters! Good heavens, why was it that no one else had discovered their appeal? If London was filled with them instead of all those marriage-mad minxes, he wouldn't be in the suds with his aunt and uncle all the time.

He glanced over at her dog, who was watching the table like a sharp-eyed chaperone, and tossed the large red terrier another piece of beef.

Preston always made it a point to charm the chaperone so when the time was right they would turn a blind eye to his misdeeds. "Does that beast have a name?"

She glanced up and blinked, as if she'd forgotten he was there. "Mr. Muggins."

"Mr. Muggins," he echoed, nodding at the dog and tossing another cut of meat at the creature. "Unusual breed," he said. "But he has a sharp eye about him."

"An Irish terrier. A tinsmith left him at the parish when he was but a pup, and I hadn't the heart to turn him out."

Preston paused for a moment. To avoid any further consideration that they might have something in common, he tossed the dog another piece of meat.

Mr. Muggins edged closer and looked up at Preston with deep, dark, adoring eyes, head resting on his paws.

"He'll never leave you alone if you keep feeding him your supper." Miss Timmons shook her head.

"I fear it is my charm coming through," he replied. "I have a talent for attracting the incorrigible." He winked at her, and she shook her head with a disapproving tilt that would have put even Hen to shame.

But Hen wouldn't have had that hint of a blush on her fair cheeks.

Truly, was Miss Timmons blushing at him?

He glanced again and this time decided that perhaps the color in her cheeks was from the wine. After all, she'd taken a few sips when she'd thought he hadn't been looking.

Certainly she wasn't blushing over him. No, no, that would never do. He glanced down at his plate and asked the first question that came to mind.

"Tell me about your village," he posed. "This Kempton and its curse."

It proved to be the perfect diversion, for it seemed the lady loved her village with all her heart, to the point that he almost envied her cozy, happy country life, her work with this Society of Spinsters or whatever it was she called it.

He even laughed at the antics of the Tempest twins and their continuing campaign to change the colors of a bunting and Lady Essex's staunch refusal to go against tradition.

Rather like Hen and her love of the Red Room.

He glanced down at his plate, thinking to add another slice of roast, only to find one already waiting for him.

Since Preston and Roxley had set out for only a day race, they had not brought their usual host of servants and valets and the like. Used as he was to having a footman adding to his plate with only a nod of his head or a flick of a hand, he might not have noticed, but he suddenly realized that as she'd been talking, Miss Timmons had been adding to his plate, refilling his glass, and without breaking her chatter, had efficiently and tidily rearranged the platters on the table so those dishes he preferred were right before him.

It was a cozy moment that reminded him of the suppers from his childhood when his mother and father and brothers and sisters would assemble for a noisy repast, with his mother or older sister tucking his favorites onto his plate from the platters around them. All that was missing now was the noisy chatter and the tug-of-war that usually happened between him and Felix as to who would find the sugar cube under the teacup—a game his father liked to play with them.

And if that sense of belonging to something more than himself didn't turn the tables on him, her next question certainly did.

"Where do you live, Mr. Preston?"

"Live?" he managed.

"Yes, as in reside," she pressed, setting down her knife and fork and folding her hands in her lap as she awaited his answer.

"Why, London, of course."

"Alone?"

"No, never," he said far too quickly, trying to catch hold of the fleeting memories of those beloved suppers at Owle Park.

She glanced up at him, for the vehemence of his answer obviously hinted at something more to be discovered.

"With my aunt and uncle," he amended. There—that ought to satisfy her curiosity.

Hardly.

"Do they approve of you gallivanting about?"

He laughed. "Not in the least."

"So whatever do you do, Mr. Preston?" She sat awaiting an answer, her gaze continuing all the while to stray toward the last serving of Yorkshire pudding.

Oh, she was just like Roxley. Truly, he needed to cultivate companions who lacked a love of Yorkshire pudding.

"Do?" he repeated, picking up the platter and sliding the last bit of pudding onto her plate.

She smiled at this, a shy, surprised sort of tip of her lips that made her look more like a lady and less like some termagant spinster.

Actually the transformation was rather shocking. Tempting, almost.

Preston froze. Tempting? He glanced not at her but at his empty glass. Perhaps he'd had too much wine.

"Yes, do. For employment," she pressed.

Employment? Good heavens, no one had ever asked him such a question.

She must have taken his gaping for a loss of hearing or a loss of his wits. "Employment? For income. You know, labor, to assist your aunt and uncle, since they have been ever so kind to take you in."

He set down his silverware. "Surely you jest?"

Miss Timmons sat up straight, like only a vicar's daughter could manage. "No, I most certainly do not."

"No, I don't suppose you do," he muttered, refilling his wineglass. No wonder her father had given her over to Lady Essex to take to London.

Her father... He caught hold of that notion and quickly changed the subject.

"What of your father?" he asked. "Will he miss you while you are away making merry with Lady Essex?" He'd meant to tease and regretted the question immediately, for she glanced over at the fireplace and he could see her already fair features go pale at the mention.

"He is gone," she said softly. "He died of a heart ailment three years ago."

"I am sorry for your loss," he said. "And your mother? Is she accompanying you and Lady Essex?"

She glanced over at him and shook her head. "Mama died of the sweating sickness when I was five. The one that killed so many people. I don't know if you recall that year or not—"

Recall it? Preston's breath froze in his chest. He glanced at her and did the math, though he needn't, for he knew exactly what year she was talking about.

The same year that the fevers had killed his entire family. Taken his cheery childhood home, which had always been filled with laughter and love and happy servants, and taken them all.

By the time his grandfather had arrived at Owle Park, there had been naught in the house save him, the servants who hadn't sickened or died having fled.

"I am sorry," she said, reaching across and touching his hand, her fingers warm. "I can see from your expression that you were—"

"My parents died of fever then," he managed, and it was more than he had ever said about that fateful day when he'd gone from being merely Lord Christopher to being his grandfather's heir. And it hadn't been just his parents, but his brothers and sisters as well. Freddie, Felix, dear, gentle Dove, even baby Lydia. Lost. Gone.

He pulled his hand back, out from beneath the warmth of her touch, her kindness.

Instead of taking offense, Miss Timmons sorted the platters and added a few things to his plate. And to her credit, instead of pressing the matter, she said simply, "Papa always said that 'life was meant to be lived, not grieved.'" She paused and looked up at him, adding, "But I do miss him, ever so much."

"Yes, I don't doubt you would. He sounds like a wise man," he agreed, getting back to the task of eating his supper. "You have other family in Kempton with whom you live?"

"Yes," she said. "After Father died, his younger brother took over the vicarage. I live with him and his wife."

"At least you had someone to care for you," he said. "Circumstances could have been much worse."

"Yes, I suppose so." She glanced away and ignored her supper for a few moments.

Preston had the sense that he was wading into a mire. The last thing he needed to discover was that her aunt and uncle kept her locked in the attics and only let her out to scour the grates, but before he could change the subject, she pressed on with her original topic: that of his employment.

Or therein general lack of...

"What is it you do, sir? I don't believe you mentioned it before."

After a few more moments of due consideration, he came up with the sort of answer that he usually tossed at Henry when he started nattering on about responsibilities. "As little as possible, if you must know."

And like his uncle, Miss Timmons did not approve in the least. She sat back in her seat and scowled.

Preston made a further note never to introduce her to Hen and Henry.

"Not all men must labor, Miss Timmons," he said in his defense. Truly, why did he even have to defend his life? He could just tell this minx exactly who he was, and then there would be no more of her impertinent questions and quelling glances.

Or her shy, tempting smiles.

Before he had time to tell himself that he was very much immune to her moments of levity, she lectured on and saved him the trouble entirely.

"A man should at the very least have something with which to occupy his time or he will…he will…" She blushed a bit and then settled her hands primly on her lap as she struggled to find the right words.

Probably trying to recall one of her father's more poignant sermons so she could recite from it. Before she went that far, he headed her off.

"Lead a life of sin and regret?" After all, he knew this lecture by heart.

"Exactly," she said, reaching for her glass and taking a fortifying gulp. As she swallowed the potent Madeira, her eyes widened. Hastily, she set the glass back down.

Preston leaned forward and smiled. "Miss Timmons, I never regret a good sin."

The lady gaped at him. When she recovered, it was

with a sputtering, spinsterly reply of shock. "Well, I never! A good sin, indeed. Is there such a thing?"

"Miss Timmons, if you have to ask, then you haven't found the right one."

Chapter 4

"What a scandalous thing to say," Tabitha scolded. "A sin is a sin."

Her devilish dinner companion shook his head. "You will be out of step in London society if you cling to such country notions."

"I am sure that decorum and a proper regard for manners are not ignored in all circles," she told him.

He smiled kindly at her. "Perhaps."

Perhaps? Whatever did that mean? And why did he have to sound like he was speaking to a child, as if trying to convince her that there weren't banshees in the closet?

There *was* good society in London. Why, one had to look no further than her uncle and aunt, Sir Mauris and Lady Timmons. And her betrothed, Mr. Reginald Barkworth. Aunt Allegra said he came from one of the finest families in England and held himself to the highest standards of gentlemanly comportment.

Tabitha sat up and folded her hands in her lap. "Have you considered that your disregard for propriety may be a reflection of the company you keep?"

If she thought her lecture on values was going to pierce his wretched hide, she was sadly mistaken.

"Ah yes, Miss Timmons," he said, waving his fork at her. "But any other company would be dull indeed."

"Perhaps you could use a bit of dull, proper company."

"No, thank you," he told her, shaking off her suggestion. "Believe me, I have had more than my fair share of dull company of late. I much prefer Roxley and his ilk, and you, if you must know."

"Me?" Tabitha sat back.

"Yes, you," he said, leaning over the table and smiling at her in something that might be called flirtation.

She didn't know for certain. She'd never been flirted with.

But whatever it was, when he looked at her so, with that intense focus—as if she was the only woman he ever wanted to see across the table from him—her heart made a tremulous thump and her usually sensible thoughts scattered about like a drove of March hares.

Especially as he wasn't done there. "You aren't the least bit dull. Or proper." He smiled at her. "You, Miss Timmons, shouldn't be allowed to mix in London society."

Tabitha sat back. So much for her delusions of flirting. "Whyever not?" she managed. Truly, whatever was wrong with her?

"Because you speak your mind. You are unlike any

other woman I have ever met. Especially in London. I hope you never change." He reached for the plate with the apple tart and began to divide it into portions.

She tried to say something, tried to speak, but her tongue had departed along with her sensibilities.

Unlike any other woman I have ever met?

Perhaps it was the wine and the three—no make that four—helpings of Yorkshire pudding that had her hearing things. For those words left her beguiled and caught in his spell.

Tabitha stole a glance at this man across the table from her, and she did her best to breathe.

He was unlike any other man she'd ever met. Then again, she had met very few, so perhaps she wasn't the best judge in these matters.

Would her betrothed be like this? Sophisticated? Chiseled? Handsome? Devil-may-care? Capable of stealing her breath away with his outrageous declarations.

This is the road to ruin, Tabitha Timmons, she could almost hear her proper and sensible nature scolding. *This man is a bounder! He says these things as a matter of course and then...before one knows it...a lady finds herself undone.*

She glanced over at her chaperone, only to find Mr. Muggins sleeping. Having had his fill of beef, he happily snored on the rug, one paw twitching as if he were dreaming of open fields filled with pheasants and grouse.

So it was just her and this man, all alone.

Oh, whatever had she gotten herself tangled up in? Was he truly flirting with her?

At least she suspected he might be until he glanced

up and continued, "However, if you go about Town thinking to correct every man's manners and the company he keeps, you'll never find a husband."

Tabitha sucked in a deep breath. Oh, and here she'd thought he'd lost his overbearing arrogance and smug tones somewhere after his third helping of pudding.

"And I didn't believe all that village nonsense about not wanting husbands." He took a bite of the apple tart and sighed. "I have to imagine the ladies of Kempton use it as a ruse to lure in unsuspecting rubes and snare them into the parson's trap."

"Oh, of all the vulgar, ridiculous notions!" she finally managed to get out. "Of course no one in their right mind believes in the Curse. It is naught but an old story that sets our village apart from our neighbors."

"A curse can do that," he heartily agreed, tipping his glass to her.

"Yes, but the reason brides are rare in Kempton is not because of any old legend but simply because there are few gentlemen to marry."

"A dearth of grooms, eh?" He shook his head. "Then I was ever so lucky to escape unscathed."

"I said a lack of gentlemen, not bounders, Mr. Preston." She tipped her glass at him. "You were in no danger, I assure you."

"Ah, ah, ah, Miss Timmons. There goes that wickedly sharp tongue of yours," he scolded, but with such approving tones it was impossible to know if he meant it. Or that he understood she'd meant every word as an insult.

"Now I see why you and your friends are off to London. Perhaps I should post a notice in *The Times*. Warn off any unsuspecting fellows who—"

"Don't be ridiculous—"

He shrugged off her objection. "Would feel terribly responsible if you beguiled one of my compatriots into matrimony with those innocent eyes of yours and then they found him with a fire iron through his heart like that poor fellow Roxley told me about. What was his name?"

"His name is irrelevant." The fact that the man's name was John Stakes—a bitter irony if ever there was one—only made the entire story of the Curse all that much more convincing, at least to the men of Kempton.

And throughout the surrounding county. And a good part of southwestern England.

"For once and for all, I am not going to London to find a husband," Tabitha told him. Which was entirely the truth. There was no finding to be done.

Her betrothed was all tied up and waiting for her, like a package on Christmas morn.

While it might be considered bending the truth a bit, it was hardly a sin, like an outright lie.

Tabitha reached for her wineglass, then set it right back down. This is what came of dining with rogues. She'd ventured out onto this narrow, slippery limb of truth and she suspected Preston carried a saw in his back pocket.

"Not going to find a husband?" He laughed. "If you are not going to London to find a husband, then why are you going at all?"

"Lady Essex," Tabitha said quickly, latching onto the most likely explanation she could foist off. "Her companion took ill and she asked Miss Dale and me to accompany her and Miss Hathaway."

Which all had a toehold in the truth. Lady Essex's

companion was indeed ill. And the poor woman's infirmary was what had cinched Daphne's spot in the carriage.

And Tabitha wasn't going to find a husband.

She sat up and stared the lion in the eye, daring him to find anything wrong with her story.

Certainly she didn't know why it bothered her or why she cared what he thought.

Yet she couldn't bring herself to tell him the truth.

Perhaps because she still couldn't reconcile the facts herself. She was going to be married. And married in all due haste.

"You might find having to spend a fortnight in Town with Roxley's old dragon of an aunt is a worse curse," he teased and, with enthusiasm, went back to eating his apple tart.

Which looked decidedly scrumptious. And worse, he had yet to offer her a piece.

As good manners might dictate.

He must have seen the envy in her eyes, for he smiled, slid a piece onto a plate and passed it to her.

And looked to be ready to skewer her yet again, so she beat him to the punch. "Why did you insist on having a dinner companion?"

His startled expression—even as quickly masked as it was—piqued her curiosity.

"It is an idiosyncrasy," he declared. "Nothing more." He dug into his apple tart with renewed interest.

And she wasn't going to London to be married, she thought, smelling a rat. Yet in her musings, she realized she'd paused for too long. He wrestled the conversation back into safer territory.

Safer for him.

"If it is the case that you aren't husband hunting—" he began.

"It is," she insisted.

"Then if we were by chance to meet, perhaps I would ask you to dance." He made it sound as if he were granting her some sort of divine favor.

Her gaze flew up. "I would certainly hope not."

Now it was Preston's turn to pause. "Whyever not?"

"Well, I think the answer is obvious."

"Not to me," he said, setting aside his fork, his hands folding together like the lofty, solid steeple of St. Edward's. "If you have no desire to seek a husband, then why not dance with me?"

His invitation ruffled down her spine even as her gaze remained fixed on his hands—strong, masculine hands. To dance with him would mean to hold one of those hands, perhaps even both, to feel him encompass her, guide her, lead her down a line of dancers...

"I do not dance," she told him hastily.

"Of course you do," he said, looking her over as if he sought some defect that prevented her from accepting his invitation.

She shook her head. "There is no need for dancing lessons when one comes from Kempton—we use our time for more useful occupations such as the Society."

"The Society?"

Good heavens, hadn't he been listening earlier? Men! Her father had been just as bad. "I told you before, the Society for the Temperance and Improvement of Kempton."

He shrugged and continued eating.

"We provide baskets to the local spinsters to aid them in their later years, and help the poor, as well as plant flowers in the cemetery and of course, sponsor the Midsummer's Eve Ball."

"Aha!" he said, perking up at the mention of the ball. "So you do dance."

"No," she said. "I am usually too busy managing the punch bowl or overseeing the supper trays."

Preston closed his eyes and groaned. "That will never do. Are you truly saying you don't know a single dance step?"

"Only a few country reels, but I have never danced them—"

"Then how do you know them?"

"Good heavens, Mr. Preston, let me finish," Tabitha said, crossing her arms over her chest. The man was utterly infuriating. Whatever did it matter what she could dance or couldn't? But from the furrow of his brow and the stubborn set of his jaw, she realized he would continue to be insufferable until he had his answers. "I have danced them. Just not with a gentleman." She glanced away.

There. Now he knew.

Not daring a look at him, she picked up her fork and took solace in a large bite of apple tart. Which suddenly wasn't as sweet as it had looked before.

Before she'd had to make this terrible confession. Yes, she was a complete country rube.

"Does this curse of yours forbid you from dancing with a gentleman?"

Oh, yes. Now the teasing and ridicule would commence.

"No, of course not," she replied. "But when there is no hope of anything else—"

It was a terribly bitter pill to admit. And now, well

away from Kempton, the things that never seemed to matter (at least on the surface)—dances, gowns, courtships, a glory box—only made the approach to London, to her intended, all that much more daunting.

Then across the table came something more tempting than the apple tart before her. An offer so inviting it took her breath away.

"I could teach you how to dance," Preston offered.

Those words—*I could teach you*—sprang loose from his lips like that ruined wheel on his carriage and sent him just as quickly careening into disaster.

If Preston could have snatched them back and tamped them down where they belonged—locked away—he would have. *I could teach you!* What the devil was he thinking?

Worse, offering? And whatever had he been thinking, telling her he would dance with her if by chance they met again.

He tried telling himself that his offer had been kindly meant. A boon for her for agreeing to share his supper with him.

Preston cringed inwardly. How honest was he being? It wasn't as if dancing with him could be considered a feather in any lady's cap, not any longer… Once, perhaps.

No, it was because he'd glanced at her half-eaten apple tart and known that once it was gone, this evening would be over. His offer was merely his own attempt to grasp at something he'd thought had been lost forever.

Owle Park. His family. He hadn't thought of them in

years—at least not thought of them and then instantly dismissed the images as too painful to endure.

Miss Timmons, it seemed, possessed a bit of magic to her, for with her across the table, the family he'd lost felt close at hand. Just within reach. And he wasn't about to let her slip free. Not just yet. Not until he'd determined the full extent of her charms.

Preston cringed.

Well, perhaps not *those* charms.

That was exactly the sort of mischief that had landed him in the suds with Hen and Henry to begin with.

Not that anyone would ever find out...

Yes, yes, he supposed that much was true. The inn was as quiet as a tomb, which meant no one would see them.

Oh, but someone always did, he knew from experience. He glanced over at Miss Timmons and wondered what his aunt would make of *this* young lady.

Miss Timmons with her tart manners and country ways. With her scolds and staunchly held opinions. Miss Timmons with the appetite of a stevedore and all the innocence of a cloistered nun.

He was wading into deep waters thinking to teach her to dance.

Don't do this, my good man. This isn't some bedraggled kitten or abandoned pup in the road but a lady. Belonging to the same ilk as the rest of those muslin menaces who had made him a pariah in London society.

But still...how could he not help? He owed her something for this glimpse backward in time she'd unwittingly given him.

Especially when she'd made such a confession—

that she'd never danced with a man before—and the stricken look in those brown eyes of hers had told him only too clearly how much such a revelation had cost her precious pride.

Then again, she hadn't exactly leapt at his offer. Only gaped at him as if he had gone mad.

Which probably wasn't far from the truth. Glancing at his wineglass, he blamed the inn's excellent Madeira, not enough Yorkshire pudding and Roxley's abandonment for this complete lapse of judgment.

No, come to think of it, it was all Roxley's fault.

"Since you've mastered dining with a gentleman," he told her, rising to his feet, "now it is time to learn to dance."

With that being said, he held out his hand.

She shied back and glanced around the room as if she expected scandal to rain down from the heavens.

Yet nothing happened. The ceiling held snugly, and not even her mongrel of a dog stirred at Preston's proximity to his mistress.

Some chaperone. Perhaps the dog was looking the other way out of courtesy.

One hound to another.

But then again, perhaps Mr. Muggins knew what Preston had sworn earlier—he was no threat to Miss Timmons.

None whatsoever.

At least he kept telling himself as he took command of the situation and caught hold of her wrist and pulled her up. Despite her rather amazing appetite, she was really quite light—no, make that thin and underfed— beneath that dreadful gown.

Good God, no one was looking after her, were they?

His fingers wound around hers, and they were met with chapped, rough calluses, the sort one might find on a scullery maid.

He glanced at her, shocked by his discovery. She was naught but a waif. A lost kitten if ever there was one.

Miss Timmons, for her part, glanced away and tried to pull her hand free—as if she still had time to hide the evidence of her labors.

Preston refused to let go, even as that warning lump whalloped in his chest.

"There is no music," she protested.

Oh, she had much to learn. "Dancing isn't as much about the music as it is being able to follow your partner's lead."

She made an indelicate snort, but whether it had to do with his assurance or the "following" part, he didn't know.

But he soon discovered.

Indeed, following was not one of Miss Timmons's strong suits. Not that he was surprised. Though he couldn't recall ever dancing with a miss who was so utterly unyielding.

"This will never do," she said, shaking her head and looking ready to bolt for the door after they knocked into the table the second time. "Without music we look foolish."

"I never look foolish," he mused, sliding his hand to her hip and hauling her closer. It was an intimate move, and for a moment they stared at each other. For all their barbs and spiked comments, standing like this, they fit.

He'd danced with dozens of women, perhaps even

hundreds, but not one had ever curved up against him and belonged. Belonged? Miss Timmons? Why, that was madness. As quickly as he'd caught her, he very nearly set her out of reach.

Nearly.

Meanwhile, Miss Timmons was staging a small mutiny, trying to bat away his hand and wiggle free.

He ignored her and held her fast. He tapped his foot slowly and then began to hum, rather loudly and off-key, before setting off on this preposterous lesson, twirling the disbelieving miss around in a tight circle.

This was a dancing lesson after all. Nothing more.

Twice, three times he moved the stiff and leaden-footed lady around the room. He was all but ready to give up, but then something miraculous happened.

Miss Timmons laughed.

Right after she'd trod rather heavily on his boot.

The merry music bubbling forth from the previously taciturn lady turned into a series of unrepentant giggles as he winced and hopped for a moment before regaining his balance and his grasp on her.

"Did you do that on purpose?" Preston came to a stop, not relinquishing his hold on her—no matter how much his toes begged him. "Because a lady never steps on a man's foot deliberately. It just isn't done, Miss Timmons."

"If you say so," she managed with a flash of mischief in her brown eyes.

But it was. Twice more.

"That is not sporting," he told her as he hopped out of her range, shaking his foot.

Even the hound glanced up at him. In sympathy, or so Preston could have sworn. Perhaps that's why their canine chaperone hadn't protested the duke's attentions toward Miss Timmons.

Mr. Muggins had known the fate awaiting him.

"I thought we were dancing," she replied, shaking away from her eyes a tendril that had come loose. It fell back over her shoulder in a silken curl of deep, dark auburn.

"I was dancing," he corrected her and his errant thoughts. "You are attempting some sort of Spanish torture on my toes."

"If you do not like how I dance, then you shouldn't bully ladies into partnering with you," she shot back, her eyes alight.

"Bullying?" he sputtered. "I will have you know, I never have to bully a woman to dance with me. Quite the opposite."

She began to laugh again, as if this was the most diverting thing she'd ever heard. "Oh, Mr. Preston, isn't that doing it up a bit?" She giggled some more. "You think I can be gulled into believing that all the ladies are lined up when *you* arrive."

Preston straightened, and it was nearly on the tip of his tongue to correct her.

At least that had been the case until a few months ago, he would have liked to inform Miss Timmons.

Now when he entered a ballroom—and only after Hen had coerced the hostess into an invitation—nearly every lady in the room turned their collective back to him, leaving only the ones too nearsighted and infirm to offer him their deepest and heartiest disinterest.

However, she continued on, blithely and unrepentantly insulting him. "I do believe you shall have to cross dancing master off your list of possible occupations, sir."

Possible occupations, indeed! It would be a cold day in hell when the Duke of Preston was reduced to teaching dancing to cow-footed, cursed spinsters—let alone fail miserably at the task.

That thought should have been enough to send him hying off after Roxley, but something else was happening…and not just that sensation was finally returning to his flattened foot.

Miss Timmons and her laughter surrounded him.

Oh, yes, she was laughing *at* him. And enjoying herself immensely as she snubbed his pretensions thoroughly.

"Ah, yes, Monsieur Preston. Dancing Master. That is, if you have extra toes to spare?"

No one ever laughed at him. At least not to his face. Preston found himself a bit off-center, for laughing at a duke just wasn't done.

Then something else happened; her infectious tones did exactly what they were meant to do—whittle away at his lofty arrogance.

For much to his disbelief, he found himself laughing. "I'll have you know I am considered an excellent partner." When he wasn't being snubbed or given the cut direct.

Miss Timmons wasn't done with her taunts. "What a happy coincidence for me then."

"How is that?" he asked, reaching down to give his boots a tug back into place.

"I doubt anyone will notice my poor skills if you are considered 'excellent.'" Dark eyes alight, mouth set in a tempting little moue—probably to keep her from laughing aloud—her hands settled on her hips as if she were utterly satisfied with the aim of her finishing salvo.

Of all the audacious, rude, presumptuous things to say. Preston set his jaw, for her teasing words weren't merely a warning shot across the bow but a squarely landed challenge.

At least to Preston.

Jerking his waistcoat into place, throwing his chin up in jaunty answer to the gauntlet she'd tossed down, he caught hold of her hand.

"There is no room to dance," she told him. "Whatever do you think you can teach me in such a confined space?"

"A Mayfair ballroom will be no different. In London, I would be forced to hold you just so." With that, he tugged Miss Timmons closer.

Being Miss Timmons, she stumbled forward and landed squarely against him. Her breasts pressed to his chest, one arm winding around him to steady herself, and her legs and skirts twining into his legs.

Then it happened again. As they found their footing, settled into place, a rare awareness of how they dovetailed so perfectly entwined around them—her in his arms and Preston holding her. Her gaze swept slowly up until it met his, wonder mirrored in those brown eyes of hers.

Yes, she felt it as well. There was no mistaking that look of shock.

And something else. Passion. A spark of passion that no spinster should still possess. One that fickle time should have extinguished years ago.

Apparently not so with Miss Timmons.

Her rosy lips parted and she looked at him, as if she expected…as if she knew what would happen next.

And once again, Christopher Seldon, the Duke of Preston, found himself caught up in something that was veering all too suddenly into a scandal.

Chapter 5

Oh, however had this evening come to this dangerous precipice?

Preston had given his word that he wouldn't ruin her, and yet here he was. Tabitha tried to breathe. He was going to kiss her.

Then again, you never promised...

No, she hadn't, trying to grasp the last bit of sensibility she seemed to possess. And with that bit close at hand, she managed one more important thought.

So whatever did one do?

Run, would be the sensible choice. Get as far away from this devilish rake as possible.

But however could she do that when her legs refused to move? Other than to tremble—with what she suspected was anticipation. When her hands were unwilling to let go of his waistcoat? When the heat of his touch burned through her gown, when his dark, usually inscrutable gaze turned into a smoky, tempting fire?

When all she wanted to do was to let him kiss her... let him...

Let him do what? Ruin her? She couldn't. *Remember Barkworth. Think of your betrothed.*

Oh, bother, however was she supposed to recall a man when she had yet to meet him? Nor had she promised anything to him. Her uncle had.

And she might have been content to take this paragon her uncle had willed to her, until Preston had come along. Arrogant, rakish, devil-may-care (and far more important, entirely improper) and stolen away her sensibilities.

Somewhere between the third helping of Yorkshire pudding and the moment he'd taken her hand and tugged her to her feet, this man, the one holding her in this delicious state of languor, had stopped being *that* Preston.

Oh, good heavens! This was wrong. She closed her eyes and tried to think of how to stop this. Tried to convince her fluttering heart, her pursed lips that all this was utterly and completely wrong. But before she could regain enough of her senses to escape his snare, her rake, her Preston, did the unthinkable.

In a swoosh, he set her out of reach.

One moment she was there in the warmth of his arms, held in his steely grasp, and the next, it was as if she'd been shoved under a rainspout. In December.

Her lashes sprang open and she found him standing a few steps away. He looked as shocked as she felt—but whether it was for the same reasons, she didn't know.

"I'm… I'm so…so sorry," she managed. "Did I step on your foot again?"

It was the only excuse she could manage for having landed so scandalously in his arms.

He shook his head. "No, no, it was my mistake," he said, looking anywhere but at her. "I fear you are correct—this room is too small for dancing."

A moment ago the room had felt as tight as a closet, but now it expanded around them like a cavernous hollow.

Empty and cold.

Tabitha shivered and realized she'd dropped her shawl at some point. Hurrying across the room to where it had fallen, she caught it up and threw it around her shoulders like it might offer some protection.

But the damage was already done.

She closed her eyes for a moment, willing herself to forget…forget what she'd wished for…what she'd thought. What she'd felt.

That shiver of anticipation. The idea that his handsome, sculpted lips would claim hers, kiss her.

That he would have to draw her closer still, closer than he already had.

She forced her eyes open and let the cold emptiness of the room, of the chasm between them, wash away the last of those warm, enticing memories.

Tabitha pressed her lips together and hoped her cheeks were not burning evidence of her previous thoughts.

Then again, she felt as if there wasn't a part of her that wasn't blushing.

"I should go," she said, glancing over her shoulder

at him. "Thank you ever so much for sharing your supper with me."

There. A mannerly retreat. Polite. Cool. Sensible.

She could only hope she appeared as unruffled as her words.

At least he couldn't see her insides—for her heart pounded tremulously and her legs wobbled yet.

Even a glance at his dark eyes, the hard line of his jaw, the breadth of his chest was enough to catch her breath, so what would it have felt like to have him kiss her?

More to the point, did all men have this power over women? She shivered at the thought.

She went over to nudge Mr. Muggins, but she stopped when Preston said, "You cannot leave yet, Miss Timmons."

The command behind his words held the power to bind her feet to the floor. "I cannot?"

"No. I'm not finished yet."

Was it her, or did his words sound as uneven as her breathing? "Not finished?"

Whatever did that mean?

They stood there looking at each other and Tabitha wondered if he truly meant to finish what he'd started—that he intended to kiss her.

"I have yet to…"—he glanced around the room—"finish my apple tart."

"Your what?" Perhaps she hadn't heard him correctly. Perhaps "apple tart" was rakish code for something more sinister, something more delightful.

Not that the apple tart wasn't excellent.

He nodded at the table. "You agreed to keep me company through my supper, and I have yet to finish."

His gaze met hers and she heard the words as clearly as if they had been spoken aloud. *Stay, Miss Timmons. Stay with me.*

He held out her chair for her, and Tabitha found herself powerless to resist. She should be scurrying out of the room like any sensible, proper young lady would (then again a sensible, proper young lady would never have found herself in this lion's lair), but the power of that unsaid plea in his eyes left her with no capacity to resist, so she sat down.

And worse, a wry little voice nudged into her thoughts. *Perhaps by staying, he might kiss you for once and for all.*

As if she wanted him to do any such thing. Which she didn't.

At least, that was what she kept telling herself.

Preston retook his seat and picked up his fork, digging into the tart as if nothing had happened.

Then again, perhaps for him nothing had. Nothing of consequence.

Tabitha stole a glance at the man and found him silently and methodically eating his apple tart as if their encounter had been yet another course to the meal.

One he'd nearly sampled and then sent back untried.

An unfamiliar pang unfurled inside her. Whatever was wrong with her? He must kiss young ladies as a matter of course, yet not her?

She looked up and found that he had stopped eating and was staring at her. Gaping, really. More like looking at her plate in horror.

And when she glanced down, she realized she'd just spent the last minute stabbing her poor apple tart into a crumble.

"Did it offend you?" he teased.

Bother the man.

"Not yet," she replied and took a bite.

Something deep and dark continued to pique inside Tabitha. A worrisome little nudge she'd never felt before. Almost like jealousy. Envy. Of all the ladies who did catch his eye…and more.

She stabbed at her apple tart, this time with a little too much ferocity, scattering crumbs across the tablecloth. Pausing for a moment, she stole a glance at Preston to see if he'd noticed her unwitting violence on the hapless pastry.

Then a more worrisome thought occurred to her—one beyond the notion that she'd just wasted a good portion of this delicious tart.

Whatever would her betrothed think when she arrived in London wearing her Kempton country finery and antiquated sense of propriety? Her intended could hardly be impressed if she came in looking like she'd just fallen off a hayrick!

Would he marry her and then set her aside as Preston had just done? Sent back untried. Oh, how very humiliating.

Just as it was now.

Worse, she had to imagine.

Tabitha's fork dove into her apple tart, and she took another bite and tried to tell herself she was being irrational.

Certainly Mr. Reginald Barkworth wasn't expecting a Diamond of the First Water. After all, theirs was an arranged marriage, a match made for mutual benefit.

A rational union of equals, as Daphne would say.

Tabitha flinched at such a cold, boring description

and ate a few more bites of tart before she stole another glance at Preston.

She hoped, nay, she wanted her future husband to gaze across their dining table at her with eyes alight with nothing less than burning desire.

Desire for her.

But would he if she looked like someone's country cousin?

"Is it ever so noticeable?" she blurted out without even thinking.

Preston sat back, looking startled by her anxious words. "Is what so noticeable?" he asked calmly, setting down his knife and fork. He glanced over at the carnage that had once been her slice of apple tart, and his brows rose.

"That I am from the country?" She set down her fork and crossed her arms over her chest.

He glanced up at her, his eyes inscrutable. "Is it important?"

"Yes." How could he ask? She hardly wanted to find herself being a point of ridicule.

"That depends on whether you are worried about how the other ladies find you or how the men in Town will give their regard."

"Either, I suppose," she told him, then hastily added, "not that I care how the gentlemen regard me, for I am not looking for a husband."

Preston's brow cocked up. "So you've said."

He needn't appear so dubious. She wasn't looking.

But suddenly Mr. Reginald Barkworth, heir presumptive to his uncle's marquisate, sounded neither romantic nor full of possibilities, not even a rational union of equals. He seemed quite daunting.

Her frantic gaze rose to meet Preston's, and for a moment she thought she spied a hint of surprise there, like he was seeing her for the first time.

Then to her shock, he leaned across the table and whispered, as if he were sharing a secret of state, "Miss Timmons, you have nothing to fear. The men in Town won't get past your bewitching eyes and that siren's head of hair of yours. You'll have them utterly charmed. As for the ladies, they will only be envious." He leaned back, a devilish tilt to his lips.

Tabitha's mouth fell open in shock.

Truly, had she heard him correctly? Bewitching eyes and a siren's head of hair? Her hand went to her chignon, the pins loose and probably tumbling about as it was wont to do. The hair her aunt called an abomination.

Truly, her? A siren? Goodness, he should be shoveling out the inn's stalls for trying to pass off such nonsense.

"I think you have had too much Madeira," she told him. Yes, that was it. The wine had loosened his tongue and his vision. "The wine has turned you into an unrepentant flirt."

Instead of being chastened, he looked quite proud. "That is an excellent suggestion, Miss Timmons."

A suggestion? "Whatever do you mean?"

"You have found my profession. You needn't badger me further about finding an occupation." He sat back and tapped his chin. "Yes, I do think that will suit. Thank you, Miss Timmons."

"A profession? I have made no such suggestions."

"Of course you have. I think I will make a most excellent flirt. Don't you concur?"

"A flirt? You call that a profession?" she shot back, a little more sharply than she intended. Then again, she was also doing her best not to look directly into his gaze, what with its mischievous, tempting light. "Why, it hardly pays."

"Ah, but it does. In ways you cannot imagine."

"Mr. Preston, I am trying to have a discussion in earnest."

Preston glanced up at her and smiled. She'd been correct earlier. He was a bit foxed. He'd have to ask the innkeeper as to who it was who'd smuggled this Madeira: it was an excellent vintage, excellent in that it had him seeing Miss Timmons, of all people, as some sort of watery nymph come to tempt him.

For somewhere after his third glass of that demmed Madeira, she'd stopped being a vexing little spinster and become something altogether different.

Whyever did she fit in his arms the way she did? And whatever had she been doing, glancing up at him with those large brown eyes and looking entirely too tempting?

That was the Madeira, he told himself. It must be. For Miss Timmons was the daughter of a vicar.

Someone Hen might even approve of. Well, not entirely, but Miss Timmons was overly respectable.

Overly respectable. Preston sat back and looked at her again, an odd plan formulating. Miss Timmons was certainly that.

Society might even find her endearing.

Even now, she was chattering on about "fitting in" and not appearing like a "poor relation" when she got to Town, and all he could think about was that for Miss

Timmons to fit into London society, her mysterious relations and Lady Essex would have to strip her of every bit of charm she possessed.

That would be a crime indeed.

His chest did that odd wallop again as he saw Miss Timmons all done up and yapping like yet another Bath-educated miss.

Oh, that would never do.

Whether it was the wine prodding him into this ridiculous notion or just that he had spied that familiar spark of passion in her eyes—a spark he understood all too well and had been ordered to extinguish in the name of respectability—he couldn't let anyone ruin her.

For if they did, they might steal away this mysterious bit of magic she, and only she, seemed to possess. She'd unlocked a hidden realm for him tonight. As if he'd awakened in a room that was both familiar and yet unknown. Had reminded him of a life he'd all but forgotten.

Why was it that when he looked across the table at Miss Timmons, he wasn't in this wayside inn but in that cozy parlor at Owle Park, the one into which his parents had loved to crowd them all, if only to while away the evenings? Together.

Gads, he hadn't thought of that room…well, ever. Not since…

Preston shook his head. Perhaps it was because he'd never met anyone like Miss Timmons.

He'd spent his entire life surrounded by Hen and her lofty ilk—nothing against Hen, but some of her compatriots… Preston shuddered. Yet that explained why he'd never discovered that a simple country spinster could be such a charming and amiable companion.

And now she was off to London to find her polish, he supposed. Well, no one was going to do that to this little charming bit of muslin.

No one was going to turn her into another Lady Violet or Miss Seales.

He glanced over at her and ignored the way her red hair, all loose and tumbling free, made him want to push it back so he could gaze into her lively brown eyes.

And not because he wanted to run his fingers through those radiant locks.

Not in the least.

He could even ignore her pert lips, the curve at the base of her neck that should be kissed. He could force himself to forget how she fit against him as if she'd been missing from his life all these years.

He would ignore all this, if only to save her. If he could, he would stop her in her tracks this very night and carry her off so she never reached London, but he suspected such high-handed actions would fall into Hen's categories of "Beyond the Pale" and "Unforgivable Ruin."

Yes, most likely, kidnapping Miss Timmons, even in the name of saving her from society, would be viewed dimly.

Even by the lady herself.

While he was sorting his plans—and rejecting most of them as impossible—she'd been going on about something to do with Almack's.

Almack's? Miss Timmons inside those halllowed halls? Over his dead body.

"Miss Timmons, what is your given name?" he asked, stopping her in midsentence.

"My what?" she asked in a distracted sort of way.

"Your given name," he said, picking up his fork. "Miss Timmons does not suit you."

"Whyever not? It is my name," she said in that stuffy I-am-the-daughter-of-a-vicar voice of hers.

He had to confess, he rather liked it. No one spoke to him like that.

Save this miss.

"Well, I differ. I don't think it suits you. And I want to know what your given name is. The one your friends call you."

She laughed and struck a haughty pose. "You, sir, are hardly one of my friends."

It was on the tip of his tongue to remind her of how close she'd been to being more than just a dining companion a little bit earlier.

When he'd held her in his arms and been about to finish off his supper by devouring her lips in the sort of kiss that came after a good meal and copious amounts of wine.

And he tried telling himself he was glad that he had set her aside. For to do otherwise would ruin everything he wanted to do...

"We are friends enough to enjoy a supper together," he said instead, but the implication was there hanging between them.

"I believe I am dining here under duress."

"Not in the least. It was an act of charity on my part."

"Charity? I thought I was here to keep *you* company."

He laughed. "That as well, but my benevolence was also intended for the rest of the inn's patrons."

"Whatever do you mean?" she demanded. Ah, so his waifish little kitten had claws.

Preston, ever the rogue, laughed. "I was also rescuing the rest of the inn's patrons from being awakened by that yawning clamor in your belly. And now, through my charity, it has, thankfully, been silenced. Vanquished, you might say."

Her eyes widened and a bright blush spread over her cheeks. Preston knew without a doubt that endearing shade of pink would be beaten out of her once the society matrons got done picking over her carcass.

"Yawning clamor? You have no decency, sir." She shook her head. "Is this what a gentleman discusses with a lady when he dines with her?"

"I wouldn't know. I've never heard a belly rumble so," he teased back.

The hue in her cheeks darkened to a deep pink.

No, she'd never get away with that color on her cheeks in Almack's.

But Preston wasn't one to give up easily, and he stole a page from Roxley's incorrigible volume of tricks. "My dear Miss Timmons, may I have the privilege of knowing your given name?" He let his words fall like a seductive whisper, tempting and intimate.

He suspected the last flickering light of the candles and the warmth of the room had her in a cozy mood. If they didn't lull her, perhaps their excellent meal had left her sated and unable to resist the languor of his words.

Lord, how much had Miss Timmons eaten? Enough

to make a shipload of sailors drowsy, but that was beside the point.

Indeed, she pressed her lips together and looked ready to give him a proper and scathing set down, so he resorted to his final, most tempting tactic.

He picked up the tart tray and slid the server under the last piece to hold it ever so close to her plate. Then he pressed a little more. "Come now, Miss Timmons, it will be our secret. What is your name?"

Her gaze fell to the tart. "Tabitha," she whispered. "My name is Tabitha."

He slipped the piece onto her plate, weighing the name against his impression of her. "It doesn't suit you."

She sat back and gaped at him. "Are you now the arbiter of names?"

He snapped his fingers. "Another occupation! By Jove, Miss Timmons, by the end of the evening you will have me completely employed."

"Oh, don't be ridiculous."

"But I am not trying to be," he replied. "It is just that I don't find Tabitha a fitting name for you."

"Of course it fits. My father gave me the name."

"He made a mistake," Preston told her. And was rewarded with a complete look of outrage.

"You don't know the circumstances."

"Enlighten me."

"If you must know—"

"I must," he replied, sitting back in his seat, crossing his arms over his chest.

"I wasn't alive when I was born—at least that was how it appeared. But the midwife persisted and finally got me to cry out. So Papa said I should be called

Tabitha." Now it was her turn to sit back, her nose tipped in the air as if to say *I told you so.*

"Ah, like the woman brought back to life by St. Peter."

Her brows rose. "You astound me, Preston."

"I am not the complete bounder you think me to be," he said, reaching over with his fork and stealing a bite from her apple tart. "Contrary to your impressions of me, I have an education. A rather thorough one."

"Yes, but do you put it to good use?"

"Every day."

"How is that?" she asked with a haughty, disbelieving air.

Touché for the little minx. She was rather like the terrier she claimed her dog to be. Overly persistent to prove her point and, from the smug expression on her face, convinced she had him on the ropes now.

Quite the contrary.

He crossed his arms over his chest and explained, "You wouldn't believe how much mathematics can save a man from wagering too much."

"Ruinous notion!" she exclaimed, though he could tell she found it amusing—her eyes sparkled as she continued in her favorite respectable tone. "You are incorrigible."

"So says my family."

"I feel quite sorry for them."

"You and the rest of London society," he told her.

"You should stop gambling and find honest employment."

"Dreadful thing to say to the man who just bought you dinner. Hardly well mannered, Tabby."

Tabby.

That brought her gaze up to his. Once again, he found himself entangled. Entwined. Snared. *Tabby.* It fit, rather like she did in his arms.

He grinned. "Yes, I will call you Tabby." He saluted her with his wineglass.

"Tabby, indeed!" she sputtered, setting down her fork.

"Yes, that is the perfect name for you." His kitten. His Tabby found. One day she would thank him for saving her. Preston was well pleased with himself, for he had it all quite settled. He'd come along just in time to save Tabby from herself and from London society and keep her just as she was.

His engaging, perfectly respectable companion—as long as he could refrain from kissing her. Yes, he could do that, he told himself, making a point not to look at those rosy lips of hers, those enticing brown eyes. He must. If he wanted to keep her as she was...perfectly innocent, impertinent, vexing and all-too-respectable.

Save he'd forgotten one important thing.

Perhaps the lady wasn't interested in his meddling.

"You cannot call me by such a name," Tabitha protested, even though her heart did an odd thump each time he did so.

Tabby.

There was something too intimate about such a nickname. It implied he knew her far better than he actually did. As if he'd actually kissed her senseless instead of setting her aside.

"I rather think I will," he said, completely ignoring her.

"Mr. Preston, please—"

He held up his hand. "No, truly, you'll thank me one day."

She rather doubted it. For this devil-may-care rake would be her ruin if they were to cross paths in London.

Cross paths... She looked up at this rogue and bounder and realized something she'd quite overlooked before.

Truly, what was the likelihood of them ever seeing each other again?

Certainly he wouldn't be gadding about Almack's. Or dropping by one of Lady Timmons's afternoons in. Let alone spending his evening at a respectable musicale or soirée.

He might be one of Roxley's boon companions, but even she knew that while the earl might have befriended him, that didn't give Preston an immediate entrée into society.

So, for all practical purposes, there was little to no chance they would ever cross paths again.

Such a notion should have given Tabitha every comfort. Instead it left her feeling a bit bereft.

This would be their one and only night together.

Not "night," she corrected herself. Night implied all sorts of things. And if just being held in his arms for a moment had been enough to knock her off balance, whatever could he do to her in a night?

Tabitha hastily set that thought aside.

"Shall we finish our evening with a wager, Tabby?" he was saying. While she'd been busy musing about his place—or rather non-place—in her life, he'd been clearing a space in the middle of the table and had set out three teacups.

A wager? "Certainly not," she told him, eyeing the cups before them. "I can't imagine that would be proper."

"Proper? Most likely not," he mused as he glanced over the table, searching for something. "But when a lady and gentleman dine together, they always end the evening with a wager."

She made a most unladylike snort. This sounded like a Banbury tale. Or a flirtatious trick.

Not that he seemed to find her quelling gaze all that pinning or capable of wrenching the truth out of him. "Ah, there it is," he said, reaching for the sugar bowl. He pulled out one lump and held it up for her to see.

Then he grinned, his lips tilted with a sort of endearing, lopsided twist and his eyes alight, and he dropped the lump of sugar into one of the cups.

Her heart made that fluttering, teasing beat again. "I don't think—"

"No, no. 'Tis a very simple wager," he explained, tipping the three cups over and concealing the lump of sugar. Then he moved them around, back and forth, waving his hands with exaggerated gestures as they moved from one cup to another—making it nearly impossible to keep her eyes on the cup with the sugar.

In fact, he redoubled his efforts, until she sat back and covered her mouth to hide the smile turning up her lips.

She certainly didn't need to encourage the man.

When he stopped, he sat back and waggled his brows at her. "Which one has the lump of sugar, Tabby? I wager you don't know."

Tabitha leaned forward and studied the cups before her. Then in a bit of glittering light from the nearly gutted candle, she spied a hint of sugar leading to one of the cups. With all his grand movements, he'd left a trail of evidence.

"What are the stakes?" she asked, masking her features.

Preston leaned across the table. "If I win, a promise, Tabby. That we shall be friends."

By reflex, she shook her head. "No, that would never do." Truly it would not. Friendship with Preston was the path to ruin.

She knew that as certainly as she knew which cup hid the sugar lump.

"Then name your stakes," he offered, "but mine still stand."

Oh, the impossible man. As if friendship with him was such a boon. It would serve him right to give him a bit of comeuppance.

But whatever could she wager?

Biting her lip, she stole a glance at him. "I don't usually wager."

"Don't you play cards?" he asked, tapping one of the cups, as if he were giving away where the sugar might be hidden.

Which he wasn't.

"I do. At Lady Essex's card parties. Penny stakes at the most."

"Then the stakes are either a penny if you win, or your friendship if I am the victor."

She would probably not have gone along with his proposition if it hadn't been for his superior tone.

Well, she would show him that while she might be a country miss from Kempton, she could outwit his Corinthian ways.

Furrowing her brow, she bit her bottom lip, as if she had found herself in the worst sort of pickle, spending a few teasing moments studying the cups before her as if she hadn't the slightest clue which one held the prize.

Then she reached out and turned over the cup to the right, revealing the lonely lump of sugar.

Tabitha grinned. "I rather like wagering with you, Mr. Preston. And you owe me a penny."

He sat up, examined the evidence before him and gaped at her. "However did you do that?" He looked down at the table again, then back at her. "Tabby, if I didn't know better, I'd say you cheated."

"What an ungentlemanly accusation," she told him, holding out her hand. "My penny, if you will."

He frowned and dug into the pocket of his waistcoat, his gaze never leaving the table, as if he were recounting every step in the process and trying to discern where he'd gone wrong.

When he was about to drop her winnings into her hand, he paused, holding the coin over her outstretched palm. "However did you know?"

Now it was her turn to preen. "The sugar left a trail," she said, pointing at the bits of evidence leading straight to the winning cup.

He drew his coin back a bit. "Tabby, you dreadful minx. You did cheat."

"I did not. I merely used my eyes," she said, thrusting her hand out again. "If you please, sir, my winnings."

"Hardly fair," he grumbled as he dropped the penny in her hand.

It landed in her open palm, and the moment it touched her hand, she had the shocking sense that she'd gained more than a penny. Something whispered to her that this coin would bind them together....

Ridiculous notion, she told herself—and even more so, for when she looked down at it, she realized something else.

"'Tis nicked," she remarked, holding it up for him to see.

"I'll give you another," he said, reaching for it.

"No," she told him, folding her fingers around the coin so it was safely nestled in the palm of her hand. "I rather like this one."

"Because it is nicked?"

"Yes, for it reminds me of you." Immediately she wished she could take her words back. For they hung there between them like a confession. Intimate and revealing.

Winding around both of them and twining them together—in ways they both knew were impossible.

Just like the way she fit into his arms. The way he'd held her and she'd thought of nowhere she'd rather have been. How this evening had changed her...and what she wanted.

What she'd never realized she wanted. And the horrible suspicion that he, this roguish, wretched man, was the only one who could open that world to her and leave her as this meal had, filled and yet ravenous for more.

More. How that word tangled up her sensibilities.

Tucking the coin in her pocket, she rose quickly from the table.

Preston got to his feet as well.

"Yes, well, thank you, sir, for dinner," she said.

"You are most welcome, Miss Timmons."

Her heart constricted. She was Tabby no more.

Moving around the table, Tabitha made a soft whistle to call Mr. Muggins, and the dog, startled out of his nap, bolted upright and nearly upended her.

To her chagrin, Preston caught her.

Caught her and pulled her close.

Oh, goodness! How had this happened? She had been bent on leaving one moment. Fleeing, actually. And now she was caught.

She had been caught, hadn't she? With her fingers curled into his waistcoat and her legs trembling, she didn't seem to possess any desire for a hasty escape.

"I think you still owe me," he whispered.

His demand teased her, but she didn't dare look at him. Become ensnared, entangled in that wicked, dangerous gaze of his.

"What say you, Tabby? Are we friends?"

Friendship? The look in his eyes called for something far more intimate.

Was he mad? Was she, for not wrenching herself free and running for the safety of her room above?

"'T'was a fair shake," she told him, trying for bravado even as her heart pounded.

"You cheated."

Tabitha's chin rose in defiance. "I used superior reasoning."

"Superior?" He laughed and leaned down, for now he had her, her gaze trapped in his. "If you had been using 'superior reasoning' you would have asked for the moon."

"The moon?" she managed in a tight whisper.

"Or more, Tabby." He gazed down at her, and suddenly it wasn't just that he held her, that he surrounded her. His arms wound around her, his hands warm against her gown, his body pressed to hers, he had her trapped and breathless.

"More?" she managed. More was dangerous. Ruinous.

And suddenly all too irresistible.

She had started the evening knowing nothing of men and now she had come all the way to this—to this passionate, dangerous madness. And that next step, to letting him steal her first kiss, was hardly as cavernous a leap as it might have seemed when she'd sat down for supper.

If this is madness...some newfound part of her heart clamored...*then let me drown in his kiss*.

One kiss...whatever harm was there in that?

Preston pulled her closer, and it was as if time itself came grinding to a standstill—pressed as she was against his chest, her legs brushing against his hard thighs. It was all so very intimate, or at least so she thought until his lips touched hers.

Then everything upended and he was kissing her.

Tabitha hadn't known what to expect, but there he was, his lips covering hers, his hands pulling her close, one at the small of her back and the other between her shoulders.

He had her exactly where he wanted and he wound his web around her and drew her even closer.

Not that she would have moved for anything, not with these beguiling tendrils of desire opening up inside her. They unraveled like spring vines, reaching for every corner and winding around anything in their reach.

Most notably, her heart.

His kiss teased at her, nibbled at her lips, begging for her response, and while she might never have been kissed, she seemed to know what to do.

She opened up to him, letting his tongue sweep past her lips, tease hers, while his hands, which weren't just holding her, explored her, roaming over her back, her hips, tracing wild paths over her, opening a floodgate of passion in their wake.

Tabitha found herself drawn closer to him as his delicious, sensuous web of desire entwined around her. Her fingers splayed out over his chest, one of them moving upward to curl around his neck and pull him closer.

His lips moved from her mouth, teasing at the nape of her neck, the column of her throat, while his fingers worked at the pins in her hair, plucking them loose and tossing them about the room like freely wagered pennies.

When the last of them fell, her hair tumbled down, and something like a groan escaped his throat.

It was desire, rough and ready, full of need. Thick, hard, masculine need.

And her body came thrumming to life at the sound, anxious and ready to answer his heady call. Her breasts tightened, her nipples grew taut against her chemise. She wanted to be touched, teased, tempted, kissed.

Her hips rocked forward, brushing against him. Against something so unmistakable, so hard and long, that now it was her turn to gasp.

She found herself aching, quaking inside. Delirious to arch against it, his lips continuing to tease her with promises of what was to come.

What could be…

And it wasn't only his lips, teasing now at the nape of her neck, but his touch—bringing her body to a chorus of a thousand traitorous notes, leaving her with only one thought.

More…

This, she finally realized, was Preston's true occupation—this dizzying whirl of desires that he spun to life within her with his kiss, with his touch—shooing good sense into a corner and making it watch in mute dismay as its mistress let herself be tumbled.

He was sin. He was temptation. If he was the lord of anything, it was the Lord of Desire.

For certainly, Preston was no gentleman.

Oh, heavens, how she wanted him. Wanted him to continue his trade, to wreak his havoc upon her. To lay her down, to cover her with his hard, muscled body.

She longed for something she didn't even understand, had never known, but now she could almost see it, a distant lamp in the darkness, and he held the only match to kindle it.

'Twas ruinous. Madness.

"Preston, I—" she gasped, reaching for that flame…

Her words, her touch seemed to nudge him.

This time as their gazes met, Tabitha knew that she wasn't alone in this hunger, this dangerous madness.

Then in a heart-stopping moment, his features went from being filled with desire to revealing a shattering awakening.

The rake blinked. And then blinked again as he took in her disheveled state.

"Oh, good God!" he gasped, looking her up and down. "Demmit, Tabby, what mischief have you wrought on me?"

Her? But before she could straighten out his memory of the events—for he had kissed her—Preston set her aside.

More like shoved her out of his arms and stumbled back from her. Then he turned on one boot heel and fled, leaving her utterly alone.

Which, as she'd claimed before, was what she wanted.

At least it had been, she thought, as she pressed her fingers to kiss-swollen lips.

Once.

Chapter 6

London
Two weeks later

"Tonight, Tabitha! Tonight you shall meet him."
Daphne practically skipped through the busy traffic
on Park Lane as they made their way to Hyde Park's
infamous Rotten Row.

"Oh, heavens, Daphne, I can't even think about
tonight!" Tabitha declared, shooting Mr. Muggins
a quelling glance. The energetic terrier tugged and
pulled on the lead, begging for a bit of freedom, the
park nearly within reach. She leaned over and patted
his head. "Not yet," she told him.

If only she could do the same to her own life. Un-
hook the tethers her family had bound her with and run
away. As far from London as she could get.

Not that any amount of distance will let you forget. Him. Preston.

It had been a fortnight since her dinner with him. Since he'd kissed her.

That kiss...

She'd replayed it over and over in her imagination. His heated touch, his lips covering hers, the way her body had come to life as he'd cradled her in his arms and kissed her into a passionate delirium.

Had she imagined it all? Oh, and those wrenching words he'd uttered.

"...what mischief have you wrought on me?"

On him? What about what he had done to her?

Her! Miss Tabitha Timmons. Respectable, innocent spinster from Kempton.

Innocent no more, she thought as she followed her friends into the park. Not when her thoughts were filled with the memory of his lips teasing hers, the steely grasp of his arms wound around her in those last final moments. Sheltering her. Keeping her close.

As if he'd never let her go.

But he had. Wretched cur. And left in his wake a passion, a flood of desires she never knew she possessed.

Now that she did know...heaven help her, they woke her up in the middle of the night, leaving her gasping for breath, her body taut with need, haunted with memories.

Preston! Every nerve seemed to cry out. *Find me again.*

Worse yet...she'd spend the rest of the night tossing and turning, filled with a dangerous longing to seek him out, if only to beg him to unwind this dangerous mischief inside her, entwine it around them both yet again.

Tabitha pressed her lips together, her fingers digging into her pocket, where she kept that nicked penny of his. It stabbed into her finger, prodding her to believe.

Yes, it had been real. Preston had claimed her, kissed her and then set her aside.

Why, he'd looked positively shocked when he'd pulled back from her. Not just shocked, tormented. A wrenching, pained light in his eyes. Enough so to send him hying off like a March hare.

Good heavens, was she that dreadful at kissing? Tabitha let go of the penny and sighed. Such a thing didn't bode well for her prospects as a happy and contented bride if her groom was destined to run away from her with that haunted look on his face every night.

Perhaps there was something to the Curse of Kempton...

"Tabitha!" Daphne was saying. "Haven't you heard a word I was saying?"

Glancing over at her friend, she realized Daphne had been asking her something about their plans for the evening.

The ones that included finally meeting her betrothed, Mr. Reginald Barkworth.

"Leave her be," Harriet told her. "If I was in Tabitha's shoes, I'd be a wreck as well."

"Is it that obvious?" Tabitha glanced from one friend to the other.

Harriet nodded. "A few moments ago you looked positively ill."

"Oh, good heavens, Harriet!" Daphne said, shooting the other girl a scathing glance. "Tabitha is radiant! And whyever wouldn't she be, when tonight she shall discover her heart's desire?"

With that, Daphne turned and continued down the path. After a few steps, Harriet and Tabitha hurried to catch up.

"I don't see why Mr. Barkworth has not called," Harriet said for about the thousandth time. "It all seems odd to me."

"He is heir to a title," Daphne told them with an airy wave. "He is allowed a few eccentricities. Besides, Tabitha was not ready to receive him—what with her wardrobe in the state that it was." She sighed at Tabitha's choice today of an old plain muslin.

"What?" Tabitha said, glancing down at her gown. "I don't want to ruin one of the new ones."

"You are an heiress now," Daphne reminded her. "You could have a new gown every day."

Tabitha scoffed at such a notion. Not that she even knew what it meant to be an heiress, since her aunt, Lady Timmons, had also been equally stringent about not taking them, especially Tabitha, out into society.

A lady of your fortune is an enticing opportunity to the worst sort of company. This is for your own well-being and safety, Lady Timmons had avowed. That, and, like Daphne, the lady had been shocked at the state of Tabitha's wardrobe, which she declared disgraceful and unfitting a lady of her future stature.

So for the last fortnight the house on Hertford Street had seen a steady stream of modistes, milliners, hosiers and glove makers, all assigned the task of turning Tabitha into a London lady.

"Mr. Barkworth will be a marquess one day, and as

a gentleman, he will expect a well-turned-out wife," Daphne noted.

"A title doesn't make a man a gentleman," Harriet shot back. "Nor is it a promise of a happy marriage."

Daphne scoffed at such dire predictions, but it was Tabitha who shocked both her friends.

"Marriage might not be so bad."

Both ladies paused and turned to gape at her.

How could she explain it to them? That marriage might mean intimate suppers, lively discussions, a bit of teasing laughter.

Kissing...

Had her evening with Preston been a peek into what a marriage might mean?

"With the right man," she amended.

"Perhaps," Harriet conceded. "Yet however will you know until you meet him?"

Before Tabitha could reply—for she shared Harriet's concerns—Daphne rushed right in. "I think it is ever so much more romantic that you are his mysterious heiress bride. You shall meet tonight at Lady Knolles's, and it will be perfectly magical."

Magic. Tabitha knew what that felt like. But would she find that same magic with Mr. Reginald Barkworth?

"I can't see how being an heiress is a good thing if you must hide your good fortune and keep out of sight," Harriet said with a sigh. They hadn't even been allowed a side trip to the Tower, much to her chagrin. "Though Chaunce agrees that your aunt's intentions are probably for the best. He says London is a wicked place, and I suspect he has good reason to know."

Harriet's brother—Chauncey, or Chaunce as he was

known in the Hathaway clan—had called on them several times. A solicitor by training, he now worked for the Home Office. Arriving in grand style, with his hat tipped in a rakish fashion, he had flirted with Tabitha's cousins until all three of them had been blushing.

Not an easy feat considering how worldly the Timmons cousins thought themselves.

"Yes, I agree with Harriet that having to hide away is rather disappointing," Daphne declared with a wide yawn. She came to a stop in the gravel, the pebbles crunching beneath her boots. "It would be much more lovely to be out here with the rest of the *ton,* and not sneaking about at this ungodly time." For a country girl, she had taken to Town hours like she'd been born and raised in London.

Not that she was fooling her friends, for when Daphne said "*ton*" she meant "gentlemen."

"We are out at this ungodly time because my aunt is not yet up and therefore cannot protest that we will ruin all her plans by being seen in public," Tabitha replied.

Lady Timmons could hardly complain about this— an early-morning stroll—for it was well before the fashionable set even considered arising, let alone making a public appearance in the park.

And no one in London knew them, since they had yet to make any sort of social debut.

In fact, they had the walkway to themselves, which suited Tabitha perfectly. She could let Mr. Muggins roam without the confines of a lead, and not worry about making some *faux pas* that would be reported back to her aunt.

"After tonight, there will be no more hiding you— or your fortune," Daphne avowed. "Perhaps Mr. Reginald Barkworth has been using this time to procure a Special License so he can marry you forthwith and save you from being stolen away."

Harriet was more direct. "If he turns out to be a regular Tulip, you might want to consider being kidnapped. By some privateer…or a duke!"

Daphne's gaze rolled upwards and she shook her head at such nonsense. "A duke would hardly need to kidnap his bride, Harriet. That, and Tabitha would lose her fortune if she didn't marry Mr. Reginald Barkworth. That's how it is, isn't it?" she asked.

"Yes," Tabitha nodded. "Uncle Winston's will provides for me only if I marry Mr. Barkworth."

Harriet thought about this for a bit and then paused. "Perhaps you will go mad on your wedding night, and then become a lovely, wealthy widow, just like Agnes did."

"Really, Harriet, if you can't add anything helpful!" Daphne exclaimed. "Agnes was burned for killing her husband, and Tabitha would end up in Newgate or Bedlam if she were to…well, if things turned out unfortunately."

"I hardly think I am going to go mad," Tabitha told them both. Not the sort of madness that would have her staking her spouse, but there was that other state of madness…

"Don't tell me you believe in the Curse of Kempton?" Harriet asked Daphne.

Tabitha paused as well to hear the answer, but Mr. Muggins had other ideas. He pulled and tugged at the leash. After a glance around confirmed that there was no one about, she reached down and unhooked the lead. The giant terrier leapt forward and danced around the ladies in excited circles before loping down the path ahead of them.

"Certainly not!" Daphne said, straightening a bit. Then after a moment, she added, "Well, perhaps a little."

They both looked at her, amazed by this confession. "Well, how can I not? I was born and raised in Kempton. Yet here we are in London, far enough away from home that…well, one begins to imagine…"

"You aren't considering—" Tabitha began.

"Heavens, no! I haven't your fortune to attract a man."

"You do have your name," Harriet pointed out. "You are a Dale, after all. That must count toward something."

"Yes, indeed," Tabitha agreed. If she had to tumble into the parson's trap… "Perhaps you might call on your Dale relations, use their connections—"

Daphne waved them off. "You must realize that for all my mother likes to toss our Dale name about Kempton, I suspect here in London it is as much a curse as being from Kempton. Did you see your aunt's face when you introduced me?"

"Yes, she did seem a bit taken aback," Tabitha agreed. Then again, Lady Timmons was not the most generous of creatures, for she'd never before shown the least bit of interest in her niece—what with three daughters of her own for which to find husbands.

Tabitha's arrival with her two friends in tow had been met with resignation—for as Tabitha later heard her aunt espouse to Sir Mauris, "We must endeavor to endear the gel to us. Think of her connections once she is married, and that fortune! La, she'll be most sought after. Remind me again why we didn't take her in when Archibald died?"

And her cousins? They hadn't exactly rushed to greet Tabitha with open arms. More like surveyed this interloper and her country entourage like one might view enemy troops approaching a closely held and jealously guarded territory.

Especially when all the new gowns and packages began arriving, addressed to Miss Timmons.

Miss *Tabitha* Timmons.

Then again, it had been Eloisa, the youngest Timmons daughter, the one the family claimed held the best prospects, what with her wit and beauty, who had pointed the way to the park to them this morning and confided that the unfashionable hour might afford her "esteemed cousin and quaint friends" a chance at some "country air," which certainly would be more "akin to their sensibilities."

Then again, Tabitha might have misunderstood, for she swore she had also heard Eloisa muttering something about a nearby coaching station and her hopes that her cousin might stumble upon it.

"Do you think we will be in the suds when we return?" Daphne asked.

"I can't see why my aunt would protest taking Mr. Muggins for a walk," she replied. "At least he isn't ravaging her house."

"Or her sensibilities," Harriet said with a giggle.

The rambunctious terrier had taken to following Lady Timmons around the house like a Bow Street runner, sneaking up behind her and then setting up a barking ruckus, one that the lady had declared just yesterday afternoon would be the end of her nerves. She'd been about to give Tabitha a terrible wigging over the matter when a cautionary cough from Cousin Euphemia had made her complaints about Tabitha's hound disappear into a forced smile on her lips.

"Do you think we might have time to venture toward Bond Street? I promise, just one milliner's shop and I will be set for life." Daphne's gaze filled with a dreamy, far-off look.

Tabitha laughed. "Just one?"

"Well, perhaps that and a ribbon shop," she added.

Harriet's gaze rolled upward. "And then a mercer's shop and then the modiste you read about in a newspaper advertisment, and then—"

"Oh, don't be ridiculous," Daphne declared. "I would never consider a mantua maker from an advertisement. I am far too discerning." This sent Tabitha and Harriet into a loud case of the whoops, until even Daphne had to laugh. "Forgive me if I just want to go shopping."

"You are forgiven," Tabitha said, for she too had started to chafe at her aunt's strictures.

"At least we are promised an outing this evening," Harriet said, and then, as if remembering the significance of the night, looked away.

"Yes, and new gowns to wear," Daphne said, adding that as if it made the prospect of meeting one's future spouse more palatable. "I do hope the color for my gown suits."

"I thought you weren't looking for a husband," Harriet reminded her.

"I am not," she replied tartly. Then her voice lowered. "Though I wouldn't mind being admired…just once."

Yes, just once, Tabitha found herself silently agreeing. And much to her chagrin, she wondered what Preston would think of her new gown—a scandalous creation Daphne had instructed the modiste to make when Lady Timmons had been called from the drawing room for a few minutes.

Not that she wanted Preston to admire her. Not in the least.

Good heavens! What if she was to run into him? Whatever would he say if he discovered the truth— that she was here in London to be married—when she'd been so adamant in her determination never to take a husband.

Something ruinous, she had to imagine. Or worse, he might do something scandalous.

"Then if we were by chance to meet, perhaps I would ask you to dance."

He'd been teasing certainly, but still, she couldn't help imagining tonight's outcome far differently than everyone else envisioned.

With Preston crossing the ballroom and taking her hand and stealing her away.

Tabitha glanced around at the line of vast trees and orderly grounds, as if she half expected to find him striding across the green, but she just as quickly realized there was little chance of running into the man here, especially at this hour. "Oh bother, it might be best if we return before my aunt arises, or worse, disaster strikes."

"I fear it already has." Harriet pointed up the path.

For while they had been comporting themselves with all the grace and manners that would have even

Lady Essex nodding with approval, Mr. Muggins had found someone new to bedevil and plopped them into the suds.

"Oh, you are in the suds," Roxley told Preston as the duke turned his new curricle onto the long, open path known about Town as Rotten Row, "if we must ride about at this time of day. Remind me again why we are out at this hour?"

"It wasn't like I rousted you," Preston replied, his head tipped as he studied how this new pair took to the straightaway.

"No, suppose not." Roxley leaned back in his seat and stretched out his long legs, folding his arms across his chest. "Demmed good night and here it is morning. Funny how that happens." He closed his eyes and began to doze.

Preston slanted a glance over at his friend, who was still in his evening attire and had come along readily at the suggestion of trying out the duke's new carriage and set.

Leave it to Roxley, feckless and idle fellow that he was, never to turn down a lark. Even if he slept through it.

Preston frowned, for a sleeping Roxley hardly served his purposes. But it would hardly do to have to nudge him awake and demand his help...

Help in finding Miss Timmons.

Tabby. Damn her and her wide brown eyes and appetite for Yorkshire pudding. And her hilariously tart opinion that he needed employment.

One kiss, and she'd turned his life upside down. And what had he done? Run away.

It hadn't been just the lure of her kiss—though that had been a good part of his flight—no, it was because Tabby held the key to a door he hadn't even realized he'd been searching all this time to discover.

What he needed to do was find her and prove to himself, once and for all, that he'd imagined that magical, delirious evening.

But how could he do that when the demmed little slip o'muslin had disappeared? Spirited away by none other than Roxley's aunt, and he had no idea how to find her.

Tabby, not Lady Essex.

Oh, he knew exactly where Lady Essex was—ensconced at Roxley's house (because Roxley remained comfortably encamped at Preston's)—but he also knew that the lady was staying at the earl's town house without any companions.

Without Tabby. A fact he'd discovered by bribing Roxley's butler, Fiske. Preston shook his head. This was what he'd come to—skulking about London hoping to discover what Lady Essex had done with Tabby between that demmed inn and Town.

He glanced over at Roxley and felt a twinge of guilt, for he knew what he must ask the earl to do, and it was unthinkable.

But Roxley was his last hope. He was also Preston's sole remaining friend, for he'd been given the cut direct even by the lowest members of the *ton*.

He couldn't get himself invited to a dogfight.

God knows, Hen had tried. He'd surrendered to her demands that he seek a wife, albeit if only to find Tabby, then only to discover that his attendance was not wished by anyone of consequence.

He'd even gone to Almack's with her, but to Hen's horror, they had been denied entrance by the patron-esses.

Sent home in utter disgrace.

Not that his indomitable aunt had given up. Lady Juniper was a Seldon at heart and had not taken the snub lightly. "They shall all rue the day when I have restored you," she kept muttering and had so until she'd managed to gain them both a single, solitary invitation.

"I wouldn't be in this demmed wretched tangle if it hadn't been for that race," Preston muttered.

"What is that?" Roxley asked, opening an eye and propping himself up a bit.

"The race. With Kipps."

"Oh, yes, that." Roxley shifted and glanced up to give the horses a discerning examination. Nodding at their pace, he added, "Bad business, indeed."

"You didn't seem to mind when you pocketed your winnings."

"I wasn't wagering with poor Kipps," Roxley re-plied. "I took Dillamore's blunt. Well, his vowel," he corrected, patting his coat pocket, where he kept his collection of notes and empty promises to pay. "Re-member, I warned you not to drag Kipps deeper into the mire. I did."

"Yes, you did." Preston glanced over at him. "I should have listened to you."

Roxley scrambled upright, gaping. "What is this? Humility from the likes of the almighty and lofty Pres-ton?" He glanced up and down the Row. "And not a soul around to witness this change of heart."

Preston laughed. "I'll deny it if you repeat it to any-one."

Roxley mustered an expression of utter indignation. "Have you ever known me to carry tales?"

"Do I have to answer that?"

"For the sake of our friendship, I think not." Roxley yawned and crossed his arms over his chest. "Besides, if I were to nose it about that you are suffering from pangs of remorse, no one would believe me. Think me mad."

"They already do."

"Remarkably convenient," Roxley replied. "No one wants to saddle their daughter to a jinglebrains." He grinned, content in his foolish reputation.

"Perhaps I should try that," Preston mused. Good God, he was already half mad to find Tabby.

"No one would believe it," Roxley said. "Same reason I never told anyone how you cracked up your carriage outside of Kempton."

"Roxley!" Preston growled in warning.

His friend chuckled. "Not a word. I shan't tell a soul. Not that anyone would believe me." The earl glanced up at the horses and changed the subject, much to both their relief. "Good pair. Solid. Nice gait."

"Yes, I thought so as well."

"Won't get skittish when you come around a corner and find the roadway filled with—"

"Roxley—" the duke warned.

His friend chuckled and Preston realized that he would probably never let him hear the end of that demmed accident.

They drove for a bit in silence until Roxley ventured, "I take it Lady Juniper—it is still Juniper, isn't it?"

The duke nodded.

"Yes, well, I take it she hasn't caught wind of that race with Walsby fortnight last?"

"No. Thank God." She and Henry would have been packed and gone.

Roxley sat back again. "Thought she'd find out for certain when we ended up in that inn full up with everyone coming into Town. Demmed rotten luck as it was, nearly running into Lady Essex. She'd have had us both in the stocks. Deplores gambling. And racing?" Roxley shuddered. "Good thing that chit from Kempton isn't one of those gabble-grinders. Sensible bit of muslin that one, didn't you think?"

Preston pressed his lips together and didn't answer. This was the perfect opening, but however did he ask his friend to throw himself on the sword of Damocles just to find her?

Roxley glanced down at his gloves and tugged at one of the fingers. "What was her name?"

"Who?" Preston feigned.

And did so miserably.

"Who, he says! Preston, you are a terrible liar. You know who I mean. That pretty little chit I made you sup with." Roxley slanted a glance at him. "And don't try to tell me you don't remember her name. Miss Tate. No, that's not it. Miss Trifle—"

"Miss Timmons," Preston ground out, wary because Roxley might seem a fool, but he had a sharp wit behind his lighthearted exterior.

Yes, her name was Miss Tabitha Timmons.

Tabby. With her voracious appetite and pert opinions. With a kiss and a way of looking at a man that left him all tangled up and lost.

Lost. That was it. Her kiss had left him adrift.

Now all he needed to do was find the little chit, kiss her, and discover that she was merely ordinary—not a siren capable of stealing his heart.

Then his life would return to normal. He just knew it.

"Ah, yes. Miss Timmons. The vicar's daughter," Roxley was saying, waggling his brows. "Thought you might end up with another scandal in your collection with that one."

Demn near had. How Preston had managed to wrench himself away from her that night was still beyond him.

Kissing her had been a momentary lapse in judgment. He'd certainly never set out to find himself entangled with her. And certainly not to ruin the little minx.

Some would argue that he already had—just by kissing her—and certainly he'd kissed any number of impudent misses in his time. But none of them had ever twined her innocent gaze into his heart.

He'd never wanted a woman more than he had Tabby.

Yet when he'd looked into her eyes, so filled with wonder and, heaven help him, desire, he'd found that he couldn't continue. Couldn't ruin her.

Something in his heart had stopped him. *Don't make this mistake.*

If anything, that warning had sent him scurrying away, all the while telling himself he'd been saving himself.

"Took long enough for you to return to the room," Roxley was saying as he nonchalantly glanced down at the state of his boots. "Began wondering if I was going to have to stand second...yet again."

Preston gave his friend his most scathing ducal glance. The one his grandfather had all but perfected. "Over that spinster? Nonsense. Besides, Hen would have my hide if I were to do something so imprudent."

"Only if she hears about it," Roxley replied as he leaned back and closed his eyes. "Scares me to death, your aunt."

"She should," Preston told him. "Managed to get me invited to a soirée tonight."

This brought Roxley fully awake. "You don't say! Who is going to receive you?"

That was the rub. Since the debacle with Kipps, no one sent round any invitations. Save one.

"Lady Knolles."

Roxley shuddered. "Poor Lady Juniper. Having to toady up to such a low creature. Rather deplore Lady Knolles. She's one of my aunt's cronies, you know."

Which was exactly why Preston needed Roxley's help.

But before he could ask, Roxley glanced up at the horses. "Fine pair. But here on the Row is one thing, out in the country—"

"They'll do. Want to give them a run tomorrow?"

"Thought you'd never ask. But you aren't racing them, are you?"

"*Et tu*, Brutus?"

"A man can only be guilty by association so many times before the old cats start tarring him with the same brush." Roxley paused. "You haven't my aunts."

"I have Hen."

"That you do," Roxley agreed. "I must say, I have

never been in the park so early—not since I was in short coats. Forgotten how nice it is...my nanny used to bring me around this time of day. Did yours?"

"Pardon?" Preston asked.

"Did your nanny bring you here when you were a child?"

Preston glanced around the park and realized how much the grand trees and wide lawns reminded him of Owle Park, the house he'd grown up in. How had he never noticed this?

"No," he replied, more to blot out the memory than to answer Roxley's question.

"Never?" the man pressed.

Preston's jaw tightened. "I grew up in the country."

"Suppose that is like being in the park all the time," Roxley mused, before he began reminiscing about his childhood in London.

But for Preston, talk of his childhood was nothing but heart wrenching. As much as he tried not to listen to Roxley's musings, he saw Owle Park come alive around him—the wide lawn, dogs bounding across the green, his brothers teasing him, his sister's merry laughter, his mother and father walking arm in arm across the estate they loved.

All gone. All lost. Of course, not Owle Park. The grand Palladian house still remained, though shuttered and closed, just like Preston preferred to keep all the memories of his lost childhood.

But since his dinner with Tabby it was all he could think about. Owle Park. The possibility that it could all come alive again.

And then, as if to keep those painful images alive for just a bit longer, out of nowhere, a large dog came racing toward them, bounding and bouncing as if it were on springs, barking madly at the horses.

The pair that had been so perfectly matched and steady just moments ago balked, sending the curricle rocking.

Preston pulled them to a stop and rose up. "Away, you mongrel! Get aw—"

Stopped in midword, Preston gaped at the hound teasing his horses.

Mr. Muggins?

The dog barked at Preston, as if in happy greeting, and then ran around the carriage and back under the horses' hooves—once again sending his previously well-mannered cattle dancing in their traces. The jolt bounced Preston back into his seat.

Beside him Roxley clung to the rail. "Where the devil did that beast come from? Looks bloody familiar. Got the manners of an Irish pugilist."

The duke ignored the double wallop his heart did in his chest as he looked up to find a trio of misses dashing in anything but a ladylike fashion up the Row, shouting something.

And the one in front was carrying a lead—but it was her determined stride and tumble of red curls escaping the confines of her bonnet that held his attention.

Tabby.

Then to his horror, the demmed foolish chit dashed right up toward his now unmanageable horses, scolding as she went. "Sir, your horses are about to trample my dog!"

Actually, they were about to trample her.

Preston would have liked to think that he was leaping down from his carriage for all the right reasons—to save Tabby from her own foolhardy nature—but that wasn't entirely true.

Nor was it to avoid the devil of a wigging Hen would give him if this vicar's daughter was harmed by his new horses.

Good heavens, Preston, is there no end to the scandal you can bring down on this house?!

Shoving the ribbons into Roxley's grasp, Preston leapt into the fray. Catching hold of the minx, he pulled Tabby out of harm's way and into his grasp.

No, it was for none of those reasons. For the moment she slammed into his chest, when his arms curled around those now familiar curves—which, he noted, no longer felt so desperately thin—and he looked down into those glorious (and right now furious) brown eyes, he realized the only person in danger of being trampled was him.

And he knew the real reason he'd leapt down from the curricle to pluck her from danger.

To have his Tabby back in his arms.

Chapter 7

Of all the men in London to find herself entwined with—rather, she corrected herself, to run into—why did it have to be him?

Preston.

And just as handsome and rakish and irresistible as she recalled. Perhaps more so, if such a thing was possible.

His arms around her, her hands splayed across his chest, his warmth, his muscles surrounding her.

Her heart fluttered, her knees wavered. Oh, yes, just as irresistible.

"Sir, if you would…would…" Tabitha drew a steadying breath. "Unhand me," she finally managed.

Then she glanced up—and what she saw in his expression stunned her. That same dangerous light in his eyes that had burned there after their kiss.

A possessive, hungry fire that had yet to go out.

"Tabby," he said, ever so softly. Quiet enough that no one else heard.

But she did. That single, intimate name whispered down her spine and curled around her heart.

She was Tabby again, and he, her reckless, dangerous lover.

"A-hem," Harriet coughed.

This prodded Tabitha's sensibilities into reminding her that this wasn't some private room in a wayside inn but the middle of London in the middle of the morning.

That, and she had no right to be this man's Tabby. Not now. Not ever again.

"You must let me go," she told him, glancing over at the horses, which Roxley had managed to settle. Mr. Muggins sat obediently next to Preston, looking up with dark doggy eyes filled with adoration—not having forgotten the man's offerings of roast beef any more than Tabitha could escape the memories of Preston's kiss.

"Please," she whispered, this time with a bit more urgency, glancing over at Daphne's scandalized expression.

"Yes, of course," he said, setting her free and taking a slight step back. "Are you unharmed?"

She shook her head, despite the fact that she stood wavering in her boots. Unharmed? She supposed not. Unsettled? Entirely.

Daphne, her ever-intrepid friend, waded into the mire, having mistaken her friend's stricken expression. "Those beasts," she began, pointing at Preston's horses, "are ill-mannered and obviously not well-handled. Why, they nearly trampled my poor friend. No wonder you are prone to landing in the ditch."

Preston, a beast of another sort, took her insult exactly as she'd intended—a sharp and hard thrust into his rather oversized pride. "Not well-handled—"

"Miss Timmons?" the other fellow in the carriage called down. "And Miss Dale?" He paused for a second longer as his gaze fell on Harriet. "Good heavens, Harry, is that you as well?"

"Lord Roxley!" Harriet exclaimed. "Lady Essex said you were out of town. When did you return?"

The earl coughed and then shot a panicked glance at Preston. "Just. Just returned," he said. "Do you recall my friend Preston?"

"Ah, yes," Preston said, setting Tabitha aside hastily and making a short bow. "Miss Timmons, is it not? Of Kempton?" He glanced over his shoulder at Roxley as if he needed his friend's assurance that he had all the facts straight, his expression now masked to be utterly bland.

But with his back to her friends, he winked at her.

"Yes," she said, ignoring the pang in her heart. No, he mustn't wink at her. Didn't he realize that it was impossible?

If only it wasn't, a voice whispered inside her. *If only...*

"I fear I must apologize for my appearance." Roxley waved his hand over his jacket and waistcoat.

"Still in your evening clothes, my lord?" Harriet teased as she reached up to scratch one of the horses. "Out all night, I imagine. Wait until Lady Essex hears this."

"No!" Tabitha, Preston and Roxley all said at once.

Daphne and Harriet gaped at the three of them, and Roxley rushed to fill the void. "Miss Hathaway, I would hope you could avoid mentioning this to my aunt. You know how she can be." He grimaced and shuddered, making a great show of it.

Harriet grinned. "I think she will be ever so delighted to know you are close at hand."

The earl blanched, and if he was already a bit worn from carousing all night, he looked positively ill at this cheery news.

"How do you like London, Miss Hathaway?" Preston asked, changing the subject.

"Not at all," Harriet told him with her usual forthright honesty.

Preston laughed, and it made his handsome features even more engaging. "How is that?"

"Tabitha's aunt will not let us go anywhere—save shopping for her—"

"New gowns," Tabitha blurted out to keep her friend from revealing too much. Suddenly she saw the real danger of this encounter—that either Daphne or Harriet would spill the soup.

"Yes, new gowns," Harriet finished, glancing sideways at Tabitha.

"Well, I suppose you have business elsewhere," Tabitha rushed in to say. "And we as well. We have… that is…" She struggled to come up with some sort of commitment that would require them elsewhere… now…nay, immediately…in fact they were late, and all she could think of was one thing.

"Dancing." She nodded most emphatically. "Yes, we must go, for my aunt has hired a dancing master, and I fear we will be late. If you will excuse us."

Daphne and Harriet gaped at her rush of words. And of course, Harriet wasn't one to be coaxed along.

"He isn't coming for hours, Tabitha," she corrected. "Your aunt said he was to arrive at half past two."

"A dancing master?" Preston asked.

Tabitha flinched and hoped the man wouldn't press further.

But of course he did. "Has this poor fellow been warned to bring extra boots, Miss Timmons? I fear for his toes if he is to teach you." His brows rose in a big arch, as if he truly expected her to answer that.

Or worse yet, *explain it.*

But thankfully, or rather mercifully, fortuitously and blessedly, Roxley leapt into the conversation. "Dancing lessons? On this, the first sunny day in a sennight? Demmed waste of time when there is so much to see in London."

"Exactly," Harriet echoed. "I would like to see the elephant at the Tower. And go to Astley's. And the theater. And Vauxhall, though Lady Essex says it is an immoral place where no decent lady should venture."

"Those all sound like the reasonable expectations on a visit to London," Roxley agreed. "Save Vauxhall, perhaps."

"Yes, but Lady Timmons, Tabitha's aunt, has forbidden us even those pleasures," Harriet complained.

"Why is that?" Preston asked, his gaze fixed on Tabitha.

She wanted to groan. Why did this man have to be so perceptive? Why couldn't he be a bit more addle-pated like the earl?

"She fears Tabitha may run afoul of fortune hunters," Harriet explained, and then realizing that perhaps she had said too much, her eyes widened.

"Fortune hunters?" Roxley exclaimed. Then after a moment of looking from one of them to the next, he laughed.

As did Preston. "Whatever do you have to fear from fortune hunters, Miss Timmons?" he asked. "I daresay it isn't as if you are here to trap a husband."

Tabitha took a step back, for whatever could she say?

Harriet happily filled them in. "Tabitha has inherited a vast fortune from her uncle. She's quite the heiress now."

The two men stilled, shock on both their faces. Roxley managed to find his tongue first. "Oh, that explains it all. Come to Town to find a husband, have you?"

No one found his ill attempt at humor funny.

"She is certainly not 'hunting,' as you so crudely put it, my lord," Daphne told the earl, coming forward and winding her hand around the crook of Tabitha's elbow. "Whyever should she, when Miss Timmons is already betrothed."

"Daphne!" Tabitha exclaimed, her gaze flying to meet Preston's.

Then to her horror, she watched his eyes darken as the truth tumbled out in the open.

There it was one second—she was his Tabby—and then it was gone. She'd never be his Tabby again. Never know his kiss. Never discover why it was she couldn't stop thinking about that night with him.

"Betrothed?" he asked, in something like a hungry growl. "Is this true?"

It seemed to Tabitha that all of London paused, the

city swirling around her in a dizzy whirl, as if await- ing her answer.

She couldn't speak, couldn't say anything. What would it matter to him? He'd teased her, tempted her and kissed her and then fled her company. *Now* her future happiness mattered to him?

Good heavens, she would never understand men at this rate.

"Of course it is true," Harriet told him. "Why else would we have come to Town if it hadn't already been all arranged."

"All this time?" Preston stepped back, staring at Tabitha as if he were seeing her for the first time.

And she knew what he was seeing. At least what he thought he was seeing. That she was one of those awful, lying London misses he so deplored.

"Why, Miss Timmons, I thought you eschewed mar- riage—men, for that matter—given your not so fa- mous Curse of Kilton." Sarcasm dripped from every word he spoke.

"Kempton," all three of them corrected.

"Yes, the dreaded Curse of Kempton," he acknowl- edged. "Destined to go mad as a banshee when you marry, isn't that right, Roxley?"

"Wouldn't catch me marrying one of you," the earl said, before he hastily added, "though I mean no of- fense."

"None taken," Harriet replied.

"There is no curse," Tabitha said.

"I should hope not for the sake of your betrothed," Preston remarked. "I must ask, whatever caused this sudden change of heart? Love at first sight? Or has he stolen your virtue and is now being forced to the altar?"

He couldn't have said anything more terrible, and Tabitha's cheeks flamed.

"You are insufferable, sir," Daphne exclaimed.

"I don't mean to be," he told her, though his gaze never left Tabitha.

"I'll have you know, Miss Timmons's betrothed is a most excellent gentleman." Daphne emphasized the last word so this Mr. Preston would know that her friend's future spouse was well above the likes of him. "He is well placed and no Tulip or Fribble like you, sir."

Preston's hand rose to his heart. "Miss Dale, you wound me. I'll have you know, I never overdress. And if your friend is marrying some veritable icon of respectability, then I wish them both many happy returns. They will be well suited."

Tabitha knew that if she had to look one more time into his dark gaze, she might burst into tears. And whatever for, she couldn't imagine.

She didn't care in the least what this bounder thought of her.

Oh, but she did. Ever so much.

All she could do was take a page from his example and turn on one heel to flee, but after a few steps, she realized Mr. Muggins wasn't following as he always did.

Rather the traitorous beast trotted along behind Preston.

"Come, Mr. Muggins!" she called out.

But the dog ignored her. Mr. Muggins didn't see any point in turning his nose up at a hand that offered roast beef.

Storming back, she fumbled with the lead as she tried to snap it back onto the dog's collar, but with her hands shaking so, it was nigh on impossible.

To her dismay, Preston reached over, took the lead from her and quickly snapped it onto the collar. "Go with her, boy," he told the dog as he handed the lead to Tabitha.

As they made the exchange, their hands brushed together, and despite the fact that they both were wearing gloves, that moment of contact, that flash of electricity sprang between them—like it had when he'd surrendered her winnings in that foolish wager of theirs. It yanked Tabitha's gaze up to meet his as if he had commanded it.

He was furious with her. Furious. Angry. Hurt.

"Tabby! How could you?" he scolded quietly so no one else could hear.

But before she could explain…oh, bother, explain what? That this engagement wasn't her idea? That she didn't want to marry Mr. Reginald Barkworth? That she had no choice but to marry and gain her fortune or spend the rest of her life scrubbing the grates?

Yes, explain this to a man who took his pleasures and his freedom for granted. What would he know or understand of how pained this choice might be?

Preston spun away from her, as quickly as he had that night in the inn, and bounded back up into the high, safe confines of his phaeton.

"Good day, ladies," he said, tipping his tall beaver hat. "Extend my deepest felicitations to your betrothed, Miss Timmons—I expect that by marrying you he will need them." Then he flicked the reins and drove off.

"Oh!" Daphne gasped. "What an utterly wretched man!"

"And I thought my brothers were dreadful," Harriet mused, adjusting her bonnet and tugging at her gloves.

"Precisely," Daphne agreed. "Who is that man, Tabitha, that he can be so rude?"

"I have no idea," she confessed. "But I find him utterly insufferable."

"Insufferable he might be, but he can be as rude as he chooses," Harriet said, stealing another glance at the departing carriage before they started back in the direction of the Timmonses' town house.

"Why do you say that, Harriet?" Daphne demanded. "That bounder Mr. Preston just insulted Tabitha. He has no right to be so rude."

"He has every right in the world." Harriet stared at them for a moment and then blinked. "Don't you know who he is?"

Tabitha and Daphne came to a stop, both of them puzzled by Harriet's question. No, it wasn't so much a question as it was a statement of disbelief.

Harriet huffed a big sigh and said, "He's Preston." When this explanation warranted nothing more than continued blank stares from Daphne and Tabitha, the girl continued, "The one your cousins have been nattering on and on about."

"Mr. Preston?" Tabitha repeated, trying to recall when her cousins had ever mentioned him, for surely she would recall a conversation about him. Certainly her cousins wouldn't ever bother over such a bounder. They only had eyes and hearts for a man with a title, a man lofty enough to snub the likes of Preston.

Lofty. That word stopped her, and once again,

Tabitha glanced one more time at the departing carriage—an elegant and expensive contraption being pulled by a matched set that must have cost a fortune.

A fortune. A worrisome niggle ran down her spine. *He's Preston.*

Harriet shook her head. "Tabitha, that man is not Mr. Preston. He's the Duke of Preston."

The Duke of Preston? Every bit of air that Tabitha had in her lungs rushed out in a dizzying whoosh.

She tried to breathe as the truth rained down on her.

Preston wasn't just some beyond the pale, ne'er-do-well? Some by-blow rake, dabbling about the fringes of good society?

Oh, good heavens. He was Society.

"That man is a Seldon?" Daphne finally managed, adding a loud huff for good measure. "That explains his manners!"

Harriet and Tabitha looked at her, as if that was hardly enough explanation.

Daphne sighed again. "He's a Seldon."

"And?" Harriet prodded.

"I'm a Dale." She looked from one to the other. "Surely, you've heard of the Dale-Seldon feud?" They both shook their heads, much to Daphne's chagrin. "Well, let it be said that the Seldons are unpardonable, indolent devils who should have been cast out of England centuries ago."

That sounded like Preston, Tabitha would have agreed, if Harriet had not waded in. "He is rather beyond the pale."

"Well beyond," Daphne added.

"Harriet, why do you say that?" Tabitha asked.

"Haven't you been listening to a word your cousins have been nattering on about?"

"I try not to," Tabitha admitted, rather put off by their mean-spirited gossip.

"Are you certain, Harriet, that he is the same one Tabitha's cousins have been discussing?"

"Oh, most decidedly," Harriet said. "Apparently he's no longer received."

Daphne shook her head. "Should he have ever been?"

Harriet paused and looked at both of them, then lowered her voice as if all of London might be eavesdropping. "He has ruined no less than five young ladies this Season."

"No!" Daphne gasped.

Tabitha faltered a bit. She might well have been the sixth.

Who was she kidding? She *was* the sixth. "You gathered all this from my cousins?"

"Yes," Harriet replied. "They are veritable fonts of gossip. I must admit their chatter is so much more interesting than my father going on about the price of corn or which tenant is behind on their rent."

Daphne kicked at a stone in the path. "I would be loath to run into the duke again, because I don't think I will be able to hold my tongue. He deserves a set down for what he said to Tabitha. A Dale set down."

"I doubt we shall encounter him again," Tabitha told her, not wanting to embroil herself any deeper into Preston's scandalous sphere. "Nor should we mention this meeting to anyone. Can you imagine the strictures my aunt would put in place if she knew—"

Both girls nodded in solemn agreement.

"Not a word," Daphne promised, though she stole a glance at the carriage and looked as if she wanted nothing more than to follow it and make good her threat.

"Still, Tabitha," Harriet began, "it would make a thrilling story. How he saved you from certain death. When he caught you in his arms and plucked you from danger, I thought I was in one of Miss Briggs's novels. Don't you remember that scene in *Miss Darby's Daring Dilemma,* where Lieutenant Throckmorten saves Miss Darby from that Spanish brigade? Yes, exactly like that. For all that the duke is a bounder, he is just as handsome and valiant as Lieutenant Throckmorten, don't you agree?"

Tabitha found them both staring at her as if they truly expected an answer—Harriet waiting for confirmation and Daphne for an outright denial.

However could she tell them that Preston up close was every bit as handsome and strong as he looked? How could she confess that the instant she'd found herself in his arms (again!) her body had come alive with languid, dangerous passions that left her knees quaking and her lips starving for his kiss?

"I fear it happened so quickly, I barely noticed," she lied, her fingers dipping into the pocket of her gown where a single penny lay hidden. Her fingers brushed over the rough, nicked portion and she sighed. "I must confess that I found the entire encounter ever so dreadful."

Because now he deplored her. Hated her. And that left her memories of the night at the inn somehow tarnished.

They walked along, and when they got to Park Lane, they had to pause for a break in the traffic.

"There is one thing I don't understand, Tabitha," Harriet said as she watched with a practiced eye a set of horses pulling a fancy phaeton much like Preston's.

"What is that?" Tabitha said, leaning over to give Mr. Muggins a scratch. The dog was busy watching all the passing carriages, probably looking for the duke and his freely shared beef.

"However did Preston know you cannot dance?"

"I think I should take a boat to Halifax and marry the first savage I find."

"Why is that?" Roxley asked.

"If you must know, by marrying some native maiden, I wouldn't have to endure the years of nagging that gels like those"—he tipped his head back at the trio of misses they were leaving behind—"promise to give a man."

Roxley shook his head at this argument. "Oh, I wouldn't be so convinced. You'd still get nagged. Only it wouldn't be in English."

Preston growled something unintelligible, not that Roxley needed a translation. Instead, he sat back and yawned. "If you didn't drive around at this wretched hour, then you wouldn't encounter such females."

"I like this hour because I usually don't encounter any females." At least he hadn't until today. Never mind that he'd been looking for this one.

Tabby. His Tabby.

His Tabby no more. Why, the lying little minx! For all her innocent ways and claims of never marrying, she'd been heading to London to get married. Preston clamped his teeth together as if that could stop the knot in his gut from rising up and choking him.

"If you are determined to avoid females, then you had best flee to the country, what with the Season and all. Town will be overrun by the end of the week." Roxley chuckled. "Bad enough when even the cursed ones are making their curtsy. No man is safe."

Cursed. The only one cursed was Preston. He'd spent the last fortnight replaying that night at the inn over and over, so much so that he had begun to think he'd imagined it.

For he'd also come to believe that he, perhaps, could have a lifetime of such contented evenings. Passionate evenings.

He'd come to think, nay, hope, as Hen had avowed, that love would find him and make his life whole.

Only to discover that the night had been a lie.

Miss Timmons was as deceitful as the rest of the Bath misses who invaded Town every year like litters of well-dressed alley cats.

"Mark my words," Preston said, having driven far enough for his temper to cool a bit. Well, maybe not that far. "That is exactly the sort of tart-tongued minx Hen is going to drag in front of me and expect me to marry if only to gain the good graces of every matron in Town."

"At least Miss Timmons is pretty. In a country sort of way," Roxley said, arms crossed over his chest and stealing a glance over his shoulder. "Can't imagine the spotted sorts my aunts would dangle in my path."

Preston pulled the pair of chestnuts to a stop and turned to face his friend. "Miss Timmons? Pretty? Good God, man, you're still half-seas over from last night if you find that chit pretty."

Actually Tabby was more like breathtaking—what

with that red hair, those brown eyes and, in the bright light of day, a nose that held a faint sprinkling of freckles. Ones he had wanted to kiss…

"I said pretty in a country sort of way," Roxley told him. "You know, not from her dress—which is ghastly—but her eyes and her hair. Gels from the country usually have nice hair." The earl nodded for Preston to drive on, which his friend did. "Good teeth, nice hair. Good gait—all that walking about and such."

"I think you're describing country horses," Preston remarked, "not country misses."

Roxley shook his head, used to Preston's moods as he was. "I will make a note to keep you and Miss Timmons well out of each other's paths. She quite puts you in the worst of humors. Certainly soured your dinner the other night. Though she hardly seemed the difficult sort when I left you in her company—"

"Abandoned me," Preston corrected.

"Rightly so," the earl pointed out without the least bit of guilt. "Still, thought you'd been caught in a *fait accompli* when you came bursting into the room—after midnight, I might note—and like the hounds of hell were after you. What the devil happened between the two of you?"

"Nothing of consequence," Preston told him. Nothing. At least now it was nothing, since the poxy little bit of muslin was going to marry another.

Roxley, it turned out, saw right through his lie. "Nothing! I saw the way you looked at her. Wouldn't have believed it if I hadn't seen it myself."

"Believed what?"

"You like that—what did you call her?—ah, yes, tart-tongued minx." Roxley paused. "Now all those questions about my aunt make sense. You had hoped to find Miss Timmons again."

Preston straightened. "Roxley, leave off."

"Oh, don't get all squiffy on me. I know you too well. You fancy that gel, and you have every intention of stirring up trouble again." Roxley clucked his tongue. "Hen would have had your hide. Bah! That gel has gone and done you a favor getting engaged before you led her astray."

"I had no intention of leading her—"

Roxley slanted a glance at him.

Then Preston saw it. His old friend—who did know him better than anyone—had led him right down the path to confessing the truth.

They rode along in silence for a good while before Roxley dared speak again. "Whatever happened that night, best forget it," he advised. "And don't go seeking her out. It will only leave you worse off."

There was something in the earl's words that held a hint of experience.

"What if I can't?" Preston hated to admit it, but even as he'd driven away, he had wanted nothing more than to turn around and gather her up in his arms and rattle the truth out of her.

"Then you will be in sorry straits," Roxley sighed. "If she is betrothed, she is lost to you."

Lost. It was a word that didn't set well with Preston. He never lost—save for that wager with Tabby.

He should have known right then she would be his ruin.

Of course, if he were to be honest, winning wasn't always the best course either. Look where beating Kipps had gotten him.

"I will admit to being a bit shocked to hear Miss Timmons was betrothed," Roxley began.

The earl was shocked? Preston had been bowled over by the news.

"Don't you think it odd that Miss Timmons is getting married so suddenly?" Roxley paused for a moment and slanted a glance at Preston. "You didn't leave her...well, you know?" He grimaced, brows arched knowingly.

It took a moment, but then it struck Preston what Roxley was implying. "Good God, no! I didn't do anything more than kiss her."

"Aha!" the earl exclaimed. "So you did trifle with her."

"Not intentionally," Preston shot back.

"Never is," Roxley said. "Still, if she isn't breeding—"

"It was only a fortnight ago, you idiot," Preston said, hoping the earl would take offense and ask to be let out.

But this was Roxley, who was well used to the duke's tempers and not insulted in the least. He merely shrugged. "Then I can hardly think of any other reason for such a hasty marriage."

His ire aside, Preston realized that Roxley made an excellent point.

There had to be a reason for this swift marriage, and as he thought about it more, Tabby had hardly lorded the news of her betrothal over him...point of fact, one might argue she'd tried to continue to conceal it.

But why? Preston glanced over his shoulder, but Tabitha was already gone from view.

"If you are plotting on how to find her and discover the truth, I shall not help you," Roxley said, for he knew Preston oh, too well.

"I doubt you have to worry about me running into her again. Miss Timmons could hardly come up to snuff to gain vouchers, let alone the lowly heights of Lady Knolles's ballroom."

Roxley wisely chose not to point out that Miss Timmons, as an heiress, was more likely to see the inside of Almack's before Preston would ever be returned to the patronesses' good graces—given the current public sentiment against him. The mere fact that his only invitation—a lowly one at that—was to Lady Knolles's was most likely due to Lady Juniper's willingness to pander to that overreaching matron, not the Duke of Preston's lofty rank.

"Why not come with me to Lady Knolles's," Preston offered. "You can keep me out of temptation's path… on the off chance…"

"Lady Knolles's?" Roxley shuddered. "Might run into my aunt."

Which was precisely why Preston needed Roxley by his side tonight.

"Coward," Preston taunted as he turned the horses into the mews behind his town house. "Where is that legion of friendship you love to hold over my head? Abandoning me not once but twice in less than a month." He muttered a *tsk tsk* under his breath and turned from the earl slightly, as if giving him a cut.

Roxley colored a bit and made a resounding *harrumph* in return. "I daresay I would follow you onto the fields of Spain, but stepping into my aunt's sights, well, that is just foolhardy."

"Then you won't mind if I suggest to Lady Juniper

that she invite your aunt for tea?" Preston repeated his *tsk tsk*, this time as a warning. "Terrible shame if the old gel were to discover you'd been holed up in my house all this time and not off 'managing your estates' as you have Fiske passing off."

The earl's response was both an affirmation of his attendance at Lady Knolles's ball—and altogether unprintable.

Chapter 8

"Gar, miss," Daphne's maid exclaimed as she, her mistress and Tabitha surveyed their work in the mirror. "You look like a princess."

The girl had the right of it, for indeed a beguiling creature in a new gown and hair done just so stared back at them. Gaped, might be the better word.

"A queen," Daphne corrected, reaching out to tuck a stray ringlet back into place. She winked at Tabitha. "You will make Mr. Reginald Barkworth the envy of all."

Tabitha glanced at herself in the mirror and marveled at the transformation the pair had wrought. Changes her friend had hinted at for years—like wearing her hair in softer ringlets than her usual tight chignon or the blue ribbon and tiny silk flowers that sat atop her head like a May Day crown.

Not that Aunt Allegra would have ever allowed such things, calling them "unnecessary vanities."

"The flowers aren't too much?" she wondered aloud, reaching up to adjust the decorative piece.

Daphne swatted her hand away. "There is no such thing as too much. It gives you the right hint of innocence and youth."

"I am hardly young," Tabitha muttered. In little over a week she'd be five and twenty—in comparison to the rest of the London misses, a bit long in the tooth.

"No one will know otherwise," Daphne insisted, pulling on her own gloves and taking a quick check of her own perfectly arranged hair.

Harriet came into the room—also done up in a new gown and just as polished—though already most of her dark curls had escaped their pins. "The carriage is here." She paused for a moment, taking in Tabitha's new appearance. "Oh, my," she said, eyeing the gown with a cautionary glance. "Why, no one in Kempton would know you."

"It is the first stare and will mark Tabitha as a lady of distinction," Daphne told her, arms crossed over her chest and her mouth set in a line that dared them to contradict her.

As if there was any chance either of them could win an argument over fashion with Daphne.

But even Tabitha thought the gown rather scandalous—no matter that it was the first stare, as Daphne averred. Certainly one couldn't find fault with the Van Dyke lace around the neckline and the pretty crisscross slashing in front, which let the sapphire blue silk beneath shine seductively through.

What had her at sixes and sevens was how the hem

stopped well above the floor, leaving her ankles on view. If that wasn't bad enough, the short, puffed sleeves and low neckline revealed far more of her figure than could possibly be decent.

Fashion or not.

Tabitha shook her head. Aunt Allegra certainly wouldn't approve. And then there was the problem of her other aunt.

"Lady Timmons will never let me wear this gown out in public."

Harriet didn't appear to approve either, given the wrinkle of her nose. "My brother George would say that gown is like fishing with extra bait."

Daphne took great offense to this, rushing over and fluffing the lace and straightening the skirt like a French dresser. "What a vulgar thing to say, Harriet. You make it sound like Tabitha must lure Mr. Reginald Barkworth to her side. That is not the case. With her in this gown, he will simply do everything he can to ensure that he has her affections secured before someone else does."

This last statement came with a significant glance— since Daphne's maid was still hovering in the background—for Tabitha had confessed everything to them on the way home from the park.

That she had dined privately with Preston. Nay, make that the Duke of Preston, and that he had kissed her.

"And that was all?" Daphne had asked, having come up short on the gravel path and refusing to move until she'd had all the details. "He kissed you and left?" Her question had left Tabitha with the impression that she hadn't been convinced.

"Yes. One moment he was kissing me and then he—" Tabitha had closed her eyes and wished she could forget that terrible, haunted look in his eyes. "Then he was gone."

"Why didn't you tell him you were engaged? That you were coming to London to be married?" Daphne had asked. Thankfully her friend had resisted asking the more obvious question:

What had Tabitha been thinking accepting the man's invitation to supper?

Tabitha had shrugged, for there had been no answer. Goodness knows she'd been asking herself the same thing for a fortnight.

And the most ready answer, *"Because the Yorkshire pudding smelled heavenly,"* would hardly have satisfied Daphne.

As it was, Daphne had paced back and forth on the gravel path. "And you haven't told a soul?"

"Who would I have told?" Her cousins? Lady Timmons?

Daphne had nodded in concession. "And you weren't seen?"

Tabitha had shaken her head.

Heaving a great sigh, Daphne had said, "Then we can be assured you will not be ruined by this unfortunate event."

"However is it unfortunate?" Harriet had asked, finally chiming in. "It sounds to me as if His Grace realized that he couldn't ruin Tabitha because he'd fallen in love with her. Overcome by the unfamiliar nature of those feelings, he fled, only to regret it later."

"Fallen in love? Over supper?" Daphne had thrown

her hands up in the air. "He's a Seldon. That he would regret anything is the most ridiculous notion of all."

They'd both looked at Tabitha for confirmation—that it was or was not impossible to fall in love in one night. She'd pressed her lips together, for until she had run face-to-face with Preston once again, she wouldn't have believed it herself...

It was utterly possible.

She had fallen in love that night. And now it was all an impossible coil.

"Oh, Tabitha, this is a terrible muddle," Harriet had said. "You don't think Preston will make trouble for you? He looked ever so angry when he heard the news."

He had indeed. Furious, really.

Whatever for? she'd wanted to ask. He had hidden his identity as much as she hadn't revealed why she was going to London.

"Of course he'll make trouble, he's a Seldon," Daphne had added. "But I hardly think he'll be at Lady Knolles's." When neither of them had replied, she'd continued, "Because, as Harriet said, he is not received."

Tabitha had acknowledged this with a nod.

"Forget about him," Daphne had continued, brushing her hands over her skirt. "After tonight, you will be well out of his nefarious reach. You will meet Mr. Reginald Barkworth, who must be a decent, esteemed gentleman, and he will sweep you off your feet in a proper, well-chaperoned courtship. Then you shall be married—exactly how it is supposed to be done."

Daphne had turned from the path, leading the way back to the Timmons household as if the matter had been finished.

Not so Harriet. She had looked over at Tabitha with a deep, silent gaze that had seemed to predict that this encounter with Preston had been merely the beginning.

"Whatever will you do if you see him again?" Harriet had whispered out of Daphne's earshot.

Tabitha had shaken her head as she'd tugged a reluctant Mr. Muggins to follow.

However could she answer, when the only thing she had wanted to do the moment Preston had taken her in his arms was to beg him for one more kiss?

Now, all these hours later, as Tabitha gathered up her belongings—her pelisse, her gloves, her reticule—she paused for a moment, once again caught in the memory of Preston's kiss.

"Are you coming, Tabitha?" Daphne asked as she and Harriet awaited her at the door.

"I'll be right down," she said, and they nodded and left her, seeming to understand that she needed a moment of privacy before this monumental evening.

But what she really needed to do was reach inside her delicate silk reticule and take out the only thing inside it.

Preston's nicked penny.

Biting her lower lip, she knew what she must do— get rid of it. Spend it, give it away, toss it in the gutter if she must.

And most decidedly, stop carrying it around like a favor, a memento.

She opened her drawer, her hand wavering over the opening and then back over her reticule.

"Oh, bother," she muttered and dropped it exactly where it belonged.

* * *

If Tabitha had hoped the ride to Lady Knolles's town house would quell her growing nerves, she quickly realized she should have walked. Nay, she should have known from the way Euphemia, Edwina and Eloisa happily joined their father in the second carriage that something was afoot.

Namely in the form of Lady Peevers, Lady Timmons's sister, who was already inside the first carriage and seized hold of Tabitha and plunked her down on the spot beside her, launching right into a recitation as to Mr. Reginald Barkworth's qualifications—that is, when she wasn't chiding Tabitha for one thing or another.

"Oh, goodness, gel, do stop fidgeting! You will make one and all think you are nervous," Lady Peevers declared.

Daphne rose to her friend's defense. "My lady, this is the first time Miss Timmons is to meet Mr. Barkworth."

"And whatever is there to be nervous about?" the lady asked, pinning her nearsighted squint on Tabitha. "Your Uncle Winston chose well for you—something I can say with assurance. My dear, departed husband was related to Barkworth."

"You're related to Barkworth?" Daphne and Harriet asked, glancing at Tabitha to see how she judged this news.

"My nephew!" Lady Peevers declared proudly. "My husband's sister was married to Lord Francis Barkworth, your Barkworth's uncle. And now, Miss Timmons, that connection will bind us all happily together."

Tabitha didn't know if she shared this lady's enthusiasm. Especially the "binding" part.

Truly? Was that going to be necessary?

"I don't know why you look so ill, child," Lady Peevers complained. "Mr. Reginald Barkworth of Acornbury, and now of Foley Place in London, is a most respectable gentleman, and one day, if all continues as it aught, he shall inherit."

"Barkworth is a man of elegant manners, so composed. Why, he has had more than his fair share of ladies cast their eyes in his direction," Lady Timmons added.

"So why hasn't he been snapped up?" Harriet muttered under her breath.

"Snapped up?" Lady Peevers sputtered, her gaze turning to Harriet. "What a vulgar phrase to use. Snapped up, indeed!"

"It is just that it is hard to believe a man so prestigious would have remained unmarried," Harriet said, holding her ground.

With five brothers and Lady Essex as her patroness, Harriet never suffered indignation as a set down.

Rather a challenge.

"If you must know, and apparently you do, Miss Hathaway," Lady Peevers said, fluffing the lace at her cuffs and shaking her fan, "the Barkworths are terribly discerning. They do not marry lightly—as they hold their family standing and reputation in the highest of regard. Not just any young lady is worthy."

"Our Tabitha is," Daphne said. "And one day she'll be a marchioness. Oh, can you imagine it, Tabitha?"

"Indeed," Lady Peevers said, taking another glance at Tabitha as if she could hardly believe it herself. "One day. And when it comes, you must never forget that I lent you my support on this very important night."

Which she followed with a "Straighten up, gel, your posture is deplorable" and an "Oh, good heavens, would you smile? This is a ball we are attending, not an execution."

When the carriage pulled to a stop and a footman came dashing down from the steps to open the door, Tabitha sighed with relief. How could whatever was to be faced inside be any worse than the drive over?

"Good luck," Harriet whispered as Lady Timmons and Lady Peevers got on either side of Tabitha and all but pushed her into the thick tide of guests moving up the steps and into Lady Knolles's house.

The only thing buoying up her spirits was the thought that at least Preston wouldn't be here—it was bad enough he knew of her betrothal, but if he were to discover that she had yet to even meet her future husband, she could imagine the lark he would make of that.

Lady Timmons began issuing a litany of instructions. "Remember, it is of the utmost importance that Barkworth finds you worthy. Smile, speak only when spoken to and show due respect to his mother. It is important that you win his favor."

"I would think," Harriet said, "that since the inheritance is Tabitha's, he should be doing his utmost to win her favor."

Lady Peevers and Lady Timmons shared a look of horror at such a notion. But that was nothing compared with their expressions as Tabitha slipped off her pelisse.

"Good heavens above!" Lady Timmons exclaimed. "That is not the gown I ordered!"

Lady Peevers stood by, speechless. Which said volumes for just how scandalous Tabitha's gown must be.

"You cannot meet Barkworth wearing that! Why, you look positively..." Tabitha's aunt stammered for the right word.

"Undone," Lady Peevers managed.

Which only served to leave Lady Timmons glancing around to see if anyone else had noticed. She caught Tabitha by the arm and was about to tow her toward the door, but stopped when she found their path blocked by their elegantly clad hostess, who stood chatting with another lady.

Lady Knolles had barely paid them heed when they'd arrived, but seeing Tabitha's gown, she shot across the foyer, her friend in tow. "Lady Timmons, how lovely to see you! This divine creature you've brought is your niece, is she not?"

"Yes, my niece," Tabitha's aunt managed, though she looked as if she wanted to disavow the relationship most vehemently.

That, or drown her in the Thames.

"What a divine gown!" Lady Knolles announced. "When I saw that print in the *Ackermann's* last month, how I wished I was young enough to dare. You will be the belle of the ball, my dear girl. La belle!" she declared before she fluttered off to greet more guests.

Lady Timmons didn't know whether to be pleased or furious, taking another scathing glance at Tabitha's gown. "I cannot take you home now," she muttered. "I only hope Lady Ancil shares Lady Knolles's verdict."

After continuing to move slowly along with the tide of guests, they finally got to the ballroom.

"How like Lady Knolles to invite such a crush," Lady Peevers complained as they looked down at the elegantly attired, brightly gowned, and overly bejeweled guests. The grand ballroom—all done in gold and deep green—shimmered from the hundreds of candles lit in the chandeliers above.

"Goodness," Tabitha whispered, and even in her new gown, she felt quite out of place. "Have you ever?" she whispered to Daphne, who she considered much more worldly.

"Never!" Daphne whispered back. "And here I always thought Foxgrove so grand."

With such a dazzling display before her, Tabitha very nearly forgot that her entire future was to be decided shortly. She followed her aunt and uncle, with Lady Peevers bringing up the rear, through the crowd to the other side of the room.

"Ah, here we are," Lady Timmons declared when they came to an open spot against the wall. "The perfect vantage point to see who is arriving."

"Especially Barkworth," Lady Peevers declared, nudging Tabitha and smiling at her.

But to Tabitha's own shock, for a moment all she could see was Preston standing at the head of the stairs about to descend into the ballroom.

Tabitha blinked and shook her head, for certainly she was seeing things. After all, Harriet had been most adamant that the Duke of Preston wasn't received. Yet there across the crowded room stood a man who quite looked like Preston…

Even as she began to doubt her own sanity, a

shocked hush came over the room, stilling all the conversations and leaving any number of the matrons openmouthed. At least the ones who weren't already turning to their neighbor to whisper a shocked "He's here!"

"My dear!" her aunt whispered, nudging her to stand up straight. "He has arrived. Do smile."

"Who?" Tabitha asked, squinting a glance through the throng. Certainly she was wrong, it couldn't be Preston.

"Who, she asks!" Lady Timmons said to her sister, shaking her head. "Barkworth, of course, you foolish girl!"

Lady Peevers reached over and pinched Tabitha's cheeks. "There! Now you don't look so pale. It won't do to appear sickly. Barkworth will need an heir, after all."

Tabitha shot a shocked glanced at the lady. She had yet to meet the man and already a union was expected...

Her thoughts flashed to the night in the inn.

Preston holding her. His hands traveling down her back, over her hips, leaving a trail of fire in their wake. Igniting her senses into a flurry of passion. His lips stealing kisses from her, his tongue teasing hers, drawing from her the very breath she could manage. She couldn't think, couldn't breathe...need filling her, her breasts heavy and taut, her thighs clenching together, her insides wavering and hungry.

"He is nearly here!" Lady Timmons whispered, dashing a bucket of cold water all over Tabitha's delicious memories and leaving her filled with nothing but panic. "Bother this press of people! Why, now he is trapped by that awful Lady Gudgeon."

"Where is he?" Daphne asked, rising up on the toes of her slippers.

"Over there," Lady Peevers said, pointing with the tip of her fan.

Both Harriet and Daphne craned their necks to see the man, but Tabitha couldn't bring herself to look.

What if Barkworth had a wen? His touch was clammy? He hadn't Preston's height and demanding stature? What if his kiss wasn't the same as Preston's?

If only she could ask her aunt if all men kissed the same. It would certainly help to keep her from being ill all over Lady Knolles's polished floor if she knew that a kiss was but a kiss.

Yet she suspected that wasn't the case.

"Oh, good heavens," Harriet gasped.

Now Tabitha knew she was going to be ill.

"Is that truly him?!" Harriet asked.

"I thought you said he wasn't received," Daphne shot back.

Not received. Tabitha's gaze flew from one friend to the other, and from their horrified expressions it meant only one thing. It wasn't Barkworth they'd discovered but someone else.

Preston.

Tabitha turned around, slowly and trying her best to maintain her composure, but even she could not keep her mouth from falling open at the sight of him.

Shaved, combed and clean, dressed to the nines, the Duke of Preston was elegant perfection.

Oh, heavens, this was a disaster.

Then Tabitha noticed something else. On his arm was an equally beautiful woman all in black.

"Who is she?" Harriet asked, directing her question to Daphne, for she was their font of *tonnish* knowledge.

Possible answers had already run their course through Tabitha's frantic thoughts.

His...sister? The widow of a good friend? His mistress...?

That seemed the most likely explanation, given that the entire room found the pair's arrival shocking. The crowd parted before them, a wake of whispers and pointing of fans rising up like a whirlwind behind them.

As handsome as Preston might be, the lady beside him moved with an elegance that was born with a knowledge that she was, quite frankly, stunning to behold, a confidence that Tabitha wouldn't even know how to summon.

A dark, deep jab of something ran down her spine. A feeling like nothing she'd ever known.

Tabitha shrank into her new gown, suddenly feeling the country cousin in comparison to this woman's elegant low-cut silk, diamond earrings and a heavily jeweled necklace that ran all the way down to the tops of her breasts.

Just then, Lady Peevers suddenly caught wind of the rising scandal in the room and, like a spaniel on the scent, raised her eyes and nose to catch any wisp of the current of gossip swirling about the room.

"Good heavens above!" she exclaimed. "It cannot be! Preston! As I live and breathe." The lady made a *tsk tsk* noise and nudged her sister. "Antigone! So shocking! Look there." The lady nodded toward the entrance, her feathers dancing to and fro in a grand, agitated dance.

Lady Timmons sucked in a deep breath. "I cannot believe Lady Knolles could be so indiscriminate. Whatever was she thinking to invite him?"

"That man is a villain, a rogue—" Lady Peevers said, again with the same disapproving *tsk tsk*.

"Precisely, sister," Lady Timmons agreed. "The Duke of Preston is the worst sort of example." She paused for a moment and then her eyes widened. "Whatever is he doing gaping at us? We have no connection to *him*."

Still, she spun around and made sure her daughters were close at hand and well behind her.

"Thankfully," Lady Peevers said, picking up her lorgnette and taking a closer examination of the infamous man. "I do say, he is looking this way. Why, I would say he is looking at—"

The lady and her sister both turned and frowned at Tabitha.

Tabitha flinched. Nor was she about to enlighten her aunt that yes, they actually did have a connection to the infamous Duke of Preston.

At least she did.

However the inspection didn't last long, for both ladies quickly dismissed the notion that the Duke of Preston was looking at their party.

"Poor Lady Knolles must have been put in this terrible position by that woman," Lady Timmons noted as she nodded at the widow on Preston's arm, "to have to extend an invitation."

Tabitha glanced at "that woman" once again, this time with more than just curiosity. So not only was Preston a terrible roué, but from her aunt's implication, the lady was just as notorious.

Whoever was she?

Lady Timmons fluttered her fan as she continued, "How she would be seen in public with him after that ruinous disaster with poor Kipps."

"Poor, dearest Kipps," Lady Peevers echoed, and the pair bowed their heads in a moment of sisterly silence.

Kipps? Tabitha pressed her lips together. Where had she heard that name before? Then she remembered. What was it that Preston had said to Lord Roxley that day in Kempton?

"Come now, Roxley? However will we ruin Kipps if we dally here all day?"

Tabitha pressed her lips together to keep from gasping. So Preston had done just that—ruined this Kipps, who apparently was held in dear regard.

Oh, the devil of a man! Her guilt about not revealing the truth of her situation eased a bit. Truly, what did she know of the Duke of Preston?

Other than that his kiss was enough to leave her trembling still.

"Poor Kipps!" Lady Peevers sighed with great feeling, as did Lady Timmons, as if this fellow had been their nearest and dearest. "So young!"

"So impressionable," Lady Timmons added. "Now lost to good society all because of *his* influence."

Daphne glanced over at her, having been listening to this exchange, and her look said it all. *I told you so.*

"Poor Kipps. I weep daily for his dear mother and sisters!"

"Yes, all of them. Ruined." Lady Peevers shuddered.

"I wonder how *he* sleeps at night." Lady Timmons shook her head.

Lady Peevers made a loud snort. "Sleep is not what

the Lion of Harley Street does at night, if you know what I mean."

Tabitha had the good sense to look away and pretend that she hadn't heard a single word, nor that she was paying the least bit of heed to the object of their scorn. Yet when she glanced around the room, she realized that most every conversation was now focused on the couple making their way through the crush.

Scornful glances, whispered comments made behind fans—as if that hid their ugly meaning—and even the cut direct as several of the gentlemen and ladies turned their backs to the pair.

"I wish he would stop staring in our direction. There is nothing of interest for him over here," Lady Timmons said in an aside that carried.

Sir Mauris arrived, having wandered off to chat with a crony, and said quite loudly and with no particular concern for discretion, "Have you all seen who is here?"

Tabitha glanced at Preston again and found his gaze fixed on her.

Miss Timmons, the wry dark smile tipping at his lips seemed to say. *How lovely to see you…again.* He paused for a moment, as if he knew she was taking in his altered appearance, and then he bowed his head slightly.

He knew that she knew.

Who he was, that is. Or rather, who he wasn't—the common scoundrel she'd accused him of being.

Not that a lofty one was much better.

She found him studying her again, this time with a narrowed gaze, as if he was considering some scheme.

Oh, no! He wouldn't! Come over here as he'd promised in the inn and ask her to dance?

He'd ruin everything.

Which she surmised would be his point.

Certainly, she might have left out the part of her betrothal when she'd dined with him, but she'd only done so out of misplaced pride.

Something he should know a thing or two about, she guessed. But then again, he might have told her who he was. Or rather *what* he was.

A duke who discarded young ladies right and left.

And now he was about to add her to his list of fallen misses.

"Tabitha, are you listening? He is here!" Lady Timmons was saying in an excited whisper, fussing over her so she might appear at advantage—like a horse at the fair.

Suddenly, she was no longer staring at Preston, for a tall figure had stepped in front of her, blocking her view. She blinked and tried to focus even as that someone said, "My dear and lovely Miss Timmons, at last we meet."

The rich, deep voice washed over her with sultry ease, the words echoing through her Preston-addled thoughts.

"...at last we meet..."

Oh. My. Goodness. Barkworth!

Tabitha couldn't breathe as she looked up into the face of the man she was destined to marry. And as she blinked again, and his features came into focus, she discovered that the man before her was nearly as handsome as Preston.

Nearly. Which was saying quite a bit.

Jet-black hair, bright blue eyes and a hawkish nose were framed by a solid, hewn jaw and a strong brow. Taking in his hair, brushed and cut in the latest fashion, and his perfectly chosen trappings, Tabitha wasn't sure if Mr. Reginald Barkworth had ever been born, more like sprung from a fashion plate in dapper style.

Flashing a blazing smile and a wry tip of his brow, he bowed gracefully and perfectly. Then, rising up, he caught her hand and brought it to his lips with all the elegance of…of…say a duke.

"Mr. Reginald Barkworth, at your service," the man whispered over her fingertips, a perfect London gentleman, the sort of counterpoint to Preston's fierce, sharp-edged countenance. The sort of man whose apparent strict adherence to propriety would keep her from being ruined by Preston's plots.

Oh yes you are, she thought wryly, glancing over her shoulder ever so slightly to see if Preston had witnessed her triumph.

But he was nowhere to be seen.

And much to her chagrin, when she looked back at Mr. Reginald Barkworth, the man her Uncle Winston had singled out for her future, she couldn't help feel a twinge that something very important was missing in all his perfect wrappings.

Chapter 9

It took Preston all of about two seconds to notice Tabby standing on the opposite side of Lady Knolles's ballroom.

Getting himself extracted from Hen took a bit longer.

So while his aunt nattered on about who was attending the gathering, who wasn't, and her list of candidates, he did his best to appear that he was hanging on her every word while he gazed across the room.

He'd nearly forgotten what Tabby's hair could look like when it wasn't knotted up behind her head. Though he knew exactly how that tempting array of curls—the sort that begged a man to find the pins holding them up and tug them free—was best viewed: tumbling adrift down her shoulders, free of restraints.

Lady Juniper prodded her nephew out of his wool-gathering. "Are you listening, Preston? Two dances with Lady Pamela. Nothing else. I am most adamant."

"But of course," he replied, knowing full well that the real scandal of the night was standing right across the room.

Tempting him like no other miss ever had. But no, he wasn't going to cause any scandals with Tabby, er, Miss Timmons. He merely wanted some answers.

Like how the hell she had neglected to tell him she was betrothed when she'd stolen his heart.

"Preston, do not try my patience," Hen warned.

"I never try," he told her. Though he could hardly say the same thing about Tabby.

"Bah! You encourage these flirtations of yours," Hen shot back, all while maintaining a perfectly serene countenance. Hen was her mother's daughter to the bone. Generations of lofty bloodlines flowed through her veins, and thus with a composed air of disdain, she also possessed the capacity to weather the stormiest social squalls, the most raging of scandals.

Even his.

Still, he raised a defense. "You know demmed well those triflings were not of my instigation."

"That might be true, but you certainly have a way of finishing them."

Preston withheld any further comment. With Hen, he'd only lose. Or bury himself, as Henry liked to point out. Instead he followed her deeper into the ballroom, ignored how the matrons gathered up their daughters and tucked them out of sight as if to prevent his predator's eye falling on their hapless lambs.

He would have told them not to bother for there

was only one woman in the room tonight who held his attention.

Tabby. And with each step closer, he longed to see more of her, not just her striking Titian hair.

Yet it wasn't until a large woman with too many feathers in her turban dodged out of his path that he finally had a clear view across the room.

Preston shook his head. Oh, good God! What had they done to her? Everything he'd feared that night at the inn.

She was every stitch *Miss Timmons,* society heiress and pending bride.

He shuddered as he tried to reconcile his Tabby with this sophisticated vision.

His strident and prim daughter of a vicar was now properly gowned and elegantly clad, presenting a temptation from on high. Worse yet, she was being dangled before the assembled *ton* so that by tomorrow, Miss Tabitha Timmons would be society's newest Original.

This regal creature, in her scandalous gown—Good God, were those her ankles?—would leave every man in the room as overcome with desire as the spinster version had left him undone.

When his gaze rose up from her scandalous hemline, he found Tabby gaping at him. And from her wide-eyed expression of horror, he knew without a doubt she wasn't overly delighted to see him.

Which could only mean she now knew who he was.

No indeed, one could even speculate she was furious with him. With him? Whatever could have her furious with him?

That you let her assume you were a low and common rake who kisses the ladies and leaves them.

Well, there was that. Not that he was likely to prove how rakish he could be, for suddenly he remembered what her friend—she would be friends with a Dale, of all people—had said in the park. Truly, how could he forget?

"Her betrothed is a most excellent gentleman."

As if one could trust the word of a Dale! He'd have to talk to Tabby about the company she kept.

Speaking of company… Preston straightened. If Tabby was here, that meant the lucky devil was somewhere afoot.

Her "most excellent gentleman."

Glancing around, he realized the room was filled with such dull paragons of virtue. Stuffed to the rafters, if he was being honest.

No wonder Roxley had yet to put in his promised appearance.

Excellent gentlemen. Preston shuddered. How he found such mincing, prancing fellows annoying. The only ornaments most of these overdone dandies were missing were a collar and a lead.

Dull sticks and hardly a match for that tart-tongued, overly opinionated and most fraudulent Miss Timmons.

He glanced over at her again and found that she was deliberately paying him no heed. He knew this for a fact because when she stole what she must have thought was a surreptitious glance in his direction, she flinched when he caught her at it.

But the real question was, where was this betrothed of hers, and who was he? He must be close at hand— that is if he wasn't a complete fool, considering the

speculative looks Tabby and her hemline were gar-
nering.

Even with this staid crowd. But still, where the devil
was the fellow, and why wasn't he staking his claim
and ensuring that nothing untoward happened to her?

Then again, with a room filled with excellent gentlemen, the only man attending Lady Knolles's ball
capable of ruining Miss Tabitha Timmons was most
likely him, the notorious Duke of Preston.

He didn't know whether to grin or chastise himself.

Truly, he had promised Hen no scandals. But then
again, he would never have made such a vow if he had
known *she* was going to be here.

"Ah, there is Lady Pamela and her mother," his aunt
was saying.

Hen's prodding tugged him out of his distracted
reverie. "Which one?" he managed to ask.

"The lovely girl in puce."

If ever there was an oxymoron, that was one. Gazing over at Hen's choice of perfect bride, Preston knew
in an instant that Lady Pamela would most definitely
laugh like a mule.

"Hee-haw," he muttered under his breath.

"He what?" Hen demanded. When he had no answer, having been caught out, she continued unabashedly, "Preston, I swear if you are planning on ruining
this evening—"

"Hen! Will you stop fussing about like one of Roxley's aunts? I have no intention of doing anything other
than as you bid. Ask. Dance. Leave."

Most importantly leave, he thought, sparing a
glance over at Miss Timmons. For the Fates were
taunting him, tempting him to risk everything for one

more taste of Miss Timmons's pert lips…one more moment of…

"Ahem!"

Now it was Preston's turn to flinch—nearly—for Hen was studying his features ever so carefully. But he wasn't the duke for nothing. He returned her icy gaze with one that could freeze the Thames in the heat of summer.

He only wished he could do the same for his insides, for right now they were boiling like a blacksmith's forge.

"As for the other ladies on my list?" she asked, her fan tapping impatiently against his sleeve.

"Memorized." Rather like one might recall the steps up to the gallows. One after another, all of them leading to the same end.

Hen's brows rose in an arched bow. Of course she didn't believe him.

To prove the point, he recounted them for her. "Miss Hollings, Miss Corble, and Miss March."

Of course he didn't add his own description of the lot: the plow-footed offspring of a penniless baron and the grasping daughters of two newly elevated knights.

Preston heaved a sigh. His boots were going to be a ruin by the evening's end. Trod upon and scuffed by nervous young ladies whom Hen had probably promised vouchers to Almack's or some other lofty denizen far above their social reach if only they would dance with her errant nephew.

A dull, lowering evening having to be done under Hen's watchful gaze…and now made worse, for it would also be witnessed by Miss Timmons.

He still could hold out hope that Tabby would find

him and give him a good set down. That might liven things up a bit.

Besides, he had a few choice words for her.

"You needn't look so put upon," Hen chided. "All you have to do is ask to be presented, dance and then make your bow."

"By God, Hen, do you really think I need to be told all that?" He'd been making his bow in public since he was nine.

"Yes. I fear you do," she replied.

Looking once again at Miss Timmons, Preston had to give his aunt credit.

She was utterly correct. For despite his better judgment (which, contrary to public opinion, he did possess) and Hen's omniscient presence, the sight of Miss Tabitha Timmons, standing there and doing her demmed best to ignore him, was inciting a host of rebellion inside his stormy heart.

For all Tabitha's concerns that Barkworth would appear like some character from a bad novel—oiled hair, short of stature, perhaps even bald, cross-eyed and with a speech impediment, she found herself face-to-face with the handsome visage of her future spouse.

More to the point, Mr. Reginald Barkworth was as elegant and mannerly as her aunt and Lady Peevers had claimed.

So much so that Tabitha considered that she might be dreaming.

Everything was as it should be, right to the way he'd gently taken her hand and brought it to his lips, his gaze never leaving hers.

This couldn't be true, this couldn't be happening.

Arranged marriages never brought the bride a groom with sharp Roman features, the sort that lent the man a chiseled appearance—from the strong brow, past a straight nose, a pair of firm lips, right down to the deep cleft in his chin.

Oh, goodness heavens! He was utterly breathtaking.

"Tabitha, where are your manners?" her aunt prodded. "Say something."

Mr. Barkworth laughed, warmly and smoothly. "Yes, well, Lady Timmons, I suppose it is natural for a young lady to be overcome in such circumstances. Give my future bride a moment to gain her composure."

Then the moment of shock wore off, for this most excellent gentleman drew back—though still holding her hand—and gave her an examining look as one might when procuring a horse, or a fine hound, or worse, a good milk cow. His gaze swept over her lines with a quick approving sweep, just pausing at her ankles, which, like Lady Timmons, brought on a slight wrinkle to his brow.

But if he disapproved of her scandalous hemline, he had the wherewithal to brush those misgivings aside, for he announced to one and all, "Perfection!" Which was only made more mortifying when he winked at Sir Mauris, who chuckled broadly.

Lady Peevers and Lady Timmons fluttered their fans approvingly, both trying to hide grand sighs of relief.

She, Miss Tabitha Timmons, country miss and sudden heiress, had passed the discerning muster of Mr. Reginald Barkworth, of the Acornbury Barkworths.

Tabitha tried to smile but found herself shivering

with a very odd note of panic. How could marriage be done like this? So quickly, with only the merest of glances? Without the least bit of common sensibilities?

Without even supper?

She forced herself not to glance at Preston, but that didn't keep the rush of memories from that night at the inn from crowding into her thoughts.

Of him serving her the extra bit of Yorkshire pudding, of her pouring his tea and discovering, with a small note of pleasure, that he took his Pekoe exactly like she did—two lumps and a large measure of cream.

Oh, bother! She shouldn't be thinking about that man. Just as she shouldn't know how he took his tea.

Doing her utmost to forget, she smiled at the handsome stranger before her. No, her betrothed, she corrected. Certainly once she knew how he took his tea, if he shared the pudding willingly, or if he deplored Coleridge, then she would no longer be filled with a sense of dread, as if she were a Christian about to be tossed to the lions.

Looking over at Barkworth, she sought some sort of reassurance that all was well, that this rushed engagement was as disconcerting to him as it was to her, but Tabitha found—much to her horror—that he'd quite moved on, chatting with Lady Timmons and Lady Peevers about some *on dit,* utterly unaware that his bride wanted nothing more than to bolt for the nearest door.

Without even thinking, she took a quick reconnaissance of the room, her gaze hunting for a door, a balcony, any route...

Find Preston. He'll get you out of here.

Oh, good heavens, whatever was wrong with her?

Thinking of Preston at a time like this. Thinking of him at any time when she was going to be married. To Barkworth. A respectable gentleman. She'd be Mrs. Barkworth, and well out of Preston's reach.

That thought should have been of some comfort to her, but yet…

"Miss Timmons, you are everything your dear aunt claimed. And more," Barkworth proclaimed, more to the audience of onlookers than to her, smiling for Lady Timmons and casting another male sort of smirk at Sir Mauris. "Our betrothal makes me the happiest of fellows in London. Nay, England."

Something about his overabundant joy put her into a pique. "Truly? We just met. I don't see how—"

"What my niece is saying," Lady Timmons said, barging into Tabitha's protest before Barkworth had the wit to notice his bride-to-be's momentary rebellion, "is that she shares your shock over how happy this impetuous match has turned out." She turned her sharp, crowlike gaze on her niece.

In fact, they all did. Lady Timmons, Lady Peevers, Sir Mauris, even Daphne. All of them staring at her and waiting.

Yet Tabitha felt this groundswell of mutiny rising up in her. Shouldn't one hope for so much more?

And once again, she thought of Preston. His kiss. The way her knees had trembled when he'd pulled her closer, how it had felt so thrilling, so delirious to be held by him, to have him gaze down at her with that hungry, passion-filled gaze just as he'd been about to…

Tabitha stopped herself right there. Certainly Barkworth, as handsome and well-formed as he was, could inspire such fervor?

She slanted a glance at her intended as he smiled blandly at her, he too waiting for her enthusiastic affirmation of their future together.

"Our betrothal is utterly advantageous," he explained to her. "For you especially, and for me—a lovely complement to my already esteemed standing. You shouldn't doubt you are most suitable, Miss Timmons."

Suitable? He found her suitable? Something very unfamiliar fluttered inside Tabitha's sensibilities. She should be pleased, thrilled that he found her so, but… Suitable? Truly? That was all he could manage?

Even Daphne seemed well pleased with Mr. Barkworth and his suitable declarations. She smiled broadly at Tabitha.

Harriet was another matter. Her dark Hathaway features, which were usually open and easygoing, were narrowed and masked.

Barkworth released her hand and turned to his aunt, Lady Peevers. "All that is left is to secure mother's blessing and then I'll go see the archbishop immediately about a Special License."

"So soon," Tabitha gasped. "What about the banns?"

"Wait all that time? You aren't getting any younger, Miss Timmons," he said, smiling about her need for an expedient marriage as if it were a marvelous joke. "Ah yes, here is Mother."

"Lady Ancil! There you are!" Lady Peevers exclaimed, fan fluttering. "Wherever have you been? You've quite missed the pair of them meeting. As I assured you, they are already infatuated."

If Tabitha had misgivings about a life with Mr.

Barkworth, the arrival of his mother only added thick, blotted underlines to those doubts.

"Mother, here is Miss Timmons—" Barkworth began, turning toward Tabitha, who had edged closer to Daphne, if only out of a rising fear and completely irrational suspicion that Lady Ancil had quite possibly eaten the rest of her young.

Lady Ancil looked first at Daphne, and her eyebrows rose noticeably. And not approvingly. Apparently the prospect of a daughter-in-law who was breathtakingly pretty did not appeal to the lady. Nose pinched, eyes narrowed, she regarded this matrimonial prospect with all the airs of a housewife finding a rat in her pantry.

"Oh, not me," Daphne told the lady brightly, as if all too happy to step out of the lady's scrutiny. "This is Miss Timmons." She pointed the way for the lady.

Traitor, Tabitha wanted to whisper. Instead, she curtsied deeply and respectfully. "I am Miss Timmons, Lady Ancil. It is a pleasure to make your acquaintance."

Lady Ancil said nothing, her gaze fixed on Tabitha's gown. Especially the hemline.

"Mother, I was just telling Miss Timmons that we are going to dispose of the banns," Mr. Barkworth said, catching his mother's hand and then Tabitha's, as if that might unite the two ladies in one smooth introduction, quite oblivious to the undercurrent of disapproval flowing from his mother like a spring runoff.

"Yes, but I would prefer to be married from Kempton," Tabitha told him, suddenly feeling a desperate need for one thing: time.

Time to get to know Barkworth, time to be certain that marrying him wouldn't be a curse in itself.

Which was most likely why her uncle had written his will the way he had. So she must make this hasty match to a respectable man and not end up snared by some fortune hunter, some ruinous rake like Preston.

The Duke of Preston, she corrected.

Oh, bother. If only he'd turned out to be the penniless ne'er-do-well she'd thought him to be.

How like that wretched Preston to be so inconveniently rich! And a duke, to boot.

"A country wedding?" Barkworth remarked. "I daresay my esteemed uncle, the Marquess of Grately, would be most inconvenienced by such a thing."

"Is it necessary he attend?" Tabitha asked.

"Necessary?" Barkworth shook his head as if he couldn't comprehend such a question. "My dear Miss Timmons, without my uncle's good favor, there would be no wedding. And until his unfortunate passing, at that time when I am to be raised to that lofty station which I am presumed to gain, I must always defer to his excellent opinion and favor."

"Get married all the way out in Kempton? Whyever for?" Lady Ancil asked. Nay, demanded, with a great shudder and a wrinkled brow. "Such unnecessary expenses when you will be living in London with Barkworth."

"As well as Mother," he added proudly, as if the inclusion of Lady Ancil only added to this burgeoning matrimonial bargain.

And if it was possible to believe, Tabitha's evening went downhill from there.

* * *

"Roxley, who the devil is that popinjay?" Preston asked his friend, who had finally managed to make his bow at Lady Knolles's. The earl had ambled up in a cloud of rum, slightly in his cups—but it was ever so hard to tell with Roxley, who always looked a bit rumpled and worse for wear.

"Eh, which one?" the earl asked. "Demmed room is full of them."

"The one in navy," Preston said, but when that wasn't enough for his friend, he added, "the one with your friends from Kempton."

Roxley wasn't fooled in the least. "You mean the fellow next to Miss Timmons?"

"Is he?" Preston feigned, tipping his head to study the tableau of guests. "Why, yes, the one standing next to her."

The earl shook his head. "I told you—"

"Roxley, might I remind you that you got me into this mess…"

"Wondered when you were going to realize that and start calling in favors," he admitted. He looked again across the room as if weighing the amount owed to what helping Preston might cost him. Then he looked over at his friend and gave way. "That's Barkworth, Grately's heir."

"Grately? That lecherous old roué—"

"Quite so," Roxley agreed. "Up the River Tick, or so I hear. If Miss Timmons is an heiress, she might be just the ticket to see that Barkworth doesn't end up inheriting a worthless title."

"How convenient for Barkworth," Preston muttered under his breath, taking a closer examination of Tabby's "esteemed gentleman."

Barkworth. Preston hated the man on sight. He couldn't quite put his finger on the precise cause of his dislike, perhaps the points on his collar were too high, his cravat overtied, the polish on his boots not quite bright enough.

If there was one thing he did know, it was that Mr. Reginald Barkworth was all wrong for her.

And if she couldn't see that, then someone needed to tell her. Immediately.

"Where are you off to?" Roxley declared, setting after Preston with the determined stride of a fox hound on the scent. The earl quickly plotted Preston's course. "Oh, no, you don't," he said, catching the duke by the elbow and pulling him up short.

"Whatever do you mean?" the duke asked as he sidestepped his friend once again.

Roxley followed, fast and furious, which meant he wasn't entirely foxed, having had just enough to drink to be dreadfully annoying.

"I am merely going to wish Miss Timmons and her Mr. Barkworth happy returns."

"You are not," Roxley declared. "Demmit, Preston, you said this morning that the chit was a menace. That one had to be mad to dangle after her skirts."

"That was before she wore that gown."

This stopped the earl, who paused to take another glance at Miss Timmons. "Yes, well, I told you she was pretty—" Roxley stopped himself and shook his head. "Good God, never mind that! You need to stay away from Miss Timmons."

"What, and be remiss by withholding my congratulations?"

"Preston, this will come to no good. Mark my words!"

"First that demmed curse you keep prattling on about and now this? Dire predictions of ruin? Really, Roxley, you need to start checking the vintage on the bottle before you imbibe. I am merely being well mannered."

"There is nothing mannerly in what you are about to do."

"Roxley, you wound me. If you don't believe me, then come along."

The earl's jaw worked back and forth as he considered the suggestion. Luckily he'd had enough rum to ensure that reason played little part in his decision. "Just well-wishes and then we leave."

"Precisely. And perhaps a dance with the lovely bride-to-be—" Preston added.

"Demmit, Preston! That goes beyond the pale. If Lady Juniper, or God forbid one of my aunts, suspects I have any hand in this—"

"Yes, yes. I know. I'll simply tell one and all you were an unwitting participant."

"Always am," Roxley muttered, running a hand through his hair.

"Tabby! Whatever are you doing here?"

Preston's voice booming right over her shoulder nearly sent her jumping out of her gown. As it was, she dropped her reticule, and he swooped over and picked it up, holding the delicate purse out to her, the tiny bit of silk nearly crumpled in his giant paw.

After having spent a good part of the evening staying well away from her—much to Tabitha's relief—now here he was, with all the appearances of a ravenous lion.

And she, the gazelle. The lame one limping at the back of the herd.

For a moment, their eyes met, and the mischief alight in his eyes spelled only one thing.

Disaster.

She snatched her reticule free of his grasp and drew a steadying breath. *Oh, bother this wretched man. Whatever does he want?*

"Ah, Miss Dale! And Miss Hathaway as well," he was saying, bowing before Daphne and Harriet before turning his full (and utterly unwanted) attentions on Tabitha. "Tabby, you wicked minx! How could you have failed to mention that you were coming to Lady Knolles's tonight when we were in the park this morning?"

Those few words—"when we were in the park this morning," if one ignored the "wicked minx" part—fell like a cannonball on their little circle, leaving one and all speechless.

Except for Lady Timmons, who made a sort of strangled sound that suggested she had swallowed her fan.

"Come now, Tabby—" he continued.

Tabitha flinched. *Of all the presumptuous, arrogant—*

"—I see you are furious with me," he was saying, more to her aunt and Lady Peevers than to Tabitha, flashing his all-too-handsome visage at them. A look that might once have been enough to lure them into his charming clutches but no longer held any sway. Not with these experienced matrons, who regarded him with stony, upraised noses. Preston, apparently no stranger to matronly dismay, blithely stepped between her and Barkworth, effectively shouldering the man aside. "Dear Tabby, you should be able to guess why I nearly missed you—can't you?"

Dear Tabby? He had not just called her that. No one called her that.

Especially not the Duke of Preston.

Meanwhile, Preston was glancing at the others as if one of them might be able to supply the answer. When no one spoke, he heaved a big sigh of exasperation. "That gown, you little minx!" He grinned and turned to Barkworth. "It has quite transformed her. I barely recognized our little Tabby until Roxley pointed you out—"

The earl sputtered in protest. "I did no such thing."

Preston waved off his friend as if the man was being far too modest. "Personally, if I were your betrothed I wouldn't have let you out in that silk. You have caused a regular stir of speculation as to who you might be. I fear your Barkley will have competition by the morning. Speaking of old Barks, where is the good man?"

Her temper, having finally overcome her shock, managed to get a sentence out. "His name is Barkworth, Preston."

"Oh, yes, but you know how I am." Preston glanced around, his features a mask of innocence, and smiled broadly at the party. Then he thrust his hand out to Sir Mauris. "You must be Barkworth! Tabby was telling me all about you this morning, though I didn't expect such a mature match." He turned to Tabitha. "No wonder I haven't seen you on the dance floor. Wouldn't do to send your betrothed aloft from too much exertion *before* the wedding."

After taking another measure of Sir Mauris, the duke glanced over at Tabitha and shook his head, a motion that suggested he did not approve of her match. Not in the least.

Not that she cared what he thought, the odious wretch. More to the point, whatever was he doing?

Sir Mauris batted away the duke's hand. "I am Sir Mauris. Miss Timmons's uncle."

Preston let out a breathy sigh. "Good news, that. But where is your most excellent gentleman, Tabby?" He looked back and forth and right past Barkworth, who was standing beside his mother. "I expected the man to be at your side all night, lest some ne'er-do-well discover you." He grinned and waggled his eyebrows, as if not one of them didn't know who the real villain might be.

Stepping out of his mother's shadow, her fiancé finally made his presence known. "I am Barkworth," he announced, slanting a disapproving glance at Tabitha as he moved to her side, retaking his place.

About time, a little voice chided silently inside her. Oh, and that wry bit of sensibility wasn't done. *Can you imagine Preston holding back to gauge a situation before wading in?*

Not likely. The duke seemed quite happy when he was up to his neck.

Much to Tabitha's chagrin.

"And you are?" Barkworth asked coldly.

"Well, Preston, of course. I thought everyone knew that." Again the flash of a grin and a wink at Tabitha.

A wink? And in front of Lady Ancil?

Didn't this insufferable...arrogant...wretched man know what he was doing?

Oh, he knew.

Tabitha tried to come up with a set down that would cast the duke on his merry way, his tail between his legs like the dog that he was... And while she could think of quite a few, none came quickly enough before Preston was at it.

Again.

"Ah, Barkstone, my good man," Preston said, throwing his arm over Barkworth's shoulder and steering him so they both faced Tabitha. "I daresay even you'd agree that your betrothed is the most beguiling creature in the room, wouldn't you?"

Barkworth's mouth fell open, but nothing came out, as if the notion hadn't even occurred to him. And when some morsel of reason did finally dawn in his thoughts, he shook off Preston's arm and stalked back to stand between his mother and Tabitha.

Preston continued blithely on as if they were all old friends. "No wonder you haven't had her out on the dance floor. I thought it odd at first, and then I realized you are a cagey fellow. Not wanting to have her ankles on display for all to see. Promising pair, don't you think?" Then he leaned back and sighed as he gazed at the enticing space between Tabitha's hemline and slippers.

"I do say—" Barkworth began to sputter.

The duke shook his head. "You were saying? Oh, yes, not dancing. Wise decision."

"I have not danced with Miss Timmons because I prefer not to dance."

"Not dance?" Preston asked, glancing around at the others for confirmation. "Criminal! Tabby should be danced with and danced with until she is exhausted with pleasure."

No! She must have misheard him. Tabitha closed her eyes and hoped she had. Though when she stole a glance through her lashes at Lady Ancil, the lady's apoplectic features confirmed the worst.

She hadn't.

"You know this man?" Barkworth asked, turning his full attention to Tabitha.

"No," she said shaking her head. "Not in the least."

"Tabby, you are shameless! Of course we know each other. We are old friends. Tell them, Roxley. You introduced us."

Roxley made a strangled sort of stammering reply. "I...that is... I never..."

"See, there you have it from the man himself," Preston said, as if the earl's answer had been as clear as day. "We met in Kempton, what was it? A month ago. And then again this morning in the park. We are old friends now, wouldn't you say, Tabby?"

"No, I would not," she told him coldly.

To his credit, he'd left out their other encounter. The one that had brought them to this state of detente.

"While I make it a rule never to disagree with a lady—just ask my aunt—I say we are. Especially after I spent our entire time together this morning listening to Tabby regale me with tales of her Barkshire. Mr. Barkshire this, Mr. Barkshire that. I quite expected to meet a man of Adonis proportions and Solomon's wisdom." He glanced at Barkworth as if he still wasn't convinced he had met the right man. "You're Grately's heir, are you not?"

"I am."

"Heir presumptive," Preston said in a tone that implied the man's inheritance wasn't the only thing he was waiting around for.

"Yes," Barkworth ground out, his face growing red with either embarrassment or fury. "Sadly, his unfortunate passing will provide me with his noble holdings."

"A marquisate, isn't it?"

"Yes," her nearly betrothed replied, his handsome features now pinched with annoyance.

"That would be worth hanging about a man's coattails, now, wouldn't it?" Preston posed, giving Barkworth a friendly nudge.

Oh, good heavens! How many insults could the man take before he was willing to do something, say something cutting and witty enough to send the duke packing?

And then Barkworth did. Or at least he tried.

"Your Grace, it is well known that you are not received."

She nearly groaned. That was it? That was his set down? *"You are not received"*?

Not that she expected Barkworth to demand seconds and put a bullet through Preston's arrogant chest, but something just below that and well above "you are not received" would have stirred a little more confidence in her.

Preston, instead of being insulted, laughed loudly and clapped Barkworth on the back. "You didn't tell me he had a sense of humor, Tabby. But of course I am, my good man. I'm here, am I not?" He grinned at

Barkworth, looking the man up and down and finally
declaring, "Truly, sir, I don't know how it is we haven't
been introduced before."

"I keep a respectable circle of acquaintances," Barkworth said, his shoulders taut, his nose tipped just so.

"Oh, so you don't entertain much, then, do you?"
Preston acknowledged.

Barkworth straightened a bit more—so much so
that Tabitha feared for his shoulder seams. "No. I am
a bachelor with only my mother to keep my house,"
he said, having utterly missed the point of Preston's
slight yet again.

"Not for long, eh, Barks?" Preston said, nudging
the other man once again as if they were old friends.
"No, I imagine soon your house will be filled with entertainments—balls, musicales, oh, and a host of card
parties, I daresay. Nothing Tabby likes more than a
good wager, isn't that so?"

"Oh, you are an odious fool," Tabitha sputtered.

Preston grinned. "I knew on further acquaintance
I would begin to win your favor, and here I have been
elevated to an odious fool already."

"Your Grace—" Sir Mauris began.

"Yes, yes, I can see from your face, my lord, that
you want to know the purpose of my intrusion, and it
is truly to extend my best wishes and happy felicitations to these lovebirds." He smiled broadly at the pair.
"That and to ensure that dear Tabby's most excellent
Barkwell was everything she'd declared him to be." He
glanced over at the other man and frowned. "Do you
ride, Barkwell?" Preston asked, again making a searching glance up and down the fellow, his face a mask
of puzzled contemplation, as if he feared the answer.

"Barkworth," the man corrected.

"Yes, yes, so you said," Preston agreed. "But do you ride, Barkle?"

With hands fisted at his sides, he answered, "Every gentleman does."

"Thank God, eh, Tabby? Wouldn't want a man who couldn't ride." He leaned over toward Barkworth and nudged him. "She's a spirited bit of muslin, but I have a feeling you'll manage her."

"Your Grace, you are referring to my betrothed," Barkworth said, his words coming out from between clenched teeth, his manners stiff.

"Yes, of course. I think we all know that she's your betrothed," Preston said, glancing around as if confused by Barkworth's furious tone. "Now as to the manner in which you will be keeping Tabby—as you can see, she has an eye for fashion. You have the necessary holdings and properties to support her?"

"I don't believe that is any of your business."

"Oh, I see, rather not reveal that you are a bit thin in the pockets before the wedding."

"Preston! That is enough," Tabitha told him. "Please, leave off."

He paused and looked at her, and she hoped he could see how humiliating he was being. "If that is your wish."

"It is," she told him.

"I am only looking after your best interests, Tabby." His words carried a hint of truth, and she nearly believed him.

Only...

"I wish you would not."

He leaned forward and looked at her. Just as if they

were still in the inn and there was only the two of them. "But I promised that I would."

She stepped back, nearly bumping into her aunt, for it was on the tip of her tongue to say the words.

Then save me, you devil. Carry me off and ruin me so I don't have to marry this fool!

And there it was. The truth. She glanced over at Barkworth, and despite such a short acquaintance, she knew exactly who, or rather what, he was.

Not the sort of man she wanted to marry. Yet those words, that plea—save me, ruin me—would land her in the briars.

She would not only lose her inheritance but she'd also be returned to Kempton (if Aunt Allegra would even take her back) to spend the rest of her days scrubbing the vicarage grates.

How could he not see that she had no choice? It wasn't like he was going to offer for her hand and truly save her.

He wasn't the sort.

Even worse, he took her silence to mean something else. "I concede to your sensibilities." Preston gazed once again at Barkworth. "Yet I cannot get over why a Corinthian such as yourself, sir, would not want to dance with such a lovely partner."

Tabitha had been thinking the same thing, waiting most of the evening for Barkworth to ask her to dance, if only so they could have a moment alone.

Well, as alone as one might manage in a crush like this one.

"I believe in an ever-present appearance of decorum." Barkworth looked out over the smiling couples and lines of partners moving elegantly together and shook his head. "Dancing should only be done when it is done well."

"A very good point, sir," Preston said. He leaned over and deftly snagged Tabitha's hand out of Barkworth's grasp. "Then shall we show one and all how it is done well, eh, Tabby?"

And with all the presumption of a duke, he didn't wait for her aunt's permission or her betrothed's blessing but towed Tabitha out toward the newly forming lines of dancers.

She glanced back at Barkworth, who should be coming to her rescue, who should be protesting Preston's tyranny, but who stood mutely at the sidelines and allowed her to be carted off by this pirate of a nobleman like she was merely paltry booty that could be sacrificed or would eventually find its way home.

Oh, bother! If he wouldn't protest, she would.

"I will not dance with you," she told the duke, digging the heels of her slippers into the floor.

"Yes, you will," Preston replied, smug and arrogant to the end. "And you know why you will?"

She pressed her lips together. She wasn't about to bandy words with him.

He leaned down and spoke so only she could hear. "Because you've wanted nothing more all night."

"I have wanted no such—"

He swung her into his arms and hitched her far too close to be decent. "Liar."

"I think you are the most odious—"

"Yes, I know. Odious, arrogant, presumptuous… did I leave anything out?"

"Yes, several," she told him, finding herself being skillfully and perfectly guided through the intricate steps. Oh, good heavens, this was just like the night in the inn…only better—for with the exacting lessons of Lady Timmons's dancing master, she could follow Preston smoothly.

It also helped that some devilish part of her longed to follow him…leaving her with nothing to do but bask in the warmth of his arms, the desire his touch evoked.

"Yes, well let me add one more thing to that list," he whispered in her ear, his breath sending tendrils of desire down her spine.

"Whatever did I leave out?" she managed a bit breathlessly.

He leaned closer still. "The part about me being the only man here capable of stealing your heart."

Chapter 10

What had he just said? Not even Preston quite believed it. Here to steal her heart? Had he gone mad?

Preston blamed Miss Timmons entirely. There was something utterly dangerous about this particular miss that had him confessing his secrets, laying his heart open.

What the devil was she doing to him? Tempting him. Creating havoc on his good sense.

Which he did possess…he did. Occasionally.

Though apparently not around Tabby, as Roxley might point out.

Well, he would argue, she brought out the worst of his common sense.

Here he had promised Hen so faithfully that he wouldn't cause any scandals, yet what was he doing? Dancing with a lady not on his prescribed list and intimating to her betrothed a familiarity that should not exist.

Ah, but it did, he thought as he looked down at her shocked expression. So his confession had left her as upended as it had him.

Good. Served her right. Coming into his life and forcing him to consider all sorts of preposterous notions.

Like opening up Owle Park.

He shook that thought off as quickly as it came to him. For it was not only preposterous but also impossible.

But when he looked into her brown, fathomless eyes (which right now were glowing with something he guessed might be a dangerous mix of fury and murder) the darkest regions of his heart began to ignite. Illuminating the possibilities.

And right now his heart pounded with the thrill of conquest, having rescued her from that booby of a betrothed—not that it had been so terribly difficult. Nor did that matter, for the end result was that he had her in his arms again.

A victory that left him unwilling to ever return her.

It was a medieval sort of feeling, something his ancestors would have understood—and acted upon—but in modern times, one couldn't abscond with any female who caught one's eye and claim ducal prerogative.

Though thankfully it did allow him to steal her away from her betrothed, if only for this one dance.

"Whatever are you smiling about?" she asked.

Preston glanced down at her and gave over to the truth. "Plotting how to get you out of here."

"Don't be scandalous," she scolded, only to his ears she hardly sounded unhappy with the notion.

"Scandalous would be to ask you to run away with me tonight," he whispered, though he stopped short of doing just that…asking her to slip away into the night with him. Tempting though it was.

"From what I understand, Your Grace, and given your reputation, such a suggestion would hardly be scandalous," she replied, "rather a familiar and well-trodden path you ought to have outgrown by now."

"Ouch," Preston laughed. "You've been listening to your Miss Dale."

"And most of London society," she added.

"Most of London society is comprised of idiots," he offered, nodding to the prancing and mincing crowd around them.

"Are you saying the reports about your…your…"

"Wrongdoings?" he suggested.

"Yes, those," she said. "The reports of your wrongdoings are merely the products of gossip?"

He shook his head. "No, I committed most of them."

"Daphne says that as a Seldon you can't help but bring the worst out in people," she told him.

"And in you?" he posed, remembering the fiery miss he'd held in his arms and kissed with abandon. And who had returned his kiss with a passion all her own. "Do I bring the worst out in you, Tabby?"

She glanced away, unwilling to answer.

"What most of these people forget—especially your impertinent Miss Dale—is that a scandal takes two. If I were to suggest to you that you run away with me—"

"Which I beg of you not to do—"

"Tabby, I have only your best interests at heart. I have promised to help you, and you have only to ask."

"I won't. Ask, that is."

"Yes, well, you've made your point on that note," he agreed as he took her hand and led her down the line of dancers, who all watched them ever so closely, as if waiting for some indiscretion. "But say I did and you refused."

"Which I would."

"Yes, so you say—"

She looked ready to protest, but he stopped her. "Miss Timmons, this is getting us nowhere if you continue to interrupt me, and I do have a point to make."

"Then make it, by all means," she told him as she circled around him and he took her back into his arms.

"I will."

"Good."

He laughed and continued on. "Since you have refused me"—he waited for her to argue the point, but she held her lips pressed together—"then my suggestion is merely ill-mannered and not scandalous in the least." He leaned closer. "But if you were to come with me now and we finished what we started that night in the inn—"

Was it him, or had she just shivered?

"—then our behavior would not only be worthy of scandal, but set tongues wagging for the next two Seasons."

"Then I am glad to have refused." She poked her prim nose in the air. "Can you not see how it would ruin everything?"

"If that is the case, then what were you thinking dancing with me?"

They had come to the end of the line of dancers and were separated as Tabitha walked down one side and Preston the other.

He looked over at the woman he barely recognized and frowned. The artfully arranged hair, the coy curls running down past her shoulders and—worst of all— this demmed gown she'd been trussed up in, with its low neckline that left the tops of her breasts exposed, ending with a view of her trim, enticing ankles.

What the devil were her aunt and uncle, let alone her betrothed, thinking, letting her out in such a rigging?

"Now what is wrong?" she demanded as they came together at the end of the line.

Preston caught hold of her and resisted the urge to pull her scandalously close…again.

However, while he couldn't see her, he could feel Hen's gaze burning two holes into his back, so he maintained the appearance of decorum.

For now.

"I don't approve of your gown." Preston shuddered. "…or your hair…or any of it." He waved a hand over her head, as if that could change her back into his funny little minx.

His Tabby.

"I don't believe my appearance is any of your concern," she told him. Then, after a moment, in which her brow furrowed in a line over her stormy gaze, she went on, "And whatever is wrong with my gown? It is the first stare of fashion, I will have you know."

"It is all wrong." This he knew without a doubt.

She made that indelicate snort that he recalled from the night at the inn—the one that made her sound like one of Roxley's dotty and disapproving aunts.

For some reason, he found her disapproval irresistible.

"It was done by Madame Moreau, and she is one of the finest modistes in London," Tabby told him.

"It doesn't suit." His worst fears for her had been realized. "You look like every other Bath miss—prowling London like a fishwife casting her wares out in the open with the single hope of catching some unwitting fool."

"I have no need of prowling," she told him. "I am already betrothed."

"More the reason to dress with a modicum of decorum." Something he knew *so* much about. "I can't see how Barkling can approve of such a display."

Instead of being insulted, a mutinous light went on in her eyes. "I would think a man of your predilections would approve of my transformation."

"Usually I would, but not with you, Tabby."

"What would you have me wear?"

"Here? Sackcloth." Then he leaned forward and, God help him, gave in to his own scandalous reputation. "And in private, nothing at all."

Preston smiled blandly at Tabitha as they moved along the line of dancers as if he hadn't just proposed he'd rather see her undone...

Naked, indeed!

Good heavens, if her aunt had heard him make such an indecent confession—let alone Lady Ancil or some other gossip—she'd be ruined, sent home in the next coach, be it a mail coach or the local freight wagon.

Wasn't it bad enough he was feigning a state of familiarity with her that did not exist?

Oh, that kiss would say otherwise, a wry little voice teased the back of her thoughts. *And the very fact that you wanted him to ask you to run away with him.*

How was it that this man seemed to undo her in ways that no one else ever had? Inspired a dangerous treason inside her that had her delirious to cast off every bit of decorum she possessed, made her long for…for…

Oh, bother, she didn't know what she wanted.

But she did. She wanted the *more* his kiss had promised. She wanted to be his Tabby, his every desire.

And mostly, she wished he'd never come along, because if he hadn't, she would have met Mr. Barkworth tonight, sensibly determined him entirely acceptable and that would have been enough.

It had to be enough, because the alternative was ruin and poverty.

So Miss Tabitha tamped down the fire Preston lit within her untried heart, shuttered the passions he stoked and pasted the most proper, bland expression she could muster on her face.

The one that hid the tumult inside her.

Preston saw right through it. "Come now, you aren't going to get all missish on me, are you, Tabby?" He grinned at her. "I thought you were made of sterner stuff."

Tabitha ground her teeth together, then glanced around to gauge if anyone was in earshot. "Stop calling me that," she scolded when she saw her chance.

"Stop calling you what?"

"You know exactly what I mean."

"Tabby, I haven't the least notion what you are nattering on about." Bother the man if his eyes didn't sparkle with mischief as he made his denial.

"No one calls me Tabby."

"But that isn't true," he declared.

"Name me one person?"

"Me," he said with all confidence, as if his insistence to name her so made it so. Then he tightened his hold on her and drew her closer.

"You do not count," she replied, ignoring the rebellious desire running from where his hand enclosed hers, where his palm rested on her hip, and all points in between. "Nor does your opinion prove the point."

He laughed. "You just proved my point, Tabby."

"However did I do that?" Really, she knew better than to ask, but the question had slipped out of her lips before she could stop herself.

"Because Tabby suits you, you little minx."

She closed her eyes for a second. Minx! Good heavens, that was worse than Tabby. "I am neither of those."

Not to you, she wanted to add.

She glanced up to find his brow arched and a slight smile on his lips. He quite thought himself the victor in this contest. Hardly. "You shouldn't call me such names. It isn't seemly."

"Yes, I suppose you are correct." His words, though contrite by definition, held not a note of penitential humility.

"You are making trouble for me. Deliberately."

"Me?" he feigned.

"Yes, Your Grace, you." She did her best to put on her most severe expression. "It is because you think it is your right."

He grinned. "It is."

"Not with me, Your Grace."

"Ah, so we are no longer Preston and Tabby." He shook his head and gazed at her as if searching for something.

For someone else.

Tabitha wanted to tell him that Tabby, his Tabby, had been naught but a product of too much roast beef, apple tart and French wine. Tabby was a dangerous, flirtatious minx and she was best kept bottled and trapped in the deepest cellar of Tabitha's heart. "We were never—"

He leaned forward and whispered, "We most certainly were."

Tabitha shivered at the intimacy, the ferocity of his words, his confession. "I should never have dined with you."

"However would I have taken that meal if you had not joined me?"

"You could have sat down and eaten it," she pointed out.

"Ever the practical miss. And I would have been able to do so—as I had planned to share that meal with Roxley—until you came along and frightened him off with your bogey man tales of his aunt sleeping under the same roof."

"Of all the ridiculous notions!" she said. "Now it is all my fault?"

"It was entirely a situation of your making," he declared.

"And you are unable to dine alone?" she posed.

"Yes," he told her.

"Why?"

A flicker ran through his usually mischievous

gaze. It was the same poignant light that she'd spied the night in the inn. And when she'd tumbled into his arms today.

It spoke of something lost, of something ever so dear, something just out of reach.

He straightened. "I prefer not to."

"Marriage would solve that," she suggested, and at that, he nearly stumbled.

Touché.

Then he managed to return the volley and nearly upend her.

"Why do you think I am here tonight?"

Tabitha's gaze flew up to meet his. "You're to be married?" Her heart did a double wallop, the same sort of furious beat that it had battered against her chest when she'd spied him with his beautiful companion.

"My aunt believes Lady Pamela"—he paused for a moment, surveying the room and then nodding toward a tall, awkward-looking girl in the corner—"and I would suit."

"The one in puce?" she asked.

"Apparently so," he said, his nose pinching slightly.

"Not in the least," Tabitha declared without thinking, something inside her wrenching the words from her throat.

Preston and this Lady Pamela? She stole another glance at this paragon his aunt had chosen.

But then again, this lady of note and breeding was the sort who did marry a duke.

Lady Pamela would never have dined with Preston in the private confines of a lonely inn. She wouldn't have wagered with him. Would never have kissed a man she believed to be no more than a rapscallion and a rogue.

Tabitha trembled. So why had she?

She was just as proper and well bred as this Lady Pamela—heavens above, her father was a vicar! Yet why had she, Miss Tabitha Timmons of Kempton, let that dangerous, roguish Mr. Preston pull her into his arms and kiss her, alighting every nerve in her body with his lips, tease her into a passion with his skilled touch?

And why couldn't she forget?

Despite her best efforts, she could not tamp down the memories of those moments, as boisterous as an uncorked bottle of champagne, whose restless, anxious bubbles refuse to stay entrapped, rising to the surface and exploding in the most unexpected ways.

Yet this man who held her now wasn't her Preston any longer, any more than she was his Tabby.

"Why didn't you tell me?" she asked.

"Tell you what?" he said, waving away her question only because he knew exactly what she meant.

"Who you were," she insisted. "You let me think—"

"I rather liked what you thought," he teased. "You were quite convinced I was…was…"

"You gave me little evidence to think otherwise," she said in her defense.

"Oh, don't deny it," he said. "You rather enjoyed thinking the worst of me."

"The worst of you? How utterly arrogant. You made a fool of me," she shot back. "You thought it a great lark to let me believe—"

"No, not in the least." He glanced around the room, his gaze moving in a grand sweep, his expression bland, as if he didn't see how all eyes were turned on them. "I enjoyed that you gave me no quarter, allowed me no liberties."

Other than the ones he'd stolen with his kiss. Even then, she could hardly call his actions thievery.

She'd wanted him to kiss her. She'd wanted more…

That was the worrisome part. The *more*…

"Let us leave all that in the past," she told him, though it was mostly for her benefit.

"Pretend we are naught but vague acquaintances?"

"Exactly," she agreed. "Proper and respectable."

He nodded and struck up a more taut position, holding her slightly out from him. "However do you like London, Miss Timmons?"

Apparently this was the safest question he knew.

"Not at all," she replied.

He leaned closer. "That was not the proper response."

"I suppose not," she admitted. "But I miss home."

"Truly?"

"Of course," she told him, ignoring the fact that she wasn't supposed to be on such easy terms with him. But whenever this enigmatic man turned his full attention on her, she tumbled toward him headlong. "The bluebells had yet to bloom when we left…and now…"

"You'll have missed them," he said, surprising her with his insight. "However, there are gardens aplenty in London."

"Oh, proper, perfect gardens," she said with a sniff. Her aunt had been horrified to find her just the past week in the garden behind the house and *not on the path*. What was the point of a garden if one couldn't get up close to the blossoms and smell them?

Preston, meanwhile, was laughing at her haughty disdain. "You do speak your mind."

"With you," she admitted.

He studied her for a moment. "Bluebells, eh?"

"Yes," she whispered.

"The color of your gown, I imagine."

"Preston," she said, trying to sound severe.

He grinned, turned her with a great flourish and then pulled her impossibly close.

So close it was hard to breathe.

More...

And now, oh, good heavens, being back in his arms, with his strong, broad palm on the small of her back, his fingers wound around her other hand, standing so close her skirt brushed against his trousers as they turned to and fro, his wide chest so very close, where she knew if she were to pluck off her glove and slide her hand beneath his jacket over the cool, crisp linen of his shirt she'd find the steady, pounding beat of his heart, the warmth of his skin invading her fingers like a fire that would spread through her limbs.

Like a fever of unbridled desires. *Preston, I... Please, Preston...*

Here in his arms, she was Tabby once again. In front of everyone, in front of...

She stole a guilty glance over at Barkworth and found him watching her—no, not her but Preston— with a disapproving furrow to his brow.

Tabitha didn't even dare a glance at Lady Ancil.

They were separated for a moment as Tabitha moved around a circle and Preston went in the opposite direction. When they came back together he took her outstretched hands, and for a second, it felt as if the world stopped.

Fireworks came to life inside her as his fingers entwined with hers.

Their gazes locked and she could see a flicker of shock, nay amazement, in his dark, mocking gaze, as if he didn't quite believe it had truly happened.

"Why are you marrying him, Tabby?"

The truth tugged at her. But to do so… He'd never understand. "My reasons are none of your concern."

"Do you love him?"

Love him? Good heavens, she'd just met the man! But she could hardly confess such a thing. Whatever would he think of her then?

Not that she should care. "Are you always so impertinent?" she said, poking her nose in the air.

"No," he said. "Usually I haven't a care."

"So why have I sparked this rare spate of concern?"

The moment she asked the question, she knew the answer. At least she thought she did.

No, it was a foolish thought. Hope. Wish.

Preston was concerned about her because he… Tabitha pressed her lips together. Ridiculous notion. She was naught but a game to him. An amusement.

"Because I promised you I would," he replied.

"I don't recall agreeing to your interference in my life," she replied.

"Our wager?"

The wager? "I won that wager—which you paid me for. There is no outstanding obligation," she pointed out.

"I disagree."

He would.

"You cheated," he said.

"Hardly."

Preston grinned at her. "Besides, I think you like my attentions."

"Not in the least," she replied.

"Liar. Just like you were that night when you told me you had no interest in marriage." He swung her around the end of the line and pulled her close yet again. "Do tell me, though, how did your Mr. Barkhall change your firmly set opinions on marriage so quickly?"

"Barkworth," she corrected.

"Yes, yes, but what secrets does this man hold on courtship that changed your mind?"

She glanced away, for what could she say? The truth? That she was marrying Barkworth to gain her fortune? That love had nothing to do with it? "It wasn't so much a courtship—"

"What?" Preston interjected. "No courtship. *Tsk, tsk, tsk.*"

"I don't expect a man to court me—"

"You should," Preston averred. "You should be courted. Wooed. Enticed."

Enticed. Here was something on which Preston was apparently an expert. One look at his handsome face should have warned her of that.

He continued on, "A lady deserves to be courted. Otherwise the man is not worthy of her affections. At least that is what Hen avows."

There was that name again. "Hen?" she ventured.

"My aunt," Preston said, tipping his head in the direction of the beauty in black with whom he'd arrived.

"That is your Aunt Hen?"

"You needn't sound so disbelieving. But yes, that

is my Aunt Hen. Or as she is currently known, Lady Juniper."

"The one you and Lord Roxley hold in such horror?"

"Whatever led you to think—"

"You mentioned her that night at the inn."

"Did we?"

"Oh, yes. But I thought she would be—"

"Older? She is, but only by six months. Hen likes to consider herself my conscience."

"Indeed?" Poor woman, that sounded like a tall order. Tabitha slanted a peek at the lady. "She doesn't appear happy that we are dancing."

Preston spared a glance. "You are not on my approved list...no, no, don't take that wrong, there is nothing improper about you...it has more to do with me."

"With you, Your Grace?" she feigned.

"Very funny, Puss." He shook his head. "My aunt is determined to see me become a respectable member of society."

"Shameful notion!" Tabitha declared.

"Indeed," he agreed. "And when Hen is determined...she's gone so far as to threaten to move out if I cause another dustup. Take Henry with her."

"Henry?"

"Her brother. My uncle, Lord Henry Seldon. Her twin in everything, save a penchant for marriage."

"She cannot move out," Tabitha teased. "For who would you find to dine with you then?"

Her jab hit the mark, and she could see that she'd dug too deeply this time. "I didn't mean—"

"—no, no."

They danced a few more steps before Tabitha waded back in. "Does Lady Juniper have any other choices of bride for you? Other than Lady Pamela?"

"Yes," he shuddered. "And don't get overly used to calling her Lady Juniper."

"Whyever not?" Tabitha asked, glancing over at the lady as if there might be some clue as to this idiosyncrasy.

"She's an incurable romantic and prone to getting married." He sighed as if he couldn't understand such an affliction. "Another few months and she'll be out of her mourning period and the house will be once again overrun with suitors." Preston shuddered. "Hen loves being courted—and then marrying the dolt who turns up with the best arrangements or sweetmeats or bit of poetry. Juniper won her hand with some bit of flirtatious nonsense."

Flirtatious nonsense. Tabitha glanced enviously over at the beautiful lady. She'd probably laugh at Daphne and Harriet's confessions that they, just once, would like to gain the attention of a man—even if it was merely an admiring glance.

A sentiment Tabitha shared but wouldn't have admitted for all of Uncle Winston's fortune. And especially not to Preston.

Instead, she held herself primly. "Courtship is overrated. Barkworth and I have an understanding that goes well beyond such—"

"Your Barkley is a fool, Tabby," the duke said. "And if he hasn't even shown up with a single posy, then he isn't worth your hand."

Tabitha bit her lips together. It would hardly do to admit that she had just met her intended. Instead, she remained firm in her defense of her nearly betrothed. "His name is Barkworth, and you don't know him."

The duke stilled for a second as they paused in their steps, awaiting their turn to move down the line. "I wager that neither do you."

Oh, bother the man. Did he have to be so perceptive?

Preston wasn't done with his lecture either. "What I find so utterly perplexing is why you, a lady so adamantly against marriage, a sentiment I can respect, suddenly decides to cast off her—what did you call it? Ah, yes—'happy situation' to leg shackle herself to a looby like Barkton."

"Barkworth."

"That is beside the point," he said with a slight shake of his head. "Truly, Tabby? That man has you tossing away your freedom?"

Her freedom indeed! When did a lady ever possess a bit of freedom? She straightened. "I have my reasons."

He glanced down at her, eyes narrowed. "Roxley thinks you are with child. You aren't, are you?"

Tabitha nearly tripped over, but he held her fast and made it appear that he'd made the misstep. "Are you mad?"

Preston shrugged. "Your Barkey is the sort on whom a lady could foist off another man's by-blow and not have him be any the wiser."

"Oh, that is beyond the pale."

He ignored her outrage and continued on, "I suppose then I must assume you aren't *enceinte,* but that doesn't explain the why of it."

"Are you going to continue disparaging my betrothed?"

"Yes," he told her, glancing over her shoulder to where Barkworth stood waiting impatiently for their return. He looked down at her, and there was no more mischief, no puckish teasing in his eyes. "Why him, Tabby?"

"Perhaps he has won my heart," she said, tucking up her chin and trying to outswagger him.

Preston dismissed her bravado immediately. "Not likely."

"How would you know where my heart lies?"

"Because if you were truly in love with that imbecile, you wouldn't be out here with another man." The music stopped just then and they came to a stumbling halt, Preston catching her before she stumbled over her own slippers. "So I suppose the better question is, why would you dance with me?"

The music ended and for a moment they paused, looking at each other, their gazes entwined, and Preston, the man who had flitted and flirted his way through London society, discovered that he didn't want to flit past this woman.

He didn't want to let her go. So he asked the question again. "Why, Tabby? Why me?" He wanted her to confess everything.

And then what? something inside of him asked. *What the devil are you going to do about it?*

He didn't know, but that thought stopped him short of pressing on to what he really wanted to know. *Why did you let me believe that you were different?*

Why did you steal my heart?

For certainly his heart was pounding right now, hammering in his chest as he gazed down into her wide, brown eyes. Her lips pursed and opened slightly, like they had the night in the inn just before he'd kissed her.

"Preston," she whispered, like a promise, a hint that he wasn't alone in his desire, but at the same time, she shook her head and stepped back from him. Out of his arms.

Then he realized something. The entire room was silent. He wrenched his gaze away from Tabby and found all eyes on them.

Oh, dear God. What had he done?

"Miss Timmons, how clumsy of me," he said, bowing low. Then he rose, ignoring the shocked stares from all corners, and took her hand, folding it properly into the crook of his arm as he said loudly and smoothly, "You must think me a wretched clod, trodding on your foot like that. I daresay, I have not danced much of late."

"No, no," she replied, managing a wan smile. "I believe it was my fault, Your Grace. I was unsure of the last step."

"Then we shall blame your dancing master," he told her and smiled as she glanced up at him, her eyes filled once again with that wary, but wonderful, mischief.

Around them, the matrons began passing the word that sadly, nothing was amiss, and quickly the room resumed its chirping chatter.

Ruin and scandal momentarily averted, Preston continued on, leading her through the room, taking the longest, most circuitous route he could manage. Not that she seemed to mind.

"Everyone is staring."

"They always do," Preston said, glancing up as if he'd just noticed. "Ignore them."

"Why do you go out if you must undergo all this scrutiny?"

"What else would you have me do? Stay home?"

Tabitha sighed. "Home sounds lovely. A cozy fire. Reading aloud. Backgammon. Do you play?"

He cocked a brow. "Ruthlessly."

"Of course. My father taught me. I never had brothers or sisters to play with, but I do love a house full of company and friends." She glanced up at him. "And you? I have to imagine you love that as well."

Preston was about to brush off her question with a blithe answer, but suddenly a memory came dashing to the forefront.

"Felix is cheating," he complained to his sister across the room.

"Am not," Felix declared.

Dove shook her head at the both of them and set aside her book to come join them, glancing over the backgammon board nestled on the small table before the fire. "You have Felix on the run, Gopher," she said, smiling at him and reaching over to ruffle his hair.

Yet when he looked up, he found himself in the overheated crush of Lady Knolles's ballroom.

Holding Tabby.

"Miss Timmons," he said, "do you truly think me such a sentimental sort?"

"Yes," she said, as if she had been in that cozy memory as well.

How the devil did she do that? Evoke these memories. Give him over to these flights of fancy that tugged at his heart. Had him saying things...

"Miss Timmons?"

"Yes, Your Grace?"

"Do you recall our wager?"

"Yes."

"Do you still have your winnings?"

She glanced up at him and shook her head. "I have no need of nicked pennies, Your Grace. Don't you remember? I am an heiress now."

"How I wish you weren't."

This gave her pause. "You begrudge me my good fortune?"

"Only the changes it has wrought on you."

They wove their way through the crowded ballroom, and as they drew closer to her friends and family, Tabby asked, "Why did you want to know about that penny?"

"I wanted to know if you would be willing to make another wager."

She laughed. "I thought you didn't like to lose, Your Grace."

"I have no intention of losing," he said, sounding as lofty as his title.

"So you plan to cheat."

There was his vexing little minx. Apparently the changes were only on the lady's perimeter. "Miss Timmons, you wound me yet again," though he said as much with a grin. "I have no intention of cheating because I have no need. I intend to win, fair and square. Besides, now I know my opponent."

The lady's lips pursed into a slight smile. "And what is this wager?"

Ah, he had her. So he leaned closer and whispered

so that no one else could hear, "That before you marry Barkworth, you will ask me to kiss you one more time."

She sucked in a deep breath and went to pull her hand free of his arm, but he covered it with his hand and smiled graciously for all the world to see.

Straightening in his grasp, she scolded him. "Your Grace, just because you have a reputation for scandal does not mean you have to prove it at every opportunity."

"Miss Timmons, with you, I have nothing to prove. You know exactly who I am." Oh, how he wished she didn't.

"You are a—"

He stopped her before she got going. "You aren't going to give me that dull litany yet again? *Wretched cur. Arrogant rake.* It is all most tiresome. And rather pointless. I know it by heart." Preston grinned at her. "So, do we have a wager?"

Tabby's mouth dropped open. "Don't be ridiculous. It is a ruinous notion."

"Not for me, and not for you…if you win."

That was enough to set her brow furrowing into a deep line. "There is no doubt you would lose, for I shall not ask you for such a thing. Ever." As if to prove her point, she smiled brightly over at Barkworth, the man nodding slightly in acknowledgement.

But she didn't fool Preston in the least. The smile was as false as her wretched ringlets and the rest of her ornaments.

"Of course you will ask me," he told her.

"You do recall I have already had the privilege of that particular favor. Whyever would I make that mistake again?"

He had to admire the cool disdain in her voice. She almost had him believing that she had no desire to ever kiss him again. Yet her eyes held a fire that said something else altogether. "If you are so sure of your convictions, take my wager. You will have nothing to lose and everything to gain."

Her chin notched up a bit, her nostrils flaring. "What? Another nicked penny?"

"If that is what you wish. You seem to have a penchant for them. But perhaps it is so you can have another to match the one you have yet in your reticule."

He had timed his comment perfectly, for they had finally arrived back at the spot near the wall, and they were greeted by a line of stony faces and stiff backs. Neither did he look at her.

He didn't need to, for he could feel her shiver.

And while he rather regretted setting her loose amongst them—almost—he had to imagine, as he glanced over at Barkless, that the more time Tabby spent in the man's puffed-up company, the more she'd be quite happy to take his wager.

And lose just as willingly.

Besides, he still had one more dance with the clod-footed Lady Pamela to endure so as to continue in Hen's good graces.

"Lady Timmons, thank you for allowing me the pleasure of your niece's company," Preston said. He made his bow and left, crossing the room with quick, steady strides.

That is, until a lady stepped in front of him. Speaking of Hen...

"Preston! Explain yourself," she demanded, folding her hand on the crook of his arm and smiling brightly.

There was nothing sunny about her tone.

"I have danced with three young ladies of no consequence, just as you asked."

"You danced with two of them," Hen corrected. "Whoever was that?" She tipped her head in Tabitha's direction.

"Miss Timmons. A vicar's daughter."

"Bah!"

"Truly, Hen. Lord Timmons's niece. A perfectly respectable lady of no consequence."

"You are bamming me."

"She is exactly who I say she is. Miss Timmons of Kempton. If you don't believe me, ask Roxley. I only danced with her as a favor to his aunt, Lady Essex."

Hen glanced over at Tabby yet again, eyeing her closely. "Really, Preston? A vicar's daughter?"

"Yes, Hen. I promised no scandals," he said, knowing he'd probably caused a bit of a ripple but hardly a scandal.

At least outwardly.

He didn't count the whirlwind going on inside his chest.

"Well, if that is true, then I shall excuse this one minor lapse."

Preston pasted a smile on his face and was thankful that for all her prowess, Hen wasn't a mind reader.

Because Miss Tabitha Timmons of Kempton had left him utterly undone and willing to risk even Hen's threats if only to kiss the impudent little minx one more time.

For about the thousandth time since Preston had returned her to her aunt's side, Tabitha cursed herself for putting Preston's nicked penny in her reticule—for when he'd picked it up, he must have felt the singular coin inside and discovered the truth.

That she was carrying it around like a favor.

Oh, bother, he knew nothing. Tabitha tightened the strings on her reticule. Many a lady had a coin or two in her purse. That nicked penny meant nothing.

Save for the memory of his kiss. Of the night when he turned your life upside down.

"I see you are obviously overcome," Barkworth was saying as he led her from the ballroom toward the foyer, his mother and Lady Peevers following close on their heels.

"Excuse me?" she managed, for she hadn't quite heard him.

She'd been too busy glancing about to see where Preston might be hiding. For she'd half expected him to return and continue causing a scandal. But even in that the duke had been vexingly unpredictable.

He'd left her alone ever since he'd returned her to her rightful position beside her almost-betrothed, and now he was nowhere in sight.

"I was saying, you appear overcome," Barkworth repeated. "And why wouldn't you be? This momentous evening is nearly over and you are bereft to see it come to its inevitable conclusion." He patted her hand and continued to guide her slowly through the parting crowd, smiling at all who sent curious glances in their direction.

Bereft was hardly the word Tabitha would use. This eager attention was hardly something she desired. One more thing she could credit Preston for— because when he'd singled her out to dance with, two questions had flown about the room with the usual efficiency of the *ton*:

Whoever is this divine creature in Lady Timmons's care?

And why has she garnered the Duke of Preston's notice?

So when she wasn't being introduced to Lady Lofty or Countess Cruella, Tabitha found her fingers being drawn up in lingering kisses by overly attentive gentlemen and lords, who added to their slavish attentions invitations to dance, to dine, and to partake in private interludes that would have put her aunt in Bedlam if she'd heard them.

All the while, Barkworth stood at her side, taking in all this adulation as if it were being laid at his feet.

As if the Enchanting and Original Miss Timmons was entirely his discovery.

"For your first venture out into London society," he said as he steered her past several leering rakes lounging by the door, "I must say I couldn't be more pleased, my dear Miss Timmons. You have surpassed even my expectations."

"Pleased?" However could the man be pleased? She'd spent most of the night as an object of unabated curiosity and untoward speculation.

"How could I not?" He bowed slightly at a matron who was watching them with her quizzing glass, and in return she tipped her head slightly. "See, just there, you gained the approval of Lady Melden. I have no doubt that by tomorrow afternoon there will be an invitation to her upcoming musicale on your aunt's salver."

"Whatever for?" Tabitha asked. For she certainly couldn't imagine that she'd done anything notable.

Save dance with Preston.

"Why, for being so utterly perfect," he declared, patting her hand yet again where it sat atop his sleeve.

What with the way he steered her and showered her with these affectionate and familiar pats on the back of her hand, Tabitha felt more like a prized pug being paraded down the lane than his future bride-to-be.

It certainly hadn't felt that way when Preston had led her through the crowd. Yes, the guests had parted before them with the same curiosity, but with Preston beside her, Tabitha had felt shielded from their scrutiny. As if with the duke beside her, he'd made her impervious to the baleful stares. That when he had escorted her, his attentions had never wavered—always been focused entirely on her.

Leaving her stirred and shaken by his steady regard, his closeness, like a dizzy, dangerous tonic.

She wished she could say the same with Barkworth, for he towed her along with a start and a stop, as if posing her for review and chatting with all those around them, barely acknowledging her unless there was a general lack of anyone else about. The only thing dangerous she felt around him was the unending urge to stuff her reticule down his pandering, patronizing throat.

She glanced behind her where Daphne, Harriet and Harriet's brother Chaunce were following. While Harriet was in a deep discussion with her brother, Daphne cast a bright, encouraging smile at her.

These things take time, her friend seemed to be reminding her.

Time! She didn't have any time. And it wasn't beneficial to her situation that she couldn't help but compare Barkworth to Preston.

Oh, if only she had more experience in these matters! Or perhaps, remembering Preston's kiss, a little less experience.

Ignorance, in her case, would truly be to Barkworth's best advantage.

"Mr. Barkworth," a brightly gowned young lady called out, stepping into their path. Mrs. Drummond-Burrell, Tabitha recalled. In a bright silk, with jewels at her ears, neck and wrists, she lit up the night with her finery. "Most happy felicitations on your most splendid news. Miss Timmons, I was just scolding your aunt for not bringing you by on my last afternoon in. An oversight, surely! I will have vouchers sent over tomorrow."

After a nudge from Barkworth, Tabitha remembered her manners. "Thank you, madame." She bobbed a curtsy, which gained another litany of rapture from this esteemed lady, who was probably the same age as Tabitha but who possessed the polish of Town and the manners of the *ton* that she, a country vicar's daughter, lacked so utterly.

Barkworth stammered openmouthed at this offer, obviously dazzled by the prospect of Almack's as much as by the infamous lady herself.

"However did you find this darling fashion plate, Barkworth? La! Here, I always supposed you to be such a dull fellow! How surprising that *you* would find her first."

Mrs. Drummond-Burrell circled Tabitha like a shark, eyeing the cut of her gown from top to bottom, all the while tossing praise at Barkworth.

"No keeping this divine creature to yourself now,

Barkworth!" she cooed. "After tonight you must share her, you devilish fellow!" With an airy wave of her hand, fan aflutter and the gems at her wrists and ears twinkling like stars, she was off to her next conquest. "Wednesday next, Miss Timmons. I shall send vouchers around. And bring Barkworth." She laughed as if it were a grand idea, and then was gone.

"Vouchers!" Barkworth said smugly, his broad chest puffing out. "To Almack's."

While it made him appear all the more impressive, Tabitha bit back the retort that he would be well advised to watch his buttons lest they pop.

"I am not surprised you have enchanted Mrs. Drummond-Burrell," he said. "Though I must admit I thought your lapses in judgment earlier might prove to be your undoing. That gown, dancing too close with that bounder—"

"As I explained before, that couldn't be helped," she rushed to say. No more than she could stop the desires that bounder lit inside her when he held her in his arms.

"Yes, yes, so you said. Still, it is to my credit that allowances are being made for your mistakes. I must say, in all humility, that my good name and reputation have carried you over what could have been a disastrous coming out."

Tabitha bit her lips together. "I hardly think one dance—"

Barkworth made a "*tsk tsk*" and continued, though notably in a much lower range, "He referred to you in the most intimate manner, Miss Timmons. Tabby, indeed! How dreadfully common! I fear he was insulting you, my dear. Or worse, attempting to bring about yet another of his infamous scandals."

"Yes, wretched man," she agreed, though not as wholeheartedly as she ought.

"Many a lady has been dazzled by the Duke of Preston, but he does not marry them." Barkworth shook his head. "But it is all forgotten now."

Not to Tabitha. If only she could forget.

"Ah, here comes the maid with your pelisse," Barkworth was saying, making a great show of being the attentive escort. For once he glanced at her and actually took stock of her welfare. "Dear God! Look at you shivering. The night air is dreadful this time of year." He took the wrap from the maid and tossed it over Tabitha's shoulders. "Don't let anyone see you shaking like that or it will be all over Town that you have a weak constitution." He paused and looked at her again. "You don't, do you?"

Tabitha was taken aback. "No," she told him. "Not that I know of." Considering she'd spent the last three years cleaning the vicarage from cellar to attics every day, she was probably as hearty as a draft horse.

"Excellent," Barkworth replied, his attention already focused on a couple passing by, whom he greeted with a well-executed bow. Then in an aside he added, "My uncle said you came from right proper stock, and we wouldn't want him to think otherwise."

"Your uncle? What has he to do with this?"

"What has he to do with this?" Barkworth repeated as if the answer should be self-evident. "If my uncle were to disapprove, why, it would be disastrous! Where would our standing in good society be if you were snubbed by the Marquess of Grately?"

Tabitha, having seen enough of "good society" to last her a lifetime, did her best to look as contrite as possible. "I leave these matters to your superior experience, Mr. Bark—" It was nearly on the tip of her tongue to say Barkton or Barkley or one of the other names Preston had worked into their conversation. "Mr. Barkworth," she finally managed.

The man smiled at her, as if he found her more demure posture delightful. "Let us forget all about this and move forward with a clean slate. Mother and I plan to call tomorrow so we can work out the final arrangements if that would please you."

"Tomorrow?" she said, and probably a little too quickly. They had reached the front steps and Tabitha faltered a little.

Barkworth didn't notice her misstep, for he was smiling and waving at Mrs. Drummond-Burrell yet again. "But of course," he said, finally having lost the other lady's attention. He turned to survey the line of carriages awaiting the lords and ladies. "However can we be married, and quickly, if we do not settle things? Though most of it has already been attended to by the lawyers—dreary details which you needn't worry over."

This was news to Tabitha. Whatever needed to be settled? She glanced at Barkworth and considered asking him how their, nay, her, future was being decided but doubted he would explain it to her—that is, if he even understood it.

Tabitha glanced over at her taciturn uncle, Sir Mauris. She had to imagine he understood where every penny of Uncle Winston's money was going and how it was going to be settled.

But would he be willing to share the details with her? She doubted as much.

Perhaps she could ask him when they got home. For even now, Sir Mauris was sending a lad off to find his coachman.

She said a silent prayer the boy was fleet of foot.

"I had thought to finish the Season in Town," she lied. "An autumn wedding, perhaps. If anything, I reach my majority in a sennight—"

Barkworth shook his head and guided her to a spot near the mews, far enough out of earshot of her aunt and his mother, but close enough to be proper. "There is no time like the present, my dear Miss Timmons. The sooner we are married, it will be for the best— our happy union a shining example to all. Society will rejoice in our love."

"Our love?" she said, more to herself. They'd just met. And now he was declaring them in love? Besides, she didn't believe in love at first sight.

It had taken a second glance for her heart to become entangled with Preston.

"Our love," Barkworth replied in all confidence.

"Don't you think that is doing it up a bit, sir? We can hardly be said to be in love."

He stared intently into her eyes. "I don't know about you, Miss Timmons, but this evening I have been struck deeply in a state of admiration over you."

A state of admiration. She looked into his handsome face, into his pale blue eyes, and waited for her heart to flutter, to beat wildly at this…this…declaration.

Yet nothing happened. And why would it? *A state of admiration.* She'd never heard such a ridiculous thing.

She couldn't imagine Preston making such a state- ment. Then again, she doubted Preston would even pause over a state of admiration, let alone waste the breath to utter such a foolish sentiment.

"I have spoken too soon," Barkworth said, taking her hand and bringing it to his lips.

Tabitha stilled as his lips tenderly touched her fingertips, as he held her hand for a second or so longer than need be, with an expectation that a spark of magic would happen.

That she would be struck by the same blinding flash of passion that drove her heart to pound wildly, that made her insides tangle into knots, that left her knees quaking under her every time Preston held her, touched her, came close.

But instead she found herself glancing impatiently up the street for any sight of her uncle's carriage.

"You needn't be worried that our acquaintance is too short to support a prosperous marriage," he said. "My parents were married with the same due haste, and my mother avers that if my father hadn't died a fortnight later of a chill, their marriage would have been most prosperous."

"Don't you think it is prudent to get to know a potential partner before becoming engaged?" she asked.

"I daresay your Uncle Winston knew exactly how we would suit when he tied us together with his inheritance."

She resisted the urge to point out that her Uncle Winston had never once laid eyes on her, let alone had known what sort of man might "suit" her.

"Perhaps instead of making arrangements tomorrow when you call, we could take a walk in the park," Tabitha suggested. "Get to know one another."

"As mother says, there is an eternity for a married

couple to fall in love," Barkworth said, waxing on as if his poetry would turn the tide of her misgivings. "And who wouldn't be in love with you? You have ensnared the very crème of the *ton* tonight. Tomorrow, all of London." He waved his arm in a grand gesture over the shadowed streets of Mayfair.

"I think it is merely because I am new to Town," she said. Truly, it didn't take a modicum of wit to realize that the novelty of her position, her scandalous gown and Preston's attentions were behind the sudden rush of interest in her.

"If it is a walk in the park you desire, Miss Timmons, I would be remiss not to give you your heart's desire. But I suspect you have chosen the park if only to give all of London another chance to see us together and so you may collect more invitations."

Actually, she was thinking about the coaching inn near the park that her cousin had mentioned earlier in the day.

Preston stepped out of the shadows of the mews, where he'd been waiting for Roxley. The last time he'd seen the earl, he'd been charming a widow in one of the alcoves.

Of course, as luck would have it, Roxley made his appearance just as Preston took a step after Tabby and Barkworth as the couple started toward her uncle's carriage.

They weren't engaged. She and Barkworth weren't betrothed. At least not formally.

There was still time to save her.

"Leave her be, Preston," Roxley advised.

"That man is a pompous oaf," Preston argued.

"Oh, you'll get no argument from me that Barkworth is a fool, but gels like Miss Timmons are offered up to fellows like him every day. It is how it is done." Roxley took another glance at the Timmons party and shrugged before he nodded down the street, where his tiger could be seen bringing up the curricle.

"'How it is done'? What the devil does that mean?"

Roxley looked over his shoulder. "You know exactly what that means. If that chit is going to inherit a fortune, then she is better off married and married quickly. To save her from being snatched up and hauled off to Gretna Green by some fortune hunter. Or worse, ruined before the deed can be done." The earl's brow arched into a sharp point.

One Preston got—having been cast as the ne'er-do-well in that scenario more than once. "He—they—will ruin her," he sputtered instead, glancing around with disdain at the milling crowd of curious onlookers, who were also watching Barkworth and Tabby.

"Better Barkworth than you. At least that nitwit will marry her."

Roxley's remark hit Preston just as it was intended. Straight in the chest.

Preston shifted, trying to catch his breath. Roxley, damn his hide, was right. Barkworth was the type to marry an heiress—all but sight unseen.

Roxley, who waited for the tiger to clamor back to his perch, climbed up into the carriage while Preston hung back.

"If you don't want to watch," Roxley said as he adjusted the reins, "go off to the country for the rest of the Season."

Preston shook his head. Going to the country meant

going to Owle Park, and he hadn't been home…well, not since he'd left it. No, that wouldn't do. Not even if it meant he had to watch Miss Timmons, his Tabby, being transformed into Mrs. Reginald Barkworth.

He shuddered. Egads. Barkworth would have her done up in some matronly gown. Or worse, in a turban with a cloud of feathers over her once pretty head. "Perhaps I could—"

Roxley shook his head. "Hen would never forgive you if you ruined that gel. Nor would anyone else. Not now. Especially now that she's made her debut and gotten half the town besotted over her. Including you…" He paused. "Which wouldn't have happened if you hadn't singled her out for that dance. Good God, man! What were you thinking?"

Preston ground his teeth together. He hadn't been thinking. What the devil was wrong with him?

Tabby. That was what was wrong with him. Tabby, with her practical exterior and her passionate underpinnings. She was like finding the breathtaking grandeur of a cathedral under the wrappings of a modest cottage.

And for one night, she'd been his. Until he'd gone too far and…

"Are we to White's then?" Roxley asked him. Hen had already left for home in the company of friends.

"Not unless you got the address for that widow you had buttonholed."

Roxley patted his breast pocket, where he kept all his notes. "Most decidedly. But the lady can wait. Had rather hoped to run into Dillamore."

"You'll never collect from him."

"I shall endeavor," Roxley vowed.

The duke laughed and climbed up into the seat next

to the earl. The height of the curricle gave him a raised
vantage point from which to watch Barkworth help
Tabby into her uncle's grand carriage with all the flourish and show of a pandering dandy. Preston shuddered.
"If she must marry, as you think—"

"I do," Roxley said.

"Then why him? Why must she marry him in such a
hellfire hurry? And again, if she must marry, why not
someone of her own choosing? Surely there is someone less of a…not so much of a—"

"Nodcock?" Roxley said, his gaze narrowing.

"Yes, exactly," Preston said as he too followed the
course of the earl's focus.

Which happened to be Miss Hathaway, who had
hung back from her party with a man who looked to be
a close relative—from their similar coloring and easy
smiles. Then she gave the man a quick embrace before
she hurried into the Timmonses' carriage.

The fellow stood sentry until Miss Hathaway was
safely inside and the coachman had clicked the reins
before he turned to leave.

"Ah, Chaunce comes our way," Roxley said.

"Who is that man?"

"Chaunce," Roxley said, as he drove the carriage
toward the fellow.

"A chance for what?" Preston asked.

"Good God, Preston, not what. Who." Roxley
laughed and pulled the carriage to a stop, doffing his
hat to the man and saying, "Preston, my good man,
may I introduce you to Mr. Chauncy Hathaway of
Kempton. Though you might want to call him Op-

portunity. For if anyone knows the answers to your questions, Preston, or can ferret them out, it is my old friend Chaunce."

Chapter 11

The next morning, Tabitha, Daphne and Harriet came down the stairs to find Tabitha's cousins, Euphemia, Edwina and Eloisa, all standing around the table in the main foyer where the salver sat.

This was hardly unusual, for her cousins spent a great deal of time hovering about the front door waiting to see who might be dropping off calling cards, invitations or other tokens.

"Ah, cousin," Euphemia said. "You have an admirer." On either side of her, Edwina and Eloisa snickered like a pair of mismatched horses. Then the trio parted to reveal the subject of their amusement.

To Tabitha's shock a single, small bouquet of bluebells awaited her. Tied with a bit of twine.

"There is no note," Edwina complained. Which probably explained a good part of her cousin's dismay—she hadn't been able to discover who was the sender.

"And they look like they were picked from the roadside," Eloisa said with a discerning sniff. She backed away from the table. "Not even from the hothouse." She and Edwina and Euphemia parted ways to allow Tabitha a closer inspection, all three of them tittering and shaking their skirts as if to remove even the hint of such wayside offerings from their lofty sphere.

Tabitha needed no note. She knew exactly who had sent them 'round.

Preston. He'd sent bluebells.

The color of your gown, I imagine.

The stems were crushed, as were a few of the blossoms, but they were country bluebells, nonetheless. She shivered and reached out with a single finger to touch the twine, if only to see if it was real.

"I think they are lovely," Daphne said loudly to no one in particular. "How thoughtful of Barkworth." She turned to Tabitha. "I imagine when you are his marchioness he will shower you with much grander offerings." Daphne smiled as she continued, this time turning toward Tabitha's eldest cousin. "A marchioness! I just can't believe it. Won't you be pleased to have such a lofty connection to mention when you go out calling, Miss Timmons?"

Euphemia nearly tripped over the carpet at this, while her younger sisters were the perfect portrait of a pair who had been sipping lemonade.

Before the sugar had been added.

Tabitha didn't correct her friend that the bluebells weren't a sign of Barkworth's affections, for it was too much fun to see her cousins twisting a bit.

She glanced at the bluebells again. *A lady deserves to be courted.*

How like Preston to send these, in stark contrast to Barkworth's clear lack of any such offering.

Then again, she'd only met her betrothed the day before…even though she'd been in London an entire fortnight. She could hardly expect that on such a short acquaintance Barkworth would be bringing her bluebells…

Oh, bother Preston! He was making her second-guess her own betrothal.

Yet why hadn't Mr. Reginald Barkworth called before their grandly orchestrated meeting? Or, at the very least, sent around a note? Hadn't he been the least bit curious to meet her, his future bride? Not even enough so to gather a small bouquet of roadside bluebells and send them along?

Picking them up, Tabitha sighed. Leave it to Preston to uncover her heart's desire before anyone else. Wretched awful man. Wading about some roadside and picking these for her just to make his point.

That image alone was enough to make her smile. The Duke of Preston out in some field, pilfering flowers! As she gazed down at the less-than-perfect little blossoms, she knew something else.

Exactly what it was like to have a man court her.

Even if he had no intention of following through, she reminded herself.

She looked up and found Harriet studying her with a wry glance that said two things:

She envied Tabitha. Not in a covetous way, like Tabitha's cousins did—for more than once they had made it clear how undeserving they thought her of

Barkworth and her future as the Marchioness of Grately.

No, Harriet envied the significance of the gesture. Probably because her knowing glance also said all too clearly that she knew the flowers were not from Barkworth.

Daphne was too busy gloating over Tabitha's triumph—for even this small bouquet was more than her cousins had received this morning—to notice the silent exchange between her friends. She looped her arm into Tabitha's and smiled brightly. "Is this not why we came to London, Tabitha? So you could get to know Mr. Barkworth? And see! He has made his intentions clear. And with your favorite flowers, no less."

"I would hardly say that his intentions are clear, Daphne," Tabitha corrected. "I barely know the man."

"And how could you? You haven't had the opportunity," she agreed. "But today will offer you the perfect chance to see his true character. You musn't jump to any conclusions about the man until you've had a chance to discover his qualifications."

"As a dim-witted ponce," Harriet said in an aside.

Daphne ignored her, and they followed Euphemia, Edwina and Eloisa toward the receiving room, Daphne continuing to chatter on about Barkworth's superiority above all other gentlemen, until they drew close enough to the room to hear not only Lady Timmons's voice but that of Lady Peevers as well.

"I aver, Antigone, it is all over Town," the matron was saying loudly, "that he chose her because he thought her naught but a—"

"Ah, dear Tabitha," Lady Timmons exclaimed, cut-

ting off her sister as Tabitha came to a stop in the doorway. "There you are, and how pretty you look."

"Daphne chose this," she demurred. She'd never
had a gown as fine as this apple green muslin, with its
modest robe front that fastened just below her bosom.
From its high neck and long plain sleeves, there was
nothing anyone could object to…especially not her
exacting aunt.

"Perfect for an afternoon call." Lady Timmons acknowledged Daphne's choice with a nod of appreciation.

Daphne smiled slightly, then slid alongside the wall
and took up a place on the window seat at the far side
of the room, muttering, "This will never do" as she
surveyed the crowded parlor.

Meanwhile Harriet followed close on her heels and
settled into the spot next to Daphne, her eyes bright as
she too took in the setting.

Meanwhile Lady Timmons shooed a sulky Eloisa
off the end of the settee. She patted the cushion and
smiled up at Tabitha. "Come sit here, so you will be
the first person Mr. Barkworth sees when he enters
the room."

And as if on cue, the doorbell jangled, and all eyes
turned in that general direction.

Tabitha hadn't even time to ask what scandal Lady
Peevers had been reporting, but it was the first subject from Lady Ancil's lips when the butler showed
her into the room.

"We came at once!" the lady announced, "to see
how poor Miss Timmons is faring."

The lady entered the room like a great hen, all feathers and fluff, so it was hard to discern her expression

until she settled into a chair, quickly vacated by Edwina. Only then could Tabitha see that it appeared she'd been crying.

She shared a glance with Harriet and Daphne. *Whatever have I done now?*

How would we know? they both seemed to answer with slight shrugs of their shoulders.

"Did you say Miss Timmons?" Lady Peevers blurted out. "How utterly like you, Lady Ancil, to be worried about our dearest Miss Timmons when this must be such a trial to *you*." Her ladyship paused for a moment, then added, "And Barkworth as well."

Lady Ancil fluttered a handkerchief in the air as if it was all she could manage.

Barkworth, who up until now had been standing stock still in the doorway, came striding into the fray. If Tabitha didn't know better, she would almost swear the man had been posed, awaiting the perfect moment for his entrance.

And Lady Peevers's heartfelt declaration proved to be just that. When the lady caught sight of him, she drew her own handkerchief to her bosom. "Ah, Barkworth! You brave, dear man!"

But Barkworth had eyes only for Tabitha. "My dear Miss Timmons, the news of your scandal has not left you overwrought, has it?" He dropped to one knee and took her hand in his, his earnest expression pinned on her own startled one.

"I fear I don't know of any scandal," she managed, glancing first at Daphne and then at Harriet.

"*No flowers*," Harriet mouthed.

Indeed, the man had arrived without so much as a petal.

Tabitha cursed not Barkworth but Preston for this. She wouldn't have noticed if the duke hadn't told her how all this courting was done.

Barkworth still clung to her hand, though his attention was fixed on Lady Peevers. "You haven't told her?"

"I was just getting to the matter," the lady replied, picking at the lace on the sleeves of her gown, her nose wrinkled at the loss of this opportunity.

"Whatever is amiss?" Daphne asked.

Lady Ancil spared her a glance and then turned back to the company at hand. "It is being said that the Duke of Preston singled out Miss Timmons for his attentions last night because he thought her quite beneath him—beyond society's cares. He meant it as a snub."

Tabitha plucked her hand free of Barkworth's grasp. "What nonsense!"

"Not at all," Barkworth corrected. "The evidence is overwhelming."

Lady Peevers nodded. "He danced with you and the daughters of several rather unremarkable families."

"Save for Lady Pamela," Eloisa pointed out.

"That was Lady Juniper's doing," Lady Peevers avowed. "She thinks to make a match, but Preston's actions said quite clearly last night he has no intention of setting up a nursery."

There were nods of understanding all around the room, save for Tabitha and her companions.

It made no sense to her. Whyever would Preston's choice of her as a dance partner be considered a snub?

Barkworth picked up her hand again. "Be brave, Miss Timmons. I am sure my uncle will see fit to give his approval to our match despite this terrible insult to the Barkworth name."

"Four hundred years of propriety," Lady Ancil was saying. "Four hundred years of unblemished and untarnished honor, and it all ends like this."

"I am afraid I do not understand how my dancing with the Duke of Preston could injure the Barkworth name," Tabitha ventured. Truly, it wasn't as if the man had ruined her.

At least not last night.

"Truly, I don't see the insult either," Daphne ventured. "They merely danced."

Cousin Eloisa just shook her head, appalled to have such dim-witted company to endure.

"It is not the dancing," Lady Peevers began, "though I daresay the duke held Miss Timmons far too close, but I fear I am a bit old-fashioned over these things—"

"The point is not the dancing," Lady Timmons interjected, "but the company he kept last night. No one save the lowest of society will dance with him, so by singling you out, he has shown one and all that you are not worthy. He meant it as an insult."

"An insult?" Harriet shook her head. "That isn't it at all." All eyes turned toward her, and ever the Hathaway, she stood her ground. "The duke is trying to amend his standing in society. That is why he chose Tabitha."

"Wherever would you get such a peculiar notion?" Lady Peevers demanded.

"From Lord Roxley," Harriet said, her cheeks pinking a bit. "He says the Duke of Preston is trying to rehabilitate his reputation and was dancing with Tabitha because she is the proper daughter of a respectable vicar."

The company gathered in the room looked around at each other as if weighing this information—each appearing to measure the notion that the *on dit* of the day wasn't the scandal that they believed it to be.

But then again this *was* society, and the notion that Harriet had the right of it and it wasn't the grand iniquity they were making it out to be just didn't suit.

Where was the gossip to be found in such a noble and respectable notion?

Tabitha watched in dismay as each of them shook their heads and refused to believe that Preston could possibly seek to reform his reputation.

Then she realized something else: it should be her defending Preston, not Harriet.

Oh, he was all the things they were making him out to be—rakish, disgraceful, ruinous. But Tabitha couldn't help but remember the pain in his eyes as he'd spoken of his mother and father...or how he had shared the last piece of apple tart...and taught her to dance.

There was more to the Duke of Preston than the reprobate ne'er-do-well that most thought him to be. Yet...if she were to explain this, then she would also have to confess to how she knew such intimate things about him.

And that would be as ruinous as his kiss—if not more so.

"Ridiculous, Miss Hathaway," Lady Peevers declared. "Truly, I would think that Lady Essex would have disabused you of any inclination toward listening to a single word that reprobate nephew of hers has to say."

"He has insulted Miss Timmons and by extension our very family," Lady Ancil said, shaking her head and looking to be on the verge of tears.

"You shan't call him out, will you, Mr. Barkworth?" Harriet asked, having slid off the window seat and come to stand closer to Tabitha.

The suggestion silenced everyone in the room, including Lady Ancil and her weeping.

Tabitha knew Harriet was only teasing—she was, wasn't she?—but everyone else in the room took her question to heart.

Barkworth blinked and gaped, looking quite like a fish out of water.

"Defend your beloved's honor?" Harriet prodded like only a Hathaway could. "Isn't that how it is done by gentlemen of honor?"

Barkworth released his grasp on Tabitha's hand and rose, tugging his jacket back into place, his broad shoulders drawing into a taut line. "I suppose I—" he began, each word being carefully and slowly issued.

And Tabitha knew exactly why.

For before he could completely commit to Harriet's ridiculous dare, the matrons in the room burst into a cacophony of protest.

"Never!"

"Scandalous!"

"Think of our name! Of your uncle's good opinion."

That was enough for Barkworth. He held up his hand to stave off their fears, smiling kindly at them. "I shall endeavor to face this trial without allowing my temper to get the better of my good judgment and your delicate sensibilities, ladies."

Harriet's nose wrinkled at such a reply and she returned to the window seat, muttering something that ended with an expression she'd probably picked up from one of her brothers.

Lily-livered...

Daphne had also moved during all this hullaballoo and now stood by the door. "If you will excuse me," she said, dipping her head to the company. "I forgot a letter I must answer before it is too late to post it."

She slipped from the room, and Tabitha—for once—envied her friend's constant and demanding correspondence. It offered an excuse to leave, of which Tabitha had none.

And right now she wanted to escape this charade of a visit more than anything else.

"No more talk of duels and scandals," Lady Ancil declared, sending a sniffy little glance of accusation in Harriet's direction. "I would rather talk of tomorrow night."

At this, Barkworth brightened. "Yes, yes, we haven't come bearing entirely bad news...though this scandal is a terrible shame—"

Again a chorus of head nods answered him. "I knew by nuncheon that quick action would be required to nip this all in the bud, so I sought my uncle's counsel."

"Dear, wise Lord Grately," Lady Ancil added sagely.

"Yes, quite so," Barkworth agreed. "And my uncle, the esteemed Marquess of Grately, thinks—nay, *knows*—that the best thing to do would be to go forward and announce our engagement tomorrow night at his annual soirée, as we've planned all along."

"An announcement?" Tabitha managed, having the sense of the air rushing from the room. "So soon?"

Whatever did he mean, "as we've planned all along"? Who'd planned? She looked over at her aunt and found Lady Timmons avoiding her gaze.

"Why of course," Barkworth told her. "When society sees—*good society*, I must say, not that low assembly of *cits* Lady Knolles passes off as acceptable—that my uncle, the Marquess of Grately, approves not only of our match but of you, my dear Miss Timmons, it will stop the veriest hint of scandal on the good name of Barkworth."

There were smiles all around, as if that settled the matter.

Not to Tabitha's way of thinking. She noted that he'd said "the good name of Barkworth," not hers. Not the good name of Miss Tabitha Timmons.

"I had thought we'd come to an agreement, Mr. Barkworth," she ventured, "that before we announce a betrothal—"

—we might get to know one another.

Lady Timmons looked ready to give her a wigging, and so, for that matter, did the always opinionated Lady Peevers, but neither lady could get a word in before a terrible discord rose up outside the closed door of the sitting room.

To be specific, a chorus of barking and yelping, followed by a large crash.

Mr. Muggins.

Tabitha flinched, for this disruption (not to mention possible damage) would only bait her aunt's temper further.

Daphne came headlong into the room. "Tabitha, you must come at once," she said. "I fear Mr. Muggins is in a state." To prove the point, Mr. Muggins invaded the room, barking madly and blindly running in circles.

"Goodness!" Lady Ancil exclaimed, clutching her reticule to her chest as if she thought the house had been invaded by an entire block of rushers.

Holding out the dog's lead, Daphne said with a bright smile, "Perhaps a walk in the park will bring him to his senses. You and Mr. Barkworth could take him together."

Tabitha lunged to grab hold of her dog even as she shot a wry look at her friend. "I can't imagine what has him in such a state."

Of course the fact that Daphne had gone upstairs and put on the new feather-trimmed pelisse she'd bought recently and had not yet dared to wear might have something to do with it.

"Please, Tabitha," Lady Timmons pleaded as she watched Lady Ancil pale and waver in her seat.

Barkworth had retreated to behind the open door and peered out at the scene before him with a look of open fear.

Oh, bother! Tabitha finally caught hold of Mr. Muggins's collar, then grabbed the lead from Daphne and snapped it on. "Whatever are you doing?" she whispered to her friend.

"Giving you a chance to be courted."

Quite frankly, Tabitha thought, looking at her cowering nearly betrothed and thinking of how Preston's blossoms had left her all tangled up inside, she'd had quite enough of being courted for one day.

Once outside, Barkworth paused on the top step, looking down at Tabitha and Mr. Muggins awaiting him on the sidewalk, eyeing her dog with both an eye of disdain and a bit of fear.

Tabitha heaved a sigh. "Shall we go to the park?"

"However shall we get there? I have sent my carriage on," he said.

"I was thinking more of walking." Tabitha tightened her hold on the leash. Off to the right a bit, Daphne's maid waited, watching this exchange with wide eyes.

"Walking?" Barkworth glanced up and down the sidewalk as if it were a foreign lane.

"Yes, that is the prescribed method of taking Mr. Muggins for a walk. Besides, it is a lovely day."

He eyed her as if he couldn't quite determine if she was teasing or not. "How quaint," he said, finally venturing down the steps, where he held out his arm for her. Once her hand was atop his sleeve, he smiled blandly and turned in the direction of Hyde Park.

"There isn't anything improper in taking a walk, is there?" she asked. "Anything to impugn your reputation? Your good Barkworth name?"

Barkworth paused and drew himself up. "Miss Timmons, your concerns do you credit. You will make an admirable marchioness one day and a most worthy addition to the Barkworth family tree."

Tabitha forced a smile on her lips, while Mr. Muggins tugged at the lead, if only to prod them both into continuing toward the park. "The Barkworths take great store in their unblemished reputation, I gather. Four centuries, I think your mother said?"

"An excellent memory, Miss Timmons," he declared. "Yes, it has been the honor and the privilege of the Barkworths to have served their king—"

"And a few queens," she noted.

"Yes, yes, under those necessary circumstances," he agreed. "The Barkworths have never wavered in their faithful service."

"No scandals, no wild cousin to blight the family name, no hints of piracy or illicit affairs?" she teased.

Barkworth's eyes widened. "Most certainly not. We have done our duty with the utmost discretion."

"During Henry the Eighth's reforms? Which side did the family take? Reform or keep the old church?"

"We followed our king."

"And later, when Cromwell cut off Charles's head?"

"Difficult times, but we remained loyal to England."

Which Tabitha took to mean that they had walked a fine line between both sides—Puritan and Royalist—and landed with Charles the Second when he returned in triumph.

"How very inspiring," she said when she could think of no other response.

They continued to walk along, Mr. Muggins behaving with more decorum than she'd ever known him to possess.

"I do say this is an excellent way to be seen," he said after passing a matron and her daughter returning from their own stroll. "Did you see the way Lady Colicott just cast an approving glance in your direction? She has the most discerning air about her. Yes, yes, I can see the advantage of walking."

"I thought we could use this time to see if we suit," Tabitha suggested, which seemed far more important than Lady Colicott's good opinion.

"Suit?" Barkworth repeated, his brow furrowing. The notion was apparently as foreign to the man as walking.

"Yes," she said, trying not to sound impatient. "So we might know if we'll be amenable marriage partners."

The light finally dawned on Barkworth's handsome face and he laughed. "Miss Timmons, you have some very quaint notions. Whyever wouldn't we suit?"

Tabitha could think of a hundred reasons at the moment, but she held her tongue, thinking yet again of Daphne's caution not to jump to conclusions about the man.

See how wrong you were about Preston.

She might have been wrong about him being someone's by-blow, but at least he sent flowers.

"My uncle said you are a solicitor?" Tabitha asked, trying to do her best to "get to know" this man her family was pressing her to wed and put Preston and his whimsical bluebells as far from her thoughts as possible. "I hope I am not taking your time away from important matters."

"No, no," he said, waving his hand. "I have very little to do with actual matters."

She glanced sideways at him. "So you do not work?"

"Work?" Barkworth paled at the word. "Why, of course not. I only studied the law at my uncle's insistence. He said I needed something to keep me occupied until…until…"

His unfortunate passing… Tabitha could almost hear him saying.

"So however do you spend your time?" she pressed. Truly, she couldn't imagine a man without some sort of occupation—thinking of her father and the constant duties of the vicarage, or Harriet's father and his vigilance with his estate. Even Lord Roxley made the occasional visit to Foxgrove to ensure that the house and grounds were properly maintained—much to his aunt's indignation that she couldn't see to the property herself.

"Spend my time? Well, as most gentlemen do, I suppose," he answered.

"However is that?"

He looked rather blankly at her, like he'd never considered what it was he did with his days. "The usual pursuits. I visit my uncle regularly."

"To learn his business and help with the management of his estates, I presume," Tabitha remarked, thinking that was why his uncle had insisted Barkworth study the law.

"No, not at all. My uncle has a steward for those mundane matters. I cannot appear to be too interested in his fortunes, for that would be rather presumptive."

For a mere presumptive heir, Tabitha wanted to reply, but she doubted Barkworth would see the humor in it.

"I call upon him merely to inquire as to his health," Barkworth said, as if that made his intentions all the more noble and honorable.

"Yes, most considerate," she said before biting her lips together, which was better than making the remark she longed to let slip past her lips.

Hallo, Uncle, however is your heart today?

"You don't live with his lordship?"

Barkworth shook his head. "Heavens no. That would be—"

"Presumptive," Tabitha finished.

"Exactly," he said. "Mother and I have the use of a house on Foley Place. It is comfortable enough—most likely quite grand compared with a country vicarage, though nothing like the grandeur of my uncle's house on Hanover Square, but I never complain. At least not to my uncle."

"No, whyever should you, when you are comfortable?"

He glanced over at her. "Yes, well, Mother finds it a bit confining and longs for a larger residence. With the prospect of our marriage, she's been on the prowl for a new address."

"She plans to move out?"

Barkworth's eyes widened with horror. "Of course not! With the addition of you to our small, but happy, family, we will most decidedly need more space, especially once, and I daresay I hope I don't offend your delicate sensibilities, we *increase* our happiness—" He waggled his brows at her.

Oh, good heavens, he means children. Tabitha suddenly saw a passel of handsome, albeit useless, Barkworths tugging at her skirt.

"Be that as it may, Mother says that with our circumstances being greatly improved due to your uncle's generosity—"

Translation: *With the infusion of your uncle's fortune into my hands, I won't be so completely constrained by my uncle's meager charity and general lack of munificence.*

Oh, good heavens. This cleared up so many of Tabitha's questions as to why Barkworth might agree to this marriage.

He clearly wanted it. Nay, he *needed* it.

Then he proved her supposition by saying, "I know Mother has already visited a house close to Grosvenor

Square. On Brook Street, I believe. The owner is in ill health and wants to rent it out, but Mother thought that while it was most suitably located, it was in such ill repair that no lady would deign to set her foot inside it, let alone inhabit it."

"She's already been house-hunting?" Speaking of presumption! "Certainly the house your uncle has provided is both economical and well appointed. I hardly see the need—"

"Miss Timmons, you are a delightful surprise. I suppose your simple sensibilities are the result of having lived your entire life in the country—and in a vicarage of all places—so much so that you will find my humble abode a castle in comparison. But by London standards…" He patted her hand, which still rested on his sleeve, and smiled at her.

Tabitha pasted a bland smile on her face to match the one on his, for there seemed no point in reminding the man that she had as yet to agree to marry him.

Why was it everyone just assumed she had no objections to this match?

Because it will save you from a life as your aunt's scullery maid…leave you secure for the remainder of your days…because this is how it is done.

All of which were sensible, reasonable reasons, ones she had agreed with when she'd come to London for the single purpose of making this match.

At least it had all made sense until Preston had come along. Now she found the heels of her boots starting to dig in with all sorts of objections.

"What about a house in the country," Tabitha suggested. "It would be ever so economical and give your mother all the room she longs for."

As in a cottage at the far end of the estate, she could almost hear Harriet say.

"The country? The country, you say? Oh, Miss Timmons, that would never do," he said, shaking his head emphatically.

"But Mr. Muggins would be much happier in the country, as well as I. I do so miss my garden and—"

"Oh, Miss Timmons, how you like to tease! Next you will be suggesting that we live out in the wilds. Wherever is it you are from?"

"Kempton. The village of Kempton," she said, wishing for a moment she could whisk him off to the *John Stakes* for a pint of ale. And a few cautionary tales about marrying a local girl…

"A village? I thought from my aunt's description it was naught but a wayside."

Tabitha bristled to hear her beloved home so maligned, but she again gave Barkworth the benefit of the doubt, since it seemed he had never lived anywhere but London.

And she was correct.

"I have never much cared for the country," he said. "Far too…oh, what is the word? Rural! Yes, that is it. The country is far too rural."

"But I rather like the country," she said. "And Mr. Muggins will be much happier there."

"Then it is probably best that he return there," Barkworth told her, eyeing the great terrier with nothing less than suspicion. "For as you saw earlier, Mother has a great fear of dogs. She much prefers cats—she has four at the moment."

Four cats? In a tiny house. With Mr. Muggins chasing them about all day and Barkworth's bland smile to greet her each and every morning.

Oh, this marriage was becoming more and more intolerable with each passing moment.

If it lasted, she mused, thinking of Agnes Stakes and how her wedding night had ended.

Tabitha couldn't help herself; she smiled up at Barkworth.

"Whatever had that animal in such a fever earlier?" Barkworth commented. "He appears quite amenable now."

"Feathers."

"What?"

"Feathers," she repeated. "Mr. Muggins deplores feathers. They quite drive him mad. And Daphne was wearing her feathered pelisse." Tabitha paused for a moment. "I daresay she forgot."

"My mother has no love for this fashion of putting feathers on everything."

"Then she and Mr. Muggins will get along famously."

The man looked down at her, his brow furrowed once again. "But I thought you quite understood. Mother does not approve of dogs."

She had meant her breezy words as a jest, but from Barkworth's puzzled expression she could see it had quite passed him by—like a feather on the wind.

Oh, dear, this was not going well at all.

How pleased Harriet would be and how crushed Daphne would be after all her noble efforts.

Still, Tabitha persisted. "Wouldn't we be able to spend part of the year in the country and part in London, like so many other families do?"

Barkworth shook his head. "I could never be so far removed from my uncle." He continued on, "By the time you are my marchioness and we move into Number 5, you will find its grandeur your due and all thoughts of the country gone." He paused for a moment. "Not that I long for my uncle's unfortunate passing, mind you."

"No, of course not," she said as gravely as she could manage, all the while her lips twitching traitorously.

"But one must always be braced for the unfortunate day, which will sadden so many," he said in a manner that sounded as if it had been repeated too many times to make it truly meant.

They walked along in silence for a while, Tabitha musing silently to herself. *Give him a chance.*

Make a list of his qualifications, Daphne would suggest.

Tabitha started right in. *Well, he's mannerly. Attentive. Handsome. Well turned-out.* She snuck another glance at him—all done up in the first stare of men's fashions, from his high collar points to his grand cravat.

Perhaps too well turned-out.

He walked in a rather straight, uncomfortable fashion, as if he were trussed. In a corset. Like the one Aunt Allegra wore.

Tabitha closed her eyes for a moment and did her best to scrub that image off her list. Then she went back to the first entries. *Mannerly. Attentive. Handsome.*

Then the others came.

Dull. Utterly without a sense of humor.

Far too attached to his mother, she could almost hear Preston adding.

She abandoned her list in hopes that conversation might add some more useful items. "So once you've called on your uncle, what do you do?"

Barkworth's jaw worked back and forth as he labored over this question. "Attend my mother as she makes her afternoon calls—which, of course, you will do once our happy joining has been completed."

Happy joining? Tabitha repressed the shudder that threatened to run down her limbs, for when compared with the breathless desires that Preston had brought forth in her, "happy joining" sounded so lackluster.

So utterly dull.

She just couldn't imagine Barkworth taking her in his arms like Preston had, kissing her as if it were his right, his due, that he would stroke her into that mindless, panting oblivion…

Tabitha stopped herself right there. No, no, that wasn't helping in the least.

In fact, all she could think of was that with Barkworth as her husband, her life would be spent just as restrained as Mr. Muggins on his leash.

They came to Park Lane and waited for a break in the traffic to cross over to Hyde Park.

This close to the grass and trees, Mr. Muggins tugged at the lead, bounding up and down, ready to find more feathers to bedevil.

"Now whatever is the matter?" Barkworth asked, pushing her hand off his sleeve and stepping back.

"He misses the country," Tabitha said by way of explanation, as Mr. Barkworth looked askance at Mr.

Muggins's exuberance. "He is used to being allowed to freely roam."

"I can't see how that would be a good notion," he said, glancing around at the busy paths ahead. It seemed a good part of the *ton* was out taking the afternoon air.

"It is different in the country," she explained.

"Apparently so," Barkworth said, nodding at an opening in the traffic and eyeing Mr. Muggins with dismay as the dog leapt forward, towing Tabitha with him.

"There is no doubt that animal must be returned to the country when we marry," Barkworth called out as he dodged his way through the traffic, his hesitation putting him between a freight wagon and a large barouche.

Tabitha had no chance to reply before they were interrupted.

"Ah, Barkworth, is that you?" a lady said, holding up a quizzing glass to examine them both. "And is this the lovely creature I have heard so much of today?"

"Lady Gudgeon! Yes indeed, it is. This is my soon-to-be betrothed, Miss Timmons. I daresay I can impose upon you to keep our pending engagement a secret?" Barkworth winked broadly at her.

The lady cackled with delight. "Barkworth, not a word shall pass my lips."

They both laughed, and Tabitha suspected that it was because the lady could no more keep a secret than she could go out without her bonnet atop her head.

A bonnet, Tabitha noted, sporting a flurry of bright red feathers.

* * *

"Do you mean to tell me that we are skulking about the park," Roxley protested, "not to test out these nags as you claimed earlier, but in hopes of encountering Miss Timmons?" The earl blew out a large huff. "My good man, have you lost all your wits?"

Well, when Roxley put it that way...

"I just thought I might apologize—"

Roxley let out a loud guffaw. "Send 'round a note."

Preston's jaw worked back and forth. *A note.* He'd thought of including one with the bluebells he'd sent over.

Dear Miss Timmons, I daresay the news of your engagement to that horse's rump made my behavior last night less than...

No, no, that would never do.

"Roxley, she can't marry that idiot," he insisted. "You heard your friend last night."

"My friend? Oh, yes, right, Chaunce. We went to White's...didn't we?" Roxley closed his eyes and pressed his fingers to his forehead. "I'd nearly managed to forget."

Preston hadn't.

Mr. Chauncy Hathaway had been a veritable font of information as to Tabby's situation.

That she'd only just met Barkworth. That the marriage was tied to her inheriting her uncle's vast fortune. That Barkworth's uncle, the Marquess of Grately, had borrowed heavily from Tabby's uncle, and in exchange for excusing the debts, had offered his nephew as collateral...if, that is, Barkworth managed to inherit.

Then Tabby could become the Marchioness of Grately. A lofty rise for a mere vicar's daughter.

"But whyever would her uncle force her into this?" Preston had asked the knowledgeable Mr. Hathaway as they'd sat in a secluded corner at White's. Roxley had wandered off once he'd caught sight of a fellow who owed him money, digging through his pockets for the vowel and muttering how the man's recent string of good luck would now be his good fortune.

"It all goes back to Miss Timmons's mother," Chaunce had explained. "She was a great beauty, and when she came to Town, she had her pick of suitors. She could have been a duchess if she'd wanted. But she spurned them all—married plain old Reverend Archibald Timmons with his vicarage in Kempton and left London a happy bride, much to her ambitious brother's wrath."

"That explains her uncle's motives, but whatever does Miss Timmons stand to gain from all this?" For what little of Tabby Preston did know, he had to suspect she took after her mother and would be more inclined to follow her heart than make an advantageous match for purely mercenary reasons.

"Escape," Chaunce had said, draining his cup, which Preston had more than happily refilled. "With both her parents gone, she's at the mercy of her relations. None of them wanted her when she was orphaned, but Lord Rawcliffe, who holds the living, made it clear to her uncle, the Reverend Bernard Timmons, he could have the vicarage—a far better posting than the one he was holding at the time—but only if he and his wife took in their niece."

"So she got to stay in her home."

Chaunce had sputtered over his brandy. "Hardly a home. Oh, they kept her. But only because it saved them the cost of a scullery maid and the vicar the wages of a secretary. Poor Tabitha's done nothing but scrub grates and keep the vicarage records for the last three years."

Preston had recalled her hands—how rough and calloused they'd been when he had pulled her to her feet for their dance that night at the inn. He'd noticed it then but had dismissed the notion, wary of wading in too deep.

A rather ironic notion now.

"Marriage to Barkworth—poor fool that he is—will be a vast improvement for her, though Harry doesn't see it that way. She wants Tabitha to cry off and come live at the Pottage."

Preston had glanced up. "Harry? The Pottage?"

"Harriet. My sister. The Pottage is my father's estate." Chaunce had paused for a moment as a tall man in a dark coat had passed the table, and he'd only continued once the fellow had been well past. Roxley had said Chaunce worked for the Home Office—which might explain his penchant for turning even an ordinary conversation into something resembling skullduggery. "Harry has been trying to convince Tabitha to come live with us for years. But she's too proud—Tabitha, that is."

"Your sister has a good heart."

Chaunce had laughed. "You wouldn't say that if she was your sister. She's an incurable busybody is what she is."

"No, no, Miss Hathaway should be commended for looking out for her friends."

"You are being polite. Harry is an impudent minx. Always has been a terrible handful. Much to my mother's despair, she's turned out like all the rest of those Kempton wags and sees no point in marriage."

"The curse," Preston had said with a nod.

"Utter nonsense," Chaunce had said with a wave of his hand. "But try to tell the citizens of Kempton that their singular claim to fame is naught but superstitious rot."

"Still, Miss Timmons could cry off," Preston had posed.

"I don't think her uncles would let her. Sir Mauris and his brother have always wanted to extend their reach into society. Their niece being a marchioness will go a long way to improve their standings."

"If she reaches her majority, which I assume she's nearly there, couldn't she take her inheritance and be rid of the lot of them?"

"Harry says she must marry Barkworth to inherit. At least that is what the will supposedly says," Chaunce had said, his brow furrowed.

Preston had sat back and studied the man. "Supposedly?"

He'd shaken his head. "I'm a lawyer by training. Such a will makes no sense. Say she does cry off, or Barkworth sticks his spoon in the wall before he can marry her—where does the money go then? There has to be a contingency for such things. There is always a contingency when it comes to money."

Preston had looked up from his glass. "What does the will say?"

Chaunce had smiled slightly, a sign that he'd approved of the duke's acumen. "That I don't know. And I would guess that neither does Miss Timmons. But I can guess who does."

"Who?"

"Barkworth. Grately. Her uncles. They all have much to gain from seeing this wedding go forward and will hardly be forthcoming."

"No. If it is as you say, none of them are likely to be overly fond of the notion of Miss Timmons crying off," Preston had mused.

"Exactly," Chaunce had agreed.

"Then how would I discover the truth of the matter, short of taking Barkworth by the scruff of his neck and shaking it out of him?"

Mr. Hathaway had grinned. "While I would love to see that, you might be better served considering a saying we have in the Home Office."

"Which is?"

"Go to the source."

"The will!" Preston had grinned, because he'd been able to see from the sly tip of Mr. Hathaway's smile that he already had a notion as to how to do just that.

Roxley had chosen this moment to come stumbling back to the table, grinning from ear to ear. "Collected from Osbourne. Wily fellow. Nearly gave me the slip."

"And now you can repay me," Preston had suggested.

"Hardly." The earl had waved off the notion. "'Sides, already put it all down on a wager over some engagement. They say Grately is going to announce it night after next." Roxley had reached for an empty glass and filled it from the bottle on the table. "As if any woman of sense would agree to marry his nephew."

"Roxley, you demmed fool," Preston had said, shaking his head. "They are wagering on Miss Timmons and Barkworth."

The earl had glanced from Preston to Chaunce and then back at Preston. "Good God! I'm done for. I wagered the chit would cry off."

Preston had turned back to the matters at hand. "You have a plan?"

"Yes." Chaunce had nudged his cup forward. "One of the advantages of having a busybody sister with an excellent memory is that she ferreted the name of Winston Ludlow's solicitors out of Sir Mauris, hoping that I might discover something to save Tabitha."

"Sounds like Harry," Roxley had added, waving his glass in a sloppy fashion so that the brandy had nearly topped the rim. "Bossy bit of muslin. No offense, Chaunce."

"None taken."

As for Preston, he liked the Hathaways more and more, especially when Mr. Hathaway had continued, "As luck would have it, I have a good friend who works in the law offices of Kimball, Dunnington, and Pennyman. And better, he owes me a favor."

This time it was Roxley who had sat up. "Are you two plotting to keep Miss Timmons from marrying Barkworth?"

Preston had shaken his head. "Whyever do you think you introduced us?"

"Ah, yes," Roxley had said. "Demmed convenient now that I've got a monkey wagered on all this."

"You'll help?" Preston had asked Roxley's friend.

Chauncy Hathaway had laughed, crossing his arms over his chest. "Your Grace, you obviously haven't a sister."

"No, but I have an aunt…"

* * *

"My aunt is going to be in ill humor if she discovers I am helping you meddle in Miss Timmons's affairs," Roxley said, his hand still pressed to his forehead as if he could stem the effects of the previous night.

"Thought you wanted to win your wager," Preston reminded him, scanning the expanse of the park for any sight of Tabby.

"I do," Roxley conceded. "But I have to consider whether it is worth winning five hundred pounds only to suffer my aunt ringing a peel over my head for the next year...or two."

"You'll manage."

"I still don't see how Miss Tabitha's future happiness is your concern," the earl pointed out, his hat tipped low over his forehead, his arms folded over his chest and his legs stuck out in front of him. "Not unless you've fallen in love with the gel."

"Nonsense!" Preston shot back, a little too quickly, a little too emphatically.

Wisely, Roxley said nothing more, slanting a glance at Preston, then giving a small shake of his head, as if the surgeon had just pronounced him on his last legs.

Preston straightened the reins. He didn't love Tabby. Not in the least. But he could no more force that denial past his lips than he could have stopped himself from coming to the park today.

And he hadn't sent her those demmed bluebells— which he'd ruined his best pair of boots tromping across a ditch to gather—because he cared. No, he'd sent them because he knew Barkworth wouldn't.

No, he had to see her for an entirely different reason.

He'd promised to be her friend, vowed to help her—even if she was hardly appreciative of his "meddling."

As her friend, he had to tell her that she might not have to marry her Mr. Barkfool. That if she, the woman who had disavowed ever getting married, was going to change her mind, she better demmed well be doing it for the right reasons.

Because she loved the man beyond all reason.

And there was no way that his Tabby, his determined, headstrong, opinionated Tabby, would ever fall in love with the likes of Mr. Reginald Barkworth.

He glanced over at Roxley, who was staring at him with a droll, knowing expression.

Demmit! He was not in love with her, he wanted to tell his friend.

"Since you are going to persist in this folly, you might want to look over there," Roxley said, pointing a finger in the direction of one of the far paths. "That appears to be your quarry, pinned between her intended—which, if you haven't forgotten, means the man she will be marrying—and…" Roxley sat up, then leaned forward, squinting at the matronly figure beside Tabby. "Lady Gudgeon." He shuddered. "I daresay Miss Timmons could desperately use your influence—the company she currently keeps is deplorable."

Preston pulled the horses to a stop and gazed across the park. Yes, Roxley was right. There was Barkworth, as well as Lady Gudgeon.

But in truth, his gaze only flitted over these others, for there was Tabby. His Tabby.

Not that he was in love with her. Not in the least. He sat back and guided the carriage over to a spot where he would be out of the way.

"Preston," Roxley said, nudging him out of his reverie—quite literally, for the earl was jabbing him with his elbow. "It appears your Miss Timmons has need of you."

The duke glanced up. "Why do you say that?"

The earl nodded across the park to where Tabitha's unruly mutt was now chasing after a surprisingly fleet-footed Lady Gudgeon.

Woof, woof, woof, the beast bellowed as he practically danced after the matron in great, bounding leaps.

And not far behind dashed a familiar figure, hat askew, a lead dangling from her hand.

"Ah, Preston, if I do say so myself, I think Miss Timmons might be your perfect match."

"Why do you say that?" the duke asked, sitting up and tugging at his cravat. Suddenly his hastily tied Mailcoach had gotten too tight. That, and it appeared he was going to have to make a dash for it.

Roxley laughed. "She appears as prone to scandal as you are."

Preston ignored his jest. Instead he shoved the reins into Roxley's hands, then jumped down from his seat. Surveying the scene, he said, "Where the devil is Barkworth? Doesn't that fool see she needs help?"

Roxley rose up in protest. "Whatever for? That's Lady Gudgeon being chased by one of hell's hounds." He grinned. "Always wanted to see that gossipy goat get a bit of comeuppance."

"Roxley—" Preston scolded as he started off.

The earl was not finished. He called after his friend, "When you do catch her, Preston, will you do me a favor?"

Preston paused and glanced over his shoulder. "What?"

"Ask Miss Timmons where I can get a hound just like that one. Might keep the aunts at bay."

Chapter 12

There is always a moment in one's life that is played over and over in the mind, filled with "if only I had—" and "why didn't I—"

The day Lady Gudgeon went running headlong through Hyde Park, screaming bloody murder as Mr. Muggins gave eager and well-meant chase, was one such moment for Tabitha.

It wasn't but a blink of an eye between the time Tabitha spotted the feathers in the woman's bonnet and tightened her grasp on Mr. Muggins's lead, and the Irish terrier, keen of eye and determined of spirit, spotted his quarry atop Lady Gudgeon's head.

The first delighted *woof* brought the lady's endless chatter to a stop. Then Mr. Muggins, a sporting dog if ever there was one, lunged forward.

It could be argued that he'd warned the old girl.

Tabitha hung on and pulled as hard as she could, yanking Mr. Muggins back, but the lead snapped and Mr. Muggins lunged forward even as Tabitha fell backwards, slamming hard into Barkworth's chest. The man, in his tight breeches and even tighter jacket, hadn't the nimble freedom to keep himself upright, let alone both of them, and they fell into a tangled heap.

After a few moments of shock, with Barkworth gaping up at her and she down at him as she lay sprawled across his chest with their noses almost touching, her nearly betrothed unceremoniously shoved her off, sending Tabitha rolling into the grass.

Meanwhile, the dog didn't waste any time. He whirled left and then right, then, finding his quarry, once again gave her loud warning.

Woof, woof, woof!

Lady Gudgeon took the dog's barking to heart. She turned and fled, scurrying away in all haste.

Tabitha sprang up and watched in horror as a delighted Mr. Muggins set off in hot pursuit, nipping at Lady Gudgeon's heels and leaping in the air in the off chance he might snag his feathered foe from atop her head.

Didn't this foolish woman have any idea of the danger she was in?

"Oh, no! No, Mr. Muggins! No!" Tabitha shouted to no avail.

Lady Gudgeon, for her part, put up a merry chase.

Tabitha gave the lady some credit. She could run.

And run the old girl did, dashing to and fro up the crowded path and then loping across the grass, darting through flower beds and around trees.

Not that she had any hope of escaping Mr. Muggins. The wretched terrier could chase after feathers until the cows were brought home.

"Get up, Barkworth!" Tabitha snapped. "We must stop Mr. Muggins."

Her esteemed almost-betrothed still lay on his back, his arms and legs pedaling in the air like those of an overturned beetle. "Ruined! Humiliated! Done for!" he complained as Daphne's maid struggled to hoist the man to his feet.

Giving up on him—good heavens, whatever had Uncle Winston been thinking in his choice?—Tabitha dashed off in pursuit, pushing through the gathered knots of ladies and gentlemen who had stopped to watch the spectacle.

Her dance with Preston the previous night would have nothing on this *on dit*.

"Excuse me...pardon me...oh, do move aside," she said as she pushed and shoved her way toward Mr. Muggins and Lady Gudgeon.

The poor lady had taken refuge atop a bench on a small knoll, and Mr. Muggins danced and barked in circles around her, having driven his quarry to ground.

Or rather, high ground.

Tabitha arrived, and she could swear her dog was grinning with pride.

"Help me! That beast has gone mad!" Lady Gudgeon pointed down at Mr. Muggins, clutching her reticule to her bosom with her other hand.

"My lady," Tabitha said, reaching for Mr. Muggins's collar but not quite catching it as the dog leapt out of reach, "it is your hat."

The woman stilled. "My hat? Why, it is of the first stare!"

"Yes, but it is what is making him misbehave."

The lady stilled and glared down from her perch. "A dog with opinions on fashion? Now I've heard everything."

"No, no," Tabitha told her. "It is the feathers. He thinks you have a bird on your hat. He's an Irish terrier—they are known for flushing birds."

"Irish!" the lady sniffed, looking askance at Mr. Muggins, who was now sitting—if you could call it that. His haunches barely touched the ground and he was all aquiver, watching her every move. "That explains the manners."

"Yes, but if you would but remove your hat—"

"Remove my hat? In public? Miss Timmons, I would rather—"

Mr. Muggins rose up and growled, inching closer to the bench, as if he finally realized he could get up there as well.

"Yes, yes, my hat," Lady Gudgeon agreed, plucking at the pins that held it in place. "I'll have you know, Miss Timmons, my opinion is highly regarded about Town as the final word in good standing"—*plunk, plunk,* came the pins—"and you have not gained mine this day. Quite the contrary." Having issued her decree, she finished it with a grand flourish of her arm that sent her hat flying well away from Mr. Muggins.

A bit of wind caught the whimsical creation, and it floated in the breeze like a kite. Mr. Muggins's gaze fixed on it hypnotically, as if he had known all along that this odd bird could fly.

Tabitha used the distraction to catch hold of his collar. She was just about to snap the lead back on when Mr. Muggins took off, pulling her over the edge of the little hill so she went tumbling headlong into a final disgraceful heap of petticoats and exposed ankles.

At least she hoped it was only her ankles on view as she teetered into darkness.

"Tabby? Tabby?" came a voice from far off. "Wake up!"

Tabitha resisted the urge to move closer to those rich, deep, masculine tones. They were far too tempting and whispered of dark desires.

Which she knew was completely true the moment she opened her eyes and found Preston's concerned and ever-so-handsome features peering down at her.

"There you are. Thank God, you're alive," he exclaimed, gathering her into his arms.

The warmth of his embrace, the all-too-familiar smell of his soap (which truly she had no right to be so familiar with) and that dizzy, heady desire that encircled her every time he held her came rushing to the forefront.

Nothing could have brought her round faster. Not even a dash of icy water or a cold compress.

Which was likely a more proper method.

But this was Preston, and he was brushing back her tangled curls and clucking his tongue over her disheveled state, leaving her with the desire to curl closer to his warmth and feign a continued state of drowsy disorder.

"Tabby, don't you dare close your eyes on me. Open them up and tell me that you are well!" he ordered, as if he had every right to hold her so, to bring her round to rights, to be his Tabby.

Which he didn't. Which she couldn't be. His.

His Tabby.

"Oh, no, you don't!" she exclaimed, scrambling out of his grasp and taking a defensive position in the grass just out of his reach. "Whatever are you doing?" She swiped her hair back and made a quick check to ensure her skirts were decent.

If only she could put her insides to rights so easily. They clamored and complained at being wrenched so savagely from Preston's grasp.

"What am I doing? Saving you, you ungrateful bit of muslin," he said, sitting back on his heels and grinning at her.

She wished he wouldn't do that. It gave his sharp, handsome features a boyish, roguish appearance that could tug at even the hardest of hearts.

"I don't recall asking you to interfere," she pointed out. "Quite the contrary, you promised me most faithfully that you would not interfere."

"Unless I was asked," he reminded her.

"Which I most decidedly did not," she told him. "I wasn't even conscious."

"Yes, but fortunately for me, your lips were moving, and I most definitely made out the slightest whisper," he said. "Something like, 'Oh, Preston.' Or perhaps it was 'Kiss me again, Preston.'" He leaned forward, puckering his lips.

"Oh, you insufferable boor!" she said, throwing Mr. Muggins's lead at him. "I did not need saving." Much to her chagrin, she went to get up and immediately collapsed in a pile. "Ow!" she exclaimed, reaching for her ankle.

And she'd been worried about it being exposed.

A shock of pain wrenched through her, leaving her gasping.

At the sound of her distress, Mr. Muggins froze from his frenzied mauling of Lady Gudgeon's hat. The feathers forgotten, the terrier trotted quickly to his mistress's side, settling down beside her.

Mr. Muggins had only downcast brown eyes and a submissive tip of his red grizzled head for her before he leaned forward and tentatively, gently licked her gloved hand.

"You wretched, terrible beast," she scolded, wagging her finger at Mr. Muggins and looking at Preston.

They both held that distinction as far as she was concerned, but never had she been so happy to see one of them.

"Let me see if it is broken," the duke said as he leaned forward and pushed her skirt away from her shoe.

Tabitha again tried to brush away his touch, but he just ignored her, examining the bone with practiced hands.

"Merely a sprain."

"This is dreadful," she replied, trying to flex her foot and flinching. "Oh, bother! How am I to get home now?"

"Like this," Preston said, rising up and towering over her like the Colossus she had first thought he might be when she'd seen him in Kempton.

Leaning over, he swooped her up into his arms and began to carry her across the park.

And if the sight of Mr. Muggins chasing Lady Gudgeon had sent the crowds into a glorious state of gossipy delight, it was all forgotten as Preston crested the hill with Miss Tabitha Timmons held firmly in his arms.

The knight-errant having rescued the lady.

More than one female spectator fluttered her fan approvingly, while just as many wore stony expressions of disapproval.

"Whatever were you doing in the park?" she asked. "Were you spying on me?"

Preston had the audacity to look affronted. "I was not. I have much better things to do with my time than skulk about after a vicar's daughter."

"Such as?"

He tucked his nose in the air, assuming a ducal demeanor. "Only you would ask such an impertinent question, Tabby."

"That's Miss Timmons to you, and it isn't a difficult question, Your Grace," she said. "Whatever were you doing in the park?"

"I happened by."

She made a "*Tut tut*," not believing a word of it.

"I will inform you," he said, "that I ride in the park nearly every day. So I might ask the same of you—whatever are you doing always hanging about the park when I am riding by? Someone might think you have set your cap to entrap me."

She gaped at him. "Of all the insufferable—"

Preston shook his head. "I warn you, others have tried and ended in ruin."

"Because Your Grace possesses no honor," she pointed out.

"No, no, Tabby, not at all. It is because I will not marry a woman I am not passionately in love with." Then he shifted her closer—scandalously closer—

and continued to parade across the park with her in his arms.

Such a statement might have meant nothing if it hadn't been for the way his piercing gaze tore away any thought of arguing with him.

Mr. Muggins had watched this exchange with avid eyes, his head swinging from one to the other, and now his curious expression rested on Tabitha, as if he breathlessly awaited his mistress's reply.

But whatever could she say? Her heart hammered in her chest and left her lungs empty of air.

Never in her life had she wanted something so far out of her reach…

To be *that* woman…the one that Preston would claim. Would love. Passionately.

For she knew all too well of the passion he was capable of provoking.

Barkworth arrived just then, out of breath and flustered. "Your Grace! Whatever are you doing with my… my…?"

"Your what, sir?" Preston stood his ground, his face stony with aristocratic bearing and Tabitha held firmly in his arms.

"My betrothed," Barkworth told him, managing to rise up to his full height and look the duke in the eye.

"I haven't heard any announcement," the duke replied. He looked to Tabitha for confirmation, but Barkworth didn't give her a chance to get a word in edgewise.

"It is a private matter and none of your concern. Now I suggest, nay, I insist, you put her down. Immediately." Her erstwhile nearly betrothed pointed at the ground between them.

* * *

"If you insist…" Preston did as ordered, tipping Tabitha gently onto her feet, and almost immediately she winced in pain. Having anticipated this, he immediately swooped her back up into his arms. "As you can see, Miss Timmons is injured." He pushed past Barkworth—annoying fellow, truly—and continued to where Roxley and his carriage waited.

"As am I," Barkworth called out, hobbling after them.

Preston threw a glance over his shoulder. "You look well enough."

"Your Grace, you cannot mean to carry her all the way to her aunt's house? Why, it would be ruinous."

Preston could have toted her all over London—she was still too thin from her relations' neglect. Mistreatment that left his insides boiling with fury.

"I am taking her to my carriage," he told the man, his hurried pace eating up the distance.

Barkworth struggled to keep up. "Then you can give us both a ride. I would be most obliged."

"Sorry, my good man. No room for you," Preston said, winking down at Tabitha. "You'll have to catch up when you can."

At this, Barkworth seemed to find a second wind and hurried to Preston's side, looking over at Tabitha with a mixture of frustration and anxiety. "I will not 'catch up.' Miss Timmons is my duty, my obligation."

Was it Preston's imagination, or did the lady flinch at this description? From what he knew of Tabitha he had to believe she'd never be happy being any man's duty or obligation.

Not even yours, a wry voice warned.

"*A lady has few choices,*" he recalled her saying. So, that being the case, what Tabitha needed most was the opportunity to decide her own future.

With or without him.

That stung, but if he was to give her her freedom, it was a risk he would have to take.

"Your Grace! The lady is mine," Barkworth continued to press.

"That may be, but at the moment it appears you haven't the means to give her what she needs." The duke grinned. "And I do."

It was a smug statement, a double entendre that had even Tabitha gaping.

Barkworth's jaw worked back and forth before he stepped into Preston's path. "You should at least allow me the pleasure of carrying Miss Timmons, or there will be talk."

The duke heaved an exasperated sigh, shifting Tabitha in his arms so she was firmly against him. "Sir, I never share my pleasures. Nor do I give a damn about gossip."

Such a disregard for society looked to be capable of giving Barkworth apoplexy. "Have you no honor?"

Preston thought about it for a moment. "No, none at all."

Arriving at the carriage, he set her in the seat, then caught up the reins from Roxley, who gave him a slight, censorious shake of his head.

"Is this how you avoid scandal?" the earl asked.

While Preston was doing his best to ignore this jab, Barkworth managed to get in front of him.

Persistent fellow.

"I shall drive Miss Timmons home," he declared.

Preston laughed. "Drive my cattle?" He glanced over at the nervous set and imagined them in Barkworth's incompetent hands. "No."

"Miss Timmons is my concern," he repeated.

Preston glanced around. "And where is her maid?"

Barkworth shifted from one foot to another. "I have sent her on an errand of great importance."

"Whatever would that be?" Preston asked, booted feet taking a wide stance.

"I told her to fetch the surgeon…and my tailor," Barkworth said, holding out his torn sleeve.

Preston glanced over his shoulder at Tabby. "Truly?"

She shook her head and looked away.

Barkworth held his ground. "Your Grace, your interference is beyond the pale, and I forbid it. I shall go fetch a hackney and take Miss Timmons home myself."

Preston looked him up and down and nodded. "If you insist."

"I do." Barkworth looked up at Tabby. "I shall return forthwith," he told her before he stormed off.

Preston waited until the man was just out of sight, then caught up Mr. Muggins and hoisted the dog into the tiger's seat. He took his place beside Tabby. "Roxley, I assume you don't mind managing your way home on foot?"

"Not at all," the earl declared, making a bow.

Giving the reins a light flick, Preston pointed his cattle in the opposite direction.

"But Barkworth—" Tabby protested.

"He's an idiot. He should never have left you alone in my care."

* * *

On that point, Tabitha could hardly argue. Still…
"You shouldn't have interfered," she told him.

"Rather too late for that," he said. "Besides, you
shouldn't be marrying that pandering nincompoop,
Tabby. He's beneath you." Preston huffed an exasperated sigh before he turned and faced her. "I won't stand
for it."

Tabitha ruffled. She didn't care that this was Preston, or that he'd just rescued her…again. If one more
person—make that a man—told her what she could
and could not do, she thought she might explode.

No wonder poor Agnes Stakes reached for the fire
poker on her wedding night.

His voice lowered. "If you want to marry him, I will
step aside. But only if you tell me that you love him."

"I must marry Barkworth to gain my inheritance."
There. While she couldn't look at him as she said the
words, at least she finally told him the truth.

"What if I told you I don't think the only way for
you to inherit is to marry Barkfool?"

Tabitha stilled. Even the pain in her ankle seemed
to fade away. "What are you saying, Preston?"

"I have presumed in other ways," he confessed,
slanting a glance at her.

"*Quelle surprise*," she replied, crossing her arms
over her chest.

"Will you listen to me, you vexing little minx?" He
adjusted the reins and guided the horses into the thick
London traffic. "I have made some inquiries."

"Inquiries?"

"Regarding your uncle's will."

Tabitha sat up and turned toward him. "Whatever for?"

"Isn't it obvious?" He gazed into her eyes, once again that boyish smile on his face—the one that made him seem so vulnerable.

"I am beginning to think you are not the seducer and rake everyone says you are but rather something quite different. Perhaps even mad." Tabitha bit her lip and looked away, unwilling to even think of such possibilities. Dare hope.

"That may be the case. So I will say in my defense and in my state of alleged madness, I spoke last night with Mr. Hathaway. You know him—your friend Miss Hathaway's brother?"

"Chaunce." Oh, yes. She knew Harriet's rapscallion brother. Already this tangle had Harriet's meddling all over it as much as Preston's.

"A most excellent fellow," Preston declared.

"*Harrrumph.*" Bothersome, rapscallion rakes, the pair of them. She shook her head.

He ignored her. "He and I are of the same mind and suspect—"

"Preston, you needn't—"

"Hear me out," he pleaded.

She pressed her lips together. Preston's meddling into Winston Ludlow's estate would ignite the collective fury of her Timmons relations. Especially Sir Mauris.

However, the duke wasn't one to easily give up. Not that she didn't already realize this about him.

"Answer me this," he posed. "Where does your uncle's fortune go if you *don't* marry the esteemed Mr. Barkworth?"

As the question and all its implications swirled around in her, Tabitha sucked in a deep breath. It was as if all of London stopped as she comprehended what he had just asked.

Where, indeed?

"I don't know," she confessed, feeling utterly foolish for not having thought of this before. In the rush of Uncle Bernard's announcement, the haste to pack and come to London, the whirl of dressmakers and dancing lessons, not once had she taken the time to contemplate such a question.

"Exactly!" Preston said, grinning as he turned off the main thoroughfare and into the more sedate streets of Mayfair.

"But my uncles both said—"

Preston's brows arched up. Truly, there was no need for him to say the words.

Why would her uncles say anything else? For Tabitha wasn't the only one who had much to gain from her marriage to the future Marquess of Grately.

Suddenly echoes from the past month began to resonate very clearly.

"*A better posting...*" Aunt Allegra had said one night when she'd thought Tabitha had been upstairs sorting linens.

"*Think of the connections for the girls...*" Lady Timmons had said more than once to her sister when she'd thought Tabitha hadn't been attending the conversation.

Not to mention the way Sir Mauris wrung his hands with glee each time he looked at her, as if he'd just found a long-ago-hidden pot of gold.

"Do you truly think—" she began, unable to say

the rest aloud, lest she curse it all. —*I won't have to marry him?*

Preston didn't answer; instead he asked, "When do you reach your majority?"

"This St. John's Day."

"Ah!" His brow furrowed. "I suspect that explains the undue haste of your match. I'd venture a guess that the terms of your uncle's will change once you turn five and twenty."

Her conversation with Barkworth from the previous night echoed through her thoughts.

...I reach my majority in a sennight—

...There is no time like the present, my dear Miss Timmons. The sooner we are married it will be for the best—

Tabitha shivered. Preston might have the right of it.

For again today, when she'd tried to put off any formal declaration of a betrothal, Barkworth had been overly insistent.

...the best thing to do would be to announce our engagement tomorrow night...

And what had her uncle said? "*You aren't getting any younger, gel.*"

All this rush for them to marry... Suddenly it held more questions than answers.

"Do you have any notion of what would happen if Barkworth decided not to marry you?"

Sitting back in the seat and folding her arms over her chest, she said, "Unfortunately, that is not an issue."

"Quite confident in your charms, are we?" Preston laughed. "Left the poor man besotted with that bonny smile of yours?"

"I believe my appeal comes in the form of a rich

purse." She swatted him in the arm. "Stop laughing. It's rather dreadful to be coveted like a prized cow at the fair."

"I would put a ribbon on you even without the benefit of your fortune."

"Do stop!"

"I'll do my best to refrain, but you have to admit it is a fertile subject."

Tabitha shook her head, and after a few more moments he burst out laughing yet again. "Now whatever is so funny?" she asked.

"Barkworth. His face. When I refused to hand you over. No wonder he looked so vexed. I was stealing his prized—"

"Preston!" she warned.

He laughed, a loud, boisterous melody that left her biting her lips together to keep from joining in.

"You should have returned me," she said, trying to rein him in...herself as well.

"I didn't think you wanted me to," he admitted. "You didn't, did you?"

"No," she admitted. "Oh, do stop grinning. I only say that because I feared he would drop me."

"Yes. If you say so," he agreed, winking at her broadly and scooting closer to her than what she suspected was proper. His thigh brushed against hers and she found herself tucked neatly against his side.

As if he were made for her.

Oh, she had to stop thinking like that...like they were...

Tabitha crossed her arms over her chest and sighed. "Preston, after you've determined the true state of my uncle's will, I beg of you to stop interfering in my life."

"No," he said.

"No?"

"Yes. Exactly. No, I will not stop."

"Why not?"

"I have very noble reasons for my interference, as you so ungratefully call it." He straightened, doing his best, she assumed, to look noble. He only looked more devilish.

After a long bit of silence, she couldn't help herself. "That would be?"

"Your family, Barkworth and his wretched lot are ruining you."

"Yes, yes, so you said last night." She turned toward him. "I will have you know I am quite the *on dit* today, not because of my family or Barkworth but because of you—"

"You are on everyone's lips, my dear Tabby, because of that scandalous gown you wore last night."

She groaned. "Oh, bother, Preston. Not my gown again."

"Yes, that gown."

"You still don't approve?"

"No," he averred. "Though it does hold the promise of setting old Grately's teeth on edge." He glanced over at her, as if a new bit of trouble had dawned in that scandalous brain of his. And much to her chagrin, it had. "That gown may be your ticket out of a marriage to Barkworth. Especially if Grately saw you in it."

"The Marquess of Grately? Whatever would he care what I am wearing?"

"Grately? Why, your soon to be uncle-in-law is the most tight-fisted, preening old goat ever to trot about

London. He sees you in that gown, he'll marry you himself."

"Marry me? Why, he's nigh on—"

"Eighty," Preston supplied. "Had four wives already trying to get an heir to replace Barkworth's father, and then your illustrious Barkworth."

Tabitha shuddered.

"Finally you see some sense," Preston said, looking quite smug.

"I rather thought of wearing the gown to Almack's," she told him. "Mrs. Drummond-Burrell is sending round vouchers."

"Almack's? Over my dead body!"

"Why not Almack's? It is entirely respectable," she told him.

"Horrid place," he told her. "My aunt was slighted by a wretch there."

"Lady Juniper?" Tabitha couldn't imagine anyone slighting that stately and aristocratic lady.

"Yes, at your respectable Almack's," Preston assured her. "And by a bounder of a fellow."

"Whatever happened?"

"My uncle—her brother—and I found the fellow and gave him a good thrashing."

Tabitha couldn't help it. She smiled. As much as she knew she shouldn't, it rather pleased her that Preston took his familial duties so seriously. "What did your aunt say?"

"She was furious."

"Did she forgive you?"

"Worse," he told her. "She married the rotter."

Tabitha laughed. "That certainly bodes ill for me."

Preston glanced over at her. "How does my aunt's marital choices bode ill for you?"

"Your interference pushed her right into the arms of the man you disliked."

"I doubt you will be so foolish as to become Mrs. Reginald Barkworth." He glanced at her, up and down, as if sizing her up. "I truly can't see you as a Barkworth."

"Why not? From what I know, the Barkworths are an old, respected family with a long lineage of service to their king and country."

"Oh, aye. The king's boot catchers is what they are. The entire lot of them. A pack of supercilious, obsequious, fawning sycophants."

"Truly?" Tabitha glanced over at him. "This coming from a Seldon."

"Leave your Dale friend's opinions out of this. You won't find a Barkworth listed at Hastings or Agincourt, or Flodden, I can tell you that!"

"And the Seldons?"

He grinned. "In the thick of it. Always. How do you think we came to our many titles?"

"And how many would that be?"

He rubbed his chin. "Eight at last count."

"Eight?"

"You don't believe me? Shall we head to the nearest lending library and check out a copy of Debrett's?"

"No, no," she laughed. "That won't be necessary."

"Then you've already looked me up." He waggled his brows at her, puffed up with his own importance.

She rather delighted in deflating him. Glancing down at her gloves, she said, "Actually, I haven't."

He glanced at her. "Truly?"

"Honestly," she said. She raised her hand as if giving an oath. "I've never read a single entry in that esteemed chronicle."

He whistled. "You are a singular woman, Tabby. An extraordinary one."

"That being the case," she said, "enlighten me."

"As to?"

"Your titles. If I am to be impressed by your lofty status and judge it against the Barkworths', I would hear a recitation."

"The dukedom of Preston."

"Duly noted."

"The marquesates of Wallington and Brinsley," he told her. "Two marquesates, not merely one, as Grately holds."

"What did you say about preening earlier?"

Preston waved her off. "Never mind that. Then comes three earldoms, Kirkburn, Danthorpe and Dimlington."

"Dimlington?" Tabitha giggled. "You are the Earl of Dimlington?"

"One does not giggle or question the titles one's king bestows."

"I suppose not," she admitted, having never considered such a thing. "Proceed."

"And finally, I hold the titles to four baronies."

"Only four?"

He shrugged. "Cartworth, Castley, Dewsbury-Poole and Rylestone."

She paused for a moment. "Wasn't that five?"

"Dewsbury-Poole is hyphenated."

"Thank goodness," she teased. "Think how overbearing you would be otherwise."

He snorted.

As she went through the titles silently, tapping them off on her fingers, Tabitha paused. "No viscountcy?"

This time the duke appeared affronted. "Do I appear to have come from shopkeepers?"

"Only around the edges," she informed him.

"Miss Timmons, you wound me. You are Tabby no more to me. I should put you down on the curb immediately." He went to pull the horses over.

"Don't you dare! I haven't the least idea where I am and haven't naught in my reticule but a—" She reached over and caught hold of his hands and the reins, turning the horses back into the traffic. For a few precious moments, they sat there, her hands covering his, Preston grinning rakishly at her and she not knowing what to say.

Let alone how to let go.

Oh, this was madness. It was the night at the inn all over again.

"Do you know how to drive?" he asked softly, his gaze still fixed on hers. She had the sense he wasn't talking about carriages and horses.

"Not at all," she admitted, feeling the warmth of his hands beneath hers, the easy, solid strength of his hold on the reins.

"Let me teach you," he said softly, winding the ribbons around both their hands, entwining them together.

"Haven't you taught me enough?"

"We haven't even begun," he said, but to her ears it sounded more like a promise. Glancing up at the horses, he tipped his head to hers so he could guide her. "The first rule is they must know what you want—just let them feel it. Gently, but firmly."

Tabitha shivered. "Are you talking about driving and horses?"

"But of course," he said, leaning closer, his lips blowing softly over her ears. "Tabby, what do you want?" He moved his hands so hers curled around the reins and his fingers wound around hers. Warm and sure, guiding her, prodding her to take hold of something just out of reach.

She glanced up at him and found herself nearly nose to nose with him. It was like the night in the inn...just before he kissed her.

What did she want? Oh, she didn't dare say it. For right now she wished he would kiss her. Devour her.

He must have been able to see the desire in her eyes, for he lowered his head, but just as his lips brushed over hers, they were jolted apart.

"Take it inside, you great toff," a man yelled out.

Tabitha looked up to find that the horses had stopped in the middle of the narrow street and were blocking traffic, much to the ire of the beefy, ruddy-faced fellow in a low-slung cap driving a large delivery wagon.

Well, trying to drive it.

"What? Can't afford a place to take her?" the man asked.

Now it was Tabitha's turn to turn bright red.

Preston gathered up the reins and said, "Yes, well, the other lesson of driving is never take your eyes off the road. You never know what hazards you will find." He gave the reins a flick and guided the horses around the wagon.

"My apologies, my good man," he said as they rounded the wagon.

The man's reply was to spit in the roadway.

"Obviously he hasn't been out riding with a lady in some time," Preston remarked in his usual smug manner. After half a block, he handed the ribbons back to her.

"I don't know where I am going," she told him. That, and she'd never driven anything more than Harriet's pony cart.

"Neither do I, Tabby. This is uncharted territory for me." He leaned back and kept a sharp eye on the traffic, reaching over only to correct her hold or straighten the ribbons.

"What? You've never kidnapped a lady before?"

"This was hardly kidnapping. A rescue of the first order. Roxley will back me up."

"Lord Roxley?" She shook her head.

"Yes, well, I doubt Lady Gudgeon would be much of a reference," he teased, turning and giving Mr. Muggins a good scratch on the head. "Dreadful trouble, mutt. You've landed your mistress in the briars."

"He's not the only one," she shot back, glancing at the pair of them for only a second. Driving took far more concentration than she'd ever realized. "Preston, I will be in ever so much trouble if I don't get home soon."

"That bad, Puss?" he mused, reaching over and taking the reins.

"Aye," she whispered.

"Where do your esteemed relations live?" he asked.

She gave him the directions and he turned the carriage at the next corner. They drove for some time in silence, until he asked, "Naught but what in your reticule?"

"What?" she asked, pulling herself out of a reverie

where she was imagining that Uncle Winston's will had consigned her to marry someone else.

A man with a lion's mercurial nature and lips that could steal her breath away with only the promise of a kiss.

"Naught but what in your reticule, you were saying earlier?" he prodded, grinning at her. "A penny, perhaps?"

Tabitha pressed her lips together and looked away. She was of half a mind to take that penny out of her reticule and toss it in the gutter. "You think far too highly of yourself."

"Well, when one possesses a vast number of admirable qualities…"

"You do?"

He grinned and leaned closer, puckering up his lips. "Would you like to discover my most popular one?"

She shoved him back. "Would serve you right to be given a viscountcy."

"I don't believe they give out titles for excellence in kissing," he told her.

"Perhaps that is how your ancestor was given the earldom of Dimlington."

"For kissing a king? Now, Tabby, that would hardly be proper."

She giggled and blushed. "Preston, you are a ruin."

"I try," he admitted. Again they rode for a time in silence.

"Preston?"

"Yes, Puss?"

"Why is it that you don't like to dine alone?"

He shook his head. "'Twas a long time ago."

"When your parents died?"

The duke nodded. "Not just my parents, Tabby," he confessed. "My entire family."

"Oh, no," she whispered.

He looked away and told the story he'd done his best to forget. Cavorting his way through life in hopes that enough indiscretions, a reputation that lent itself to gossip, would keep everyone far enough at bay so as not to press too close to the truth.

"The fevers came so suddenly. Everyone got sick, myself included."

"I remember how fast my mother succumbed," she remarked.

"Yes, I was sick, lost in fever. I remember my mother by my side, and then she was gone. And my sister, Dove, replaced her, and then she was gone. And then it was my old nurse, and by the time I woke, there was no one."

"No one?" Tabitha's eyes welled up with tears.

"No one alive," he said. "I wandered through the house trying to find someone, anyone. I was all that was left. My parents, my brothers, my sisters, the servants. All of them either gone, or dead in their beds."

She sucked in a deep breath.

"I didn't know what to do," he confessed. "I went into the dining room and sat down in my father's chair. It hadn't even occurred to me that I was now the heir, for my brother Frederick had been the eldest, but I took the place because it gave me comfort."

The image of the stalwart but frightened child in his father's chair broke Tabitha's heart. "How long were you there like that?" *All alone.*

"Two days, or at least that is what my grandfather determined." He looked over at her. "Someone had sent word that there was illness and he'd come at once, but it had taken some time for him to reach Owle Park. I remember the sharp sound of his boots as they crossed the marble floor in the foyer and how he flung open the dining room doors and gathered me up, brought me to London. He never said a word. And I haven't been there since."

"Oh, Preston," she said, tears falling down her cheeks. She dashed at them and took hold of his arm. "I am ever so sorry."

"You shouldn't be. You're the first person I've ever told that story to," he confessed.

Tabitha glanced around at her surroundings and realized they were getting close to her aunt and uncle's house. She wanted to say something, but she knew there were no words that could assuage his sorrow. Yet there was something she had been remiss to do, something she could say.

"Thank you for my bluebells," she said, leaning her head against his shoulder for only a second.

"Did they help?" he asked.

"They made me smile."

He nodded. "Because they reminded you of home."

Tabitha thought about that and shook her head. "No. Not for that reason."

Preston glanced over at her, his face confused. "Why not? Did I pick the wrong ones?" He turned down the street and glanced around for the address.

Tabitha pointed to the one in the middle of the block. "No, not at all. They were perfect."

"Then what made you smile?"

Smiling again at the memory of the crushed stems and the bent blossoms, she said, "I was too busy imagining what you looked like climbing across a ditch to gather them than to think about home."

"What I looked like?" he laughed. "Like a bloody fool, that's what I looked like. Ruined my boots getting through that field. My valet will probably quit."

She laughed as he held out his leg for her to examine. Indeed, his Hessians looked very shabby compared with his usually polished, enviable boots.

"Ruined!" he told her. "I hold you accountable."

"You would," she shot back as they came to a stop in front of Lord and Lady Timmons's London residence.

They both laughed, and in that instant, he reached out to cradle her face. "You, Tabby, astound me."

"You surprise me, Your Grace," she said, breathless to be held so. She couldn't help herself, she tipped her chin up.

So he could kiss her.

And once again, Mr. Reginald Barkworth showed her the one thing he excelled at.

Timing.

"Miss Timmons!" Mr. Reginald Barkworth cried out.

Tabby froze, Preston's lips just a breath away. Oh, good heavens, she was ruined.

The duke sighed and winked at her, then made a great show of straightening her bonnet. "I deplore this fashion for wearing bonnets askew, Miss Timmons," he remarked to no one in particular. He leaned back and eyed her. "Somewhat better," he said, glancing up at their audience with such an innocent expression that it was hard to believe he was the same man with the wicked light to his eyes and the devil-may-care smile that could entice even a worldly bit of the demimonde to blush.

"Your Grace! Unhand my betrothed," Barkworth said, nay, demanded.

Preston sighed. "However can I do that when I have yet to 'hand' her?" He glanced at Tabitha and shrugged as if to say *do you know what he is talking about?*

Tabitha shifted in her seat and turned to find not only Mr. Barkworth—frozen in place, his face a mask of horrified shock—standing on the front steps of the Timmonses' town house but also Lady Ancil, her pickled expression never seeming to change out of its universal state of disapproval, alongside her aunt and uncle and, back behind them, Harriet on her tiptoes, peering over the crowd to gain a peek.

She would have wagered anything that her cousins were peering out one of the windows, having not ranked a spot on the front steps but unwilling to miss one delicious moment of their cousin's fall from favor.

Barkworth didn't remain fixed in place for long. He dashed down the steps to the side of the carriage, thrusting out his hand toward Tabitha. "Come now, Miss Timmons, before this day turns to utter ruin."

Preston, ever the helpful rake, leaned over and said loud enough for all to hear, "How do you know it hasn't been already?" He waggled his brows and winked up at Lady Ancil.

"Your Grace is no gentleman!" Barkworth declared.

The two men glared at each other until Tabitha grew weary of both of them. Wretched Preston for implying that he'd ruined her and Barkworth for being so... well, Barkworth!

She swatted Barkworth's hand aside and went to

climb down from the carriage, until she got to the curb and sidewalk and her ankle protested. She cried out and caught hold of the carriage. Mr. Muggins leapt down from his spot and took up watch by her side.

Harriet pushed past the crowd on the steps and came to her aid. "Tabitha! Whatever happened?"

"I twisted my ankle in the park," she explained as Harriet helped her up the steps.

"Barkworth said nothing of you being injured," her friend said loudly, sending censorious gazes at both Lord and Lady Timmons, as well as Lady Ancil.

Lady Timmons eyed her niece. "What has *he* done to you?"

"Nothing," Tabitha told her. "The duke merely brought me home from the park after I fell. He was there with his carriage, and since it seemed improbable that Mr. Barkworth could carry me home—"

There was a loud sniff from Lady Ancil at this suggestion.

"—His Grace offered to bring me home." She glanced at Harriet, who looked ready to murder someone.

"Mr. Barkworth arrived with a wild tale that the duke had spirited you away. That Mr. Muggins had attacked some lady or another, and that he—I mean Barkworth—had been injured saving her." Harriet huffed an exasperated sigh. "It all sounded like a great bouncer to me, though no one would believe me."

"Oh, how ridiculous!" Tabitha replied. "I fell and the duke gave me a ride home. Truly, I do not understand how anyone could find anything amiss in his kindness or why there is this need to invent such tales."

Something Preston had said, about making her own

choices, had lit a fire inside Tabitha. Or perhaps she was more than a little annoyed at having lost the opportunity to kiss him again.

Her heart still hammered a bit unevenly, and when she realized how close he'd been to stealing that kiss if it hadn't been for Barkworth's interruption, she clenched her teeth in frustration.

Lady Ancil, having also grown weary—or perhaps worried that Barkworth would grow rash and issue some insult grievous enough to warrant seconds and an early morning meeting on some grassy knoll—called over to her son, "Reginald, we are leaving." Then she turned to Tabitha's aunt. "This is unforgivable. I will not have my son ridiculed for some hoyden's lack of modesty. All Barkworths possess an exacting standard of decorum, and your niece..." Her nose wrinkled up and she shuddered.

"Lady Ancil, you cannot mean—"

That she would insist her son cry off? Tabitha glanced from one to the other, her fingers crossed. Oh, if only it was that simple.

"I do indeed!" Lady Ancil declared. "Hear me clearly on this: keep that gel under lock and key until they are wed or I shall hold you personally responsible, Lady Timmons."

Lady Timmons blanched but then held her own, saying, "My niece is naught but an innocent in all this."

Her staunch defense surprised Tabitha, until she realized it wasn't just her reputation her aunt was defending but those of her daughters as well.

Her unmarried daughters.

"Inside," Lady Timmons instructed, pointing the way. She turned to the carriage before her house and said to the duke, "Your Grace, my husband and I are indebted for the help you provided our niece, but please understand that your assistance is no longer required."

Harriet smiled over at Tabitha. "I do believe your aunt just told the Duke of Preston to shove off."

Her aunt didn't know Preston very well. He wasn't one to "shove off" in the least. Rather, such a threat would only make him more of a rapscallion.

Tabitha caught one last glimpse of him before her uncle slammed the door shut. While the sight of his solid jaw, upturned handsome lips and the bright light in his eyes stole her heart, utterly and completely, when she looked over at her aunt and uncle's stony, furious expressions, Preston made her wish—yet again—that he'd never come along.

"Hathaway! There you are!"

Mr. Chauncey Hathaway opened one eye and peered up at the young man standing in front of the chair where he'd been dozing. The eager, grinning fellow had probably only been with the Home Office for a few months.

Or else he wouldn't be grinning over his discovery.

For Chaunce was in no mood to be found. He'd spent a good part of the night breaking into the offices of Kimball, Dunnington, and Pennyman. And even so, he'd only managed to catch—he glanced up at the grand clock just down the way—an hour's worth of sleep before he'd hied himself off to White's to find the Duke of Preston.

Yes, yes, he'd told Preston he had a friend in the office, but that had only been to hold off the man from doing something stupid.

Oh, he knew Preston's sort. The duke would go blustering over to the solicitor's offices, all high-handed titles and demands, and the next thing you knew, one of the clerks would be dispatched to Grately, and then Barkworth, and finally Sir Mauris, alerting them all that the jig was up.

In an hour's time, one, or all of them, would have Tabitha bundled up in a carriage on the way to Gretna Green.

No, that would never work, and Chaunce knew well enough that Harry would hold him personally responsible for such a travesty. "A dreadful tragedy," she would call it. Then she'd spend the next ten years lamenting that he should have "done something" to prevent it all.

Rather like she still blamed him for losing her best fishing rod in the pond when he was fourteen and she only ten.

So he had done something. He'd lied. And then done what he did best. Gone to the source.

Still, it had been no easy feat getting in, discovering where Winston Ludlow's will was filed, copying down the extensive points, and then escaping Temple's Inn before being caught. He'd nearly broken his neck getting out of the second-story offices, and then he'd been chased by one of the guards at Temple's Inn for farther than even he would like to admit.

Shifting from one foot to another, the fellow eyed him quizzically. "Sir, you are required at the Home Office. Immediately."

Chaunce eyed the fellow and didn't even bother to get up. Not that he would have been overly impressed and sprung into immediate action if it had been a more senior fellow.

He rubbed the back of his head and groaned. Next time he'd find a source on the ground floor.

"Mr. Hathaway? Sir?" the man before him repeated, reaching out and giving him a shake. "The minister has had us all looking for you since past midnight. He wants to know where you've been." And apparently so did this fellow. Likely so he would have something to nudge about the office.

Found Hathaway at White's looking as drunk as David's sow, and you'll never believe what he'd been doing...

"Here," he replied. "Must have fallen asleep. Quite a night." Wouldn't do for the minister to find out he'd been moonlighting for an addle-pated duke who just didn't realize he was in love.

"Yes, if you say so, sir." The young man cleared his throat and eyed him suspiciously. "If you are ready, I have a carriage downstairs—"

"I can't go yet," Chaunce told the anxious fellow. "I have something I must do first."

And as luck would have it, down the hall a commotion began to brew and Chaunce leaned forward to eye the gathering storm. Ah, in the middle of it all stood Roxley. Not surprising and perfectly well-timed.

Roxley would know where Preston could be found.

"The minister said—" the young man badgered before Chaunce glared at him again. Clearly this fellow was well on his way into management.

"Yes, yes, I'm sure old Iron Drawers said to haul me in, even if you had to clap me in chains." He pinned a piercing stare on the younger man as he got up. It helped that he was a good head taller than this underling. "Did you bring any manacles with you?"

The fellow stepped back and glanced around. "Certainly not," he said in a hushed, reserved voice. "This is White's."

"Just as I thought. A moment then, Mr.—?"

"Mr. Hotchkin."

"Yes, well, Hotchkin, I've a bit of business I need to tidy up and then you can haul me before the minister, your mission a success." Pushing past the junior clerk and heading toward the knot where Roxley stood facing down another man, Chaunce paused for a moment to gauge the tide before him.

"A vowel?" Roxley was complaining. "Poggs, you lost—fair and square—and you never once said you were going to pay your winnings with a vowel!" The earl stood nose to nose with the other man.

A baron, Chaunce recalled.

Lord Poggs appeared hardly concerned by the earl's ire. "'Tis all I can do at the moment, my lord. 'Tis an honorable offer. I've got a horse running this afternoon, and when I collect—"

"When you collect! I've got pockets of promises like that and no one ever pays them," Roxley complained, plucking several out of his coat and holding them out as evidence.

"Ought to find plumper pockets to pick, eh, Roxley," a lounger nearby tossed out.

Roxley looked ready to kick up a dust, so Chaunce shouldered his way into the fray before it did turn into something more. "My lord, a moment of your time."

"Eh?" Roxley looked around and blinked. The man always had the appearance of being half-seas over, but Chaunce knew better. "Ah, Hathaway! You devil! What are you doing here?"

"I wondered if you knew when Preston was going to come by. I have that information for him." Chaunce held up the sheets of paper he'd jotted the notes down on.

"Information for Preston?" Roxley shook his head. Then the light dawned in his eyes. "Oh! *That* information." He nodded. "Give it to me."

Chaunce snorted and took a step back.

"Good God, man. I'll make sure he gets it. I'm staying with Preston. At least until my aunt returns to Kempton." The earl held out his hand, and when Chaunce paused, Roxley shook it, as if to emphasize his point.

"Mr. Hathaway, will you be much longer?" The young fellow from the ministry was back at his elbow adding to Chaunce's already present headache. This fellow was going to end up the prime minister one day, or found in the Thames drowned by his subordinates.

So, pressured from all sides, Chaunce—against his better judgment—surrendered the pages. "If you can't get them to Preston, tell Harry that 'the lady in question must get that gentleman to cry off.'"

"Cry off?" Roxley asked, blinking.

"Yes, yes," Chaunce told him. "Tell Harry that they must find a way to get him to cry off. She'll know what to do."

"Harry always does," Roxley replied as he stuffed the papers Chaunce had given him into the inside pocket of his jacket, along with the rest of the vowels and nonsense he kept tucked away in there. "Give the papers to Preston and call on Harry. Get 'im to cry off. Yes. Yes. I've got it."

This did little to assuage Chaunce's misgivings, but

what else could he do? He could hardly waste another hour or so hunting down either his sister or the duke.

Besides, the fellow they'd sent to herd him back to Whitehall looked as persistent as a sheepdog. And willing to bite if necessary.

"Now, Hotchkin, you have the honor of having found me," Hathaway told the younger fellow. "Take me in."

"Oh, sir, thank you," Hotchkin enthused.

Chaunce smiled. Fool. Obviously a Cambridge man, or he'd remember the old adage about shooting the messenger. Old Iron Drawers would probably give them both a thorough wigging.

Guilty by association, and all.

As Chaunce strode toward the stairs, Hotchkin at his heels, he could distinctly hear Roxley saying, "If it must be a vowel, then summon the man to fetch a pen and ink. I've got a piece of paper here—"

And for once in his life, Chaunce ignored the ripple of warning that ran down his spine.

As it turned out, Harry never did let him forget it.

Chapter 13

Banished to her bedchamber, Tabitha wanted nothing more than to pace the floor in frustration. However, her ankle prevented her from even that bit of relief. With it propped on a pillow, she looked out over her prison and frowned.

While Daphne was there to keep her company, she sat bent over the desk, writing a letter that held all her interest, her arm curved around it. She wrote quickly and avidly, unlike her usually carefully crafted compositions.

Though she could hear the occasional sound of the bell ringing or her uncle stomping about below, no one ventured upstairs to see them. Not even Eloisa, who was prone to gloating and would probably see this as a perfect opportunity.

Though it was good that she hadn't, because Daphne

had sworn that if Tabitha's pert cousin rapped on the door, she would personally sew feathers into every bonnet the girl owned.

The only diversion had been from Harriet, who had spotted Roxley lounging against the streetlight across the way and had snuck downstairs to meet him, despite Lady Timmons's threat that if one of them set foot outside their room, she would pack the lot of them home to Kempton in disgrace.

Tabitha sighed, for her thoughts were awash with everything that had transpired with Preston—his rescue, the drive, the way he'd held her hands, his confession.

He'd stolen her heart anew, and she felt the fresh sting of tears in her eyes. When she glanced up and found Daphne watching her, she dashed them away.

She hadn't even noticed that her friend's letter was now carefully blotted and folded.

"I'm afraid I owe you an apology," Daphne said.

"How so?"

"Barkworth is not the man for you," she replied.

"Even if he is a gentleman?" Tabitha posed in a teasing voice. "And in line to inherit a fine title?"

Daphne waved her off as she tucked the now folded missive she'd been answering into a packet of similar letters all bound up in a red ribbon.

Before Tabitha could get to the bottom of this change of heart, Harriet came rushing in. "I have the best news, and I think this is even better news," she said, holding up a crisp white letter closed with a fancy seal. "I stole it off the salver before your cousins caught wind of it."

Tabitha glanced at the note. "Is it from Preston?"

Harriet shook her head. "No, Barkworth."

Sinking back into her pillow, Tabitha didn't want anything to do with what could only be a lecture on her general lack of decorum.

"Tabitha, this could be excellent news," Harriet insisted, thrusting the note into her hands. "Read it. Quickly! I am dying to know—"

Sighing, Tabitha slid a finger under the wax and broke the seal. Unfolding the letter, she skipped the superfluous portions and got to the most salient point.

She looked up at Harriet. "He still intends to marry me." For a man who took such great pride in his family's sterling reputation, whatever was it about her that had him overlooking every trial she laid at his doorstep?

She could guess that it had everything to do with Uncle Winston's fortune.

"He does?" Harriet shook her head. "That will never do!"

"You think?!" Tabitha snapped and immediately regretted it.

Harriet paid it little heed, waving her off. "No, no, you are right to be vexed, especially when I tell you what Roxley had to say—he brought good news from my brother."

Tabitha's eyes lit up. "About my uncle's will?"

"Yes!"

Daphne sat up. "What is this?"

"Preston… I mean… His Grace believes that my uncle's will more than likely has provisions that allow me to inherit without marrying Barkworth."

Daphne's eyes widened. "Whyever didn't we think of that?"

Harriet nodded. "Chaunce procured a copy for the duke, and just in case the duke couldn't get to you in time, he sent Roxley over with a simple instruction."

Getting to her feet, Daphne came over to stand next to Tabitha, taking her hand and holding it fast. "Which is?"

Taking a deep breath, Harriet conveyed her message. "Get Barkworth to cry off."

"Cry off?" Daphne said. "Oh, that is an excellent notion."

It was. But there was only one problem.

Tabitha sank onto her narrow bed. "That will never happen."

Harriet's brow furrowed. "He looked ready to cry off this afternoon. His mother threatened just that when she gave your aunt that wigging."

"She can threaten all she wants," Tabitha said, having looked back down at the letter she still held and scanned a few more lines. "Despite my 'general lack of understanding of the propriety that is expected of the future Marchioness of Grately'"—she shook her head—"he says he and his mother will endeavor to see that I am fit for the task and have a clear understanding of 'my duties' before the unfortunate day arrives when I shall rise so far above my station."

Even Daphne shuddered. Tabitha suspected it had to do with the word "duties."

Frankly the notion of "duties" with Barkworth didn't leave her shuddering so much as ill right down to her toes.

"I cannot marry him," Tabitha told them. "I cannot!"

"I agree," Daphne said.

Harriet's gaze swiveled at this. "You do?" Especially since Daphne had been one of Barkworth's most ardent supporters.

"What? I don't have the right to change my mind?" Daphne poked her nose in the air. "Upon a closer acquaintance, I have decided he is an insufferable boor."

"That is self-evident," Harriet muttered.

After sending a pained glance at her friend and issuing a large sigh, Daphne laid out her list. "That he would continue to insist on your marriage even after your disgraceful behavior—"

"My—" Tabitha protested, but she was cut off by a pinning glance that was the Dale hallmark.

"Yes, your scandalous behavior," Daphne repeated. "His acceptance indicates he is only marrying you for your money." She shook her head, for such a notion was repellent to someone even as practical as Daphne. "Therefore he is not a gentleman."

"He's a boody-witted nobcock," Harriet corrected.

"That as well," Daphne agreed, which was a momentous concession in itself.

"Preston promised to help me send him packing, but what am I to do? Barkworth writes that his uncle will announce our engagement tomorrow night!" Tabitha shuddered. There would be no turning back once that announcement was made.

Harriet and Daphne sat down on the small sofa and frowned at this turn of events.

Then Harriet perked up. "There is always the Kempton Curse. Barkworth may go mad on your wedding night and then you will have your freedom—as a lovely widow."

Daphne shook her head, as if she'd never heard such

foolishness. "Harriet, it is the bride who goes mad. Barkworth just ends up dead. That will never do. Even for a nobcock like Barkworth."

"I think I might go mad at the very thought of having to marry him," Tabitha confessed.

"Refuse," Daphne told her. "They cannot force you."

"Yes, I fear they can," Harriet said. "I overheard your cousins when I went downstairs. Your Uncle Bernard has been summoned up from Kempton to perform the ceremony, since he will have no qualms about marrying you even if you protest. I fear you may have no choice in the matter."

No choice in the matter...

"Oh, dear," Daphne said. "Whatever is to be done?"

Not what, Tabitha realized, *who.*

"There is always Preston," she said more to herself.

"The duke?" Daphne asked, her head turning toward her friend. "Whatever would he do?"

Tabitha slid her hand into her pocket and felt the familiar knick of his penny. "Hopefully something unforgivably scandalous."

Yet even as she thought of asking him to help her, quite possibly ruin her, she knew she couldn't.

Oh, the consequences for her would be dire, but for him? She couldn't ask him to help her—not if it meant his aunt and uncle would move out and leave him all alone.

Not when it would cost him so much.

The next evening Preston bounded up the front steps of his town house in a jubilant mood.

Tabby. The little minx. She'd caused quite a stir in

society. He'd spent most of the past twenty-four hours being quizzed about her.

However had he found such a creature?

Was it true her dog had chased Lady Gudgeon up a tree in the park? No, just a bench, he'd corrected.

Did she have a sister or two about?

Where could I get a hound like hers?

Preston had done his best to overlook the remarks about her being nearly betrothed to another.

Well, the man didn't deserve her.

Nor would he have her now, Preston would wager, thinking of Barkworth's furious expression when he'd set Tabby down at her uncle's house and the excellent news Roxley had passed onto him when they'd crossed paths at White's several hours earlier.

If Barkworth cried off, Tabby would be free. Free to inherit, free to choose her own path.

Most likely her house in the country, with its comfortable rooms, cozy fires, where she could surround herself with friends and family, he supposed.

And he'd be... Preston paused halfway up the steps as he considered his place in this perfect scenario.

He'd still be in London. No, that wouldn't do.

"Welcome home, Your Grace," Benley, his butler, intoned with all the proper respect of a London servant as he opened the front door, interrupting Preston's plans.

"Good to see you, Benley! Where the devil is everyone?"

"In the Red Room, Your Grace."

Preston paused and glanced over at the table where the salver sat. Since it had been empty of late, he'd given it little notice, but today it overflowed with letters. In fact, the entire side table was littered in notes. "More lonely hearts for Lord Henry?"

"Yes, Your Grace," Benley replied with his usual brevity.

Preston suppressed a laugh. "With who? Looks like half of London has written."

"The female half, Your Grace." Benley shuddered.

Heaven help poor Henry now that Hen had taken it in her mind to make him sort through them.

Preston continued past with only the slightest twinge of guilt, taking the stairs two at a time. When he rounded the landing, he heard voices coming from the Red Room, and when he entered, he found Hen looking particularly splendid, dressed to the nines—obviously on her way out.

"I told you this morning over breakfast that I wanted you to escort me there tonight," she was complaining to Henry.

"Good God, Hen, you natter on at breakfast every morning," his uncle was replying. "However do you expect me to remember everything you want me to do?"

This was familiar territory. Hen loved going out, and Henry deplored it. And despite having the advantage of being a widow and being able to choose her own entertainments, Hen clung to propriety and refused to go out without a respectable escort (Henry, or, if all else failed, Preston) or a suitable chaperone—one of her mother's old cronies.

"Have Roxley take you," Henry said, nodding over at the earl, who sat in a large chair before the fire, his long legs stuck out in front of him.

"Me?" the earl said. "Demmed if I want to spend the night at Grately's! The supper will be inedible." The earl glanced up and spotted Preston. "Ho, there's your reprobate nephew. Make him pay the piper."

"Ah, Preston. Finally come home to roost," she remarked, glancing down with a critical eye at her gloves.

"I do live here," he said, crossing to the sidebar and pouring himself a brandy.

"Yes, but it seems I will not be. Truly, Preston, did you have to wade into that scandal in the park yesterday?"

"Why wouldn't I?" he said, nudging Henry out of the way as he made his way to the other end of the settee. Settling down, he crossed his arms over his chest. "I thought you wanted me to be an example to society."

Hen let out a loud, huffy sigh. "If that were the case, you would have lent aid to Lady Gudgeon."

"Whyever would I do that?" he asked, glancing over at Henry for support. "She isn't anywhere near as pretty as Miss Timmons."

"Miss Timmons!" Hen shook her head. "Whoever is this lady? Her name is on every tongue! A vicar's daughter…" She paused, then looked again at Preston. "The same vicar's daughter you danced with the other night, isn't she?"

This was no mere question from Hen; it had all the ominous air of the beginnings of an interrogation.

"Yes," he answered warily, shifting in his seat.

"And you carried her across the park?"

"Yes, but she was—"

"*Tut, tut*—" Hen warned. "I don't want to know. Not that it matters now, for by tomorrow she will be beyond even your reach. You should come with me instead of Henry—"

"Please, Preston, take her to Grately's for me—" Henry begged.

"Yes, save us both," Roxley intoned.

"I daresay not," Hen replied, as if that settled the matter. "He wasn't invited."

"Grately's? That dull old skinflint." Preston shook his head and settled further into his seat. "What entertainment could he be offering that would interest me?" Or Hen, for that matter, he wondered, eyeing her resplendent gown and jewels.

The gown was new—not black, but mauve—a declaration by Hen that she was leaving off her widow's weeds and moving into half-mourning. Which was one short step from venturing back into the Marriage Mart.

Heaven help them, Preston nearly groaned.

"He's throwing an engagement party," Hen replied, glancing inside her reticule.

This stopped Preston cold. Barkworth wasn't crying off? Good God, that meant—

If the shock registered on his face, Hen gave no indication that she saw it. Taking one more glance at the mirror, she gave her hair a satisfied little pat, then gazed expectantly at him. "Well, now, I suppose I will just have to go alone. Though I so loathe—"

"Wait!" Preston said, bolting to his feet. "I'll take you."

She shook her head. "You weren't invited. You know how the marquess is. He has very exclusive attendance at his parties."

"And you think you are going alone?"

Hen shrugged. "Perhaps it is time I ventured out a bit. As you are always telling me, I should—"

Preston's jaw worked back and forth. He had to stop that announcement. He'd promised Tabby he'd help her.

Not for the world would he let her down. Abandon her now.

Ever...a soft voice whispered in his ear.

Meanwhile, Hen had gathered up her belongings and was headed out of the room.

"I forbid it!" Preston declared.

Hen stopped at the door. She turned around slowly. "You what?"

He straightened into his most ducal stance, something very much like what his grandfather would have taken great joy in displaying. "I forbid you to leave this house unescorted."

"You wha-a-a-t?" she sputtered, glancing over at Henry for help.

Not that he was any help. He was too busy gaping at their nephew as if Preston had suddenly gone round the bend.

"I forbid it!" Preston repeated, this time actually sounding like their father. Like a duke. "You will not attend that party without me."

Hen bowed her head. "If you insist, Your Grace."

"I do," he replied.

For a moment, they all stood there, measuring this sudden change in the house, the subtle shift that Preston had finally managed.

"Then you had best get changed," she nudged, tipping her head toward the clock. "So we don't miss the announcement."

"Yes, quite," Preston agreed, glancing down at his plain coat and breeches. "Can't miss that announcement."

"Announcement?" Roxley muttered. "Tonight?"

Lady Juniper heaved a sigh. "Yes, haven't you been listening?"

"I try not to," he replied.

There was a snorkle of laughter from Henry, which was squelched with a hot glance from Hen. "Remember, Preston, no scandals."

He bowed to his aunt and said, "Most assuredly, my lady."

Which meant he'd just have to find a way to ruin Miss Tabitha Timmons without Hen finding out.

"Despite yesterday's unfortunate events," Barkworth said, "my uncle is most taken with you, my dear."

How Tabitha wished he wasn't. Good heavens, whatever was it going to take to get Barkworth to cry off?

How she wished Preston had been just a little quicker with that kiss. She gave herself a moment to delve into the delicious possibilities that said kiss might have offered, but then she shivered, and once again, Barkworth intruded into her reverie.

"Miss Timmons, you have the most dreadful habit of shivering. Someone is going to think you in ill health," he complained. "My uncle has a great dread of infection."

Who can blame him, she thought, *knowing you will inherit?* She just smiled and straightened, for she had no desire to come under the marquess's scrutiny any more than she had to.

As Preston had said, the Marquess of Grately was an odious old goat, who'd come up and inspected her like a horse at the fair, stopping just shy of checking her withers.

"Excellent, Barkworth. Excellent," he'd cackled as he'd walked around her, eyeing the low cut of her bodice with a lecherous stare.

Meanwhile, Lady Timmons and Lady Ancil had looked on approvingly.

Even now, with Barkworth at her side, and his mother and her aunt right behind them, there was little room for escape, not that the two matrons were leaving anything to chance. Even worse, Barkworth continued to go on and on about the Special License he had procured this very afternoon so they could expedite "their happy and joyous union."

What would have been "happy and joyous" would have been to awaken this morning with her ankle swollen to the size of a small pumpkin and her unable to attend the marquess's ball. Yet once again, her long hours of labors at the vicarage had left her able to rebound quickly—and her ankle had presented hardly a twinge.

So unless Tabitha could manage another injury, it appeared there was little time left to stop Barkworth's uncle from making his announcement.

Please, Preston. Save me.

"Good heavens above!" Lady Timmons gasped. "What is she doing here?"

Lady Ancil sniffed. "Scandalous creature. Three husbands, indeed! How can she call herself a lady?"

Three husbands?

Tabitha looked up and spied Lady Juniper coming into the ballroom. The stately lady was like an answer to her prayer. For if Lady Juniper was here, then Preston must be close at hand...

Rising up on her tiptoes, Tabitha craned her neck to find him, but much to her disappointment it wasn't the duke escorting Lady Juniper this evening but the Earl of Roxley guiding her into the crush of guests.

No, no, no! Tabitha wanted to cry out. *Oh, Preston, where the devil are you?*

Harriet, who stood off to one side with Daphne, met her gaze and nodded, understanding in her eyes and a slight smile on her lips. Without a word, she slid away into the crowd.

Tabitha knew exactly where her friend was going: to Roxley. Which was a scandalous notion in itself, but not one Lady Timmons would notice, for she was too busy keeping a tight guard on her niece.

Meanwhile, Barkworth continued on, blithely discussing the merits of a vacant house near Hanover Square that a friend had mentioned. "The morning room is supposed to have a lovely view of the garden," he was telling her.

Tabitha feigned interest, all the while thinking of the clutch of bluebells Preston had picked for her. That he'd gone out into the countryside and found them just for her.

You, Tabby, astound me.

You surprise me, Your Grace.

Her insides trembled as she recalled how he'd leaned down and she'd thought, nay, she'd wished with everything she possessed that he would kiss her again. Leave her so breathless and insensible that he'd pick up the reins and steal her away, take her far from London before she ever gained the wits to protest.

However had this happened? She'd been able to convince herself that their night at the inn had been naught but the results of hunger (on her part), too much wine (on his part—and hers, if she was being honest) and a setting fraught with intimacy—as well as a less-than-stellar chaperone.

But even surrounded as they had been in Lady Knolles's ballroom, Tabitha had discovered that an entire world could exist between two people. A stage of sorts that was theirs, and theirs alone. Secrets shared, a touch that sent shivers of promises through one's limbs, the desire to get lost in an intimate gaze.

Again, she tried to convince herself that the night had been inclined to romance—dancing with a handsome duke, the music, her scandalous gown, a night she never could have imagined before…

Just as now, she had come to realize how no two men were alike. Or that her heart, once it had discerned the difference, could not be swayed.

Preston…and his wretched bluebells…and his lopsided grin…and his teasing manners.

She wished him to perdition. She wished he'd taken that corner by the oak with all due care and continued through Kempton so that she'd never met him. She wished he'd never come into her life and turned it so very upside down.

She wished him at her side this very moment.

If only to turn it all to rights by doing his very best to turn it all to ruin.

"And how could I fail to mention that uncle has invited us to Grately House for the autumn shooting season. Can you imagine that? It is a compliment on my choice of bride, I do believe," Barkworth was saying. "There, my dear, you shall have your jaunt to the country yet."

An entire month of the old goat ogling the front of her gown at every opportunity—Tabitha's stomach rolled. She glanced away lest he see the tears rising in her eyes, and there across the room she thought she saw him.

Preston. A tall figure done up in black standing to one side. Could it be him? She dashed at her eyes with the back of her glove.

Just then, Harriet came rushing back from her foray. "Tabitha! Oh, there you are. Most excellent news. Lady Essex is here. You must bring Barkworth over to meet her."

"Lady Essex? Indeed!" Lady Ancil enthused. "You know Lady Essex?"

"Yes, ma'am," Tabitha said. "She kindly brought us all up to London."

"Lady Essex holds Tabitha in the highest of esteem," Harriet said, which was doing it up a bit but nonetheless gained the desired results.

"Oh, that is wonderful," Lady Ancil said, a bit of admiration and approval showing in her eyes, where most of the night she had regarded her future daughter-in-law as a necessary evil. "She is hosting a breakfast next week that is supposed to be quite exclusive."

"We've been invited," Harriet said, glancing at her gloved fingers. "At least Tabitha and Daphne and I were."

Lady Timmons sniffed.

Apparently, Lady Ancil had not been and was even now seeing her opportunity. "Yes, yes, we should all go over and pay our respects to Lady Essex."

She moved forward and Barkworth went to follow, towing Tabitha with him, but unfortunately, Harriet had not been paying attention and trod down on the hem of Tabitha's gown so that it ripped.

"Oh, no!" Harriet said, dancing back a bit, her eyes wide with horror.

Tabitha, having played enough games of charades with her friend, knew it was all an act.

Lady Ancil glanced down and shuddered, for the gold overskirt of Tabitha's gown was torn—noticeably so. "You clumsy girl," she scolded Harriet. "However can she go up for the announcement looking like that?"

"Oh, I've ruined everything!" Harriet bit her lip and looked ready to cry. "Tabitha, will you ever forgive me?"

Then Daphne waded in. "Harriet, take her to the retiring room and fix it." She glanced over at Lady Ancil. "As awkward as Harriet is, she is ever so good with a needle." Winding her arm into Lady Ancil's and her other into the crook of Barkworth's free arm, she continued, "Have I told you that Lady Essex is a Dale? A very distant one, but she holds such a fondness for family. I know if I were to ask her—"

"Do you think you might, Miss Dale?" Barkworth interjected, his tattered bride-to-be all but forgotten.

However, Lady Timmons wasn't so easily diverted. She glanced down at the ruined hem and frowned. "Come now, Tabitha. That gown must be repaired."

Daphne wasn't a Dale for nothing, for she glanced over her shoulder. "Lady Timmons, aren't you coming? I am ever so sure we could secure invitations for you and Tabitha's cousins—if you were there to remind Lady Essex of her obvious oversight in not including all of you to begin with."

The lure of invitations to the most coveted breakfast

in London proved to be the lady's undoing. "Tabitha, why are you still loitering about? Go have Harriet fix your gown and return as quickly as possible." She shooed her off, then hurried after Daphne and Lady Ancil.

"Come quickly," Harriet said, towing Tabitha in the opposite direction.

"But I thought I saw Preston," she whispered. "Over there—" She tipped her head toward the other side.

"He has found the perfect place," Harriet said.

"The perfect place for what?"

They had come to a stop in the foyer, which was empty, save for the footman standing well outside the front door on the steps, awaiting any latecomers.

Harriet grinned. "For your ruin, what else?"

Harriet all but shoved her through a narrow door, and Tabitha landed squarely in Preston's firm embrace.

"Tabby, whatever are you doing here?" he murmured into her ear as he held her close.

Tabitha knew she shouldn't feel this way—but whatever was it about this man that made her long to be with him, rub against him like a house cat? More than that, Preston smelled heavenly—like a man ought—of a bit of bayberry rum soap and something else that she couldn't put a finger on but her fluttering senses recognized.

A masculine, sensual air that had her inhaling deeply.

"Didn't they tell you it was a betrothal party?" he scolded so very firmly that she might have thought it a ducal reproach if it hadn't been for the twinkle in his eyes. "And after you promised me so faithfully that you would not engage in such tawdry matters. *Tsk, tsk, tsk.*"

She smiled at his teasing. "I am hardly here by my own volition, Your Grace."

"Preston," he corrected.

"If you insist," she said, knowing very well she would never think of him otherwise.

"I insist," he told her. "It is my right."

"You are a scandal," she shot back, then glanced around at their surroundings. "What is this place?"

"The footman's closet."

Indeed it was, tucked partially under the stairs, with lamps on hooks, umbrellas at the ready and all the other tools of their trade. As well as an old sofa in one corner for the poor man who had to tend the door late into the night.

"A perfect place to cause a scandal, don't you think?" he mused, holding her out at arm's length and looking her up and down from head to toe.

Tabitha shook her head and stepped out of his grasp. "If you ruin me… Think of what it will do. What if your aunt makes good her threat? Then where will you be? Preston, I won't have it."

"Then we will have to make sure this doesn't turn into a great dustup. Just enough to give Barkworth a case of cold feet."

"I don't know," she said, shaking her head.

"This from my perpetual damsel in distress." Preston circled her, looking her up and down.

"Whatever are you doing?"

"Wondering why you wore that gown." He eyed the white embroidered muslin with the gold silk overskirt.

"Whatever has my gown to do with getting me out of this betrothal?"

"Everything," he told her, digging into his coat pocket, "but we will get to that in a moment." He held up a piece of paper covered in a scribbled hand.

"Is *that* a copy of Uncle Winston's will?" It was dog-eared and barely legible.

He nodded. "I fear Mr. Hathaway had to jot down the particulars in great haste."

She laughed and rushed back into his arms.

"I hate to say it, but your admiration should be directed at Mr. Hathaway—he was able to procure this," Preston told her, though he didn't let her go. "Though perhaps in his case, an enthusiastically worded note of appreciation will suffice."

"Yes, but you made it happen," she replied, ever so happy he was her knight-errant. "Is it true? As Harriet said, I need only get Barkworth to cry off?"

He nodded and guided her over to the table, where he lay the paper down. He caught up one of the lamps and held it aloft.

"There's hope?" she whispered, gazing at the piece of paper, trying to decipher Chaunce's dashed cipher.

"Tabby, there is always hope." He stabbed one paragraph. "Here is your key to freedom."

Article 3, Section 1, If the designated party in Article 2, Section 5, declares his intention not to marry my niece, Miss Tabitha Timmons, or he is married at the time of my death, or he has departed this world, she shall inherit the entirety of holdings upon reaching her majority, to be held in a trust...

The note ended there.

Tabby looked at him. "So it is true—if Barkworth cries off, I keep my fortune?"

"Indeed."

"And I don't have to marry anyone else. My uncle doesn't have another such creature in line for my hand."

Preston laughed, "If you don't want to marry—"

"I most decidedly do not want to marry—" She stopped herself as she looked up at Preston, for she feared what would come tumbling out.

No, not Barkworth. Especially not Barkworth.

But if she were ever to dream of a husband, then he would be just like the man before her. Willing to wade in and catch her when she was falling—or even after she'd tumbled. Willing to share the last piece of apple tart.

A man whose kiss kept her awake at night wondering if it had been real.

And more so, what would happen next if ever Preston kissed her again...

As she gazed up into his handsome features, into his endless blue eyes, she dared to suspect that he might... Oh, it was too much to believe. Too much to dare consider... But what if...

In an instant, he tore his gaze from her, and an odd, awkward silence filled the room, as if they'd been overly conscious of the intimate moment that had just passed between them.

Tabitha coughed a little and stared down at the paper, while her mind could only think of one thing.

Perhaps Preston cared for her.

No! Why, it was too ridiculous to believe.

Then he gave her every reason to hope.

"Do you trust me?" he asked. His fingers twined in a loose tendril of her hair and gently pushed it back from her face, sending shivers down her spine.

The answer came easily. "Decidedly not."

"Excellent," he said, grinning. "This is what we are going to do…"

Chapter 14

Harriet had made her way to stand beside Lord Roxley.

"Hallo, Harry," he said.

"Miss Hathaway, my lord," she said, nose in the air.

"You'll always be Harry to me," he told her.

She shook her head. "Can't you see? I'm no longer that child." She held out her skirt and gave him her best all-grown-up-and-in-London pose.

He cast a sideways glance at her. "No, you aren't." Folding his arms over his chest, he sighed. "And if you ever dance with Fieldgate again, I will inform your brothers. He is not good *ton*, Harry."

"I found him charming," she shot back. "And if you won't ask me—"

"I'm not one to stand in line," he told her.

"And I am not one to wait."

Her answer came out hot and testy, and it made Roxley grin. "You aren't going to floor me now, are you? Like the last time I refused you?"

"My lord! How can you bring up such a thing?"

"Because it isn't every day one gets a marriage proposal and a black eye."

"How like you to keep bringing that up, my lord."

"I keep hoping you will call me by something other than 'my lord,' like you used to."

"It isn't proper," she said softly.

"Not even when we are nearly alone, as we are now?" he asked, turning toward her and hiding her from the host of guests.

And then, something changed. They were no longer children in Kempton—Roxley having been brought down to his future holding by his grandmother to visit Lady Essex, and the Hathaway children brought over to entertain the future earl.

Roxley gazed down at Harriet Hathaway and saw her all over again. "Given up on marrying me, have you, Harry?"

Her lashes fluttered—actually fluttered, all coquettish and meant to stop a man cold. Where the devil had Harry Hathaway learned to do that?

"How many times can a lady ask before she gives up?"

The note in her voice haunted him. She was right. One day she would give up on him and find someone else. Like that idiot Fieldgate or, worse, some fellow who actually deserved her, was worthy of her.

Looking into those emerald green eyes of hers, the invitation in them so very clear, it was all he could do not to lean over and kiss her.

Oh, good God! Kiss Harry? What the hell was he thinking? Never mind the fact that her brothers would kill him for such an affront—five times over.

Roxley pulled back, the very thought of a firing squad of Hathaways enough to cool his ardor. "I'll continue to refuse you, imp," he said, turning around so he stood next to her, his back to the wall. "You would deplore being married to me."

"Yes, most likely," she replied.

He glanced over at her. Well, she needn't sound so sure of that.

"How long have they been in there?" she asked with a nod toward the foyer and a quick change of subject. "The timing needs to be perfect."

"You aren't just getting rid of Barkworth, are you, Harry?" Roxley glanced down at his gloves, trying to put up the appearance of being bored out of his mind. "Matchmaking, are we?"

Harriet ignored him for as long as she could manage before she turned to him and demanded, "Whatever would be wrong with that?"

Roxley grinned. Ah, so Harry's fire hadn't been extinguished by that proper silk gown and all her Town manners. "Nothing."

They stood there for another few minutes, watching the clock as the hand slowly made its trek up toward midnight.

"How long does it take to ruin a lady?" she asked as one might the directions to Hyde Park.

He coughed and nearly fell off the wall. "Depends on the gentleman..." Then he took another long, sideways glance at Harry. "And the lady, of course."

Much to his chagrin, Harriet wasn't looking at him.

"They've missed her," she said, nodding across the ballroom toward Miss Timmons's relations. "Dash it all, I think they need more time."

"I promised Preston I would arrive at the stroke of midnight," Roxley told her.

"Couldn't we give them just a little more time?" Harriet pleaded, and demmit, if she didn't do that thing with her lashes that left him all tangled up inside. Made him nearly forget who she was and the devil's load of trouble he would be in if he ever did overlook that.

He managed to nod. "Yes, if you insist." Better to give in to her demands than to give in to what he suddenly desired more.

Probably always had if he was being honest. *Can't have her, Roxley. And you know it.*

"You go divert the ladies," he told her, sending her across the room, "and I will take care of Barkworth." Who was, even now, striding toward the foyer, right past Roxley.

Trying to think of some way to delay the man, Roxley did what he always did best. He improvised.

"Ah, Mr. Barkworth, a word with you," he called out.

"Not now, my lord," Barkworth said, about to continue past.

Roxley shrugged and resorted to Plan B.

He stuck out his boot and sent the very respectable and always dignified Mr. Reginald Barkworth catapulting into the foyer.

"Preston, I won't ruin you," Tabitha told him. "There must be another way."

He nodded at the door. "I could fetch Roxley to do

the task." He started for the door, and she anchored him by the arm.

"No!"

"Do you want my help or not?" he asked.

"Ever so much." She was talking about his help, wasn't she? Tabitha slanted another glance at him and shivered.

How could she think of anything else with her gaze fixed on the masculine cut of his jaw, the hard line of his lips, the covetous way he looked at her that left her feeling like the last piece of apple tart—wanted, desired, enticingly delicious.

Her. Miss Tabitha Timmons of Kempton. Enticing to a duke. It was a heady, unbelievable notion that had her almost believing she was a beauty, like Daphne, or daring, like Harriet.

Oh, bother the man. He was distracting her from being reasonable. And he must have seen the hesitancy in her eyes.

"This is my decision," he told her. "I want to help you."

"Not even for my freedom," she said, "will I sacrifice your happiness. I won't have you left alone just to save me."

"It is my choice," he told her. "Just as I long to give you your choices. Your freedom," he confessed as he drew her into his arms, unwilling to hear any more arguments on the subject. He gazed down at her for the barest of seconds before his lips captured hers and he kissed her.

Tabitha melted inside the moment he claimed her. It wasn't just his kiss, but Preston. Holding her, pulling her up against him so she was pressed to his chest, his arms wound around her.

She was trapped, ensnared, delirious.

Then she discovered he had yet to work his magic.

His lips teased hers, whispered over hers, tugged at her. She opened up to him, surrendering beneath his eager assault. Perhaps she should have put up a better fight, but honestly? She was in no mood to protest.

Her body had ached for weeks for him to return to her, to awaken the lingering threads of desire he'd plucked to life before. And the notes, the music, the way her body tightened as he continued to kiss her, his tongue sliding over hers, tangling with hers, lapping and pulling at her desires like the persistent flow of a river.

Come with me, follow me, drown in me.

Drown she did. As he kissed her, as he touched her, one hand stroking her back, the other beneath her breast, gently cradling it, his thumb moving to her nipple, which tightened into a knot as he rubbed it, sliding his thumb over her again and again, waves began to crash inside her.

The tumult spread, careening through her limbs as his lips moved from her mouth. She could breathe, but only for a moment, as he dipped his head to the nape of her neck, just behind her ear and began to nibble and tease her there.

Tabitha gasped for air. "Oh, my! Oh…"

Preston's head dipped further as his lips explored the tops of her breasts, his hands lifting them so he could nuzzle against them.

Tabitha rose up on her tiptoes, her thighs clenched together, for the twisting, aching desire that had settled there made her want to hold onto it and at the same time find some way to set it free.

He glanced down at her, his dark eyes smoky with desire. Without a word, his fingers slid inside her bodice, touching her. No longer was there the silk of her gown between them but the warmth of his bare fingers sliding over her trembling body.

His lips returned to that spot on her neck, the one that left her writhing with need, while his fingers were tracing a new path of desire.

"Oh, Preston," she gasped, her legs beginning to give out. She didn't want to stand up anymore. As much as she didn't know about all this, her body seemed to understand.

She wanted to lie down…she wanted him to cover her…to ease this ache he was building inside her with his touch, with his kiss.

He looked up from his conquest and grinned. And she could have sworn he was about to sweep her off her feet when all of a sudden the clock in the hallway beyond began to chime.

The deep sound startled them, and they both took a step back, Tabitha's heart hammering in her chest. Almost immediately she was surrounded by the chill of the room as it scolded her heated limbs.

Yet for all the room was cold, she was still warmed through by his kiss, by his touch. By the fire he'd lit inside her.

"Oh, goodness," Tabitha whispered. If anything, his kiss improved with time. Or she was getting better at all this.

At least he hadn't left the room in a blind rush. Thankfully, for her body was atremble with desire.

"Yes, my," he said, straightening up and looking everywhere in the room but where she stood. "Yes, that ought to do the trick...you look..."

Tabitha stilled. She looked what?

He didn't finish, just gazed at her, his mouth slightly open, like the lion he always reminded her of—hungry and ready to devour his prey.

They stood there for some time, and finally Tabitha's patience began to wane. "The earl isn't here yet," she said. "Perhaps we should kiss again."

"If you insist," Preston said, closing the space between them and catching hold of her in a heated rush.

Preston had known desire for a woman, but he'd never known how ravenous desire could make him with the *right* woman. Their lips fused together and they kissed deeply, hungrily, as if the minutes apart had been a lifetime.

"Tabby," he whispered into the nape of her neck. She smelled of wild roses, spicy and tempting, leaving him with the desire to inhale, to taste deeply.

He cradled her breast again, and this time he didn't wait to explore them, sliding her gown from her shoulder and pulling them free, her puckered nipples like ripe raspberries, begging to be tasted.

Taking one in his mouth, he grew harder as he listened to her gasp in surprise and then moan softly, her body rocking against him with that familiar, anxious cadence.

He teased the rosy tip to a tight bud and then kissed the other one, while Tabby, his insistent Puss, rubbed against him, purring like a heated cat.

Yet he was still hungry for her, desired so much

more. He rose and kissed her, his fingers working the pins in her hair free so it tumbled down in a ginger veil. All fire, she was his siren temptress. No more the tart spinster.

Well, tart, perhaps, he mused as she kissed him back, insistent and hungry. Her hands slid over his back, down his hips and then moved to the front of his breeches. With one bold move, she touched him, tracing her fingers over his entire rock-hard length.

To hear her sighing with longing nearly left him undone.

How had he come to this ragged need?

At first there had been this slow rekindling of that fire that had sparked between them at the inn, but now having her this second time, he found himself combusting. Burning to lay her down on that narrow sofa and ruin her completely, utterly…until she cried out his name and he had claimed her thoroughly…

"Preston, please," she whispered anxiously in his ear.

To him, her pleas were as intoxicating as her kiss. As her anxious touch.

He glanced at the sofa, imagining her there, her skirts thrown up, him burying himself inside her. He couldn't think of anything he wanted more. To claim her as his own.

But then his gaze strayed to the single door that any moment Roxley would be leading Barkworth through. This time he wasn't about to let that man interrupt them.

Never again. Because as far as he was concerned, she was his. For now. Forever.

So he set Tabitha aside and went to the door.

* * *

Tabitha teetered on her wobbly legs. Good heavens! Whatever was Preston doing? He wasn't leaving?

Not now! her body clamored loudly. *Please, not now.*

She rushed around him, as fast as she could move with her ankle, and threw herself across the closed door. "You promised."

He looked at her. No, he gaped at her.

Tabitha glanced down and realized her most proper gown was off one shoulder and her hair had tumbled free from the pins. And she knew why. This man. This rakish, devilish man. He'd left her so utterly undone. She looked up at him.

"Yes, you do look properly ruined," he told her.

Glancing over at the door, Tabitha bit her lower lip. "Whatever is wrong? Wouldn't it be more convincing if you were kissing me when we are discovered?" She tried batting her eyes.

He laughed. "Tabby, you are my undoing, aren't you?"

"You are the one who came along and insisted on saving me," she pointed out. *Now save me...*

"Agreed."

She reached out and laid her palm on his chest. Beneath her fingers, his heart hammered. "And you said that Roxley would be here at the stroke of midnight?"

"He was supposed to be," Preston conceded.

Her other hand clung to the doorknob, unwilling to let go...to let him pass.

"Then it will hardly do for him to bring Barkworth here to find us arguing over whether or not we should be kissing," she told him.

"There is no argument on that point," he said, in a voice thickened with desire. "But if we continue—"

"You'll ruin me," Tabitha finished. "Which is, I believe, the point of all this."

He reached around her and Tabitha stilled, waiting for him to pry open the door and leave her to her ruin.

Alone. Anxious. Hungry. Did she leave out delirious? Yes, that as well.

"Whatever are you doing?" she whispered.

Preston leaned closer and said softly into her ear, "Locking the door."

Tabitha stilled as his hand came out from behind her, holding the key.

Then, to her amazement, he pressed it into her hand. "It is your choice when to open it."

Never, she wanted to cry out as she looked down at the cold metal piece in her hand. She looked up into his eyes, where the fires still blazed, her fingers curling around the key.

The key to her virginity...

Outside the door, there was a bit of a hue and cry being raised in the foyer. It was only a matter of time before they would be discovered.

Time...choice...discovery. It all ran together in Tabitha's whirling thoughts with only one clear answer.

She tossed the key onto the little side table where the lone lamp illuminated the narrow room, and she stepped into Preston's arms.

The duke enveloped her in his grasp...and was it her, or did he let out a long breath as he did? Relieved that she'd returned to him.

What did it matter, for their lips fused together,

all the more hungry. His tongue ran over hers and Tabitha's insides tightened.

She arched toward him, suddenly wanton. "Preston!"

He swept her into his arms and carried her over to the sofa.

"Tabby. My ruinous, beautiful Tabby."

She sighed at his praise and felt exactly as he'd described her—beautiful—as he set her down, his eyes all smoky passions as he gazed down at her. He kneeled between her legs and kissed her. Her lips, her earlobe, her neck, the tops of her breasts.

Her nipples… Sucking them deeply into his mouth, one, then the other, until Tabitha stretched like a cat.

His hand reached down and edged her skirt aside, running his fingers up her calves, to her thigh, his fingers sending tendrils of desire through her already anxious limbs.

As he came higher, she had a moment of panic, her slippers digging into the carpet, her hands clinging to his jacket, a moment which subsided instantly when his fingers brushed over the curls there.

He stroked her slowly, softly, while he plied her lips with kisses, teased her tongue in a lavish dance, running alongside it, over it, beneath it. And when his finger slid inside her, it was at the same time his tongue teased over hers and she felt something so breathless that she rode up on his hand, if only to feel all of it.

She was wet and taut, and all she wanted to be was filled. Filled by him. Reaching for his breeches, she opened them, her hand going inside, and she curled her palm around him, lifting him out and running her hand up and down his solid, hard length, stroking him as he continued to tease her.

Dizzy with need, she looked up at him, then, easing out of his grasp, leaned back on the sofa so she lay on its length. "Please, Preston."

He moved over her, and he caught hold of one of her legs and wrapped it around his waist, while he slid his other hand under her hip and hitched her up, even as the tip of his member came into her cleft, sliding slowly at first, in and out.

Tabitha gasped as he drove himself deeper into her, for he was long and thick, and she felt so very full. He continued to stroke her, kissing her as he moved deeper, and when he got to the barrier that said all too clearly that no man had ever had her, he paused only for a second.

Choices, she could almost hear him saying. *You will always have a choice with me.*

"Please, do this. Take me completely," she gasped as she tried to arch up.

And he did, thrusting into her, finally and completely ruining her.

For any and all others.

Then Preston revealed his true profession, the one that was his calling, as he made love to her, slowly, quickly, gauging the fever in her eyes, in her soft, urgent cries. He built an anxious fire inside her, inside himself, she had to assume, for he too moaned, thrusting hard and quickly as the dance between them became a restless, greedy, driving race for one thing.

And what that was, Tabitha hadn't the least notion, until suddenly the waves, the river's flow that had pulled her along, now tossed her into a ravine, over the cascading torrent she fell… Fell and crashed over the rocks, unable to breathe, breathless as wave after wave swallowed over her.

Consumed her.

She gasped and cried out, what she didn't know. Didn't care.

She clung to Preston and hung on, for he too was thrusting into her, crying out her name and filling her with his hot desire.

Preston looked down at the lady in his arms and had never felt both so sated and so possessive in all his life. As if he had found his home. His heart.

No, it wasn't possible. And yet…

Tabby. Oh, Tabby. However did you do this to me?

This spinster had driven him over the edge. Left him without an iota of control, and now he'd made love to her at her own betrothal ball. It was beyond even his own notion of scandal.

Oh, dear God, he realized. She hardly looked the penitent miss. Not with that starry look in her eyes—a light that burned there for him and him alone.

No, Miss Tabitha Timmons wasn't ruined.

He was.

Leaning closer, Preston kissed Tabitha, softly, gently, quietly, despite the tumult raging inside him. For when he kissed her, all those old fears, all those empty places seemed to glow with a light that seemed capable of chasing away the darkness.

A light that could guide him home.

* * *

"Get off the ground," the Marquess of Grately barked at his nephew.

Barkworth scrambled to his feet. "I was tripped." He glared at Lord Roxley.

"Tripped?" Roxley shook his head. "Yes, by the steps. Doesn't do to get so foxed at your own betrothal ball, Barkworth. One would think you didn't want to marry the gel."

"I am not drunk. I'll have you know I never—"

"Oh, do shut up," his uncle said, pushing past Barkworth and coming to face Roxley. "Where is Miss Timmons?"

Roxley gave them both his best wide-eyed, innocent expression. "How would I know? She's not my betrothed." He glanced over at Barkworth, who was brushing off his pants and jacket. "Lost her already? Doesn't bode well if you can't keep her in hand, now, does it?"

"Roxley, I'll shoot you myself if you don't tell us where Miss Timmons is!" Grately thundered.

The earl stood his ground and mutely faced the irate marquess.

The older man's face grew even more red. "Where is she?"

"Well, I am rather at a crossroads," Roxley replied. "Did you mean to say you would shoot me if I didn't tell you or if I did?" He glanced around at the growing party that now included Miss Timmons's aunt and uncle and a few others. "I'm utterly confused now."

"Bah!" Lord Grately said, waving a hand at him. "Search the house," he ordered Barkworth. "You as well," he told Sir Mauris and Lady Timmons. And finally he turned to Roxley. "And don't you move."

"I daresay I must," Roxley told him. "I have a terrible itch right here." He scratched his shoulder and sighed happily as his fingers dug into his jacket.

"Idiot," Grately ranted as he began to climb the stairs, the entire party and every available footman trailing in his angry wake.

Harriet passed him and winked. "Well done."

Roxley bowed slightly and leaned back against the wall opposite the footman's closet, looking anywhere but at the closed door across the foyer.

The search for Tabitha ranged through the Marquess of Grately's house, from the attics to the ground floor.

"Get a lantern," the marquess ordered one of the footmen, "so we can search the cellars."

Sir Mauris let out an exasperated sigh. "She wouldn't be in the cellars. She's escaped!"

The footman looked from one lord to the other and did as Grately told him, even if he privately shared Lord Timmons's assessment that this bird had flown. Yet when he went to the closet, the door was locked.

"Whatever is taking so much time?" Grately fumed.

The footman tried the door again, but the handle wouldn't turn. "The door's locked, my lord. It's never been locked afore."

Lord Grately and Sir Mauris exchanged glances.

"Kick it open, you fool," Grately ordered.

As Preston looked at Tabitha's tousled state, her swollen lips, her half-lidded expression of bliss, there would be no doubt to anyone as to what exactly had transpired between them.

Hen would never forgive him for this new scandal. Henry would take her side and follow his sister as she moved out.

But the real disaster lay elsewhere…in his tattered and lonely heart. But before he could fathom this change inside him, the doorknob rattled ominously.

The rattle was immediately followed by a rumble as the door shook on its hinges, bringing them both to their feet in a frantic hurry to recover their clothing and some semblance of modesty.

Tabitha straightened her gown and sighed as she tried to tuck her hair back up into its elaborate waterfall of curls, even as he was tugging on his breeches and boots.

He couldn't even remember when they'd come off in the hurried, torrid rush that had been their lovemaking.

Neither of them spoke. What was there to say?

Too much, he supposed. And neither of them knew the words.

Say what is in your heart.

Preston stilled. No, that was too much. He'd vowed never to do that. There was too much to lose when one loved entirely.

Instead, he went over to the side table and picked up the key. "Ready?"

Tabitha nodded.

He pushed the key into the lock and turned it. The old lock gave a loud click, and he stepped back.

Which was fortunate, for the door almost immediately swung open.

Grately came through the door first, with Barkworth and Sir Mauris crowding into the narrow room.

Any hope Preston had of keeping this scandal to a minimum was quickly doused, for he could see that while the room's size prohibited a large audience, that didn't mean the grand foyer prevented any number of the *ton*'s biggest gossips from elbowing their way into a front-row seat at the door.

For those who couldn't see in, there was Lady Peevers, who announced to one and all, "Good God, what has Preston done to her?" This was followed by a stunned pause, the time it took for the lady's jaw to drop and then find its way back up. "Oh! That!"

Yes, *that*.

"Dear heavens," Lady Ancil began before stuffing her handkerchief into her mouth and breaking into sobs.

Impotent fool that Barkworth was, the man's lips flapped and fluttered, while no words came out.

Tabitha's uncle wasn't so encumbered. "Get away from my niece," Sir Mauris ordered.

Nor was their host, Lord Grately, his face blazing with apoplectic fury. "You wretched bounder! How dare you! And in my house!"

Preston wasn't too sure if the man was mourning the loss of a wealthy heiress or that his name would now be tied to this scandalous scene. By tomorrow—given that Lady Peevers was the first witness—the story would be repeated across London and filling every gossipy letter leaving Town.

You will never believe what happened at Lord Grately's last night...

He glanced over at Tabby, her lips plump and rosy

from his kisses, her eyes alight with passion, and he couldn't help himself—he grinned. He'd saved her.

From a wretched marriage. From her family's machinations. Even from her uncle Winston's carefully wrought provisions.

Or so he thought.

"I should have known how you would turn out," Grately was saying, his dark gaze blazing into Tabitha. "Your uncle was an insufferable mushroom with no honor—thinking he could use my debts to blackmail me into agreeing to this match. I won't stand for it."

"But Uncle—" Barkworth began.

"Don't 'But Uncle' me, you sniveling, worthless reminder of what I don't have! An heir worthy of our family name. You'd have me welcome that devil's byblow as yours?" Grately made a guttural noise that had Lady Ancil yanking her only child out of his uncle's line of sight. "Get out of my house!" the man fumed. "All of you!"

Sir Mauris crossed the room. "You foolish, stupid, girl!" He stopped in front of Tabitha and looked to be about to strike her, his hand rising in anger.

Preston moved faster, pulling her behind him and stepping up to the other man. "Harm her and you'll answer to me."

But Sir Mauris wasn't easily cowed. "Bah! You're the one who should be answering for this. And you will, by God! I promise that you will—"

"Not here," Lady Timmons said, having pushed her way forward, now that Barkworth and Lady Ancil had retreated to the foyer. "Do not add to this," she warned both of them. Her ladyship caught hold of

Tabitha, and, with a raised eyebrow, she dared Preston to naysay her.

He was going to protest, but he looked up and found Hen in the doorway, her face round with shock.

Preston bowed his head and let Lady Timmons take Tabitha. She hauled her wayward niece out of the room so quickly that he nearly missed the quick glance Tabby threw him over her shoulder.

Even as she was pulled past Lady Ancil, who drew in her skirts, and Barkworth, who gave his former nearly intended the cut direct, she mouthed to him and him alone two words. "*Thank you.*"

He tipped his head slightly in acknowledgement. He'd saved her.

Oh, but had he?

Meanwhile, Hen caught up her skirts and turned her back to him, taking advantage of the wake left by Sir Mauris and his disgraced party. She hadn't said a word.

Then again, she didn't need to.

This left only him, and all eyes turned in his direction. Gazes filled with disgust, dismay and outright anger.

He'd laughed and dismissed his tenuous place in society for months. Gadded about Town as if it were his private circus, as Hen had once said.

But no longer. He'd ruined an innocent vicar's daughter—was there no end to his vile conduct?

It isn't like that, he wanted to tell them. *It is different this time. She is different.*

Very different. Up ahead, Tabby was being pushed into her uncle's carriage, and as it wheeled quickly away, Preston felt as if it was taking a part of him with it.

His heart. With that carriage went the only chance he'd ever had to regain what he'd lost all those years ago.

Owle Park as it should be. Open and filled with laughter. A life spent squabbling over the last piece of Yorkshire pudding and apple tart. Spending days riding, and walking, and keeping Mr. Muggins in line.

And nights…nights in the most heavenly ways possible.

He wanted her always and in every way. He wanted her because…because…

Egads, because he'd fallen in love with her!

Preston came to a sudden stop, the notion knocking the wind out of his chest. *He loved Tabby.* He loved her because she'd made him believe again.

Lady Essex took full advantage of his halted progress and stepped into his path. Leave it to Roxley's formidable old aunt to say what everyone else was thinking. "You horrid man! You've ruined the girl. Now no one will ever marry her."

No one save me.

The realization left Preston grinning at the old girl. Then he caught her by the shoulders, leaned close and bussed her on both cheeks. "I know. Isn't that the most perfect solution!"

Chapter 15

Preston spent three days waiting for someone to call. Three days! Usually it only took one before an outraged father, a furious brother, a guardian with a grudge arrived—seconds or witnesses in tow—and demanded satisfaction.

Or more to the point, that Preston marry the flirt and make an honest woman of her. What they really wanted was for him to elevate this reckless chit to the rank of duchess. His duchess.

Which, of course, being him, he'd refuse. Refuse to duel, refuse to marry their wayward, all-too-forward slip-o-muslin, refuse to be blackmailed by their complaints and impotent threats. Then he'd have Benley show the entire party to the door.

That was how it was supposed to be done. On this, one could be assured that the Duke of Preston could be considered an expert.

But not this time. No one came.

Not Barkworth, not Sir Mauris, not even Grately had found his way to Preston's prominent address. Not one of them had come to Harley Street demanding satisfaction for Tabby's ruined honor.

He'd woken up this morning, exasperated with the entirety of Tabby's family, though he'd held out a small hope of finding Miss Dale and Miss Hathaway outside his address, tossing rotten eggs at his front door.

Much to his disappointment, not even that plucky pair had deigned to visit.

"Good God, I am going to have to do this all myself," he muttered to no one in particular over a nuncheon in the Red Room that had yet to be interrupted. That was because there was no one to interrupt it. No one at the door, no one in the house.

Save Preston and the servants.

The emptiness made the duke's residence a veritable tomb. Not that he'd noticed overly much. He'd been too busy: hunting down his mother's jewels, issuing orders and letters to have Owle Park reopened, servants hired. Making all sorts of plans that he would be able to put in motion if only Sir Mauris would show up.

Leave it to a mere baronet to get this all wrong.

Preston heaved a sigh, pushed aside his cold cup of tea and ordered Benley to fetch his carriage as another possibility came to him: Sir Mauris, having never caused any bit of a dustup, least of all a ruination, might not have any notion as to how these things were done.

If only Preston had realized this sooner.

Dashing off to his carriage, Preston wondered if

he shouldn't enlist Roxley to go over and set Tabitha's uncle to rights. No, no, that would never do. First, he hadn't seen the earl in days, and secondly, he'd get it all mixed up.

So as it was, Preston went over to the house on Hertford Street, only to be informed that his lordship was out and then have the door slammed in his face.

Coming to White's had seemed the logical next step, but much to his chagrin, he discovered that Sir Mauris wasn't even a member—a Boodles man, of all things!—and was about to leave the hallowed halls of White's to ferret the baronet out on his turf when he spied Roxley.

As he got closer, he could see the earl had finally found his man—the ever-elusive Nelson Dillamore. Slippery eel that he was.

"You owe me, my good man!" Roxley complained. "I have the vowel here, and I expect payment. No more of your excuses."

"I don't recall any vowel or wager, Roxley," the fellow bluffed. Crossing his arms over his chest, he continued his brazen denial. "Produce it."

Preston groaned. Roxley and his vowels. He was forever collecting them and nearly always losing them.

As it was, the earl was digging into the pocket inside his coat and producing a veritable litter of notes and vowels, which began fluttering down around him like errant petals in a summer breeze.

"Need some help?" Preston asked, reaching over to retrieve the ones that lay on the floor.

The earl turned around. "Preston? Is that you? Thought you'd left Town."

"I never leave Town."

Roxley thought about this for a moment, then nodded in acknowledgement. "No, I suppose not. Forgot that. Devil of a week," he complained. Then without even looking, he caught hold of Dillamore, who had taken the opportunity of Preston's arrival to try and skulk away. Having caught the man by the back of his collar, the earl hauled him back to the table and shoved him into a seat. "Don't press your luck, Dillamore. I've enough of your excuses. About time you owned up to your obligations. Isn't like you haven't got the blunt."

Preston resisted the urge to smile, instead crossing his arms over his chest and glowering down at the other man.

Roxley's words were true enough. Dillamore's father had been a second son who'd been sent to the West Indies to make his fortune and had shocked his family to no end by doing just that. Now the wretched little weasel, having inherited his father's wealth, was as rich as Midas and lived an elevated life his more lofty relations could barely afford.

Nor was he inclined to share his wealth, not even when obligated by honor or duty.

"Come now, Roxley, you had better produce a vowel to back up this high-handed treatment," the haughty man taunted. "Or I will complain to the membership committee."

Roxley's gaze narrowed into a murderous scowl. You could insult the earl on a number of issues, but he held his place at White's, nay his standing as a gentleman of honor, in high regard. "Did you hear that insult, Preston?"

"Aye, I did, Roxley. But I've better things to do than stand second to you over this fool." He held out the papers he'd gathered up. "Find the demmed vowel and I'll hold him while you clean out his pockets. And next time—" Preston blundered to a halt, his gaze falling to the back of one of the papers he held, where an odd handwriting caught his eye.

"Pick my pockets?" Dillamore squawked in complaint. He tried to clamber his way up, but Roxley shoved him back down in his seat.

"Got to be here somewhere," Roxley was saying, reaching for the papers Preston held, but the duke pulled them back.

"Preston!" Roxley protested, reaching for them yet again.

The duke swatted the earl's hand aside, plucking one paper free from the clutch of notes and vowels. He handed the remainders to Roxley but stared in shock at the one he held.

"Owe him, do you?" Dillamore smirked.

"Shut up," Preston told him with a firm tone and enough ducal air that the fellow clamped his mouth shut and sank into his chair.

His gaze danced over the hastily written words, adding them up as he went. This was a vowel of another sort.

Article 3, Section 2 In the event that my niece reaches her majority without the benefit of marriage and inherits my entire estate, the money shall be co-managed by her uncles, Sir Mauris Timmons, Bt. and the Revd. Bernard Timmons, who shall oversee the investments, and provide an allowance to her that is deemed proper and necessary for her care

and upkeep until such time as she marries.
They shall also be fairly compensated for these
obligations and duties.

Preston stared down at the paper in shock. There was more to Winston Ludlow's will than the one page Roxley had given him.

He saw all too clearly what had probably happened—Hathaway in a rush had given the pages to Roxley to pass along. And the earl being, well, the earl, had stuffed them into his collection of vowels and forgotten that there was more than one page.

Oh, good God! He'd plucked Tabby from one fire only to drop her into another. With her uncles' talons wrapped around that fortune, they'd hie her away and never let her marry.

Or provide for her in any way other than how they already had: as a poor servant at their beck and call.

"What day is it?" he shouted at Dillamore.

The man nearly fell backward out of his chair. "What day?"

Preston caught him by the collar and hauled him up. "What day is it?"

"Friday," Dillamore managed, clawing at Preston's grasp.

"No. What day of the month is it?"

"The twenty-second," the man gasped.

"Then I have 'til Sunday," Preston muttered.

Less than two days before Tabitha's uncles would make sure she was far from any man's reach. Save theirs.

Preston would see about that. He shoved Dillamore aside and caught hold of Roxley, shaking him out of his distracted sorting of notes. "We need to find Miss Timmons. Is she still at her uncle's house?"

"Hardly," Roxley told him, staring down at the way Preston's hold was creasing his sleeve. Preston released him, and the earl smoothed the wool back into place. "Back in Kempton. Lady Essex took her, with Sir Mauris bringing up the rear. Poor chit. Probably took a wigging the entire way."

"We have to go," Preston told him. "We have to follow them."

"What? To Kempton?" Roxley shook his head. "Not when I've got… Demmit, Preston. Now look what you've done!"

Distracted by his own churning thoughts, Preston glanced up at his friend. "Whatever have I done?"

Roxley pointed at the empty chair. "Gone and let Dillamore escape."

"I'll help you track him down the moment we get back from Kempton."

"I've heard that promise before," Roxley complained.

"This time I mean it," Preston told him as they went to dash down the stairs. "Come along. We have to get to Kempton."

Roxley dug in his heels. "Do you recall that is how all this started?"

"Yes, and now it must end there. Look at this." He held up the rest of Hathaway's note.

"Good God! Those uncles of hers will empty those accounts in no time." He glanced up. "But she's already reached her majority, hasn't she?"

"No." Almost, but not quite.

"Truly? I thought her a bit long in the tooth myself," Roxley said, rubbing his jaw.

"Not in the least," Preston told him. "And if my suspicions run true, once she turns five and twenty, they will hide her away."

He caught hold of Roxley's arm again and all but dragged the fellow along, that is until they reached the main staircase, where he found his way blocked by none other than the Marquess of Grately.

"Preston! How dare you show your face in public."

"Not now, Grately," Preston told him, trying to side-step the older man, but the codger caught hold of his arm and hung on.

"I have a few words for you, you feckless devil! Put my family in the suds you did! Got my nephew running off, determined to marry that light skirt. I'll not have your by-blow inheriting my title. I won't!"

Preston turned a murderous gaze at the marquess. "Miss Timmons is not to be spoken of that way." He shook off the man's grasp and was about to push past him when the rest of what Grately had said came to roost.

"Got my nephew running off, determined to marry..."

Oh, good God, no!

Grately snorted, stamping his cane to the floor in an impatient gesture. "Yes, that's right. She won't be Miss Timmons for long. Cut that idiot nephew off without a farthing, and his solution? Marry the gel anyway!"

"Never!"

The marquess shook one of his bony fingers at Preston. "I blame you first and then that mother of his. Greedy bitch that she is. Never content with her lot in life, always wanting more. And that Timmons gel offers them all the blunt she could ever spend." He snorted again. "Rapacious pair of vultures. Well, he'll marry that gel and then they can see the shame she brings on them."

"It won't matter," Preston told the man. "If Miss Timmons reaches her majority—which will happen Sunday—her uncles will control her fortune."

The old man's eyes widened. "How the devil—"

"How did I discover the truth? I got my hands on a copy of Winston Ludlow's will."

"But I told those fools never to let anyone—" Grately began and then clamped his lips shut tight.

Preston eyed him. "I suppose you thought keeping a tight rein on Pennyman and his partners would prevent anyone else—especially Sir Mauris or Miss Timmons—from seeing all of the provisions in Winston Ludlow's will. I fear your trust in Pennyman was misplaced. I've read it, and I'd wager Sir Mauris has by now gained a copy as well."

The old man's jaw worked back and forth, but he didn't admit a thing. Not that he had to. "What do you intend to do?" he finally demanded.

"I plan on putting an end to all this. Stop your nephew and Miss Timmons's uncles from using Tabitha as a pawn." He nodded to Roxley, and the two them pushed past Grately.

But the marquess wasn't done. "I might forgive you, Preston, if you stop that nephew of mine. I won't have him marrying your leavings."

Preston nearly turned around and flattened the old man for saying such a thing, but he hadn't time.

Nevertheless, Grately continued after them. "Barkworth left hours ago. He'll be to Kempton and have that gel as his bride if you don't stop him. Don't see how you'll do it."

Preston's gaze narrowed. "He hasn't my cattle."

As they hurried out the doors, Roxley tucked his hat down atop his head. "Truly do not like that man."

"Agreed."

"Did I hear him correctly? Barkworth is going to press his case."

"Yes." Preston stood at the corner and whistled loud and clear for his tiger. "I know I've put you in suds of late, and I have no room to presume, but could you... that is, would you mind..."

"Help you stop a wedding?" Roxley grinned. "Be my pleasure. Probably leave my aunt so vexed with me she won't come to Town for at least two, maybe three, Seasons."

Preston grinned back.

"What do you have in mind?"

"Ride that chestnut of yours ahead and find Barkworth."

Roxley nodded. "Find Barkworth. Got it. Stop him?"

"Yes. Any way possible," Preston advised as his friend climbed up onto his horse. "Do you think you can manage?"

Roxley tipped his hat. "Never fear. I shall improvise."

"And while you endeavor to do that, I shall do what I do best," Preston said, taking up the ribbons and wrapping them around his hands.

"Ruin young ladies?" the earl quipped.

Preston laughed. "No! Drive like the devil and beat Barkworth to his bride."

* * *

"Where are you sending me?" Tabitha demanded, facing her irate uncles, Mr. Muggins at her side. Her aunts hovered in the background. They were all crowded into her attic room at the vicarage in Kempton.

Aunt Allegra and Lady Timmons appeared to be dressed for the evening—most likely planning on going to the Midsummer's Eve Ball.

That boded well for what she had planned—two less pairs of ears to spy on her. She'd tried for three nights now to slip away, but they had kept a vigilant watch over her. Tabitha had to imagine tonight may well be her and Mr. Muggins's last chance for escape.

"You heard me—it is none of your concern," Sir Mauris told her, glancing around the attic with an air of disdain. "You are being moved for your own good. Now pack your things."

"Yes, for your own good, Tabitha," Lady Timmons repeated, peeking around her husband's shoulder. "You have proven far too susceptible to the deceptions of unsavory gentlemen."

Preston wasn't unsavory! He was her hero. Her knight in shining armor. How she would like to inform her aunts and uncles that when Preston kissed her, she felt as if she were being carried to heaven.

Then again, she suspected that wouldn't do her current cause any favors.

"Yes, this is for your own good," Aunt Allegra added—then again, she always had to make her opinion known. Though she needn't sound so pleased about the situation. "We must safeguard you from the villains and knaves who will only seek to steal your fortune."

Mr. Muggins growled at her, as if he, like Tabitha, knew they were standing in front of four such villains.

Oh, they thought Tabitha didn't know what they had planned—for her and Mr. Muggins—but she knew the vicarage inside out, including all the spots from which to listen from. No, she wasn't proud that she'd spent the last few days doing her best to spy on her relatives' conversations—without getting caught by Mrs. Oaks—but since no one would tell her what they had planned, she'd had little choice.

Not that she'd liked what she'd heard. How they intended to take over her fortune and use it to their benefit. With Uncle Bernard and Sir Mauris as the trustees, they could do as they pleased with her money. But only once she reached her majority.

Which would happen at the stroke of midnight. She'd be five and twenty. Which she knew had everything to do with their haste.

If only Preston would come along in the nick of time.

"I will not pack until I know where you are taking me," she repeated stubbornly.

"Do not take that tone with your betters, miss!" Uncle Bernard scolded in his most pious tones. At least he hadn't reminded her of how "unworthy" she was— which he did at every chance he could.

"I will take this tone when I am being forced against my will to leave my home. This is a kidnapping," she said, shaking a finger at all of them, a reminder she hoped might send a twinge of guilt through one of them.

"Not if you are unworthy of such considerations," Uncle Bernard said, looking quite pleased at being able to work his condemnation into the conversation—finally. "You are a wicked girl, unbalanced by your predilections to sin."

There were nods all around, as if that was the agreed-upon story.

And then she saw it. At least how they were going to spin this lie of theirs. *Poor Tabitha. Gone mad by her perilous affair with a London rake.*

She also knew where they meant to take her. Or rather, to have her locked up. To a madhouse, far from anyone who might be able to help her. She swayed slightly as she realized just how perilous her situation had become, and she reached for the steady assurance of Mr. Muggins beside her.

No, this couldn't be happening. She wasn't the one who was mad—they were, with greed for Uncle Winston's fortune.

Worse yet, what they had planned for Mr. Muggins was unthinkable. Her fingers twined in the rough hair around the dog's head as she silently vowed they wouldn't harm a single one. Not as long as she had breath left.

"Preston will not allow this—nor will my friends here in Kempton." Tabitha straightened and glared at them, every bit the marchioness she might have been.

"If the man is so in love with you," Lady Timmons posed, "don't you think he would have followed you? Been here by now?" She glanced toward the window, then the door. "Where is he?"

Tabitha's resolve began to waver. She'd spent the last five days looking over her shoulder, peering out her window, praying for any sign of Preston coming to save her. Where the devil was he? He had the most indomitable knack of arriving when he wasn't needed, but right now would be a good time for him to go against his nature.

She'd even had a rare moment yesterday when she would have been willing to be cheered by the sight of Mr. Reginald Barkworth. But not even that fortune-hunting fool had managed to show up.

"Where is he, you foolish girl?" Aunt Allegra asked. She looked over at Lady Timmons. "Still in London enjoying the favors of another young innocent, if I were to guess."

Lady Timmons laughed, as did Aunt Allegra, while her uncles nodded in agreement.

Tabitha shook her head. "Preston will come for me."

But he did need to hurry up.

Uncle Bernard wagged a finger at her. "Best you reconcile yourself that he is not coming for you. No one is."

She would beg to differ, for she knew that Sir Mauris's carriage, which had brought them here to Kempton, had suddenly broken down; the brake lever was mysteriously missing, and there was a crack in one of the spokes. The Fates hadn't stopped there—the harnesses for Uncle Bernard's modest coach were now missing. Further, not a single resident of Kempton would loan the pair another conveyance, no matter how much Sir Mauris blustered and bribed.

Personally, she suspected Harriet of these crimes, and it buoyed her spirits to know she hadn't been entirely forgotten. Further, Lady Essex had called daily, demanding to see Tabitha, if only to check on her welfare.

How Sir Mauris and Uncle Bernard had managed

to turn the determined spinster away was a testament to their resolve to steal her fortune.

"Pack your bags, miss, or I will take you in the morning with nothing save the clothes on your back," Sir Mauris ordered as he turned to leave. "Bernard, what did that blacksmith say about my carriage?"

"That it would be ready by dawn." Uncle Bernard shuffled his feet and coughed. "Country ways, brother. This village is utterly backwards. I cannot wait to leave."

Sir Mauris huffed. "In London they would have had the task done in half the time. But if we must leave at dawn, so be it." They departed, but Tabitha could still hear her uncle's imperious voice as they descended the stairs. "Pennyman is to meet us at the posting station so we can sign the necessary papers. Then we can be well rid of her."

Her aunts followed their husbands, though Aunt Allegra was the last to leave.

Tabitha got to her feet. "You still haven't told me where you are taking me."

"You will find out when you get there." And with that, the door to the attic was slammed shut and locked.

Preston walked around the vicarage for the third time, trying to gauge the best way to gain entrance and steal Tabby away.

He'd arrived to find that the entire village of Kempton was empty—even the John Stakes public house was shuttered and closed—not that he needed directions to find the vicarage.

The steeple of St. Edward's Church rose like a beacon over its smaller, tidy neighbors, leading Preston directly to its hallowed ground and, indirectly, to the vicarage.

Since he'd watched the ladies leave—one of whom he recognized as Lady Timmons—he suspected that Tabitha's uncles had remained behind to keep their niece from escaping.

Especially since their prize—her majority and her fortune—were just hours away from the taking.

One advantage of being a notorious rake was that Preston rather excelled at slipping in and out of unfamiliar houses. And the vicarage was no exception. He'd managed to locate the kitchen door, the study window, and he guessed that Tabitha was up in the attic, for one of the windows there glowed from the light of a candle, the thin curtains drawn tight.

However, the kitchen was manned by a terrifying-looking housekeeper—the woman looked capable of tearing an ox limb from limb. A theory he did not want to test.

Encamped in the study were Sir Mauris and a man who looked to be his brother. The pair were sharing a bottle of port, while the baronet espoused one thing after another. It appeared his hapless younger brother was left with the task of simply agreeing with the man, which he did with anxious nods and earnest smiles.

Preston had come to the conclusion that while he might be able to just slip in via the front door, eventually it would be a choice of facing Sir Mauris and his brother or the stevedore masquerading as a housekeeper.

"Ho there," someone whispered behind his back.

Preston nearly leapt out of his skin. "Good God!" he

exclaimed, then clapped his hand over his own mouth as he found himself facing Roxley.

"Yes, well, now that we've gotten that over with," Roxley said, grinning, "what have we here?"

"Did you take care of Barkworth?"

"Oh, yes. Advised him of your plans to come and steal his heiress, and he's doubled his pace."

Preston slanted a glance at his friend. "The plan was to deter the man, not give him an advantage."

"I did give him an advantage," Roxley gloated. "Of a shortcut past the large oak. Told him to drive like the devil. If he takes that corner as I advised him to—"

"Roxley, you are a genius," Preston told him, slapping his friend hard on the back.

"About time you noticed," Roxley replied, straightening his coat and glancing toward the front door. "Plan on just going in and taking her out?"

"Yes."

"Simple and straightforward." Roxley nodded in agreement. "Rather like a pair of rushers."

"Exactly," Preston said, pulling out a pistol.

"Always wanted to be a housebreaker when I was growing up," he said.

"Why am I not surprised?" the duke muttered as they stole toward the front door.

It was not locked. This was a vicarage, after all.

They made their way down the front hall and were about to mount the stairs that would hopefully get them up to Tabitha's attic prison when from behind rose the wrenching clatter of a tray being dropped.

Again Preston nearly leapt out of his skin, and he whirled around to find the sound of breaking crockery replaced by an unholy screeching.

"Help! Thieves! Fiends!" screeched a woman. "We are all to be murdered!" The housekeeper came rushing forward, one meaty fist balled up, the other having retrieved the now empty tray.

Roxley moved so quickly that the woman didn't have time to change course. He yanked open a door to his right, and she ran right into it. Roxley moved around the door and, seeing it was a closet, pushed her, in her befuddled state, inside. Then he closed the door and leaned against it. "Fetch that chair," he said to Preston, pointing at a narrow chair that sat near the base of the stairs.

With it tucked up under the latch, the woman was trapped.

But she'd done her work all too well, for stumbling out yet another door, the one to the study, came Sir Mauris and his brother.

The brother brandished a pistol. "Ho, there! This is a vicarage! What sort of villainy is this?"

Preston strode forward, putting Roxley behind him. He raised his own pistol. "Drop it, sir, or I shall shoot you where you stand."

Luckily for Preston, Sir Mauris's brother had been perfectly chosen for his calling—he certainly hadn't the nerve for a career in the military—for his resolve folded as quickly as it had been summoned.

"Now, see here," the man said, shakily setting the pistol down on the floor and taking a step back. Notably behind his brother and out of harm's way.

Roxley came up, grinning, and retrieved the vicar's pistol.

"Where is she? Where's Tabitha?" Preston demanded, pointing his gun at the baronet.

Sir Mauris blustered and steamed. "You blackguard. I'd rather die than hand her over to you!"

Preston shrugged and pointed the gun at the vicar, who was still trying to hide behind his brother. "Do you agree, sir? That you would rather die than surrender Miss Timmons?"

The man grew wide-eyed and pointed toward the stairs. "She's locked in the attic."

The baronet turned around and cuffed him. "You stupid, blundering fool. He would never have shot us!"

"For kidnapping the woman I love?" Preston edged closer until the pistol's muzzle rested against the man's forehead. "Stealing her rightful fortune? Do not test me, Sir Mauris."

The baronet blinked and turned even redder, but he said nothing more to provoke the duke.

Preston waved them both down the hall. "Take me to her."

And the Timmons brothers did, mounting the stairs at a slow pace, arguing the entire time as to who was at fault.

They got to the attic door, and when Sir Mauris declared he knew not where the key was—nor did the vicar seem to know how to find it—Preston saved them both the trouble and kicked it in.

Surging into the room, Preston held his breath for the sight of his future bride. His Tabby.

But the room was empty.

Miss Tabitha Timmons hadn't waited for the duke to come along and save her.

Not this time.

* * *

Tabitha felt rather proud of herself as she and Mr. Muggins slipped from the vicarage unseen. Fortunately for her, Uncle Bernard and Aunt Allegra had never taken much pride or interest in their residence or they would have discovered, as Tabitha had with a lifetime of exploring the ins and outs of the ancient house, that it held any number of secrets.

Including an old priest hole in the attic—as well as a hidden staircase that led down to the kitchen—so one could be ferried in and out of the vicarage without detection.

Kempton had come to the new religion as it came to all change—slowly and stubbornly resistant.

A factor that had now restored Tabitha's freedom.

She moved quickly up Meadow Lane, Mr. Muggins bounding joyously ahead, while her overflowing portmanteau banged against her hip. She had finally taken her uncle's advice and packed. Though she had no intention of going anywhere he might have planned. When she reached the intersection with High Street, much to her elation, she spied a swiftly moving curricle, driven by a tall figure coming into town.

Preston! her heart sang. He'd come at last. Late, she mused, but here at last. She'd let him apologize profusely, beg for her absolution (and her hand in marriage) and then she'd forgive him.

How her body ached to forgive him, the memories of his lovemaking never far from the surface, sending tendrils of desire racing through her.

"Here I am," she said, waving her arms at the driver to get him to slow down.

Which he did, managing to get his horses stopped

just before they trampled her. She rushed around the carriage, only to come to a stumbling halt.

Oh, good heavens, no!

"Miss Timmons! This is most fortuitous!" Mr. Reginald Barkworth exclaimed.

Fortuitous was not the word Tabitha would use.

Barkworth leapt down from the carriage, and before she knew what he intended, he folded her into his awkward embrace. "My poor, dearest lady! The iniquities you have suffered! But never fear! I have come here to save you."

Oh, how she wished he hadn't.

After discovering that Tabitha was not in the vicarage, Preston and Roxley locked Sir Mauris and the Reverend Timmons in the cellar. When they got to the lane where Preston's carriage and Roxley's horse awaited them, they spent a moment determining which way she might have gone.

"If I were to guess," Roxley said, "we should try the Pottage."

"Miss Hathaway's?"

"Yes," Roxley said. "Or—"

Woof. Woof. Woof.

The earl's suggestions came up short as Mr. Muggins came bounding up toward them.

"There you are. Good dog," Preston said, giving the dog a friendly pat on the head and looking around for Tabitha. But to his concern, she didn't appear. "Where the devil is she? She wouldn't leave this mongrel behind."

"Not likely," Roxley agreed, then sighed, looking up the road. "Though I am loath to suggest it…" He glanced up the lane to where it intersected with the main road. "I suspect she's gone where everyone else is tonight."

"The Midsummer's Eve Ball," Preston supplied.

Roxley looked up at him, surprised.

"Miss Timmons mentioned it. Once or twice."

"Most likely twice. It is all they talk of around here for months." Roxley reached over and gave Mr. Muggins an affectionate scratch behind the ears. "Then we are off to Foxgrove." They began to walk up the lane, both of them leading their horses, Mr. Muggins following right at the duke's heels. "My aunt will not be happy to see me. Or you."

"Is she ever?" Preston quipped.

The earl snorted. "She complained quite vigorously before she left Town that you kissed her at Grately's." Roxley slanted a glance over at his friend, one brow arched high.

"I'd rather not discuss that," Preston told him, looking straight ahead.

"I'd rather not hear about it," Roxley told him. "Ever."

Preston and Roxley arrived at Foxgrove a little while later, and the earl led the way around to the back of the grand house. Easing up through the shadows, Preston looked through the open French doors of the ballroom and tried to spy Tabby, but she was nowhere to be seen.

Demmit! He was of half a mind to storm Lady Essex's house, but then that might just raise the alarm with Lady Timmons and her sister-in-law, and they would finish what their husbands had failed to do—spirit Tabby away.

Then all of a sudden a lithe, blonde beauty walked by the door, and Preston, with his well-known prowess at stealing young ladies right out from beneath their protective maman's watchful gazes, leaned inside, grabbed Miss Dale's hand and tugged her out the door, even as his other hand swept over her mouth to keep her from crying out.

For a moment, she put up a good fight, until she spied his face and he nodded at her. Her gaze changed from panic to fury.

An infuriated Dale. Heaven help him. But this was the best chance he had at finding Tabby. He released her. "Miss Dale—"

"Your Grace," Daphne said in a strained voice. "Unhand me! Isn't it enough you've ruined Tabitha, now you must include me in your nefarious ways?"

Roxley leaned back against the wall and shrugged, as if to say *Well, she does have a point.* Mr. Muggins, meanwhile, had settled down at the earl's feet and watched the proceedings with his gaze still fixed on Preston.

"Miss Dale—" Preston began.

"You fiend, you badger-witted—"

"Badger-witted?" Roxley laughed. "That's a new one."

Preston shot him a hot glance, and the earl managed to stifle his ill-timed humor.

Preston hardly needed Roxley's help when he had to deal with Miss Dale.

Dales! Lofty tempers and endless parries with words. Preston hadn't any patience for either. "Miss

Dale, you know why I am here. I must find Tabby." He paused. "Miss Timmons."

"What? To ruin her yet again?" She shook her head and began to gather up her skirt. "Leave it to a Seldon not to know when enough is enough."

He heaved a sigh. "Miss Dale, I know we have a shared dislike for each other—"

"Harrumph," she shot back. "Seldons!"

Yes, well the feeling is mutual, he would have liked to have told her. Dales! Overly insolent, supercilious… He took another deep breath. What he needed to do was put aside his own Seldon pride and find Tabitha.

Doing his best to sound conciliatory, if not sane, he said, "Just this once, I would like to ignore our familial differences in the name of saving your friend."

Miss Dale's eyes widened. "Save her? You ruined her."

So much for a peace accord.

"Demmit, Miss Dale! This is going nowhere! Now, are you going to help me or not?"

"Of course she is," Harriet Hathaway said as she came tumbling out the open doors in her usual forward way.

"Ho there, Harry," Roxley called out.

The lady glanced over her shoulder. "Roxley! Best not let your aunt see you. She's in a rare state. Something about the duke kissing her and you not around to avenge her slighted honor."

Roxley grinned at her, and Preston could have sworn Miss Hathaway blushed a bit before she turned toward him and showed him why her brothers feared her wrath. "About time you arrived, Your Grace," she scolded, hands fisting to her hips. "I was beginning to think you'd never get here. And after all the trouble I've gone to to see that Sir Mauris couldn't leave Kempton."

"What did you do, minx?" Roxley asked.

"I might have taken apart his carriage a bit," she admitted. "Daphne helped."

"Not so you could save her, mind you," Miss Dale told Preston tartly. "But rather to give us more time to find a way to get Tabitha out of the vicarage."

"Now that you are here, Your Grace," Harriet said, "where is Tabitha?" She glanced around, looking for her friend. "If you've got Mr. Muggins, then Tabitha can't be far away. She'd never leave him behind. Not willingly."

"She's not in the vicarage," Preston told them and then quickly recapped what they had found when he and Roxley had stormed St. Edward's.

"Then you must find her, and find her quickly," Harriet told the duke.

"Harriet! He's a Seldon," Daphne said, stepping between Preston and her friend. She tossed another disparaging glance over her shoulder at him. "He has ruined Tabitha and means her no good."

"Oh, good heavens, Daphne, he's here to save her," Harriet said. "If you had your way, you'd have us all believing the Seldons roast their young and defile ladies as a matter of course."

Miss Dale's expression, a "you-shall-see-that-I-am-right" smirk, suggested that she had no doubts he had a pot in the back of his carriage for boiling stray orphans and spare virgins strapped to the front of his carriage on the off chance he ran out of his usual daily course of nubile sacrifices.

Harriet went to open her mouth, but Daphne caught

hold of her arm and gave her friend a good shake. "How can you trust *him* so implicitly with Tabitha's future happiness?"

"Because Roxley trusts him," Harriet said, nodding toward the earl. "And Chaunce says Preston has more wits about him than one usually finds in a duke."

Preston groaned, pressing his fingers to his temple. He would never get used to these ladies from Kempton. "Please, Miss Hathaway, where is Tabby?"

"Harriet—" Daphne began to warn.

This time, he truly lost his patience with her and her Dale presumption.

Towering over the lady, he leaned down until they were nose to nose. "Demmit, you impertinent little snip! I intend to save her from her uncle and Barkworth."

Her eyes widened at this.

"Yes, Barkworth, who is even now on his way here to steal her back before she reaches her majority."

"But—"

"No buts. Further, I intend—if it is any of your business—to see that she inherits her uncle's estate. And finally I intend to give her the choice of being my duchess. The choice. Not force her into some marriage that is convenient for everyone but her. I want to make her my wife. My beloved, dearest wife. Or not. It is entirely her choice. Either way, she will have a fortune at her disposal and the freedom to do as she pleases. Is that enough to warrant your demmed assistance or not?"

Wide-eyed, Daphne pressed both of her lips together and simply nodded.

Preston rose up, straightened his jacket and was about to add a nearly honestly meant *Thank you, Miss*

Dale when a vision stepped out of the shadows in the garden.

"Woof!" Mr. Muggins barked, bounding to his feet and nearly upending Roxley in the process.

"Tabby," Preston gasped, impertinent snips forgotten as he crossed the space between them and gathered her into his arms. His lips sought hers and they kissed, hungrily, eagerly.

It was like coming home, a feeling he hadn't understood—no, had more like avoided—for so many years that it nearly left him undone.

He cradled her face and drank in the sight of her. "Tabby! Where the devil have you been?" Not that Tabby could get a word in, what with Mr. Muggins racing around the pair of them, barking and grinning as only a terrier could. And not after Preston got a closer look at her. "Good God! What happened to you?"

Her muslin gown had a large rent down one side and looked like it had been rolled in the dust. She had the beginnings of a bruise on her cheek and was skinned up on both arms.

"What happened?" he repeated.

"You didn't come along in time, so I had to improvise," she confessed, smiling up at him.

"Always my best plan," Roxley added, though no one was listening.

"My uncles locked me in the attic—"

"The devils!" Daphne declared.

"But neither of them knows of the priest's hole up there or the staircase that leads down to the kitchen. All I had to do was wait for Mrs. Oaks to take a tray to my uncles, and when she did—"

Preston grinned. That was his Tabby. Resourceful to the end.

"So I didn't need to come rescue you after all," he said.

"I wished you had," she told him. "I ruined my gown jumping out of Barkworth's curricle."

"Barkworth?" all four of them said.

"Yes, Barkworth," she told them. "When I got to High Street, I saw a carriage coming toward Kempton at a breakneck pace and thought it was you." She grinned up at Preston and leaned against him for a moment, as if she just had to reassure herself that he was real.

Yes, Tabby, I am. And I will never leave you again.

However there was one point that needed clarification. "You thought Barkworth was me?"

"Yes, I know, rather embarrassed by it all, but in my defense it was dark and I hadn't had my supper yet."

"You are nearly forgiven," he teased.

"I give you leave to taunt me with that fact, but only once a year," she told him.

"So noted."

"But what happened when you discovered that it was Barkworth?" Harriet pressed, eager to hear the rest of Tabitha's adventure.

"I was rather shocked, because before I knew it, he swept me off my feet and tossed me up in his carriage."

"Barkworth?" they all four asked at once.

"Yes, Mr. Barkworth. Apparently being cut off by his uncle—at least until the man's unfortunate passing, which I don't think Mr. Barkworth will find the least bit unfortunate—"

"No, hardly," Daphne agreed.

"Yes, well, being cut off has given him a new lease on life—at least one that had him seeking my hand and fortune no matter the cost. I tried to get out, but he was determined to rescue me. Refused flatly to bring me here, or bring Mr. Muggins, and then he took off at a devilish pace, until just before we reached the main road—"

"He turned onto a shortcut—" Roxley said, jumping into the conversation.

"Yes, exactly," Tabitha said. "However did he know about the Old Oak Road?"

The earl shrugged and scuffed the toe of his boot into the thick tiles that made up the terrace outside the ballroom.

Tabitha shook her head. "Yes, well, someone had informed Mr. Barkworth that it was the fastest way from Kempton to the London road."

"Doltish man!" Roxley protested. "I told him exactly the opposite."

"And neglected to mention why it is called Old Oak Road?" Harriet asked.

"Might have left that part out," he admitted.

"So you did," Tabitha said. "He had a hold of my arm and was driving with the other and had the horses going far too fast, and when we got to the corner—" She held out her skirt to show exactly what happened. "He let go just in time for me to jump. I thought I might do in my ankle, but I landed in the hedge—"

"Yes, I know that hedge well," Roxley said, sending a scathing glance at Preston.

Tabitha nodded in understanding. "I saved myself, but I fear Mr. Barkworth wasn't as quick."

"Mr. Barkworth is dead?" Daphne gasped.

Tabitha shook her head. "No, but he's trapped beneath his carriage. Had the audacity to ask me to fetch someone to rescue him. Oh, and a tailor to repair his best driving cape."

She reached over, scratched Mr. Muggins behind the ears and grinned up at Preston. "I promised to send help, but I have yet to find anyone."

"Yes, might take some time," he agreed.

"Hours," Harriet agreed, smiling over the entire story.

"I would think he might be there until morning," Tabitha said.

"Serve him right," Daphne added. "But, Tabitha, you cannot stay here. This is the first place your uncles will look, and your aunts are inside. We cannot let them take you away."

"They won't dare now," Preston said, folding her into his arms again and kissing Tabby thoroughly, his heart hammering all the while to a new beat.

Home. Hearth. Love. Home. Tabby.

"It is the Midsummer's Eve Ball. I had hoped... That is, I thought..." She looked up at Preston in wonder, her eyes aglow with what he could only hope was love.

"No," Preston said. "If I know you, Tabby, you came for no other reason than to discover what color the buntings ended up being."

She laughed. "What color are they?"

He glanced over her shoulder so he could see inside the ballroom. "Lavender."

"Excellent. Some things shouldn't change."

They spent a starry-eyed moment gazing at each other, and Harriet caught hold of Daphne and Roxley and towed them both into the ballroom, leaving Tabitha and Preston blissfully alone.

Save for Mr. Muggins, who, they all knew by now, was a wretchedly poor chaperone.

"You don't think some things should change?" Preston's heart trembled for a moment. "But others? Should they change?"

"Have you?"

"Would I be here if I hadn't changed?" He couldn't help himself; he gathered her closer to him. "I came along to save you. But mind you, Tabby, this is the last time."

"You drove all this way just to save me?" She smiled with a coquettish little grin that made his heart hammer even harder.

"Yes."

"From my uncles?"

"Yes."

"How did you find out what they had planned?" she asked.

"It was rather by chance," he admitted.

"Harriet's brother?" she asked, thinking he meant Chaunce.

"No, actual demmed luck," he told her, explaining how he'd found the other page of Winston Ludlow's will.

She sighed. "However am I going to repay you, Your Grace?"

He scratched his chin and thought about it. "You're an heiress now, it ought not to be very difficult."

She playfully slapped his chest. "You bounder."

"Your friend called me a 'badger.'"

"That too," she agreed.

"I thought you might save me from my aunt," he told her.

"Lady Juniper?"

"Yes, that one. She's determined that I marry. Marry anyone."

It was her turn to tease. "Have you met anyone respectable and proper enough?"

"Yes. I wasn't overly fond of her. Especially after I met you." He paused and let go of her, falling down to one knee and catching hold of her hands. "I want to marry you."

She smiled at him. "I should confess, I already know that."

"Eavesdropping, Tabby?"

"Yes, I was. I am surprised Lady Essex didn't hear you browbeating poor Daphne."

"I wasn't browbeating Miss Dale," he said in his defense. Actually that he'd refrained from throttling the overly opinionated chit was to his credit.

"She will be hard put to believe that you mean me anything other than further irreparable harm," Tabitha informed him. "You don't intend to steal my fortune, do you?"

This took Preston aback. "Bother your uncle's fortune. Didn't you hear the rest of what I said?" he said. "About making you my duchess?"

"Yes, I heard all that," she said, crossing her arms over her chest. "But I want to hear about my fortune first. And my ability to make my own choices."

He might have thought himself done for if it hadn't been for a wicked little twinkle in her eyes. So he nodded in concession and explained himself. "Your uncle's will holds that if you reach your majority unmarried, your uncles become the trustees."

"My uncles are hardly trustworthy!" she told him. "They meant to put me in a madhouse."

"That is excellent news," he told her.

"Not for me."

"Yes, but it will prove they are unworthy of their positions, and Mr. Pennyman, as the solicitor of record, will be obliged to appoint a new trustee. And since I have moved a rather large portion of legal work to his offices, I do believe I may have some influence in the matter."

"Information that might have been helpful last week before you ruined me," she pointed out.

"Yes, well, that is the problem with using Roxley as a messenger," he told her, reaching out and taking her hand. "When I learned the truth—"

"—you came along to save me?"

"It seems to be my fate," he told her, trying to sound humble, which was rather difficult when one was a duke.

"Just fate?" she teased.

"Tabby, I love you. When I realized that, it rather changed my opinion of marriage."

Gooseflesh ran down her arms and her eyes stung with the rush of hot, sudden tears that welled up but didn't quite fall. "You love me?" she whispered.

He bounded to his feet, and, once she was in his arms, he was kissing her. "Good God, woman, how could you not know?"

His practical, straightforward Tabby told him. "You rather neglected telling me."

Preston's chest puffed out. "I'm more of a prove-my-point sort of man."

She nestled closer, her hand reaching up to cup his face, her bare fingers warm and soft against the stubble there.

"Then, Your Grace, what are you waiting for? Prove it."

Chapter 16

London
A fortnight later

Tabitha smiled as she read the carefully engraved words on the thick piece of vellum she held.

The Most Noble the Duke of Preston
Requests the honour of your presence
at his marriage to
Miss Tabitha Timmons
Commencing
On the morning of
Wednesday, the eighth of August
in the Year of our Lord, Eighteen Hundred and Ten
Owle Park, Surrey

"Four weeks!" Preston complained, looking down at the invitation Tabitha had brought over to show him.

They were in the Red Room of his London house. Mr. Muggins lay curled up on what was probably a very expensive rug near the fire, his tail beating in a happy refrain. For an Irish terrier with no manners, he had quite taken to ducal life and turned over a new leaf. Well, nearly.

For he was still a bad chaperone. After all, he'd let Tabitha and Preston spend an indecent amount of time together alone in the gardens ("wretched Seldons," Daphne had complained), yet when they had returned to the Midsummer Eve Ball they'd announced their betrothal, which, as Harriet had said, "was how it was supposed to be all along."

Much to the chagrin of Tabitha's uncles. But Lady Timmons viewed this change of fortune with a more pragmatic air.

"Think of the connections, my dear," she told her outraged husband, who had finally managed to escape the cellar. "Why, our dearest Tabitha will be the Duchess of Preston!"

Lady Essex had immediately taken charge of the bride-to-be and brought her to London to help her pick out her trousseau and to declare to one and all that she had been instrumental in bringing the notorious Duke of Preston to heel.

"He kissed me once," she was wont to say.

And while Preston had vowed their return to London was only to gain a Special License and a quick wedding, Tabitha refused.

"I will have the banns read and a proper wedding,"

she repeated to him this day, as she had every day since they'd left Kempton.

"Yes, yes," Preston agreed, though he was still of a mind to hasten the entire process along. He'd been convinced that after a fortnight under Lady Essex's strict care, Tabitha would change her mind.

But he was learning his bride-to-be had a stubborn streak that rivaled his own.

"I ordered my gown yesterday, and it will be ready in time to take to Owle Park for the house party," she told him.

Owle Park. Preston couldn't believe it. He'd driven down to the house with Tabitha the previous week, Hen and Henry coming along to chaperone.

All his fears had washed away as he'd stepped down from the carriage and looked over the lush green lawn, the warm stone facade and the line of servants awaiting him.

When he'd taken Tabitha's hand and guided her out of the carriage, the servants had cheered heartily.

And he'd sworn the old house had as well.

"Welcome home," she'd whispered up at him.

"Yes, welcome to *our* home," he'd replied.

Everything had been ordered for a house party that would culminate in their wedding. And now the invitations were being sent out.

"I am still holding out hope of convincing you of the decided advantages of a Special License," Preston said as he looked down at the invitation. Four bloody weeks!

Tabitha shook her head. "I will be married properly. On the church steps, with a new gown on a Wednesday."

"Leaving nothing to chance?" he teased, smiling at her traditional leanings and superstitions. This bride from Kempton was taking no chances.

As for Preston, he glanced around the Red Room and decided to take this opportunity, while Lady Essex was downstairs with Hen looking over china, to give Tabitha a long overdue kiss. "A Special License," he teased as he nibbled at her neck. "And you could spend tonight in my bed."

"No," she told him with that determined air that he loved so much about her.

"Gretna Green?" he tried. "That's only a few days away, and longer if we find a cozy inn with a large bed."

There was another shake of her red head.

"What if your most esteemed Mr. Barkworth were to steal you away before I can marry you myself?" Preston teased. "He's back in Town, or so I hear."

"He wouldn't dare," Tabitha said, grinning and tugging Preston closer for another kiss.

He indulged her and kissed her soundly yet again, until his Tabby, his dearest, beloved Tabby, was breathless.

As was he.

"I know I can convince you otherwise," he said, leaning down for yet another attempt.

She put her fingers on his lips and looked him squarely in the eye. "Care to wager on that, Your Grace?"

* * * * *

SURRENDER TO SWEET TEMPTATION FROM
NEW YORK TIMES **BESTSELLING AUTHOR**

Along Came A Duke
978-0-06-208906-9

The Duke of Preston spies a rebellious streak in Tabitha Timmons that
matches his own. And when he discovers that she is about to enter an
arranged marriage that will turn her into a wealthy heiress, he makes it
his mission to save her from a passionless match.

Lord Langley is Back in Town
978-0-06-178351-7

The wily Lord Langley will keep his word and follow Lady Standon's
rules for their faux engagement. That doesn't mean he won't use every
rakish trick he knows to get Minerva to break her own proper rules.

Mad About the Duke
978-0-06-178350-0

Level-headed Lady Elinor Standon will not allow her greedy step father
to wed her younger sister to the highest bidder! The only way to stop
this evil plan is for Elinor to quickly marry and gain control of her
sister's guardianship. But her plans go awry when she discovers that
beneath her solicitor's rumpled coat is a man too desirable to ignore.

How I Met My Countess
978-0-06-178349-4

The improper daughter of an infamous spy, Lucy Ellyson
is now living a new life in the heart of Mayfair. But proper society
hasn't taught her to mend her scandalous ways, and when the
Earl of Clifton happens upon her, she's landed in the sort of trouble
that only a hasty marriage can solve.

New York Times **Bestselling Author**

Memoirs of a Scandalous Red Dress

978-0-06-137324-4

What if all you have are the memories of a rake…
and the scandalous red dress that nearly brought you to ruin?

Confessions of a Little Black Gown

978-0-06-137323-7

She spied him in the shadows and in an instant
Thalia Langley knew the man before her was no saint.

Tempted by the Night

978-0-06-137322-0

Lady Hermione Marlowe refuses to believe that the handsome
gentleman she's loved from afar for so long could be so wicked.

Love Letters From a Duke

978-0-06-078403-4

Felicity Langley thought she knew what love was after years of
corresponding with the staid Duke of Hollindrake…until her footman
unlocked her passionate nature with his unlikely kiss.

His Mistress by Morning

978-0-06-078402-7

An impudent wish—and a touch of magic—lands a very
proper Charlotte Wilmont where she always dreamed she'd
be—in Sebastian, Viscount Trent's bed…and in his heart.
But not in the way she had imagined it.

EBB1015

At Avon Books, we know your passion for romance—once you finish one of our novels, you find yourself wanting more.

May we tempt you with . . .

- **Excerpts** from our upcoming releases.

- Entertaining **extras**, including authors' personal photo albums and book lists.

- Behind-the-scenes **scoop** on your favorite characters and series.

- **Sweepstakes** for the chance to win free books, romantic getaways, and other fun prizes.

- Writing **tips** from our authors and editors.

- **Blogs** from our authors on why they love writing romance.

- **Exclusive content** that's not contained within the pages of our novels.

Join us at
www.avonbooks.com

AVON *An Imprint of* HarperCollins*Publishers*
www.avonromance.com

Available wherever books are sold or please call 1-800-331-3761 to order.

Give in to your Impulses!

These unforgettable stories only take a second to buy and give you hours of reading pleasure!

Go to *www.AvonImpulse.com* and see what we have to offer.

Available wherever e-books are sold.

AVON
IMPULSE

AVONIMP0815